FIRE LIKE THE SUN

FIRE LIKE THE SUN

MICHAEL BOND

ST. MARTIN'S/MAREK
NEW YORK

Grateful acknowledgment is made for permission to reprint from the following:

An Area of Darkness, © 1964 V. S. Naipaul, Penguin Books.
"Connection," Rolling Stones (© 1967 Jagger; Richards), London Records.
"Visions of Johanna," © 1966 Bob Dylan, Columbia Records.
Oeuvres Complètes, © 1962 Montaigne, Éditions Gallimard, Paris.
Qu'est-ce que la littérature?, © 1948 Jean-Paul Sartre, Éditions Gallimard, Paris.
Noces, © 1950 Albert Camus, Éditions Gallimard, Paris.
"The Waste Land," T. S. Eliot © 1930, © 1934 Harcourt, Brace, and World, Inc., New York.

Design by Doris Borowsky

Library of Congress Cataloging in Publication Data

Bond, Michael, 1943–
    Fire like the sun.

    I. Title.
PS3552.O5973F5   1985   813'.54   85-2547
ISBN 0-312-29195-7

10 9 8 7 6 5 4

*To Richard F. Bond
and to the memory of Isobelle C. Bond*

The world is illusion, the Hindus say. We talk of despair, but true despair lies too deep for formulation.

—V. S. NAIPAUL

The persons in this account are real; their names and specific recognizable characteristics have been changed. Nearly all their actions occurred as narrated, although identifying circumstances have been altered.

To be hunted confers a certain terror, beyond dread of death, that is henceforth inextinguishable. The only exorcism of this terror is a reversal of roles, the prey becoming hunter and the hunter prey. But such occasions are few in the forests of life, when the doe, malcontent with her fate, stalks the leopard, the hare the hawk, or the man of peace the man of war.

FIRE
LIKE
THE
SUN

1

THE RIVER THUNDERED OVER the bamboo footbridge, snatched his ankles and smashed him into the rail. Rain roared down his face into his eyes and mouth; wind whipped the bridge, its rope rails ripping his fingers. Bare feet skidding on the slats, he shook the rain from his eyes and inched forward. Before him the bridge skipped and darted above the black churning waves, its far end ascending toward a trail notched into the cliff. A tree swirled past, its roots clawing his leg. A chunk of the canyon broke loose and boomed into the river. Wanting to quit he glanced back; the bridge yawed wildly.

Through veils of wind-lashed rain he glimpsed the others watching helplessly from the trail: Alex and Paul bellied out on the cliff edge steadying the bridge hawsers, Stihl and Eliott huddled under glistening ponchos, ten near-naked Nepali porters squatting beside their loads, Goteen the Sherpa hunkered motionless to one side.

The bridge lurched sideways and he dove hugging it, turning to see Alex crawling toward him. He waved Alex back, shifting his weight; the bridge spun, the river surged up and yanked him under, his fingers skating from the slats; freezing water crushed his ears and bones, his fingers wrapping round a trailing cable in the terror of death as the gale snapped the bridge from his grasp.

I won't die. Fingers numbly slipping. Not now. This cable. Knot at the end. Oh God my arm. Please let go. One hand closer. Jesus the pain. I will not die. Another handhold, slipping. The bridge lunged higher, whipping his head above the icy, eye-sucking current. Oh God air. How lovely air. Another hold. Hold no matter what.

Hands without feeling, pain beyond pain. Will not die. Can see. One hold closer. Please let go. Not now. God save me save me. New hold, hand over hand now, hook fingers over slat, now bite this edge, one arm up, over bridge. Pull. Inch by inch he dragged his chest atop the slats, lay choking and gasping.

Over screaming wind and battering rain Paul was speaking into his ear but he could not hear him, only feel his presence. Paul grabbed his arms and crawled dragging him along the bridge toward the far canyon wall and up onto its foot-wide trail.

It seemed the rain had lessened slightly. He leaned back against the cliff, legs over the edge, mind vacant, eyes on the snakelike whirl of wind-driven rain over the roiling river. I was dead. This is all new. Paul brought me back. My beloved brother Paul.

The wind ebbed, increasing the river's roar. He inspected his lacerated underarms and chest, tried to breathe deeply but that hurt. "Didn't figure it," he rasped.

"Shoulda turned back." Paul's voice was hoarse.

"Too scared." He watched the river flexing her sinews like a cold black panther. "She had me."

"Kali Gandaki." Paul spit into the river. "Mother of the Ganges. You're nuts—you know that, Cohen? Why outmacho Stihl?"

His own voice sounded faraway, a boy's or an old man's. "Why didn't she take me?"

Paul put a hand on his shoulder and boosted himself up. "'Cause she didn't want you, right then."

"For a moment I stopped caring—almost let go. Something held."

"The body loves to live." Paul reached down. "C'mon, you been hit. Walk it off."

Cohen stood, bare toes over the edge. He turned to smile at Paul's back-tilted features, his warlike blade of a nose, high-boned ebony cheeks, his classic Greek head on its column of muscled neck. "We gotta cool Stihl off."

"Crossed my mind to kill him, right then."

"He must sense that." Cohen dragged his gaze from the river. "Too much bread."

Paul leaned out over the edge to massage his calves. "It keeps us in Nepal."

"We gotta get tough."

"He's unreachable, man. It's insane, this rush upriver to Changtshang. We're letting *him* push *us*." Paul thumbed mud from

2

between his toes. "Ever since Katmandu he's been wired, every night hustling to get a few kliks further, hard-assing the porters, while they got eighty pounds and he's got nothing."

"Just his silly cameras."

"That's his world, those kinda people. Nepal ain't real till it's plastic—a transparency to view on the idiot box while you eat ice cream."

"You know how long since I've had ice cream?"

"Two years, same as me."

"I've never missed it. Not one iota of that world." Cohen snickered. "Maybe we just can't tolerate working for anyone else."

"This ain't work." With one toe Paul nudged a rock off the edge. Spinning wildly it clacked off the cliff and spumed into the river. "They're ugly people, Stihl and Eliott. No joy."

"So we should feel sorry for them? We can't lead them to Nirvana, only to Mustang and back. Then they'll take their plastic Nepal back to the States."

The slit of light atop the steepled canyon walls had grown brighter; rain now softly stippled the slaty, rushing river. Cohen bent to rub mud from his bare arms and legs onto his soaked T-shirt and cutoff jeans, took his glasses from a pocket, tried to clean them on his shirt, pocketed them again. He took a deep breath, forcing a grin at the pain, climbed the trail a hundred feet or so until it widened toward the first switchback up the canyon wall.

Rumbling pewter clouds ruptured against the canyon rims; a spear of sunlight struck the river, bleeding it golden, its boulders black and shiny. I'm still here, he wondered. You're still here too, Kali. As if nothing's changed. He smiled down at the river. I'm always feeling different but nothing ever changes.

He returned to help Paul hold the hawsers as Alex crawled down the far side of the bridge and pulled himself toward its sagging center. Without the wind and heavy rain Alex crossed easily, climbed up beside them on the trail, shook the rain from his hair, and stood. "I don't believe you're still alive, asshole."

Cohen grinned. "I . . ."

"Don't say it." Alex grabbed him by both biceps as if he were a child. "Don't make no excuses—nothin'." He shoved him against the canyon wall and stepped past. "Let's go."

Cohen felt his face redden. "And leave them?"

3

"I don't give a sweet fuck." Alex turned on him. "Don't ever do that again—let him bait you like that. The little cocksucker."

Cohen tried to shake off his embarrassment. "Look—it's my life—I know what . . ."

"A sweet fuck it's your life! We're in this, too—we're responsible, too, for getting that little cocksucker to Mustang and back—we're getting paid, too, just like you—we're the ones'd have to search that frigid fucking river for a week for your lousy waterlogged body—so don't tell me it's your life!" He scowled across the river. "We wait for them in Bagling. If Stihl wants us to guide him there'll be no more pushing against time."

Cohen smiled at the hairs plastered to Alex's muddy shins. "Let's wait for them here? And tonight set them straight in Bagling?"

Paul turned from picking at his scraped forearms. "This's he-man shit. I got *no* use for it."

Cohen stared tiredly at the roiling current. "It isn't like we expected. Stihl and Eliott are even bigger assholes than we figured. How come there's so many more assholes than people in the world? It should be one for one."

"They got some fear," Alex grinned. "Something's pushing them."

"Fear? Culture shock."

"So we leave them."

"And the money?" Cohen nodded at the far side, where Stihl was hesitantly descending the becalmed bridge. "How do we stay in Nepal without money? What about next year, Macha Pucchare, all that?"

"I still don't understand," Alex said. "Why pay us so much to guide them to Mustang?"

"The other people he had first must've really laid it on him, expenses and all. So when they couldn't make it, he turned to us, or rather the Embassy turned him on to us, he says, and now here we are. Escorting a dipshit to Mustang." Cohen made a disgusted sound in his throat. "For the bread, how can we kvetch?"

Stihl reached them, shivering, shinnied gingerly up on the trail and squeezed back against the cliff. "You should've waited, Sam. I didn't realize—I thought . . ."

"Don't think, you'll hurt the team." Cohen spat into the river. "That's what my old high school coach used to say."

4

Alex took up a rock and began to polish it with his hands. "You didn't think nothing, Stihl. Because you're a nothing and nothings don't think. But you push us once more and I throw you in the river."

Stihl watched Cohen. "It must've been terrible—that rain, wind. . . . Why didn't you turn back?"

"We're reassessing our role, Clem, whether we want to work for you any longer."

Stihl shrugged and beckoned across the river to Eliott. "Whatever. You realize, though, I can't afford to pay you anything if we stop now?"

"Clem," Paul interjected, "why all this hurry?"

He faced each of them in turn. Like a spider, Cohen thought, with three flies in his web. Stihl smiled. "You know we've got to reach Changtshang before the river rises. That means one more crossing—at Bagling. After that we cruise. All downhill."

"All uphill," Alex corrected.

"Metaphorically."

"Goteen says the bridge is out at Changtshang," Cohen said. "We'll have to wade across from Bagling."

Stihl rubbed his palms together, started to stand, glanced over the edge, and sat again. "I know you boys've been stuck here in Nepal a long time, and the world's gone on without you. Why shouldn't I come here doing articles, travel stories, about a trip to Mustang? It's way back against the Tibetan border and nobody's been there. The Himalayas have always been remote and mysterious for Americans, for all westerners. Where there's mystery there's money. Good money. And I'm paying you more than fairly."

"Yeah," Alex grunted. "And where there's Mustang there's the CIA training Tibetan guerrillas, the Khambas—where there's mystery there's danger."

Stihl grinned. "Are you telling me that you, an American, a Vietnam vet, a former All Conference wide receiver, a mountain climber, are afraid of a little danger?"

Alex's nostrils widened. Cohen put a hand on his arm. Do I let it fall apart here? Shit no, I need the bread. "Let's work it out tonight," he smiled. "In Changtshang."

Stihl returned his smile. "You said this morning we'd reach Kagbeni by dark. So why stop at Changtshang?" He stood carefully, his back against the cliff, patted Cohen's shoulder. "Think it over, huh?"

"Sure, Clem, sure." Cohen turned to watch the porters padding across the bridge. I think with my body, Stihl, not with my head. I'm not you, couldn't be. The body's free and chooses quickly, fears death and injury, but only at the moment. It doesn't fear consequences. He stretched his bruised chest muscles. Then why do I do this, when something warns me not to? Been around you too long, Stihl, your white man ways. Contagious.

When the porters, Goteen, and Eliott had crossed, Cohen led them quickly up the steep, switchbacked trail toward the widening gap of light above the canyon walls. They broke over the rim into sunlight and the sight of terraced green hills stepping northward up to tawny ridgetop yak pastures under the ice-ribbed Himalayan wall.

At noon they descended to the disheveled outskirts of Bagling, sunlight plunging between the canyon walls to sparkle puddles in cobbled courtyards and lift steam from dungbrick walls and soggy thatch. A cock crowed warning and children pattered up to them with dark, unreadable eyes. Goteen joined them silently in the village square. *"Daju,"* Cohen said, "Older Brother. The river rises."

"Stihl wishes to cross?"

Cohen peered across the river at the randomly clustered huts of Changtshang. "You have waded here?"

"Not in spring snowmelt. Once, there was a bridge."

"What's he say?" Stihl interjected.

"That it may be impossible to wade."

Stihl shifted ground, lug soles sucking mud. "This's the last bad crossing until Tshele, right? Let's try. Before it's too late."

"The porters're tired," Cohen said. "And hungry."

Stihl's blue eyes were unshifting, pleasant. "Afraid to cross?"

Cohen snickered. "Of course. Someone could drown, a porter with a load."

"The water's rising, Sam. You want we sit here a week?"

"In Nepal," Alex said, "you respond to circumstances. You don't dominate them."

"That's Buddhist bullshit," Stihl called over his shoulder as he clumped down the path to the gravel bar at the river edge.

6

"If we go," Goteen said, "it should be quickly."

"Wha'd'e say?" Eliott tugged Cohen's elbow.

Cohen translated, watching sunlit mist shift before the now-shadowed huts of Changtshang under the opposite canyon wall. He walked down the path and across the damp, clacking gravel into the river, his feet and ankles numbing at once, stones shifting under his toes. Again Stihl's challenging me, forcing me to choose. Why? Does he hate me? Because I'm free and he's chained? What's he chained by? Water's cold. If we're crossing, better be soon.

Paul grabbed his shoulder, leaned toward him, shouting, Cohen hearing only "too deep."

Downstream the river curved eastward, to their left. "It'll carry us over," Cohen yelled. Paul grinned, his body steely beneath the drenched blue T-shirt, his skin coal-colored with wetness and cold. He dove and the current yanked him downriver, his head sliding along its dark surface, arms sparkling as they thrashed him toward the far canyon wall.

When Paul reached the opposite bank Cohen retreated to the gravel bar and took a coil of nylon cord and three sections of yellow climbing rope from a porter's load. He tied them together and looped them over one shoulder, found a block of waterlogged bough in the shallows and waded back into the river.

Paul had returned upstream to chest depth. Cohen tied the end of the nylon cord round the block and, holding the coil loosely in his left hand, threw the block across the center of the river, above Paul. The cord drifted down and Paul grabbed it, pulling it in as Cohen paid it out. Paul climbed the far bank and tied the rope to a tree. Cohen recrossed the gravel bar and drew the rope tight around another tree.

Alex crossed first, hand over hand along the rope, then Stihl and Eliott. The porters looped their tumplines across one shoulder and went over one by one. Cohen untied the rope and lashed it loosely under his arms, waded the river to the deep channel and dove in, Alex and Paul pulling him across.

Changtshang had a defeated, resentful air. Women crouched silent in doorways; yellow *pai* dogs hunched like hyenas down rubbled alleys. Tibetan ponies, their red-haltered heads drooping with exhaustion, clustered in a train under a dead banyan in the village square, sinewy dark men with long sabers and black braids checking their riggings and hooves.

Stihl and Eliott stood to one side talking with two Tibetans from the pony train. "Sam!" Stihl called, beckoning.

Cohen bent to watch another Tibetan tighten a girth under a pony's belly. The pony's hair was soggy and white with sweat. *"Kata janahuncha?"* he asked the Tibetan—where you going?

The Tibetan eyed him under the pony's belly. "Mustang."

"Sam!" Stihl yelled.

"What you carrying?" Cohen said to the Tibetan.

"Food for my people." The Tibetan stood, the pony's flank shifting against Cohen. "Why care, white man?"

"I am a curious white man." Cohen crossed to where Stihl and Eliott stood with the two Tibetans. "You're suddenly chummy with the natives."

"Hey, these two speak some English." Stihl waved his hand to include the two short, wiry men at his side. "They crossed earlier." He shouldered Cohen slightly, lowered his voice. "They say there's robbers up ahead, invited us to join them."

Cohen snickered. "There's no robbers on the Kali Gandaki."

"They heard it in Tatopani. I think we'd be well advised to team up with them."

"I disagree. We'd have to slow to their pace."

"They're mounted."

Cohen turned to the nearer Tibetan, who was tossing cucurbit seeds from his palm into his mouth. "Who said there are robbers?" he asked in Nepali.

The man grinned, showing flakes of white seed against his small ivory teeth. Wisps of unshaven hair hung from his angular chin. "Gurkhas say many bandits raiding Kali by Muktinath trail."

"Where do you go?"

The Tibetan turned aside to spit a fragment of seed. "Mustang."

Cohen shook his head. "In every village there'd be a scramble for food. It's too big a party."

"It's super photo material. That's why we're here, isn't it?"

"You told us you wanted to get to Mustang. You got the permits, I don't know how, but you did. All we agreed was get you there and back."

"Sam, I've got thousands of bucks of photo equipment on a

porter's back. If it's safer to travel with these Tibetans, then I think we should."

Cohen moved away to watch the river glinting through the banyans. Such a schmuck this Stihl. Like so many Americans he thinks what he wants is important. But why do I care? Why bait him? He turned back. "C'mon, man, these Tibetans are arms smugglers. They say they're headed to Mustang, but they're the CIA train to Tibet."

"Oh, I heard those stories, checked them out with the embassy. They're just not true."

"How long you been in Nepal, Stihl?"

"A month."

"I've been climbing in the Himals for two years; so have Paul and Alex. You're paying for that experience. I don't want to be tied up with smugglers, lose my visa."

"No gang of thieves is going to attack either arms smugglers or salt traders, which is what these boys are. Come on, Sam." Stihl gave Cohen's shoulder a friendly punch. "Give me a break. I'm stranded way up here, dependent on you guys. Don't you owe me a little faith?" He smiled. "Please, talk to Alex and Paul. These boys want to leave soon."

"The porters have to eat."

"That won't take long."

Paul shrugged when Cohen asked them. "I don't care if we travel with the Penn State marching band." Alex merely grinned, nodding at the Tibetans. "Might as well trek with old Kali herself."

"So what are they going to do," Paul laughed, "steal your Swiss Army knife?"

"Levis, man, levis. Snatch 'em right off your ass."

"Speakin' of that," Paul chuckled, "do you remember Gabriel, the guy from Chamonix who went with the Italians up Dhaulagiri Three? He offered to trade a Tibetan guerrilla a pair of jeans for a Chinese watch. So six weeks later the guerrilla returns from Tibet with the watch, still strapped around a Chinese soldier's rotting arm."

"Gross. Did Gabriel keep the watch?"

"I believe so. But it took some time to scrape the skin off."

Alex shuddered. "Endless killing. What do they hope to gain?"

"They're pissed, man. Had their houses bombed and kids killed

9

and temples destroyed and all that other shit by the Chinese. The Dalai Lama chased out. How do you think *you'd* feel?"

The porters finished their noon rice, squatted against their loads, slipped the tumplines over their brows, and rose to cluster with Goteen near the village edge. One of the two Tibetans who had spoken with Stihl approached Cohen and Alex. He pointed up the trail. "Now go?" he said in English.

Cohen answered in Nepali. "There are no robbers."

The man's eyebrows lifted. "Gurkhas say . . ." He shrugged, switched to Nepali. "Surely we are safer together." He glanced up, hearing the crunch of Stihl's boot.

"What the fuck you guys waitin' for?"

"Cool it, Stihl," Alex chuckled. "You'll get a brain hernia."

"We can make Kagbeni before dark."

"You should take a copter, you're in such a rush."

Stihl shook Cohen's shoulder genially. "C'mon, let's hustle."

"What do you think, Alex?" Cohen said. "You wanna join these guys?"

Alex scratched the week-old whiskers on his chin, put his hand on Cohen's shoulder to turn him aside. "You're gettin' a little compulsive, Sam. Who cares about Tibetans? If Stihl, here, thinks they're a story, then let them be a story." He licked his lip. "Do you realize we haven't been to Thailand in three months? I'm gettin' a little bored with five-fingered Mary, but after this trip we'll have enough bread to bang cock in Bangkok till the monsoon's over. So keep your mind on pussy, where it belongs, and we'll muddle through."

Cohen pulled away slightly from Alex's grasp. "It feels weird. Can't explain."

"You want to dump Stihl here, go back to K'du?"

"We should do what we agreed to."

Alex shrugged. "So we stay a little stoned, ignore Stihl and Eliott, enjoy the mountains for five more weeks, and return rich to K'du." He crouched, picking pebbles from the earth, stood and threw them one by one into the river. "You don't like Stihl 'cause he reminds you of the States."

"Who knows?" Cohen squeezed Alex's shoulder and turned back to Stihl. "Paul and Goteen can lead. You and Eliott with the Tibetans. Alex and I take up the rear."

Paul and Goteen led the ten porters out of Changtshang and up the precipitous canyon path, Stihl and Eliott behind with the Tibetans and the ponies. Alex crouched waiting with Cohen on the cliff edge, pulled a leather bag from under his shirt and removed from it a small convoluted brass pipe and a plastic bag. He tucked a thumbful of ganja into the pipe, lit it with a waxed match that he tossed over the edge. Cohen watched the match diminish, fluttering featherlike in the wind, and vanish into the rushing Kali Gandaki. Alex inhaled deeply and passed the pipe. "Remember last time in Bangkok, that girl I met by the Great Temple, our last night?"

Cohen chuckled. "I can remember several."

"Dark-haired, golden tits?"

"They all have dark hair and golden tits."

"We did it seven times, that night." Alex took another hit, waited. "I'd like to marry her."

"Has she accepted?"

"I've known a lot of women, Sam—we've both been lucky that way, but to me she's the first one who's impeccable. You know the word 'unique,' how meaningless it is?"

"That's what advertising does, ruins all words."

"Well, she's unique, in the way that word was meant, in the way she made me feel. Not in love or any of that shit, but at peace, at peace in myself, in the world. For sixteen hours I was with her—her eyes, the way she would look at me, without fear or embarrassment—her way of holding herself . . ." Alex shook his head. "She has some deep level of self-respect—not egotism—*self*-respect, I've never encountered before. After all I've done, why go home and marry an American girl? I want to live in, be part of, the whole world. Christ, I think about her all the time on the trail. The last time, I was so sore but she did it all with her lips."

"You're horny. Besides, how many guys has she fucked?"

"A thousand, probably. But how many girls have we fucked, back in the glory days? I don't care. There was absolutely no distance between us. That night—it was like we'd been together forty years. Even if she never loves me, her extraordinary decency would be better than most people's love."

Cohen inhaled from the pipe, his shoulder against Alex's as they crouched side by side. "We're going to have to get you out of

11

the mountains," he exhaled. "I fear for the goats." He hugged him by the neck, passed the pipe. "So did you feel the earth move?"

"With her? We were on her houseboat so I couldn't tell. But we sure made that boat move . . ." Alex relit the pipe. "You never think of being married, having kids?"

"Not any more. Too many lovely women in the world to live with just one."

Alex stepped downwind and took a leak off the edge. "Bullshit."

"She's been dead three years, Alex. I'm over it."

"Maybe." Alex stepped up onto the trail. "But you miss caring, don't you?"

"If I were married I'd miss the mountains." Cohen took a last glance down at Changtshang. "With the money we're making from Stihl we can fuck ourselves to death in Bangkok and still have plenty to pay for the funeral."

Alex reached up and banged his knuckles on Cohen's head. "Knock on wood."

"When I fell off that bridge," Cohen said, "I had a moment when I didn't care—live or die."

"Like I said, you're missing something. Me too. Emotional neutral, that's where we are. It's easy for Paul, he's got Kim. They love each other and she's right here waiting in K'du. But you and I got nobody."

Alex put away the pipe. "Ever since Nam I've been outside looking in. Or sometimes not even bothering to look in. Hating the human animal."

"Shit, man, don't make it hard on yourself." He hugged Alex as they walked. "So tell me about this woman in Bangkok. I might want to fuck her myself."

"She wouldn't touch you, Cohen."

"I been thinking of maybe soon going back to Paris. If I can face that place I can face anywhere. And it's my home, really." Cohen plucked a grass blade, began to chew it. "You really want to marry her?"

"I want her with me. I want to see her face every morning, have babies with her. Want to feel her back and shoulders inside my arms."

"Maybe I need that too."

"Remember how it goes—time wounds all heels."

"You'd know."

12

"The drag about takin' up the rear is all this horse shit between my toes."

"Growing up in Montana I learned horses always shit more on the uphill. One of the seven immutable laws of the universe."

"With those loads it's no wonder. It's Nam all over again."

"What are they?"

"Mostly M16's. A few grenade launchers—which means the grenades must be somewhere, on some lucky horse. Hard to tell beneath the canvas."

"Fuckin' CIA. Don't they ever get tired of war?"

"Big business, war. The biggest. You know, one of the poorest kept secrets about Nam was we got into it to protect the CIA—their drug smuggling rings out of the Golden Triangle."

"No, I don't believe that."

"You ask any guy who worked in Air America, the CIA freight line, in the sixties, and he'll tell you about the tons of heroin they shipped out every month, out of Laos and Cambodia and South Vietnam—Hell, on river patrols we'd sometimes bring a boatful of the shit right down the Mekong. The CIA put it on planes and sent it Stateside, kept the locals high and mellow and made the CIA billions of bucks they spent on actions Congress or the generals wouldn't go for." Alex kicked a stone from the trail. "When we split Nam, the CIA lost its major source of funding, baby."

"You're a conspiracy freak, Alex."

"If so, my fears're based on what I seen, what I know." Alex slowed to look at the trail where it narrowed ahead of them and began to climb the cliffside. "Landslide territory, with the rain, those heavy horses."

"For me that was the final turnoff, about the States . . ."

"What?"

"That we're a society based on war, that we can't exist economically or psychologically without someone to hate."

"That's why we invented the good old Commies. Those folks I was fighting in Nam'd never even heard of Communism. They were defending their homeland from aggression, same as any American would."

"Before them we hated the Germans and Japs, and before them the Spanish, the Mexicans. Before that, the English." Cohen paused to pull a thorn from his sole. "Some day we'll be friends with the Russians and hate the Italians and the Dutch, or the Samoans and Madagascans."

"Don't let it eat at you. Hate only leads to more hate, like war only leads to more war. Here we are in these magical mountains, not back in the States. Forget those assholes at the Pentagon and the taxpayers who feed them, and enjoy what we have."

"We've got trouble, that's what we have." Cohen ran forward as a pony slipped on the trail edge and fell to its knees, a front and rear leg over the cliff. The others tied in front and behind it reared against the sudden yank on their ropes. The pony tilted sideways and dropped with a scream toward the Kali. Two behind and one in front peeled off the trail after it. A Tibetan leapt forward and with a sharp flash of his saber cut the rest free as the fourth slid off the edge.

Cohen and Alex dashed from the trail to a ledge dropping to the river. One of the Tibetans had fallen with the ponies; he was yelling and waving his arms as the river twirled him about and sucked him away.

Cohen pelted through the shallows toward a pony lying broken-backed over its load. He tugged its halter up to raise its head above water. Its nostrils and eyes were wide; its forefeet thrashed erratically. Its load had burst open and he could see the black sparkle of rifles through the flitting water.

"Sam!" Alex's yell was almost inaudible over the Kali's roar. Cohen ducked a flying hoof and knelt to shove the pony's head up onto his shoulder, skidding barefoot on the riverbed. "Sam!" Alex was wildly waving him over. He shook his head, pointing to his pony. Two Tibetans were inching down the cliff; others were running back down the trail to the ledge Cohen and Alex had taken to the water. Alex screamed his name again; Cohen released the moaning pony and struggled upcurrent to the knee-deep rapid where Alex stood beside a pony with splintered legs. "Look!"

Cohen bent down and saw a gray metal object, perhaps part of a pump or compressor, cylindrical, less than three feet long, in the shallows where the pony's load had opened. Alex crouched in the water, trying to feel along one side of the object. He reached beneath it.

"What is it?" Cohen yelled.

"Bomb!"

"Get away from it! Jesus Christ!" He grabbed Alex's arm and shoved him toward the bank; Alex stiffarmed him and broke free, ran splashing to the bomb and knelt beside it.

14

"Alex!" Cohen ran at him, shaking him. The river undercut him and slammed him downstream, banging his knees on boulders. He scrambled to a stop and waded angrily upstream. Alex was running ashore. The first Tibetan splashed in and waded past him into the current. Alex yanked Cohen up on the ledge. "Gonna die unless we run. A detonator!"

"A what?"

"Plutonium detonator. For an atomic warhead."

Cohen quivered with shock, then ran behind Alex up the ledge to the trail and past the ponies standing silent in the hands of the other Tibetans. Stihl and Eliott were edging between the cliff face and the last pony. "Clem," Alex yelled, "got to get rope—pull out the horses."

Stihl blocked the trail. "Are there guns?"

"Who knows?" Alex shoved past him.

They reached the porters. "Bad men," Alex gasped at the lead porter, pointing at the Tibetans. "They'll kill you all. Leave your loads, run into the hills. Run!"

Goteen and Paul were scrambling downhill toward them. "Go back," Alex screamed.

Paul, panting, held out his big palm. "Slow *down*, baby! What's up?"

"Down there's a detonator for a nuclear bomb." Alex caught a breath. "The rest of the bomb's probably on a couple of other ponies."

"Who says?"

"Naval ordnance—Vietnam—had to be able—take them apart—know by heart. Stihl's in it. They'll kill us. Christ, we're all gonna die." Stihl was clambering from the river, waving at the Tibetans with the ponies. One Tibetan flicked out his saber and slashed the canvas from a pony load.

Ahead of them the trail snaked up the canyon wall, without cover. Behind them the porters had slipped past the horses and were running toward the bend in the canyon leading to Changtshang. The Tibetan pulled a rifle from the pony pack.

Alex shoved Cohen into a narrow defile in the canyon wall as high, fast popping exploded downslope. Goteen screamed and Cohen grabbed for him but he dropped backward off the trail, face spattering red. Alex tumbled onto the trail, blood spilling over his chest.

Cohen tossed Alex over one shoulder and ducked into the defile. He grabbed the rockface lefthanded, his right clutching Alex's body, his legs pumping, Paul shoving them up.

15

2

THE DEFILE DIED OUT in steep talus sheering up an avalanche chute. Cohen put down Alex's body and wiped bubbly gore from the bullet's exit hole in his chest, shattered ribs staring uprooted from the pink flesh.

"He's dead, Sam." Paul's voice seemed faraway. "Time to go."

He could not see, turned to go down after them, to kill them now, here and now, but Paul grabbed him. "Later!" Paul screamed, driving him upward. The avalanche chute soared northward up the canyon wall, sheltering their climb, the Tibetans' voices ascending invisibly beneath them. Halting breathless on a ledge, Paul dug a chunk of rock from the wall and twisted round.

A Tibetan appeared in the chute, climbing fast, two hundred feet down. "Throw!" Cohen hissed, fingering the wall behind him for a rock.

Another Tibetan appeared, a rifle on his shoulder, Eliott behind him. Paul's arm zipped; the rock accelerated downward and smashed Eliott's head, his body hurtling outward and down. Seconds later its rattling thump echoed up the chute. Bullets hammered the underside of the ledge. Cohen edged up a sidewall, Paul following. They traversed again to the chute, then cut back in a vertiginous gulley that led them to a windy notch atop the canyon.

Paul hurled another rock, missing. "They're closing in," Cohen panted, "both sides."

"They'll bring up the horses. Split up and one of us might make it." Paul's voice was calm. "Me through Thorungtse and Braga, you back down the Kali, over to Pokhara." He ducked back as a bullet smacked off the edge, whined into space. "Meet in K'du, my place, five days?"

Bullets drummed the cliff. "A backup!" Cohen screamed.

"Where?"

"The Serpent—Paris!" He sprinted along the cliff edge, up a

16

brushy gully, thorns tearing his legs and feet, across a goat pasture, through a juniper grove, up a ravelled creek bed, and along a buffalo trail bending southward high above the canyon, the river flashing somber far below. From an oxbow in the trail he looked back but saw only five dark figures approaching fast, a half mile behind. He turned and ran hard for several miles, but they stayed close.

Above Jamosom the river was joined by a broad, crashing tributary that drained the high peaks to the east, forcing him to run down its darkening canyon as the last daylight dispersed in the west. He hesitated, wanting to follow its streamside trail plunging toward the Kali Gandaki, but fearing other Tibetans were already there, on horses. He waded the icy current and clambered up the opposite canyon wall under cover of darkness as voices and the clink of guns descended behind him.

At the top of the canyon he stumbled and fell, legs quivering, lungs gasping, pulse hammering his brain. Below, five shadows crossed the white rapids of the stream. Can't lose them. He ran cursing his rubbery legs, falling over rocks, forcing himself to remember the years of running that had conditioned him to climb, that had given him the physical and mental will to win where others lost. With the passing miles his legs grew weaker, his mind more confused. More and more often he looked back. Can't lose them. I'm dead. A dream, this. Dead and don't realize. "Dead and don't realize," he panted, over and over, until the words fell into cadence with his stride, pacing him across the rubbled hills like a metronome.

In the starlight he could see nothing, hear nothing over the thunder of blood in his head. Head down, palms on knees, he inhaled, exhaled, inhaled, exhaled. No matter how tired always go farther. No matter how hurt, one more step. With each step, force out one more step. Head high, thinking one more step, one more step, he stumbled on till his breathing again deepened, and in the clarity of pure exhaustion ran steadily southward under the cold light of the stars.

Hours later he halted on a bluff above terraced rice fields, seeing nothing behind. Slower but still rhythmically he ran, midnight air sharp in his lungs, all thoughts lost in the throbbing ache of his legs, arms, and chest, the mantra "I'm dead—don't realize—I'm dead—don't realize" his only awareness. Ten miles further he circled a village where a *pai* dog caught his scent and barked listlessly. Beyond the village he drank from the coolness of a flooded paddy and took a buffalo trail southeast, under the high Himalayan front, toward the steep ridges above the canyon of the Mristi Khola.

At the first ruby tint of dawn over the eastern crests he cut a quarter mile uphill to a clump of junipers creviced in the hills, and collapsed. Minutes later he woke and glanced round the pungent brush expecting to see Alex, Paul, and the others snoring peacefully beside him in the crowded, malodorous dung-brick shelter of a trailside *butthi*.

He reached out in the darkness to comfort Alex. Go deep. I was always telling you go deep. For a moment the old feeling, Alex blowing downfield past the cornerback and cutting for the post, his long light legs soaring over the choppy grass, Cohen seeing him over the thrash of helmets and waving arms, throwing the ball so hard and impossibly far in front of him, the ball arcing in the late afternoon sun, drawn magically downward into Alex's distant hands. And now you've gone so deep I'll never find you.

Gone deep. To the end of the world. Beyond. Every bird, blade of grass, child's laughter, woman's love. Gone from you. You who were a magic universe are not. They killed you. They'll kill us all.

Hallucinating. Crazy. Come out of it now. See, all's fine. He sat up and looked around, rosiny cypress tickling his lip, sharp branches tinted from the lightening east. Been hit, Paul said. Walk it off.

"Alex?" he whispered. He fingered the ground prickly with dry needles. "Alex!"

It's true. He cupped his legs in his arms, face on his knees. It's true. "Paul!" he cried, sparking a bird's call in the brush. A bomb. On its way to Tibet on horseback like a stone age weapon. Delivery from the CIA? Who do I tell?

Now what to do? Don't give up. Outrun them. Be waiting for Paul. Tell the Embassy. Paul—are you dead? Oh God poor Kim. Oh Christ Alex don't be dead.

As a moth at a flame his mind reverted once more. "Stay in touch," Eliott had said, cocking an eyebrow at Cohen in the early spring evening outside the Peace.

18

"I'm always in touch," he had countered, annoyed by the inherent command.

"We've a trek going in a couple weeks," Stihl had smiled—always a thin smile. "Might be looking for assistance. With good pay."

"There's five million Nepalis out there. All but a hundred of them are hungry." Cohen had begun to step away.

"I mean weathered climbers. Who know the ropes, parlay the local gibberish. Who can put together some porters, Sherpas."

"Some Yugoslavs just tried Kanchenjunga. Ask them."

Stihl had picked at an incisor with a slim fingernail. "We prefer our own kind."

"What kind is that?"

"People we can trust."

"You're safer trusting Nepalis than westerners." Cohen had turned away. It seemed now not weeks but days ago. He had felt vaguely used, yet curious to know their plans. He had avoided the Peace; they had appeared at his two-room hut off King's Palace road. This time Eliott had been more blunt: "We need two American climbers right away for a photo trek to Mustang. It's short notice, but the guys we planned on ran into trouble. Wanna go?"

"Up there's off limits without a permit."

"We're working on that. We may even want to reach the border."

"Tibet?"

"Where else?"

"To climb what?"

"Depends on what's there."

"I can tell you what's there and it's all off limits."

"There's five grand in it for you and five for your buddy," Stihl had interposed. "You let us worry about the permits."

"Which buddy?"

"The guy you climb with—what's his name? Vlasic?"

"Alex Vlasic. He's one of the guys I climb with. Paul Stinson is the other."

"Stinson? Lives with a white girl, doesn't he." Cohen had nodded, conscious of Eliott's smiling drawl. "How's his stamina in the cold?"

19

"Better than yours, or mine." Cohen had glanced toward the open door. "I don't think we're the people you want."

"We've made a mistake." Stihl stepped outside to tip cigar ashes. "We didn't realize you three worked together. In that case Stinson should come."

"With five in it for him?"

Stihl had hesitated. "We could go maybe twelve, for all three. Four grand apiece."

"That's a ridiculous lot of money."

"There's a lot to be made. Photo sales, magazine articles, a book." Stihl had puffed his cigar gently.

Cohen had gone that evening into a walled garden to knock on a carved door beneath suntala trees, and Paul had given him rice wine and Tibetan hash while Kim sat on pillows behind a trestle table knitting a sweater for her niece in Oregon.

"Stamina in the cold?" Paul had chuckled. "Who is this boy?"

"A Texan," Cohen had grinned.

When they had discussed it next morning at the Globe, Alex had been more precise. "I don't like the sound of that mother-fucker."

"Which one?"

"Either." Alex had stopped to lift a piece of *rango* from his stew to his mouth. "But I can use four grand."

Paul had laughed. "I'm a poor boy too."

Alex had licked his fingers, stroked the lapels of his homespun Sherpa vest. "The secret is to act rich."

"I vote we go, then," Paul had said. "So I can act rich too."

He was shivering. Dampness had risen to the hills, cold on his back, knees, and feet. A scuffling grew louder from the east, the silhouette of a porter hunched under a load. As the light strengthened, more followed, tumplines taut around their brows, loads tall above their heads.

By sunup no one had passed but porters and a few women hurrying to neighboring rice fields. With a fingernail he scraped dried blood from the gashes in his feet, stood and stretched his aching legs, descended to the trail, and took off at a steady lope. As his muscles warmed he ran faster, imagining each person he passed describing him later to mounted Tibetans—"*Ho,* one barefoot sahib, running east."

20

The day turned hot, sweat cutting channels through the dirt on his chest. Repeatedly he switched trails, always choosing the less travelled, misleading the few Nepalis who called out *"Kata janahuncha?"*—"where you headed?"—by yelling *"India-ma janchu."*

In late afternoon he forded the Mristi Khola and ran steadily up the zigzag trail on the east side of its canyon, stopping a half hour later to catch his breath at the summit. The low sun inflamed the dusty, high air, washing out color and depth, but in the distance, on the far side of the canyon, three horsemen trotted onto the trail leading down to the river. The moment they dropped out of sight into the canyon he sprinted from the trail up a stony track into the hills.

When the sun sat fat and orange over the lower crests of Dhaulagiri he bolted a *chai,* tea boiled with yak's milk, in a *butthi* at a fork in the path. "The sun sets, sahib," the *butthi* man said.

"Ho."

"You will stay?"

"Huena."

"It is wiser not to travel when the leopard hunts."

Cohen gave him ten pence. "To Hell with leopards."

"This one does not eat the goat, but the man who watches the goat."

"How far to the next *butthi?*"

"Tensan Bazaar. Perhaps two hours."

He ran eastward, leg muscles screaming, on the springy earth between terraced rice fields that glinted like emeralds in the sun's reddish afterglow.

Atop a forested knoll he checked his backtrail. The land tilted westward in pinkish gray ridges and aquamaroon valleys, the sky's magenta streaked by leaves. Boughs rustled in a cooling breeze; a tinkle of water waxed and subsided. In the hazy western distance, movement that might be a farmer with two water buffaloes, going home, or perhaps two riders. He rubbed his glasses on his shirt and squinted, shook his head, and glanced around at the rugged scrubby hills settling into darkness.

Two hundred feet below him a leopard slipped onto the path and raised her green eyes to him. She flicked her tail, stretched languidly, claws kneading the earth, her back quivering. She shook her head from side to side like a dog, glanced round once and trotted uphill.

Frantically he sought a tree. Only rhododendrons, low and spindly. He raced down the far side of the knoll but the path vanished in a ravine choked with magnolias. Dead—don't realize, sprawling into a stream, tearing his hand, smashed through the magnolias and up the far side of the ravine. Thorns ripped his knees; rock spilled away underfoot and clattered down the slope. The leopard bounded over the knoll into the ravine.

Steeper. Dashing along a ledge till it narrowed to inches. The leopard slipped through the trees, crouched on her belly at the side of the ledge, grinned, licked her nose. Huge bone-white saber teeth, one top fang missing. Ears flattened, muscles rippling, she glided toward him, a silky ribbon of saliva drooling from her jaws. He fell, jammed his fingers into a seam. Belly arching, yellow claws gritting the stone, she padded closer, sniffed his bloody hand, slashed at him, fanning his leg.

He could not free his hand. The leopard edged forward, balancing carefully. She was slightly above him now and he could see a row of pink nipples through her belly hair. She clawed at him and he twisted away, toes scrambling for a hold. She was purring, a hideous rumble of pleasure deep in her chest. He slid back down; she raked at him. Swinging sideways, he found a crack with his other hand and pulled himself up, yanking his fingers from the seam. Above this crack he found another, and then a slanting crease that took him hand over hand up a cliff face to a grassy shelf. Below on the ledge the leopard rose on hind paws, seeking a way up the cliff.

He scrambled across the shelf to the edge of the precipice, swung on a root across to the steep wall of the hill, and dashed over the top into a muddy field. Beyond it a tiled roof was silhouetted against the dusk-red snow of Macha Pucchare.

Two football fields. She'll get me. His feet slogged in the soft earth; breath thundered in his ears; his spine ached with terror. Dreamlike, the roof drew no closer, the leopard gaining invisibly behind him. He hurdled a wall into a courtyard, yelled "*Namasté!*" Far away a dog barked. The door gaped open. He pounded down a corridor patched by dim light from open rooms.

The first room had no door. The next had a thick door with a rusty bolt he kicked home. Gasping, head spinning, he crossed the room. Its vacant window stared into the garden four feet below. He stumbled back from the window to the door but the bolt was jammed, ran to the window and climbed through it up a prickly cypress to the second floor, stones crackling as the leopard soared over the wall into the courtyard.

The cypress teetered with his weight. From its top he could not reach a second floor window. The leopard's lithe shadow crossed the starlit courtyard like a shark through dark water. Plaster rattled in the corridor. The leopard shot through the window, green eyes gleaming. Shuddering with fear he shinnied higher but the cypress tipped sideways and down toward the leopard. Hastily he slipped down several branches, closer to her. The treetop righted.

The leopard vaulted into the courtyard and stretched up the cypress, her claws rending bark and shivering the boughs under his feet. The tree lurched sideways. He grabbed a second floor window sill as the treetop tilted past it. The tree sprang upward, the leopard snarled and dove for the window as he squirmed through it, her claws shredding the sill as she crashed into the courtyard.

She lunged up the cypress. He tore a stone block from the lintel. As the cypress tottered and she tensed for another spring at the sill he hurled the stone into her green eyes. She roared in surprise, tumbled to the courtyard. He prised loose another stone that hit her neck as she jumped into the cypress.

The corridor. In the other rooms no doors. Through a slack-jawed window a field and the glow of huts under the Himalayan wall. Dog's bark.

Scrabble of plaster on the stairs—she exploded into the corridor. Screaming he bolted the door as it shuddered under her claws. He ran to the window but she careened downstairs into the courtyard, charged at his window, fell back with a crash and leaped into the cypress.

She halted near the top, huffing, her eyes the pure green of ice burning underwater, green eyes of the Devil, mirthful and pitiless. He flung another stone that thudded into the cypress. She moved higher, leaned the cypress toward the window and caught the sill as he sprang into the corridor slamming the door, her claws splintering its planks. He bounded the stairs and garden wall and raced for the huts.

3

His feet leaden with mud, the deserted building looming end-lessly over him, the leopard closing silently. He roared into the yard of the first hut and pounded on the door. A chained dog ran whim-pering to him.

"*Ho!*" A man's sleepy voice.

"Open! The leopard!"

"Who's there?"

"Help! The leopard comes!"

Light shifted through cracks in the door. The dog growled high in its throat. "It's the leopard," a woman's voice whispered. "Don't open!"

"No!" Cohen wailed. "I'm running from her."

"Go, Leopard Demon, go!" the man screamed. "You cannot trick me, Devil Leopard!"

"Help. A *butthi!*"

"This is not the *butthi!* It's on the Pokhara trail."

Cohen glanced behind his back. The dog whined, rubbed its shoulder against his knee. He scratched its ear unconsciously, pounded again. "The leopard!"

"*Butthi chaina!*" the man repeated shrilly. "*Pokhara-ko bato-ma cha.*"

The dog growled into the darkness, retreated on its chain to paw the door, licked his hand, then howled as he sprinted uphill past other huts where firelight snuck through window bars and un-der doors, children chattering inside like swallows. The leopard flashed across the darkness behind him—he spun round to face her. The dog screamed, a snarl of rage from the leopard, the ping of the chain snapping, choked gurgling of blood in the dog's throat. The trail forked, its east branch sinking toward Pokhara. He banged at the last hut.

"*Ho?*"

24

"*Butthi cha?*"

"*Butthi cha.*" The door opened. Lamplight yellowed the *butthi* man's stubbled chin, his stained and crinkled topi. "Good you are just one, sahib. My house is full." He waved his arm into the dim room, where half-naked porters squatted round a rice-oil lamp. "Yet scarce would I leave you for the leopard."

Cohen shut the door and leaned panting against it. "In the village—they called me—Leopard Demon."

The *butthi* man's black eyes appraised him. "Kali can adopt the human form. They feared her in you."

Cohen sank gasping to the floor. "Better the two-step snake, than the leopard."

"So says the proverb." The *butthi* man bolted the door. "Either seems a fearful fate."

He sat cross-legged among the porters, their talk muted by his alienness, in the bittersweet haze of green woodsmoke and ganja. The *butthi* man had bandaged his hand with hazel leaves; a bowl of *dhal bhat,* rice and lentils, lay untasted in his lap. The room, low and smoky, the porters, emaciated and sour-smelling, the glimmering coals and the needle flicker of a rice lamp, the coarse grain of the bowl in his palm, had no meaning, no presence; like a man awaiting execution he felt equally numb in the tangible and the dream. Dead but don't realize. He stared at the porters fingering their food. They too.

One by one the porters rolled into their burlap sacks on the hardpan floor, the room quieting to their breathing. The coals shrank silently toward the center of the hearth till two yellow eyes remained.

He clenched his arms round his knees to stop their trembling, bit his wrist till blood flowed. Alex is dead. Nothing I can ever do in the whole unrolling universe of time will wake him. Nor Goteen. Stihl killed them. Stihl and his bomb. Perhaps Paul's dead too.

I've never given up. Have I? Haven't I always fought back? How easy that was: football games when we were behind, or teams that blacklisted me over Vietnam, hardened minds hating me for what I'd done. Mountains that would not be climbed. But when Sylvie and my folks died what did I do? Gave up, ran to Nepal. Gave up love. Quit the fight.

War's just a symbol of the fact we're already dead. Only a person whose soul's dead could want to kill, could stop another's life.

Then my soul *is* dead. For now I *will* kill. Baptized in Alex's blood, I'll kill every killer. First Stihl, then those who sent him, then those who sent the bomb. The people in the factory who made the gun that killed Alex. Kali, Mother of Death, Daughter of Death—I swear this to you. Leopard Demon, I give myself to you forever; give me your help in return.

I will become like them. I will kill them. For you, Alex. For you and the two million of Vietnam, for my half-sisters and half-brothers in Buchenwald and Dachau and on the bonfires of Spain, for every victim since the first day of time.

He unbolted the door and stepped into the lanceolate shadows of the rhododendrons. Under a scimitar midnight moon the village lay bathed in gray silence. A silvery wire looped northwest up the nearer hills: the Tatopani trail. Beyond these hills rolled higher, darker ones, and over these rose foamy clouds. Above the clouds towered the black, icy Himalayan wall, and soaring from it, severed from the world, sailed the glittering peaks whose bleak jaws rent black space and blotted out the stars.

Macha Pucchare's great white spire sang of hope founded on incomparable beauty, on a savage, pure elation that now only angered him. He scrutinized the Tatopani trail; nothing moved along it either mounted or on foot. I should go now. The thought raised waves of fatigue quivering from his thighs up his back and across his shoulders. A little sleep, then go.

He reentered the hut's odors of curry, burlap, ganja, and sweat, moving cautiously round the sleepers lest he step across one with the sole of his foot and thereby injure him in a future life.

"*Kata timi janchau?*" whispered the *butthi* man from a corner by the barred window. "Where do you go?"

"*Pisab garna pardaichu,*" Cohen answered.

"It is better to hold your water when the leopard hunts."

"The leopard had dog to eat this evening. He will not hunger till tomorrow."

"If he's filled his belly."

"He surely has. Who would not prefer a dog to man?" Cohen pulled up his burlap and adjusted his hip into a niche in the hardpan. Something bumped his knee; he raised the burlap. A yellow foot, horny and flattened, lay against him. With his own foot he pushed it down.

Hands behind his head, he stared at the dark patterns in the thatch, hearing the porters' steady exhalations. *I should have stayed with Paul. The route through Thorungtse's harder. Maybe he's already dead.* He gripped his temples with both hands to squeeze out the thought, but the thought remained, and with it the rerunning mental film of Alex thrown backward in a hail of bullets. He sat up, leaning forward, head on his knees, biting back the words. *I should have stayed with Paul.*

Maybe Alex was wrong. It wasn't the bomb, but just some machinery, a pump or something. He snorted in derision at his own wishfulness. Whatever it was, it was important enough to kill for. To kill Alex. He cringed at the picture in his head, bullets punching lung and bone through Alex's chest.

Who'd send a bomb to Tibet? Who was sending guns? The CIA. In the Chinese civil war the CIA helped prepare Tibet as a refuge for Nationalist armies. Then the Nationalists under Chaing Kai-shek retreated to Taiwan instead. But to protect their flank the Chinese invaded Tibet in 1950 against ferocious but poorly armed opposition. The CIA was soon in the business of outfitting Tibetan guerrillas for their war against occupying Chinese armies. But would they, could they, send that bomb? Why? A cynical acceptance of one form of exported violence quails before imagination of the other. Who'd put the bomb together, and where? There were no answers to such questions, and he twisted and turned against the hard ground as if to find some solution there.

Before the moon had sunk into the western hills he rose again. By the door a stub of twine flickered in a saucer of rice oil. An untouchable, his forehead grooved by the tumpline, sat cross-legged before it.

"You wake early, father," Cohen whispered. He folded his burlap, took his glasses from his shoe, and cleaned them on his shirt.

"Burdens are lighter before the day is hot." The untouchable snuffed the wick and tucked it in the rags about his waist.

"Why the lamp?"

"The flame?" The untouchable stood, bony-kneed, calves like

wrists, naked but for his cotton waistcloth, and pointed to the center of his brow. "As I go I watch it, with the third eye."

"I see."

"You do not. But you could. Light a little flame, and sit before it. As you watch it, do not think. Let the flame simply appear as it wishes. Later, when you need to see it, it will be here." He touched his brow.

"What good would come of that?"

"Even those like you who are favored by fortune are blind in both eyes. Only with the third eye can we see the world which does not pass away."

The pain screamed inside him. "Do not say, father, that I am favored."

The old man scanned Cohen's face in the near-darkness. "To be favored by fortune is a great impediment to wisdom." He opened the door and dragged a frame of loaded kerosene tins onto the trail, squatted and adjusted the tumpline round his brow, leaned forward, feet splayed, and stood, the frame groaning. "When I was young, I thought I understood this world, but did not. Now I am old I see I don't understand and that it doesn't matter. Is this not wisdom?"

The *butthi* man rose, coughing and spitting, and fried Cohen *duita phul,* two eggs in yak butter, while the porters, rubbing spidery hands before the dim stove, waited to warm their morning palmfuls of rice.

The eastern sky flamed coral as he paid the *butthi* man five rupees and asked the direction to Tatopani and the Kali Gandaki. The man pointed out the wire line against the tan, eroded hills.

Once beyond the man's gaze Cohen dropped from the trail down a path between fields of new rice and recrossed below the village to pick up the Pokhara trail. From a ridge he glanced back through the ascending haze of morning fires but saw no horses, the land quiescent.

By noon he had walked and run another thirty miles yet felt no exhaustion. The trail was busy with barefoot porters bent under their tumplines, with red-saried women who stared at him openly. He stopped at a trail shrine to drink thirstily from the grinning face of a stone waterspout, a stump-nosed leper watching him vacantly from the twined shadows of a banyan and pipal tree.

In the valley after the shrine, *pai* dogs ran at him barking where seven huts clustered by a sparkle of water; beyond them a man followed a wooden plow and a water buffalo round a tiny rice plot. The trail snaked out of the valley to a cobbled, brushy ridge.

Atop this ridge he glanced back as a horseman crested the valley's western edge and leaned forward in his saddle to speak with the leper at the shrine. Cohen dove into the thornbrush, crawled fifty feet from the trail and squeezed on his back beneath a butterfly bush. The *pai* dogs began barking when the horseman reached the huts. Soon a clink of shoe on stone sounded over the twitting and scuttling of sparrows in the bushes. The water buffalo bellowed, a clear, lonely sound. "Twik-twik," called another bird, deep in the scrub.

A stripe of sunlight shifted on the branch above his face. He tried to look up but it lay on the periphery of his vision. Gently he turned his head. The sunlight slid toward him along the branch, iridescent jade, hand-to-elbow long, diamond-headed. The yellow eye with its black slit pupil blinked, the translucent sheath slipping down and away. It swayed above his forehead, one loop over the branch, split tongue flickering.

He did not breathe. Bony scrub encased his legs and ribs. The snake's swollen mouth was framed by globular white lips tufted with glossy scales. The topaz eye with its black slit winked. The head descended.

Sweat stung his eyes. He fought the urge to blink. Pulse fluttered in the snake's neck. The horse whinnied. Gravel crunched as the rider dismounted. The snake's coldness brushed his forehead. He twisted from a sudden pain above his eyes.

Time for two steps before I die. Don't move, slow the circulation. Falling into a core of light. A gaunt, bearded face before me, eyes that drink me in. I feel no fear. I love You and my heart is at peace with You. I may have been apart from You but never have I ceased loving You. A warm calm sea was inside and all around him. Thoughts passed away.

A small chittering went on near his ear—a child, crying from afar, over a broken music box. It grew closer, clearer:

> *Connection,*
> *I just can't make no connection,*
> *and all I want to do*
> *is to get back to you.*

*   *   *

The strangeness of this dying overwhelmed him. He was in a warm winter's apartment in Paris, surrounded by music, a woman near. Sylvie, it's a dream. Sadly she shook her head. "To be favored by fortune," she said soundlessly, "is an impediment to wisdom." He opened his eyes.

A cobalt sky loomed over bright leaves. A gold spider twirled from a twig. The music wavered, distanced. He reached a tentative hand to the trace of pain above his eye. Blood mixed with sweat came away on his finger. The chittering subsided.

A small yellow bird lay shivering on its back, vermilion underwings fanned out on the dead leaves. The two-step snake lay atop one wing, its slimness undulating over the bird's body as a man over a woman in the aftermath of love. Cohen rubbed the scratch in his forehead where the bird in its terror had clawed him. He slid quietly from under the butterfly bush and inched upward till he could see through an aperture in the leaves. The horseman was a portly Newari boy clutching a black plastic tape deck to his high-fronted saddle. Cohen shivered and turned back to the snake.

It had unhinged its jaws around the bird's head. He dug a stone from the soilless earth. He raised it, then remembered his own sure death moments earlier. The feeling of unity returned, and with it reverence for life. On his sleeve lay a yellow feather, down-tufted at its stem. He pocketed the feather and cast the stone away.

He threaded through the brush to the trail, inspecting each branch for snakes. At the trail's edge he knelt to sip from a slender runnel. Beyond his tanned and unshaven reflection, two butterflies linked and spiraled skyward, toward the blue apex in the pebble-bottomed mirror of a palm-sized pool.

Beyond the next valley the trail switchbacked up a southwest ridge, then descended into a purple-shadowed forest ringing with birdsong and the chattering of monkeys. Travelers were fewer and he made good time on the downgrade, stopping once for a glass of *chai*.

At dusk the forest opened on a valley where horses grazed knee-deep, their tails painted red by the setting sun. Stone houses

30

rimmed a paved yard cut by a stream whose susurration merged with the arhythmic tinkling of horse bells and the failing wind's whisper in the rhododendrons.

A bent woman in a black sari watched him from a garden. "*Namasté,* grandmother," he called. "This is the Pokhara trail?"

"*Ho.*"

"How many days?"

She raised three crooked fingers, holding in her other hand a plank she had removed from the streambank to divert water into the garden. "If there are no landslides." Wrinkles jammed the corners of her mouth. "Now the dark comes. You may stay tonight in the house of my brother."

"I must go tonight to Pokhara."

"It is impossible. Three days."

Cohen turned toward the fields behind him. "They are fine horses."

"My brother's."

"I seek such a horse to go to Pokhara."

"These do not leave the mountains." She replaced the plank. Water sank from view into the dirt, pebbles glistening.

Raising her sari hem, she crossed the stream and led him to a two-story stone house, the first floor open facing the yard. Herbs and bulbs hung from the beams. To one side a man crouched on his heels among naked children, a stemless pipe cupped in his hand. A girl with onyx eyes and mahogany skin sat beside him, one hand on his knee. He detached himself, grasped a cane, and stepped into the yard.

"You travel to Pokhara?"

"*Ho.*"

"The river eats the trail." In place of one eye was a half-closed pit. "In the morning I will tell you the old way to Pokhara."

"I must go tonight. I would pay well for a horse."

"Sit down. Have *chai.*" As the man spoke the children scampered from the firepit. "Even the porters do not travel it, since India fixed the trail."

"Why?"

"Two days ago, four fell into the river. Now, their families will starve."

"I have no family."

The old man smiled. He lit and proferred the pipe. "What is your name?"

"Cohen. And yours?"

"Hem, though I tire of it. Perhaps I will give myself a new one."

Cohen exhaled the smoke slowly, tasting it. "I would change more than my name, Hem. But first, I would talk with you of horses."

"They cannot be sold." Hem jostled the fire with a hardened stick. "In the morning we can talk Pokhara. Tonight my daughter will kill a chicken for curry, and you may sleep in the tallest part of the house." He grinned. "It is there the bedbugs are fewest."

Cohen watched the dark slink of water across the stone yard. Its sound was like many tiny bells. He glanced past the woven leaves of the porch to the trail breaking the tapestry of darkness at the forest edge.

"I must ride the metal bird at Pokhara tomorrow noon."

"The trail is very dangerous in day. At night, impossible."

"And the old way?"

"Is longer." Hem shook ashes into the fire. "There are some who seek you, Koan?"

"Why do you ask?"

"You look often at your back trail. And why else would you wish to travel at night, in the mountains?"

Cohen stood, stunned by a photograph on the wall. "From where comes this picture?"

"He was a young king of a far land. Years ago one like you gave me his image. Even in these mountains we knew him, for he was fair, and loved all children of God. Soon after, he was murdered. His death is not yet avenged. Perhaps you know of him?"

"His name was Kennedy; he was the leader of my country. After his death my country suffered a long and painful war. It suffers still."

"War is the punishment of nations, as sickness and pain are the punishment of men." Hem gestured to the onyx-eyed girl, crossed the stream to the pasture, and whistled. The nearest horse raised her head, a tuft of grass in her mouth. Cohen followed him to a stone shed, where Hem took two blankets from a stall.

"I must not stay."

"These are for the horses. Or do you wish to ride without a blanket?"

"You will go also?"

"You would not find it alone."

The horses approached, heads nodding. Hem looped rawhide bridles over the ears of a spotted gray and a bay roan, strapped a blanket on each with a leather girth. Their unshod hooves clattered on the stones as he led them to the stream. Over the sucking of the horses Cohen could hear children laughing behind the huts; from faraway downwind came the steady thunk of a rice mill. "There are others in this valley?"

"Where the river meets the trees." Hem handed him a woolen cloak and a topi. "In the darkness, your face hooded, you are Chetri."

They washed down a quick meal of *dhal bhat* with *chai* and rode into the shadowed valley. At its far end Hem turned the gray along an irrigation ditch. To their left passed the blunt outlines of huts, here and there a trace of lamplight.

For several hours they descended the canyon of the Modi Khola, fording finally at a gravel bar where stones rumbled on the riverbed, then turned eastward along diked fields where star reflections darted like minnows among stems of young rice. Hem reined in to point out a faint cluster of huts. "The *butthi* of the first day."

They climbed through cedars and junipers, then wind-torn scrub, then higher through ice-fractured rock, the wind stealing their voices, lashing skin from their faces, sucking air from their lungs, numbing their fingers round stiffened reins, freezing the horses' lips to their iron bits. Petrified buttresses of jagged stone spired over them into the wind-tortured darkness, the stars shimmered fiercely against the higher, black-ribbed peaks, the gasping, shivering horses broke belly deep through hardened snow that the wind snatched westward in tinkling fragments, the moon a razor creeping from the wind-sharp eastern crests.

Down the far side the trail was a frozen stream bed that became a rushing creek, then a torrent, the horses slipping and hoof-slapping back and forth through it. They dismounted, their feet soon numb in the near-frozen water, their clothes hardening against them. Cohen felt Hem's hand on his shoulder, could barely hear his yell above the crashing water, "It is here India fixed the trail."

Soon the canyon brightened. The stream cascaded over a ledge, shattering luminously and soundlessly on the cliff far below. They followed the clifftop westward to the old trail, coming out in a wedge of wind-stunted pines overlooking a dark valley.

"Here the danger begins." Hem grasped Cohen's shoulder and pointed to a filigree of moonlit ledge against the black cliff. "The trail is narrow there; the fall is long. In the valley below are leopards, which scare the horses. They smell them now."

Hem descended first, leading his horse. The ledge immediately narrowed to body width, the horses rubbing shoulders against the cliff. It narrowed again, and then more. The horses hesitated, huffing nervously. Cohen bumped a rock from the cliff with his elbow. Ten heartbeats later it clicked distantly against the cliff, then clicked again.

He inhaled, relaxed. The roan made a shivering murmur behind him. From far below rose a clatter as the rock reached the valley floor. Hem was invisible. Cohen urged the roan forward, trying not to lose his balance by pulling too hard on the rein. They stepped over a depression cut by a seep across the trail, the footing even more narrow and slippery.

After an hour the tops of the valley trees reached up to them. At the first widening of the trail Hem whispered, "Now we will go quickly, Koan, through this valley of dangers. We will not stop, or talk, but run, as the horses wish."

The trail disappeared under the black canopy. Twigs tore at their faces, louder than the horse hooves on the sod. The forest was redolent with rotten, leaf-damp, mushroom odors overlain by the sweat and manure smell of the horses. Cohen squeezed his shoulder blades against the empty feeling between them.

4

MOONLIGHT SLIPPED DOWN HEM'S back and across his horse's rump. Then Cohen saw his own horse's head illumined, her ears bent forward, her head casting steadily from side to side, before the moonlight slid across his hands and face and he too reentered the darkness. Hem flitted through another moonlit patch, his silvery image etched in Cohen's mind when he again had vanished. It seemed a very odd and old feeling, horsemen riding through the mountains in the darkness; it made him think of war. Now I too am at war. Where and who is my enemy?

Soon the forest thinned; ahead light gleamed among the trees. Hem rode unconcernedly on; Cohen urged the roan forward to warn him but saw that the gleam was a clearing into which moonlight poured. Hem halted. "The *butthi* of the second day."

"The leopards?"

"Behind us." Hem leaned forward to caress the gray's neck. "Before noon you will be in Pokhara." They left the trail and circled the clearing through forest whose resinous branches hissed against the horses' flanks.

As the first birds began to call they broke out on a tapering burnt ridge, below which a pocket-mirror lake gathered in the fading stars. The moon had set. They descended the ridge as dawn spilled red over eastern peaks, toward a long valley of villages and farms, toward the crowing of a cock and the wavering, unanswered bray of a buffalo.

The rusty clock inside the Pokhara terminal shed said 11:35. "The Katmandu-going plane comes at noon?" Cohen asked a Gurkha who sat splay-legged on a crate polishing the sheen of his crescent *kukri* against a khaki trouser cuff.

"Possibly," the soldier yawned, eyeing him down the blade edge.

Cohen stepped past a cyclone fence to Hem and the horses. "Soon."

"I do not see it, the bird."

"It comes now, from Bhutwal."

"The soldier said?"

"It does each day."

Hem shook his head. "Do not so depend on things, Koan."

Cohen scanned the field. "I must pay you for the horses. And for your help."

Hem grinned, empty eye socket crinkling. "I have watched as you spoke with the soldier. No one here hunts you."

"Because you brought me swiftly."

"They give up, Koan?"

"No."

"Then cease to be the one they hunt. Was it so good, your life? Before they came to hunt you?"

He watched wind devils twist across the field. "No."

"Our lives derive from what we are. There are no accidents."

Cohen turned his head to a distant whisper. "The bird comes." He took a wad of notes from his pocket. "We haven't discussed the money."

"Perhaps the young king on my wall was killed by those who hunt you?"

"*Huena*. Not the same ones."

"But the same kind?" Hem shortened the reins. "Some day you will be with a wife and children. Bring them across the water to my home. The sun is warm. Your children will play with my grandchildren. Your wife will sit with my sister by the stream. You and I will talk." He mounted the gray. "*Namasté!*"

"The horses, Hem. I must pay you."

"When you return!" Tugging the roan behind, Hem trotted through the outskirts of Pokhara toward the hills, his stiff right leg jutting from the gray's side.

Over the rumble of the descending plane Cohen noted for the first time the noises of Pokhara: chugging rice mills, the complaining dusty wind, the gnashing wail of a sawmill, the babble of school-children as they ran past him barefoot, clutching thin books bound with red string.

36

Nothing moved along the edges of the field but a hungry dog; no one approached from the town. He took a deep breath, fatigue slumping his shoulders and aching down his legs into his ankles, his eyes gritty with exhaustion and windborne dust. How long since I slept? How can I change, when I don't know who I was? When the one I was is dead?

He returned to the galvanized shed as the plane bounced down. His fellow passengers seemed unlikely foes: three overweight Newaris in red topis, a hill man with four goats, two old women in saris whispering and nodding, a teenager slipping back the sleeve of his cotton shirt to glance at a chrome digital watch with a black plastic wristband.

In the plane they sat on benches on both sides of the fuselage, held in by a rope running from front to back, goats and baggage in the middle between them. Lulled by the vibration of the propellers he nodded into watchful sleep till they turned south under the soaring Everest wall and drifted nose high up over the edge of the Katmandu valley, over a dusty farmer and his buffalo cart, the tan and blue silhouette of the city wide on the plain before them.

Katmandu Terminal squatted brightly in the noon sun. He descended amid the Newaris, eyeing the reflective terminal windows as he crossed the tarmac. Before the door he slipped behind a fuel truck, crossed a grease-slick unloading bay, hurdled a fence, squeezed between two panting buses and ran unhindered across the parking lot and along the road toward town.

He took an approaching taxi to Katmandu's center, ran, always glancing back, through thronged streets rank with feces, curry, and smoke, turned into a shoulder-wide alley in the Sherpa bazaar, waited but no one followed, crossed a paved square still sticky with the blood of a newly slaughtered buffalo, and knocked softly on a carved, worm-eaten door.

The steely-haired woman in a red shirt and leather skirt smiled as she asked him in, arranging pillows for him to sit on by the coals. "There is still a touch of winter in the house, Koan." She leaned through a wool-string curtain to the second room. "Seral, it is Koan."

Cohen knelt to hug the little girl who ran to him. "And Phu Dorje?" he asked.

"At the bazaar, coming soon. You have eaten?"

"Not since yesterday. But I bring sorrow."

Her eyes narrowed. "You are hungry?"

"*Ho.*"

Seral brought him meat stew, *chai,* a clay bowl of rice wine. She sat by him, silent, one hand on his knee. When he was done he took her into his lap, tucking back her braids. "Such a silent one thou art, little snowflake."

"Thou art also quiet, Koan-*daju.*"

"*Ho.*"

"My mother too sits silent in the other room. But I am happy to see thee."

"And I thee."

Phu Dorje entered softly, slipped his sheepskin coat from his back and sat on the far side of the fire. "I am surprised thou art not in Dhuala Himal."

"All has gone wrong, my brother."

"Where are thy friends?"

"Thy brother Goteen is dead. Also Alex. Paul perhaps has escaped."

The Sherpa crossed his legs carefully. "An avalanche, then." His face was calm, eyes tiny and black. He motioned to Seral; she stood and ran quickly into the other room.

"Above Changtshang. Where the trail cuts to Muktinath . . ."

"No danger is there."

"Stihl and some Tibetans killed them."

"Why?" Phu Dorje whispered.

"Because of what we saw."

"Saw?"

"It was not to go to Mustang that Stihl wanted. At Bagling we met Tibetans on horses. Stihl wished to travel with them up the Kali Gandaki, because of some robbers, he said. But it was guns they were taking into Tibet, to fight the Chinese."

"And so? Since the Chinese first marched into Tibet, have not the Americans sent guns upriver to the Tibetans?"

"But Stihl was of them, in secret. He and the Tibetans had a great bomb, taken apart, on the ponies' backs."

"Bomb? What is?"

"A great fire, like the sun."

38

"How did thou not see this great fire, at first?"

"It was locked in metal. Later, they would release it among the Chinese, perhaps in a large city."

"To do what?"

"It would destroy all the houses, kill all the people."

Phu Dorje shook his head in negation. "In a city are women and children."

"It has been done before."

"Who would do this?"

"Americans. It was war."

"Even in war one does not kill women and children." The flames hissed as Phu Dorje spat. "How did thou escape?"

"They shot Alex and Goteen at once . . ."

"How did he die?"

"Instantly. His body fell into the river."

"Then?"

"Paul and I climbed the canyon wall and separated. He went up the ridges toward Thorungtse."

"In that valley are many Tibetans." Phu Dorje rose and stepped through the curtain. Cohen removed his glasses and rubbed the ridge of his nose where they had indented to the bone. Phu Dorje returned. "My family will go to the village. We will tell Goteen's wife. Then we will find Stihl."

Cohen shook his head. "I will find him first."

Phu Dorje took his hand. "Two years thou hast been here, a blood brother to my tribe. Not like the other white climbers for whom we carry oxygen, tents, food, boots, the flags they plant at the top of the world. Not one who climbs a mountain with our help only to exult that he has climbed it, when it is we who have made that possible. Thou hast danced at our weddings and climbed like a Sherpa. Thou speak the Nepali tongue, which many of us do also, thus we do not have to use our childish English with thee. But it would be better for thee to leave the Himal, going home."

"I shall wait here for Stihl. And for Paul." Cohen replaced his glasses, caught momentarily by the room's sudden detail, by a kukri and a red cotton bag hanging on the tan wall.

"And the Gurkhas—if thou goest to them?"

"That is unwise. I saw the Mustang permits that Stihl had, permits that are impossible to get. He will say that we tried to rob him, that we killed Eliott. Stihl is American, with the power to get such permits. The bomb and the guns were American."

"And thy people?"

"I go to them now."

"I do not want thy people to punish Stihl." Phu Dorje eased back. "Stihl is a grain of snow on Annapurna; I will kill him because he killed my brother. But he is not the cloud that brings the snow."

"He can tell us . . ."

"If he knows, and if we kill him slowly." Phu Dorje bent to relace his rawhide boots. "And Paul?"

"If he's alive he should reach Katmandu within two days."

Phu Dorje stood. "I must call together my family, so that we can grieve for my brother." He looked up at Cohen. "That is all thy clothing? No shoes?"

"All our things were with the porters and are lost. This cloak was given me by an old man with one eye, who took me three days' journey in a night."

"It is Chetri."

"*Ho.*"

"One cannot trust the lowland people."

"He was of the mountains."

He moved quickly through smoky alleys hung with bright linens and littered with human excrement over which *pai* dogs fought bloodily, emerging on a broad boulevard of motorbikes, rickshaws, trucks, and buses. Ahead, beyond the trees drooping in the heat and dirty air, the august portals of the American Embassy flanked by two Marines. His steps slowed. What can I say, in my own tongue, to my own people? How can I explain what we have done?

Yet how reassuring the hard-jawed faces of the Marines, the tan four-door Dodge parked before the Embassy. It's been so long. Suddenly seeing his mother's face, lined and worn as it had been the last time he had seen her—for there is nothing to see in a closed coffin housing the cindered remnants of a plane crash. As he stepped from the curb she seemed younger, her skin now not desiccated by Montana's harshness, and he was running to her, she kneeling down—as he had an hour before with Seral—to comfort him against the impact of older boys in this new country laughing at his Jewish face and Irish accent, backing up their contempt with their fists. "Aye, and ye'll learn to beat 'em, Sammie, sure ye will."

Crossing the street, the Marines noticing him now. It's been so long, feeling grateful, strangely, to be American again, part of a worldwide network of might and privilege. To be protected. Strong, clear faces. To have someone to tell. The Embassy door opening, two men, one in a tan bush jacket, the other in a suit. Stihl in the bush jacket seeing Cohen transfixed in mid-traffic, Stihl grabbing the other's arm and pointing, yelling now at the Marines awakening from their somnolescent stare of hostility and peering open-mouthed about them, one unlimbering his rifle as Cohen stood rooted to the street.

The man in the suit already across the sidewalk, hand under his lapel, Marines with him, Stihl retreating to the Embassy door, calling inside. Man in the suit ten yards away, pistol in hand, yelling "Hold it!" as Cohen swung his fist and slammed him to the street, ducking the black blur of one Marine's rifle and barefooting him in the groin, swinging the pistol against the other's head so that his cap sailed across the street.

Stihl darting out the door with others, checking his stride at the sight of Cohen bearing down, pistol in hand, Cohen squeezing round after round into the elegant, thin-lipped face as it jigged frantically back toward the door, blood spraying the Embassy wall, Cohen dropping the pistol and sprinting down the street until there were trees, parked trucks, and then buildings between him and what had happened.

The narrow, darkened alleys milled with late afternoon crowds; leaning buildings traded ornate shadows. No one seemed to notice him; unshod, threadbare, and filthy, he was unlike the overloaded, skinny, and underdressed mass only in his few days' beard, an absence of umber in his skin, and the burnt sienna of his curly hair. He sat with a cool bottle of Indian beer in the back corner of a dirt-floored bar, alert to the faces flowing past the door.

Clenching his trembling hands he bit down the terror to run, run anywhere. Simply to run, running only, as if that simple act would free me. Now surely dead. The Gurkhas watching now, waiting now. Every trail out of town is a trap. Christ, I'm more afraid of the Gurkhas than my own people. . . . The Embassy won't tell them about the bomb. There'll be some other story. His shaking calmed. Very careful, very strong. Coming into a game in the fourth quarter, four touchdowns behind. Almost nothing can't be done.

41

For a moment he smiled, looking down at his hands, thinking Alex's words: "You're a guy with much more confidence than brains." Who will believe me now?

With Stihl and Eliott both dead how do I find the source? How do I find where they came from and kill their friends? Piss on nuclear war—it's due anyway. Divine retribution. But they killed Alex. . . . A Gurkha popped his head in the door, yammered at the barman, stared into Cohen's corner, and left. No, that's not true—I *do* care about the bomb. But long ago I gave up hope about it. Since she died I've given up hope about everything. Haven't I? He peered at the dark street, put on his glasses. Kim's home now.

A chill pervasive fog had slunk down from the mountains, the streets nearly empty. The alleys all were silent but for the hum of an occasional streetlamp casting its weak pool on the damp, uneven, dung-stained cobbles, the sorrowful bellow of a tethered rango, or the faraway rattle of a bus fighting the slight grade up from the *stupa* grounds.

He stopped, confused by the fog, retraced his steps. Gravelly footfalls approached, halted. He held his breath and backed against a wall. Leather-bound silent feet, a quick shape, braided hair above a variegated cloak, slipping past the rim of streetlight at the corner.

The steps paused. He could hear the man's breathing, deep and steady. Lost like me. The steps returned. Fabric brushed the wall. A shadow crossed the light, trailing an odor of green woodsmoke and curds. The Tibetan reached the corner, hesitated. He looked back the way he had come, shielding his eyes from the dim bulb, then trotted down the side street, kicking up a rock that rattled among dry dung in the gutter.

Cohen moved away from the Tibetan, keeping far from the lights. He ran down an alley leading to the *stupa* square where a giant beehive temple, beribboned and prayer-flagged, gave a suggestion of mass against the wheeling fogs. He crouched beside a bush and waited. For fifteen minutes no one came. He followed another smaller alley to a broken whitewashed wall behind which a cubicled white house sat in a tiled garden among suntala trees. After watching for a long time he knocked softly on the door.

She held a dishcloth in her hands as she opened the door, her short amber hair tucked in a maroon Newari scarf, her jeans torn at one

42

knee, a Coors T-shirt drawing his eyes automatically to her small high breasts. Her smile faded. "Sam, you look awful! What're you doin' back?"

He entered and locked the door. The same Tibetan rugs on the walls, the same worn gray boards of the knee-high trestle table, with thick cushions piled against the wall behind it. The same posters, of Big Sur, Santana, and the Bernini Fountain. ("Paul has a body like Bernini's *David*," she had once said.) By the door to the kitchen, the same silk scroll painting: a great convoluted mountain with its tiny figure of an old man stooping at a forested pool below a waterfall.

"You should change your pictures, Kim."

"What's gone wrong?"

"Alex is dead. I don't know where Paul is."

She lit a kerosene lamp and centered it on the table. She sat on the table edge. "How?"

"Shot. By Stihl and some Tibetans."

"Who else?"

"Goteen."

"Where's Paul?" Tremolo now in her voice.

"I don't know. We split up to evade them. He should be here in two days."

Bending away, she was crying now, fighting to hold back. "You asked for it—I told you, I told him!" Her face scarlet, tears thick on her cheeks now, she buried sharp nails in his arm. "Mustang! I hate it, hate it, hate it! Oh how I hate that word! He'd be here now. He'd be here tonight! We'd have had dinner like we always do, and talked and read and made love and held each other. You! You had to drag him away—to Mustang!" She tore at his arm. "You always know best! Don't you? Don't you? Men always know best. Don't you!"

She sat sobbing on the table. "And we're always your victims. Aren't we?" She faced up at him. "You bastards! When was the last time a woman ever killed anyone? When?"

Sitting on the table edge he told her all he knew, leaning against her, from time to time rubbing her neck at the shoulder or holding her hand wet with the tears she rubbed from her cheeks. After a while she got up and made tea. "Alex was your friend long before I knew him, Sam. Yours and Paul's."

"I keep expecting him to show up, as if nothing's happened."

He sipped the sour tea, letting it burn the membranes inside his cheek. "I always learn too late."

"He loved the mountains. It's not your doing."

"But I knew it was wrong. Stihl didn't add up. And I did it anyway."

She wiped at tears with the back of her hand. "I begged Paul not to go—something ate at me. . . . He wouldn't pass up Mustang."

"We all wanted the money. It's like death, money." He tugged her close. "You have to leave, Kim."

She pulled away. "I'm waiting for Paul."

"You'll have to wait for him in the States." He held her face in his palms. "Paul's dangerous now, like me. He killed Eliott. They'll blame him for Alex, maybe for Stihl. You have to get away and stay away."

"If you're dangerous I shouldn't be with you either. In any case I'm going to keep on doing what I've been doing, till he . . ."

"Keep teaching?"

"Yes! Every day nine classes of ragged little Newaris with gentle, hungry eyes, their festering sores, their blindness, cholera— God, Sam, do you know how many of my kids've died this year? Half the children die before they're five!"

He sat again on the table edge and looked into her reddened hazel eyes. "It's a joke, life. I used to love it, but it's a vicious trick. It makes you love it, then snatches itself away like a cockteaser. It makes you love people then kills them. God, whoever He is, is a malevolent bastard."

"God tries, Sam."

Cohen rubbed exhaustion from his face. "Why do the best die, and the ugly and the evil live? The old man on the Modi Khola who gave me this poncho had a picture of Kennedy on the wall of his hut. Way back in the mountains of Nepal, back in the stone age— and he loved him too. Kennedy's dead, and his beautiful brother too, and Martin Luther King and Medgar Evers and Malcolm X, while an evil, ugly, craven cheat like Richard Nixon, or a malignant Barbie Doll like Ronald Reagan lives on! Why's that?"

She began to set things straight in the tiny square room. "How different things would have been . . ." She looked down at his feet. "You must be cold!"

"They're sure to be watching my place. By tomorrow they'll be here, too. I gotta go—you too."

"You'd have to kill me, Sam, to make me leave."

"That's crazy! Go to Rayamaji's, anywhere."

"You go! Take some of Paul's clothes—in the bedroom."

"I guess it's me they want. Maybe it's safer for you not around me." He resisted the chest-crushing urge to drop his face into his hands. "Seems unreal. So far away. I've been dead, Kim, dead all this time."

She stood on tiptoe to kiss him. "Put on some clothes. Hurry!"

In the bedroom a pale nightgown tossed on the bed, dresses and skirts hanging from a pole across the corner, white underpants crumpled on the floor. Beside the bed with its four posts set in tins of water to deter bedbugs was a leather trunk filled with clothes, Paul's and hers, among which Cohen found a clean undershirt, socks, shirt, and worn jeans. Beneath the hanging clothes were two sets of climbing boots, inners and outers, and a pair of running shoes, frayed in the toes, that fit him loosely. He sat on the floor tying the shoes. The clothes smelled like Paul, the blue and white shoes so reminiscent that Paul's absence was almost more than he could stand.

He faced the mirror. I do not realize each second I am alive how deep life is. That's the measure of my failure. That is how I've been dead, how I must change. His severe, tanned features were pinched with fatigue, the wide thin lips blistered, the oft-broken nose sharp under narrowed, bloodshot blue eyes, the crinkled brown hair tangled with dirt and dried sweat, the beard reddish-brown and uneven, a boy's. "You're not very handsome, shitbird," Paul had once said.

"At least I'm white."

"Yeah," Paul had chuckled. "That's the essence of your problem."

On a shelf above an ice ax with a bent tine was a football, its pighide worn slippery, its laces tanned by years of sweat and countless rains. It felt perfect in his palm, nothing but an extension of his arm, laces matching his fingertips. "I can remember," he said to Paul, "when just the touch of this would bring me peace." He took Paul's razor into the kitchen, heated water, and shaved. He finished the new tea she had brought him and put the cup in the basin. "Let's go."

"Where?"

"An empty garden somewhere. A few hours' sleep. I'm so tired I can't figure anything out."

"I'm sorry, Sam—I've been so upset . . . You've killed a man—it must be awful."

He reached for her. "I'd kill him a thousand times over for what he's done. My only regret is now I have to run and can't face them openly. That now I can't expect anyone to believe me. Give me a blanket, some matches?"

She brought a blanket from the bedroom and a box of wooden matches with a leaping tiger on the cover. He started to tell her about the leopard but stopped, thinking of Paul.

Her lips were trembling again. "I'll not take the chance of missing him." She grimaced brightly. "No one'll bother me, anyway."

"If he's late, or if I can't stay in K'du, we've got a backup. In Paris, a bar called Le Serpent d'Etoiles. Where we used to hang out."

"Before my time."

"So if anything goes wrong, that's where to find me."

"If *anything* goes wrong?" She shook her head. "You must be crazy, Sam. Everything's already gone wrong."

"You should sleep." He dredged up a smile from the depths of exhaustion. "So tomorrow you can cast eloquence before the unwashed."

"They're cleaner than I am, Sam."

"I didn't intend it like that." He brushed at the hair pasted with tears to the side of her cheek. "It's just that all human effort seems a waste. . . ."

"They starve; the ones who survive are always hungry. Their parents die at forty. Still they're happier than we. I can see it in their eyes. Grateful for the blessing of life."

"It is a gift, God-given. How we trample it." He took her hand, feeling her head and shoulder against his chest. The lamp wavered in a draft, stilled. Far away a dog moaned in hunger.

5

HE UNROLLED THE COARSE, itchy blanket and sat up to scratch bedbug bites. The light was gray, its edges sharp with cold, acrid with cooking fires and pungent with human and animal dung. "Welcome to exotic Katmandu," he mumbled, in his mind a Samoan beach, a dark girl in a white bikini, white orchid in her hand, and below her the words, "The first day of the rest of your life."

Unmelodious tinny complaint of Hindi song from a distant radio, mutter of hens, aggrievement of a donkey. By his head, a stone block engraved with a snake ingesting its tail. The two-step snake. He shuddered. It's a gratuity, what I have now. I was meant to die back there.

Yellowed suntala leaves floated on a murky pool; tendrils of algae reached up from its shallow bottom. Ants traced one edge; he stepped round them and watched the mist fill with dawn between the nearby crouched huts and sloping walls. A cock crowed; he ducked as a bicycle jingled down the alley beyond the wall.

He folded the blanket and stuffed it between the wall and the clustered trunks of a magnolia, tightened the laces on Paul's shoes. One snapped and he relaced and retied it, climbed the wall and dropped into the alley.

A rickshaw clanged past, a fat Newari pulled by an emaciated puffing man in a knit cap whose feet slapped wetly on the pavement. By the *stupa* grounds a naked child squatted, *pai* dogs circling nervously. As she stood they leapt between her feet for the sallow tumulus of excrement, knocking her down. Without tears she rose and moved away.

Women in thin saris crouched over twig fires between sagging huts, fragrances of chutney, curry, lentils, and tea rising from their dented, blackened pots. Fog blocked distant views and sounds, muffling his steps, Katmandu in the mucilaginous light seeming more an endless village than a city, its serpentine alleys branching on unpredicted vistas that hinted at open country then inturned to reveal new facets of the city.

He ducked through a skin door into a smoky hut. Blue flanks of meat and stalks of brittle herbs hung from its beams. A swarthy, squat woman shifted pots on a low woodstove.

"*Namasté, daju,*" she called.

"*Namasté,* little sister."

Two men in leather vests drank *chai* at a table near the unlit fire; they did not look at him. The other tables were empty, flies lifting from them briefly in the breeze of his entrance.

"So, *daju,* you have been in the Himal?"

"For two weeks."

"And your friends?"

"They stay. I go back."

"The wife of the black one, she comes often."

"You are with what today, little sister?"

Her grin showed a gold tooth. "We are with *baisi,* eggs, rice, even goat—but that was last week's."

". . . and Nescafé?"

"We are with."

His back against the rough wall, he watched the single half-window whose crude glass fractured the light into unrecognizable shapes and colors as shapes of passersby flitted across it. She brought him thick slabs of *baisi,* water buffalo cow, in a sage and curry sauce, brown rice, a cup of hot water, a tin of instant coffee, and a rusty spoon.

He stirred the dark powder into the water, inhaling its weak coffee odor that was not Paris, not espresso in a sunny midmorning café while a waiter swept chestnut leaves from under his table, a slim lovely woman in brown tights stepping up from the metro and crossing to his table.

She bent to kiss him, her dark hair coiling down his chest. "*Qu'ils sont salauds.* Bastards! *Ils sont vaches, fils de putains, couillons—merde! Ils sont pas gentils.*"

He grinned and steadied the table as she sat. "You didn't get the part?"

"*Si tu peux voir,* the *bête,* the dog, they gave it to—if you could see her!" She flipped her bag onto the table, rummaging for a comb. "*J'ai pas faim.*"

"That's just because you're mad, Sylvie. Have an *express*, a brioche . . . It's good you didn't get the part."

"*T'es fou?*"

"I have a better idea."

"*Mais je l'ai tant voulu!*" She paused, coppery eyes damp, tucked her chair close to his. "I hate to lose. I so wanted that part. It was *perfect* for me!" She folded his hand over hers and kissed his fingers. "*Mais que je t'aime!* And I won't ever let anyone else get you. *Jamais, jamais, jamais.* I'm the only one who'll ever be allowed to love you. So what's this fine idea?"

"Let's go back. I'll never make it in European football—I don't have the leg agility. And I can never play in Canada again with this shoulder, but I can coach. I want to go back to Canada and coach. Or maybe now Vietnam's over they'll stop boycotting me in the States. I love Paris, but I have to face that I'll never make it here."

"You must give it time, Samuel. Oh! How you are impatient!"

"Let's go back and get married in Quebec. Your father would love it. My folks'll fly in from Montana—they can all meet each other." He touched her cheek with the backs of his fingers, feeling its warmth. "I'm tired of fooling around. I never want to love anyone else in the world. The football talk's pretext. Why're you smiling?"

"I'm thinking of my father in his bar telling all his customers his daughter's coming home from Paris to Quebec to get married. You're right, he would so like that."

"And your hunger?" A voice at his shoulder.

"*Ho,* it is gone, little sister. Yet I seek more."

"What?"

"Eternal Snow, that comes from your land."

The Tibetan woman laughed. "You faraway people think only of hashish!" She took his plate. "Soon one who knows will be here."

He drank more coffee, watching the door. The room filled with dark men in sheepskins and dirty wool blankets, black braids down their backs, their faces scarred and hardened by the weather. A tall, slender man leaned over his table. "I am the one you seek."

"Coffee?"

"*Ho.*"

The man sat awkwardly, not familiar with benches. The woman brought him a cup of hot water. Cohen swirled Nescafé into the darkening reflection of the ceiling beams and passed the cup to him. "Eternal Snow," Cohen said, "like many fine things, comes only from Tibet." The man bent to sip. Cohen waited till he had straightened, then continued, "I seek one who is with."

"In what amount?"

"As large as possible."

"In . . ." The Tibetan sought a Nepali word, hands unfolding upward.

". . . return for?" Cohen replied.

"*Ho*. In return for what?" The man raised his chin, black slitted eyes on Cohen's, his eyebrows arched from the flat planes of his cheeks over his jutting nose, above the flat seam of his lips.

"What is most valuable in Tibet?"

The hands turned over. "It is a poor country . . ."

"Little sister," Cohen called, "you are pleased to bring hot water again for my guest?" He spooned out more coffee. "But Tibet is a brave country."

"Bravery in itself is nothing."

"Without bravery, life is nothing."

"It is difficult to fight tanks and planes with stones."

Cohen was silent. The tall Tibetan lifted a small clay pipe and a leather bag from a fold in his blanket. He took a chunk of hashish from the bag and shaved some into the pipe, stood the pipe on the table, walked to the stove and returned with a small coal between his fingertips, placed the coal atop the pipe, and offered it.

The smoke was sweet and very strong, blending with the coal's wood taste and the adobe flavor of the pipe. The tall Tibetan smoked in turn, stopping to shave more flakes into the bowl. Beyond his shoulder the window shimmered like a sheet of ice, like snow blown before the sun, a pool of stars. Cohen saw the slab-cheeked men hunched under their braids, their faces betraying nothing. He sensed himself a cave man midst an alien tribe. These are the people who killed Alex. Who will kill me the second they recognize me. But who are my only clue. "Soon I cross the water," he said. "I would purchase Eternal Snow for my friends there."

The Tibetan's bronze lips parted in a smile. "As you say in Nepali tongue, 'in return for?'"

50

Cohen did not speak. The greasy, rough-hewn table was suffused with meaning. He felt that if he never spoke again it would make no difference. Flies rimmed his cup; he watched them indifferently. "My friends are with many guns, from the war of Vietnam."

"I do not know this war. It is now?"

"It is finished."

"Your friends win, then?"

"*Huena.*"

"How are they with guns if they lose this war?"

"There were many guns."

"They will not be good."

"It was not lost by reason of the guns. A large country fought a small, brave country, as China fights Tibet."

The tall Tibetan waved his hand in a scoffing motion, flies rising from the table in alarm. "You speak too simply."

Cohen watched the flies settle. "That is true."

"You wish to take Eternal Snow across the water, in return for guns?"

"*Ho.*"

"The juniper on the mountain has many leaves." The tall Tibetan played loosely with his cup, his fingernails pitch-stained and attenuated. "I am but a leaf on a juniper in the Himal. I am not the tree. The tree is not the mountain." He stood and adjusted the long knife at his belt. "*Bholé* I come, here to the Globe."

"Tomorrow is too late."

"You faraway people do not understand time."

"We must talk now."

"I will speak now, then, with the juniper. In our tongue his name means Undying. You are curious why?"

"No."

"He was a boy when the Chinese cut his throat on Gunthangla, the High Plains Pass. His blood stayed in him. Twice more they have killed him with bullets. Yet he lives, and those who have crossed him are dead. It is wise to deal with him clearly."

"Have no fear."

"It is not for me to fear, but you." The tall Tibetan stepped through the skin door, letting in sunlight and noises of the city.

Cohen paid and cautiously inspected the alley. Nothing suspicious in the medley of passing voices and colors. Above the shop next door a carved balcony overlooked the street; he paid the shopkeeper ten rupees to let him sit there in the warming sun, out of view of the street yet able to observe it. Yes, if we'd stayed in Paris Sylvie wouldn't be dead. Nor Alex, nor Goteen. Why am I never satisfied? He rested his head on his folded arms; after a while he dozed, waking every few moments to glance into the street.

Footsteps halted beside him. The leather boots were fringed with blue beads; above them threadbare levis, a sash with a bone-hafted knife, a leather shirt, long braids beaded and twined with varicolored cloth, a hawk face haloed by sky.

The man squatted; the tall Tibetan stood behind him. This one was older, his face narrower, his eyes almost invisible under black brows. As he adjusted his stance, his chin lifted to reveal a thumb-wide glossy scar across his throat from jawbone to jawbone. "You are the one with guns?"

They conducted him through the crowded, hot streets to a dusty road of weathered huts, and beyond to the Tibetan refugee camp, where the white tents of the U.N. and Swiss aid programs speckled the grassless hills and blackeyed children played at war, ducking under the bellies of tethered ponies, with guns of sticks and stone grenades.

He lost direction as they twisted and turned among the endless tents. A boy in a beaded cap was splitting kindling with a kukri; Cohen realized he had seen him ten minutes before. "I am enough lost," he said to Undying. "Take me to the mountain."

Undying said nothing, his soft-soled boots treading a clump of cropped, spiky weed. A young bare-chested man was currying a shaggy pony, a Kalashnikov assault rifle dismantled on the grass beside him. With a sudden hollow stomach Cohen recognized him as one of Stihl's guerrillas on the Kali Gandaki. He moved quickly to the far side of the tall Tibetan. Undying strode steadily before them, his bone-hafted knife swinging loosely in its sheath.

Undying motioned him into a tent and disappeared. Inside, airlessly hot, it stank of grease and canvas. He faced the door. If that guy with the AK47 saw me I'm dead. Nothing I can do. Dead. Dead. Dead. Cut me up alive and throw my pieces to the ravens. Relax. Run. No, relax. His body, cold and sweaty, felt suddenly thin, weak. He bit his lip and waited.

52

Against the tent's sidewall was tilted a backboard with a sleeping baby. Flies clustered like grapes over the baby's eyes. Finally Cohen sat crosslegged on the ground; the tall Tibetan hunkered down facing him, back to the door. Cohen ignored the urge to chase flies from the baby's face, knowing it would be seen as a sign of weakness. The tent flap jumped aside and Undying entered, an old man behind him.

"This is the one?" The old man's eyes were sardonyx under spidery brows, their light utterly without warmth. Scars radiated over his face; his teeth were large and thin. Stringy muscles rippled under the hairless chestnut skin of his arms. From one elongated earlobe a cameo earring dangled.

Cohen took off his glasses. "Undying has told you . . ."

"Undying speaks for himself. What are the guns?"

"M16's, some pistols, grenades."

"Where?"

"Two days from Katmandu."

"Why art thou with guns in India?"

"Perhaps they are not in India."

"Where else, two days away?"

"They are to fight Pakistan." Cohen flicked his hand; the flies buzzed angrily round the baby. "I come to take Stihl's place."

"Who says this?"

"Our chief."

"Stihl is in the Kali Gandaki."

"He is dead in Katmandu."

"Only three weeks past we bring much Eternal Snow to the Americans, exchanging for guns. Why now more?"

"Many in America now prefer to be friends with China. Yet Eternal Snow gains more value in our country, is easy to find in yours."

The old man spoke in Tibetan with Undying. "Thou," he said to Cohen, "bring some guns for us to see. Then we discuss payment." He rubbed his chin. "For years the Americans bring Russian guns, that are better. Why now American guns?"

Cohen took off his glasses and cleaned them on his shirt. "When it rains, do not complain of thirst. These are what we are with."

The old man stood. "In two days, then."

"In four. Two going, two coming back."

"How is Stihl dead in Katmandu, and not with our people in the Kali Gandaki?"

"Because the bomb is broken. He failed and was killed."

"*What* is broken?"

"The fire like the sun."

"I do not know it."

"The bomb to kill Chinese."

"I do not know of this." The old man glanced at Undying, who shook his head. "Only guns were to be in the Kali Gandaki. It is of Stihl, this fire?"

"*Ho*. It is broken in the canyon below Muktinath. Who of your people knows of it?"

"No one, if not I." Again the old man looked at Undying.

Cohen stood. "You are with the name of the new contact?"

"What is the name?"

"Show me the name and address you are with."

Undying ducked from the tent. The old man bent to follow him, turned to Cohen. "We will wait for him outside."

"I will stay here. It is best not to be known."

The old man crouched back down. "As thou wish." Undying returned with a slip of paper. The old man turned to Cohen. "I cannot show thee this until Stihl tells me."

"He can never tell you now, and I cannot give you the new name until you show me the old."

"Why?"

Cohen allowed himself to smile. "How do I know you are the one?" He crossed to the exit. "Without the name of the old contact I cannot give you the new, nor can I make an agreement concerning guns." He stepped outside, the sun-bleached dusty air almost cool after the tent. The guerrilla with the Kalashnikov was not visible. Perhaps one o'clock by the sun: Paul could be at Phu Dorje's now. With the name of their contact we can get them all. He faced the old man. "You are with paper?"

"For what?"

"My instructions are to give you the name of the new contact . . . in exchange for the old."

The old man nodded his chin at the plain of white tents. "My people's lands were stolen by the Chinese. Our children slaughtered, homes, fields, and temples destroyed. Our sacred books

54

burned. Yet, we will never be defeated. We will never give up." He smiled. "It would not be wise to betray us."

"If you fear that of me we should speak no further."

"I fear that of everyone." The old man hesitated, then passed Cohen the slip of paper:

KOHLER IMPORT-EXPORT
293 Fulton Street
New York, N.Y.
U.S.A.

Cohen tore it up. "I will write the new words." He printed an imaginary Upper East Side address on the paper that the tall Tibetan had brought and gave it to the old man. "Mark these words on an envelope and send it, and someone will come to you."

"But in four days thou return." The old man motioned to the tall Tibetan, who took the leather bag of hashish from his blanket and handed it to Cohen. "A token for thy journey," he grimaced, then gripped Cohen's elbow. "You are familiar with our treatment for those who betray us?" He jabbed his fingers under Cohen's ribs. "Cutting here, we reach a hand beneath the ribs and squeeze the beating heart. Not too quickly, letting it come back then squeezing again. After some time, perhaps hours, perhaps days, we crush it. It is a painful death."

Cohen grinned. "He who fears death does little."

"Sometimes there is even more to fear of life," the old man smiled, "than death."

55

6

THE FLIES HAD BEEN in it for several hours, a few becoming stuck as it dried. Others now wandered its crust with impunity. It had gone deep rust, almost black. Her eyes glazed, her neck sliced to the white-red bone, Seral lay twisted in its center. Her parents sprawled face down behind her, the boy beneath his mother.

He stumbled into the other room and fell on the floor, coals from the hearth warm on his face. Vomit came up; he forced it back; it went down the wrong way and choked him. He spat into the hearth.

Life's a joke, Seral. It had no meaning. It wasn't real, it wasn't there. Don't mourn it. Better to be dead. Death's done you a favor. Seral's black shining eyes looked into his. "To be favored by death?" her lips said silently.

"I don't believe . . ." he ran screaming into the other room, his shoes crunching dried blood, her body sucking free of it as he took her up in his arms. A red glob squirted from her throat; he wiped it from his knee. Putting her down he knelt beside Phu Dorje and cut the bandanna gagging his mouth and the rawhide tying his hands behind him, then did the same for his wife.

A while later he found himself leaning over, knees and forehead on the floor. He shook himself. The posture of one awaiting execution. And so I should be. For I killed them. By coming here yesterday. Somebody's watching.

He stroked Seral's braids. At what moment did they kill you? Was I drinking coffee with the tall Tibetan? Was I calmly eating *baisi* and rice? Was I bullshitting with them at the refugee camp? And pretending I was in danger? Was Undying laughing inside, watching me, while it was being done? Or does he even know? Is their New York contact, the Kohler Import-Export place, real? Are they all playing with me? God, too? Waiting for me to lead them to Paul? To then kill us both? Seral . . . at what moment . . . ?"

Kim! He lurched to his feet, grabbed the kukri from the wall and dashed into the alley tripping over two women hunkered on the step. *"Namasté, sahib!"* one called, laughing.

Sprinting through the Sherpa bazaar he snatched a bike from a protesting Newari and raced to Kim's school. The headmaster was a slight, graying, bowing man in a white topi. "She is gone this hour with two who came for her."

"Who?"

"Far mountain people."

The bicycle chain broke by the *stupa* grounds; he dashed through the crowded, loud streets, knocking over animals and people. Her gate was ajar, the house empty. "Kim!" he screamed. "Kim!"

She lay face down under suntala trees by carved antique stones Paul had rescued from a ruined Rana palace, flies testing the edges of the blood still flowing from her throat. He carried her into the living room under the scroll painting of the old man and the waterfall, her head wobbling on the spine, her cut throat gaping.

A milky sunset illuminated the Big Sur poster, highlighting the cyan luster of the Pacific and the virid crowns of redwoods stepping up the cliffs. There were voices in the street; he placed her gently on the pillows and stepped over the trestle table to the window. A child ducked from the window and ran to the gate, where faces peered expectantly.

A Gurkha rapped his kukri on the gate, his khaki uniform pea green in the waning sun, the stainless steel of his kukri handle flashing. Cohen glanced down at his jeans streaked with Kim's blood. The Gurkha rapped on the door. Cohen darted into the bedroom, grabbed the football and a pen from the shelf, knocking over Kim's things, scrawled "Serpent—Easter" on the worn pigskin and shoved the football back on the shelf. The Gurkha shouldered open the door as Cohen ducked out the back, under the suntalas past the Rana palace stones, skidding and falling on Kim's blood. "He runs, policeman!" a voice yelled from the road.

He leaped the wall into a buffalo pen, a blunt-horned old *rango* lurching up, its leathery balls swinging like a pendulum. Ducking its horns he slopped through manure and dove over the gate into an alley blocked by an old man selling pans from a wooden framework supported on his shoulders, women in pink saris arguing round him, the street thronged by people shouting and pointing. He smashed through the women, the tinker falling with a yell and clatter, dashed right at the corner, then left at the next through streets jammed with porters, women, children, and dogs, and ran steadily westward past the town center and northward on the Pokhara road.

On the first crest he halted to look for Paul on the road ahead. Behind him, in a dusty haze riddled by Katmandu's frail lights, mounted Gurkhas cantered through the streets. A truck rattled toward him, dropping Gurkhas two by two up the hillside. He scrambled from the road into a magnolia clump. Headlights jigged over the leaves; the truck geared down and halted, valves rattling.

Swish of feet through grass. He slid the kukri from its sheath, held his breath. Two shapes against the city lights below; one glanced into the magnolias. The steps receded. He sheathed the kukri and exhaled.

Soft steps behind and in front. More left and right. The kukri blade pinged as he yanked it out. He squirmed through the magnolias, crushed grass thundering in his ears. Kukri between his teeth he bounded downhill on toes and fingertips, grass hissing over his legs. Glint of a blade in the starlight, two dark shapes ahead. To his left a ravine deepened toward the valley; he tossed a pebble tinkling down its ravelled canyon. The man-shapes halted whispering; as they edged toward the ravine he circled them. A stick snapped, they yelled and he was up and running down the chunky slope, across a wide paddy in the starlight, feet splashing behind him. He sprinted upslope through a farmyard where chickens scattered squawking, a pig ran farting and squealing, its tether tripping Cohen into a cesspool gashing his knee, driving him faster up to forest whose startled birds chattered far overhead.

The Gurkhas spread out as they reached the farmyard, one slapping down the farmer when he came yelling, lantern in hand, into the yard. A voice called, followed by the snapping of rifle bolts, Cohen tripping into vines and creepers, thrashing at them with the kukri, hobbling breathlessly upward and falling again.

Above the forest the slope opened for a half mile, every bush and boulder visible. To left and right the forest faded into hills empty of cover. The first Gurkhas had reached the edge of the trees; Cohen sheathed the kukri and scaled hand over hand up a vine into the darkness.

Birds twitted furtively around him; the branches were slick with their pale, foul droppings. Beneath him the Gurkhas quartered and searched the glade, the only sound an occasional whisper of an officer and the constant snick-snick of kukris slicing through creepers and saplings.

After an hour the Gurkhas deployed up the open slope. When they were well above the glade, Cohen descended the vine part way, then lower. The birds did not stir. He dropped farther, wrapped his thighs around a bough, cleaned his glasses on Paul's shirt, and stared down into the glade.

For a long time he saw no movement. He moved down, unable to see the lookouts the Gurkhas had posted, decided they would be watching the slope going down to the farm. He slid to the ground. Nothing stirred, and he crept up the open hill behind the Gurkhas, veering westward along a horizontal path.

After a half mile he stood and ran lamely along the path, crossing the far western end of Katmandu's valley at midnight. Halting to remove Paul's too-large shoes, he massaged his blisters and the searing, torn edges of his knee and continued barefoot. Never get to Paris now. Never track them down, Kohler Import-Export, in New York. Can't walk much longer. Maybe fifty rupees left—seven bucks. Should have taken some from Kim. Oh God Kim you can't be dead. What have I done, what have I done . . .

Villages and farms passed in a dream. Dogs barked; once a man's voice called, "*Kata jané, daju?*" A buffalo bolted from his path. In the long part of the night the pain in his knee grew unendingly; the cold was unbroken. Finally the stars dimmed.

Birds called, a dewy, solid sound. The hills took shape; the trail swam over them like a snake over green-black waves. Above tree-soft silhouettes the east inflamed as if dawning on the smoky remnants of a sea battle. Stars winked out like streetlights of a vaulted city, like airplanes shot down one by one till none remained. Sun burst over the jagged peaks, at once warming his face, drawing up steam from the road and gossamer mists from the east-facing slopes.

Himalayas trailing scarves of windblown snow walled off the north. The sun glinted on their black granite scarps and the gelid white of glaciers and snowfields. Shortly after sunrise the trail broke on a small village. In a *butthi* he asked for *chai,* rice, and eggs. The *butthi* man shook his head sadly up and down, meaning no. "All the chickens have died, sahib. But," he smiled, "we are with rice."

Ten miles farther he reached the Bhutwal road and flagged down an ancient Ford truck heading south. *"Kata janahuncha?"*

"Thori janchu," the driver said, revealing a few tooth stumps behind a bristly grin.

"I go to the splitting of the Thori road. You can carry me?"

The driver rubbed tiredly at his cotton headband. "Ten rupees."

Cohen sat gingerly on spiky horsehairs padding the bare springs. The driver pushed the gearstick forward into first. The truck lunged, slowed, then gradually gained speed. The engine noise was too loud for talk; Cohen fought a nodding sleep as the truck labored over the sunbaked hills. The driver braked where dung-brick huts and tin sheds huddled meanly under bare-branched trees.

"Half way!" the driver exclaimed triumphantly.

Swollen-bellied children were gathering to hold out yellow palms, their eyes reproachful. Cohen glared at the driver. "Bhutwal is yet half day from here."

The driver inspected him calmly. His wrinkled simian fingers hung loosely over the wheel. The gearstick with its blue-and-white Ford knob vibrated erratically against his knee. "For a few more rupees, Bhutwal very close by."

"Give back my ten rupees!"

"Why give back?" The driver appeared affronted.

"If I Nepali," Cohen said, "you ask no rupees."

"But you not Nepali," the driver answered softly.

Cohen unclenched his fists. He twisted off the gearshift knob, stepped out, and threw it over the bare trees. It dipped across the blue sky, pinpointed with distance, and dropped with a silver flash into a rice paddy.

Where the road crested beyond the village he glanced back. In the emerald paddy beyond the desolate huts a lone figure in a cotton headband, trousers rolled to his knees, bent searching in the knee-deep reflection of the sky. Cohen trudged on. I become what I hate. Spread sorrow and death like a plague. On the hungry, the poor. On the least—the best—of my brothers.

The heat worsened. As he approached each new village, children met him, palms upward. When traffic increased he followed a path under the cathedralled canopy of a rhododendron glade. At the rim of a steep ridge he lay down on a small plateau edged by banyans. Below him the canopy of rhododendrons was unbroken but for the road's sinuous traverse.

With Paul's shoes for a pillow he lay in the banyan shadows, Phu Dorje's kukri clutched to his chest. That which is, is not. That which is not, is. I'm untouched. Dead. Have to be alive to feel. No one who has ever lived has felt what I feel. A tinkling disturbed him, three girls in red saris watching from the forest. "*Namasté,* sahib," called the tallest, stepping closer. Her face was bony, her wrist angular as she held out her palm.

"I have nothing," he murmured, waved them away, and fell asleep.

Chattering, screaming everywhere. Thick-tongued and sweaty, he jumped up, midslope sun in his eyes. The plateau was cut into shadow and light. Drops pattered on dead leaves. He looked up; a drop struck the corner of his mouth. Branches tossed in the banyans overhead.

A lemur peered down at him, its face yellow, sagacious, wrinkled below the cheekbones. Long fingers parted the leaves; another face joined it. Other lemurs ran gibbering along a branch. More drops spiralled down, smelling of ammonia. He hobbled into the clearing. The lemurs cavorted in the nearest high branches. He flung a rock, hitting one in the ribs. It screamed and fell, caught a lower branch. The others yelled, baring their teeth.

On the road below a motorcycle rounded a curve, vanished and reappeared, soon audible between lemur noises. It stopped in a patch of sunlight. Its rider, a blond man in a gray windbreaker, waved toward the edge of the forest. Three smaller figures dressed in red stepped onto the road. The man in gray bent down, took something from his pocket. One of the three red-saried figures pointed up at the plateau. The man reached over the handlebars to stuff something into her hand. He tipped the motorcycle back on its stand, readjusted his jacket, and slipped into the forest.

In the clearing, knee-deep grass nodded in a slight wind. In the forest, flat leaves caught the sunlight; compact white cumulus chased each other over undulant sea-green hills. The lemurs had quieted; one looked down at him over her shoulder as she nursed an infant.

He slipped into the forest, crunching leaves, skirting the thickest grove of rhododendrons, and crouched holding the kukri on his good knee. A leaf spun indolently down. A bird called, shrill and fast. He eased along the hillside, bent behind a tulip tree.

An ant ran over his hand. The bird called again. A stick cracked downhill toward the road. He moved his foot. No sound. He brought the bad leg forward, let it down; a twig crunched. He raised the foot, set it elsewhere, slowly, quieting his breath. Lemur screams exploded overhead. Branches cracked like rifles; urine spattered him. Echos of their hooting rebounded from the hills. The lemurs pursued him, screeching, from tree to tree. The man in the gray jacket held a pistol on him, ten feet away.

"A novel approach," the man smiled. "Stalking lemurs with a kukri—sporting, rather. Or is that what you were up to?"

"They pissed on me. I was going to climb up after them."

"See how easy it is," the man replied, "when you're properly equipped . . ." He raised the pistol, his right wrist in his left palm, and fired. A lemur tumbled head over tail through the branches and bounced once on the brown leaves, ". . . to achieve the results you seek?"

"What the fuck you do that for!"

"A specimen, naturally." The man lifted the lemur's head with his toe. "A death for science is a creditable one, don't you think?"

"No."

"You were going to kill them just for peeing on you."

"I was hardly able."

"Intent's the thing, my granny always said." The man's wide-set eyes were cheesy blue. He extended a hand. "Sydney Stowe. London."

The hand was limp as a piece of kelp. Cohen tried to smile. "What brings you to Nepal?"

"Primates. You?"

"Just traveling through."

"Where to?" Stowe was kneeling by the lemur, deftly cutting its skin away from the rib flesh. The forest was silent.

62

"You scared me with that gun," Cohen replied.

"Imagine my surprise bumping into an American with a pigsticker like that. Why don't you put it away?"

Cohen complied. "What made you come up here?"

"Saw some girls on the road. Asked them had they seen any monkeys. Simple as that." Stowe slipped a bloody leg free of its skin. "At first I took you for a monkey man. Where you going?"

"Monkey man?"

"Ever since Schaller and Goodall the woods are full of earnest young Americans stirring up the wildlife." Stowe's smile revealed an asymmetry of yellow teeth. "Long in Nepal?"

"I came yesterday. Don't like it here."

"Why?"

"Nobody speaks English. I hate rice. I was going to Katmandu, but've decided to hitch back to Delhi." Cohen glanced down at his bloody trousers. "And I've fallen and torn my knee. Shitty country."

"I've just come from Katmandu. Had rather a tiff getting out." Stowe turned from the skin to look up at Cohen. "The roads out of town are barricaded. The Gurkhas're hunting some American who killed four Sherpas."

"What's that, some kind of sheep?"

"Can see you're one of the great unwashed." Stowe tugged the skin away from the lemur's back, stood with the pink carcass at his feet. "I'm going part way to Delhi, if you'd like to ride on the back of Sue."

"Sue?"

"Suzuki to you." Stowe held the lemur skin, head still attached, away from his trousers. When they reached the motorcycle he stuffed it in a saddlebag.

"You going to ride with that pistol in your coat?" Cohen asked.

The pasty blue eyes wavered over Cohen's. His hair, Cohen noted, was pale and thinning above the forehead. It covered the ears. The face was cratered with old acne scars. "May see another specimen, don't you think?" Stowe climbed on the seat. "Here are your foot pegs." He reached back, pinning Cohen's arms round his waist. "Safety first," he shouted. "Just lean as I do, no more, no less."

The engine's roar and the sensation of speed were overwhelming. The foothills slumped gently toward the Indian plain; bony dogs yapped in the ditches and empty-faced children ran toward them, hands outstretched. Gradually the hills receded and they reached the parched Terai, the fields and villages even poorer, children too apathetic to beg. "Where will you find monkeys here?" Cohen yelled.

"Can't hear. Wait till we stop."

Stowe leaned into a turn, gearing down. Tall spiky grasses blocked the view. Water buffaloes had crossed, leaving slick piles of dung. The bike skewed, slammed over the dirt embankment and cartwheeled into a field.

Cohen stood rubbing his shoulder. The tan earth, prickled by yellow stubs, rotated at an angle as he tried, each time it passed, to catch a fleeting view of the motorcycle. He stumbled, sat, stood again.

The earth's rotation was subsiding. The motorcycle, front wheel gyrating, lay on its side. He tried to approach it.

Before him lay a patch of what looked like snow; he reached down for its coolness. It was slippery. Paper, glossy. Two others. He glanced at and dropped them, wandered toward the motorcycle. Stowe lay beneath it. One saddlebag was open, contents strewn. Stowe moved his head. "Crushing me, get it off."

The wheel stopped. Cohen lifted the motorcycle and leaned over Stowe. "Can you move?"

"Don't know." Stowe's face was scraped, dirty. He raised his head. Through his open jacket front Cohen saw the pistol.

Cohen looked for Alex.

"Think I'm all right," Stowe said. "Bloody buffaloes!"

Alex is dead. But he was just here. Cohen glanced around. The photo. Alex's photo, lying on the ground. From the saddlebag.

Stowe sat up. He readjusted his jacket. The photos lay behind him.

"Wait!" Cohen said.

"Huh?"

"You're bleeding. Back here." He rubbed the back of Stowe's coat.

"Where?"

64

"Here." He grabbed past Stowe's neck for the pistol strapped under his armpit. Stowe's fist smashed his face; he twisted and pinned it down. It jerked free and plunged into his crotch. With a hand and knee he pinned it again, then yelled with pain as teeth sank into his knee. He spun Stowe over, punched him twice in the temple, Stowe butting him in the crotch. Fighting back nausea he squeezed Stowe into a half nelson, twisted out the gun and leaped away. "Get up!"

Stowe stood, wiping his mouth. "This is truly excessive."

Cohen backed past the motorcycle. A slightly younger Alex stared up at him, shorter-haired, without his Himalayan tan.

"Where'd you get the pictures?"

Stowe looked down, raised his eyes, smiled. "The Gurkhas, simple as that."

"Gurkhas."

"At the barricade. Said to look out for these Americans. Killed the Sherpas. And an American girl."

"Turn over the other two."

"This has gone too far, don't you . . ."

"Quick!"

Cohen saw himself in the photo as Stowe sprang. They tumbled backward; he tucked up his knees and rolled them over. The gun punched his palm, a shot loud like dynamite. Stowe arched. His legs straightened, heels gouging the earth. He raised one hand briefly.

Cohen's own face was mirrored in Stowe's chalky eye. Dark blood seeped from a pinhole under the chin. He rubbed a toe over the eye. It did not blink. He gathered the photos: one each of himself, Alex, Paul, his own the same as his passport's.

A water buffalo bellowed. It was a *rango,* a bull, standing in the field perhaps fifty yards away. He raised the motorcycle. The headlight was cracked, the right handlebar and brake lever bent. The key was on. He turned it, swearing as the bike bucked forward. He shifted to neutral and tried again. It revved at once. He accelerated a hundred yards down the road: the gears were fine.

He rode back and turned it off. Again he bent over Stowe, chased a fly from one nostril. Perhaps he did get the photos from the Gurkhas. Now I've killed him. I'm turning to dirt. Scum. Avoiding the warm blood, he reached inside the jacket pockets, found a wallet and a passport.

The face in the Australian passport was the same, but the name was Derek Willard, place of birth, Canberra. The wallet contained several hundred dollars, assorted rupees, two English driver's licenses in different names, and two scraps of paper. On one was scribbled, "An Ethnology of the Primate World," on the other, "Bess, her place, 8 P.M., Claret."

Cohen glanced at the person for whom such words had had meaning. The face was marbled slightly; dust filmed the eyes. Ants were running along the widening pool of blood that carried crumbs of earth and grass at its edges.

The *rango* had disappeared. There was not a shrub or boulder behind which it could have hidden. "I'm going crazy," he shrieked. "Help me, please." He stared open-mouthed and silent at the empty land.

The *rango* was back. It stood as before, watching him sideways, chewing steadily. He stepped around Stowe and limped toward it. It swung away, tail high, and sank into the earth. He followed it to the edge of a sinkhole. Water lingered in half-crusted hoofprints at the bottom. The *rango* glared up at him, huffing, its concave flanks white-sored. He returned to Stowe's body and dragged it into the sinkhole, wiped off the gun and put it in Stowe's hand, scuffed out the slender trail of blood, and mounted the motorcycle.

In the coolness of speed Paul faced him. "Everybody lose eventually. Everybody die." Paul spun a football small in his shoe-polish palm. "But we don't want to fear it. We don't want to *think* we're going to lose."

Water glinted beyond the road's descending arc. Before the bridge was parked a truck. Gurkhas in olive uniforms spanned the road.

7

A GURKHA RAN FORWARD, pointing his rifle. Cohen drifted the Suzuki sideways to a stop, gritted his teeth as his bad leg took up the load. "You go too fast," the Gurkha said in clipped English.

"I was surprised to see you. Nearly an accident."

"You must slow for the border. Ahead, India. Documents, blease."

Cohen offered one of the Australian's driving licenses.

"Your bermit?"

"Pardon?"

"Your bermit!" The Gurkha jerked his chin at the motorcycle.

"I bought it in Katmandu. The guy didn't give me a permit."

"It is unlawful in Nebal without bermit."

Cohen glanced across the river. "Raxaul isn't far."

The Gurkha stepped in front of him. "In India bermits also are necessary."

"I'll get one in Calcutta, then."

The Gurkha crossed to the truck and spoke into the radio. Cohen edged closer trying to hear. Two other Gurkhas swung their Enfields to move him back. Wide terraces paralleled the river. No cover there, slow running on furrowed soil.

The Gurkha stepped down from the running board. "No bermit is necessary for you to leave Nebal."

Cohen smiled. The Gurkha also smiled. "However, to enter India one must have bermit. As would one entering Nebal."

"Like I said, I'll get it in Calcutta."

"You must get it in Katmandu."

Cohen's eyes wandered to the muddy river and its corroded, sagging bridge. Beyond the bridge the empty road wobbled in the heat.

The radio squawked. "A moment," said the Gurkha. Cohen nodded, extended his hand. Surprised, the Gurkha shook it and turned to lean into the truck. Cohen remounted the motorcycle, switched on the key and coasted down the slope past the Gurkha's back. He slipped into second and released the clutch. The engine caught; another Gurkha raised his Enfield and stepped to the middle of the bridge. Cohen accelerated, straightarmed him flat in the face, gripped the weaving, screaming motorcycle as it pounded faster and faster over the riveted plates of the bridge toward the U-shaped chunk of sky beyond, his back arching in terror against the bullets singing past; he zipped past the astonished guard at the Indian checkpoint and into the flat, arid countryside.

The speedometer jiggled and the broken headlight rattled as the motorcycle pounded wide-open over potholes and ruts. Telegraph poles zipped past; he eyed the wires as if trying to outrun the words flitting along them. He skirted the first disheveled village, then abandoned such stratagems and tore through the rest, scattering chickens, dogs, laundry, and children, leaving a new coat of fine dust to settle on centuries of old, stopping once for gas cranked by hand from a broken-gauged pump by a girl with white, unseeing eyes.

Twenty-three days, Paul. Easter in Paris. Le Serpent d'Etoiles. I'll get there—will you? From Paris just a hop across the ocean to 293 Fulton Street. Kohler Import-Export. We're running from them now, Paul. But not forever.

It was dark when he reached New Delhi. A few lights glimmered, giving the streets a Chaldean air. The airport was poorly lit. He parked the motorcycle as the last dirty mauve of day turned charcoal in the west.

The Air France flight to Paris would leave in two hours. Stowe's money would get him to Athens with a few dollars left for food. I can hide out there till it's time to meet Paul in Paris. Or maybe Yugoslavia, somewhere out of the way? From an airport telephone he made a reservation for three people in a false name, then bought bandages, iodine, a razor, toothbrush, shoes, and clothes in airport shops. In the men's room he cleaned and inspected his knee; the cut was long and when he pulled it apart the kneecap showed whitely. He soaked it in iodine, dressed it, washed quickly with paper towels, changed, shaved, and tossed Paul's clothes in the trash. A flushing toilet startled him, an alien sound. Hobbling to the motorcycle he emptied its saddlebags into a rubbish can, tore up Stowe's licenses and passport and the three photographs and scattered them in the wind, and left the Suzuki with the key in its lock in long term parking. "You won't be here long," he said, patting its fuel tank.

Five minutes before takeoff he bought a ticket to Athens. The plane was half empty. He took his seat by a window at the rear and collapsed against the headrest. The plane picked up speed, sucking him down a whirlwind of exhaustion.

Kim lay beside him, still his friend's lover but also his wife. And also my sister? Or are you Seral? She did not answer; as she turned away he saw the jagged gash crossing her throat from jawbone to jawbone, her flesh peeling in yellow-green chunks from her cheekbones, Seral's glossy black braids falling away in his hands. He jumped agonized to his feet but the awful pain in his knee forced him down. I should have made you go, Kim; I murdered you. I'm no different than I was. No one will ever believe me. He stared astounded at his surroundings. The few passengers near him slept slumped across their seats in the semidark cabin; the black ridges of Afghanistan crept by flat and lightless under the stars.

When the plane shuddered and slowed he woke quickly to a spray of lights; low desert huts swept under the wing as the plane descended to Teheran. Few passengers descended; five Shiites boarded, talking animatedly and holding the hems of their striped robes free of the steps; amid the Shiites was a tall, lean man with rimless spectacles, a black moustache, and a tan scarf over his blue wool suit. The engines caught; the plane inched from the ramp. Cohen eased down in his seat. The plane lurched and halted; the engines died. Four uniformed men rolled a mobile ramp to the plane. He unclipped his seat belt and stood. The nearest Emergency Exit was forward, over the wing, the rear door directly behind him.

A terminal door flashed. A tall woman in a gray suit banged a suitcase through it and across the tarmac. Her auburn hair gleamed in the landing lights as she trotted up the ramp. He removed his glasses and closed his eyes.

Again Paul was close enough to touch. After Sylvie was gone, there were times I could almost reach her. Now I've deserted you. I couldn't wait in K'du, Paul, they were hunting me everywhere—and then outside K'du, the Gurkhas—I was leading them to you so I turned south, went by Bhutwal, got them away, got away. Didn't I?

You'll never see the football. You'll be dead before you get there. And I killed the monkey man. For nothing. He'd been given the photos by the Gurkhas. Cohen shivered wearily. Bullshit. Two driver's licenses, with different names, a different passport. I mustn't wear myself down with doubt.

He rubbed his face in his hands. It's true, the monkey man was hunting me. Why didn't he kill me? Where are his friends? 293 Fulton Street, that's where they are. If they aren't there maybe I'll go after the CIA in D.C. or wherever and kill them all. Every killer there. Twenty-three days.

The woman in the gray suit was in the next row of seats, tugging her skirt down over crossed knees. When he noticed her again she had fallen asleep, a pale finger poised against her cheek, her skin luminescent marble under the yellow cabin lights, her hair fine and fully glissading down her shoulder and breast.

She scratched unconsciously at one knee. How apart we are. Her voluptuous world, its sleek silks and shimmering nylons, seemed polarized to his. A mahogany-colored leather handbag lay tucked in her lap; he stared at it and at her as if they were omens of another incarnation, as a Nepali peasant might. Cunt, she has no cares.

He took off his glasses and rubbed the bridge of his nose, stepped back to the lavatory, washed his face with a miniature pink bar of Air France soap, cleaned his glasses, and combed his hair with his fingers. To kill the pain in his knee, he cut some of the tall Tibetan's Eternal Snow into the clay pipe and smoked it, sitting on the toilet flap, feet propped against the door.

In his hand a box of Tiger matches. Kim held these. She lit her stove with them, in the mornings, thinking of Paul, wanting him home. Now he'll never come home, and she'll never be there. Oh God, to have things as they were. They were so fine and I never knew it.

Don't. Don't think of Seral or Kim or anyone. Just do. A time to kill and a time to die—that's how it should go. Vengeance is mine, I will repay, says the Lord. Fuck you, Lord. Now I'm vengeance, Lord, I shall repay.

Going crazy. Crazy and don't realize. Concentrate. What next?

70

Making no mistakes on the hitch from Athens to Paris, that's next. Salonika, Skopje, Belgrade, Trieste, Milano, Lausanne, Dijon— I've done it before, the other way. How soon will the police, or the CIA, track me to this flight? He lowered his jeans and watched the red-yellow stain advancing through the bandages. Can't hitch with this. Hole up in Athens? Crete? Yugoslavia? Three weeks till Easter—plenty time for Paris. Should get it stitched but don't dare.

He waited for the air to clear, snapped back the lock, and stepped into the corridor. The woman halted before him, pinned him down with her green eyes. "We were already high enough."

He did not respond; she went in and shut the door. He stood momentarily in her French scent, hearing the swish of her garments through the thin panel.

The plane was quiet, cabin lights extinguished. Under the gold orb of her lamp the woman read a blue-bound copy of *Der Spiegel,* her head tilted slightly in concentration, long legs tucked beneath her. The lamp gilded her hair with sunset reds; from time to time she would weave a loose strand behind her ear and pat it down with her fingertips.

Where are you now, Paul? Today—no, yesterday—you'd have reached Phu Dorje's. Was that yesterday, the Tibetan camp?

If you came in from Pokhara you'd go first to Phu Dorje's. Seeing that horror. Then Kim. Have they taken her body? In Cohen's mind Paul stood before her corpse—jaw muscles rippling under the black skin, eyes knowing yet unbelieving, the turning away into darkness, conscious of punishment meted again to the union of black and white. How many ancient wounds, Paul? Since the beginning of time?

In a penumbra of cabin lights he limped the sticky carpet, watching through the galley window a slender moon on crystal clouds, returning to the lavatory to urinate into the chemical toilet, breath held against the stink. How much better to pee in the open air. A bit perilous, though, at thirty-five thousand feet. His hollow face glowered from the mirror. Six nights and so little sleep.

Back in his seat he eyed the woman. Fuck her. Never known pain. Never known hunger. All dressed up like a turd in a rainbow. Better the ones Alex and I used to screw in Bangkok, ratty water slapping bamboo branches against the pilings, small tight cunts, brown little nipples, eyes that never turn away. Licking the clitoris up through its silky black forest.

If only Alex had married the whore in Bangkok. Can't remember her. Fat little slant-eyed Alex babies running barefoot, round little baby buns brown in the sunlight.

A whisper of silks and nylons as the woman changed position. So cold. No fire underneath waiting to be lit. Nothing sunny. Glacier Face. Chiselled cheeks sheer and dangerous as the south wall of Macha Pucchare. Such a farce, life. The beautiful stink when they're dead, too. He scowled at his reflection in the perspex.

What goes on in her head? Thinking of humping some guy who's got a Mercedes and a hundred-foot yacht. Two years I haven't seen a well-dressed western woman. Thai women look better. What's it like to be her, inside that pearly skin, those soft hands with their delicate fingernails, those avocado tits, those long, long thighs, that vacuous western brain?

Six nights, so little sleep. Comatose. All that comes together suffers dispersal. Molecules and nations. Universes and the flesh of women and men. He felt his swollen knee. CIA's closing in already. Waiting in Athens. I'll die not knowing why I've lived.

Despite the knee he wandered forward again, glanced out the galley window. The moon was hidden. Cold and lonely to die. I'm losing faith. But faith's a habit. After all, what is there to lose faith in?

As he returned to his seat the woman raised her eyes. "Can't sleep either?" A brief smile. "It's your grass that's done it."

Her eyes were iceberg green. Or are they blue? Slightly tilted, a cat's. Her voice throaty yet soft, an abrupt breathless style of speech, an almost theatrical lilt. A Vassar voice. Jesus protect us all from Vassar voices. Atop the cleft of her breasts glinted a heart-shaped diamond pendant. Wonder who gave her that. And what he got for it. I know the answer to that. "It was hash—should make you sleep."

"That's why you're pacing?" He shrugged; she added, "Where you coming from?"

"Thailand." His voice echoed inside his head as if his ears were blocked.

"Sounds more fun than Teheran."

72

He rubbed his knee irritably. "Then why go there?"

"For a story, but it didn't pan out. The good old Shah, friend of democracy, is building a summer palace covering half an island in the Persian Gulf. It's all hush hush—too many starving Iranians might get upset. . . . And they don't approve of women doing anything except making babies and taking care of men."

"You're a journalist?"

"Free-lance. Politics mostly. You?"

"Just wandering."

She grinned. "Sounds like fun." One of her top teeth, he noticed, was chipped. "I've always wanted to do that." She closed *Der Spiegel.* "It takes money to be free."

"Money's slavery, too. The worst kind." He settled into his seat and closed his eyes.

Her voice again. "I bet you're hungry. I am. I'm like a cat—feed me and I sleep."

The leopard's unwavering green eyes on the cliff below Tensan Bazaar. In the cypress outside the deserted Rana palace. She would have slept well with me in her belly. "What day's it?"

She glanced down. "Saturday, three-twenty A.M., Teheran time." She stood and walked up the silent aisle, pushed aside the First Class curtain, returned moments later with four sandwiches in plastic and two bottles of wine, and sat beside him opening a bottle. "'Antidote to grief and anger, dispels all care . . .'" Her voice deepened, semidramatic, "'. . . although one's father and mother both were dead, and though his brother had fallen before his eyes . . . .'" She smiled primly. "Homer, speaking of Nepenthe, an Egyptian drug."

"How'd you . . .?" He turned away in shock.

"Oh I was a Classics major, can reel off hundreds of lines like that—*very* dramatic ones: 'Behold me, princes of Thebes, the last daughter of the house of your kings,—see what I suffer, and from whom, because I feared to cast away the fear of Heaven!' Antigone, nearing the end." She put the wine glass in his hand. "Only an Iranian could be opposed to Montrachet. Come, cast away fear of Heaven!"

He calmed his face. "Who *are* you?"

"Who *am* I? Claire Savitch. Twenty-seven. Till tomorrow, that is."

"Who are you going to be tomorrow?"

She giggled airily. "Then I'll be twenty-eight. So how long were you in Bangkok?"

"How did you know?" His voice stumbled. Stop it. Dreaming things.

"You *told* me, silly. Said you'd been in Thailand. So I assumed Bangkok. Was I right?"

He tried to watch her face but the light was wrong. A sign of madness is when every phrase has portents. "Yeah, I was in Bangkok."

"How long?"

"Three or four times, last two years."

"Hmm. Did you miss the States?"

"Never."

"I don't either. Been gone for nearly four years—occasional necessary visits only. If it disappeared from the face of the earth I'd hardly notice, though once I was rah rah—quite the patriot."

"Our recent actions aren't much to be proud of."

"What country's are? Oh how lovely!" she added, tucking back her hair and bending past him to look out the window, where saffron moonlight tinted the wing.

He breathed deeply, sat back in his seat. "As a free-lance journalist, do you write things and hope people buy them?"

"Not that simple. Have to be where the action is—or I do in-depth stuff when I can't hit the earthquakes."

"Earthquakes?"

"You know, all people really want to read is about the deaths and sufferings of others—wherever there's gore, I go. But mostly I prefer the in-depth politics, behind the scenes."

"How do you set those up?"

"I get assignments—a magazine wants a quickie on political murders in Indonesia, say, and they check with the agencies to see who's free and close by. Maybe I get picked. Or I have an idea, send a query. Sure it's hand-to-mouth, but it beats the nine A.M. obeisance five days a week."

"What kind of in-depth politics?"

"NATO, SEATO, war and economics—human interest stories."

74

"Why so cynical?"

"It goes with the territory. Journalists look beyond what people—politicians—say, to what they do. Usually they're lying."

"Who, the politicians or the journalists?"

"Sometimes both. But often the politicians, the 'statesmen.' Though most journalists do a lousy job—contented to file the official version and go back to the bar. Like whores, most of us don't put our hearts in it."

"Do you?"

She grinned. "I'm learning more and more to take an interest in the truth that doesn't get out. Trouble is there's no end to levels, to truths. At one level a man commits a crime, at another level he may be a hero, patriot. At a certain place you leave journalism and enter art—what was it Picasso said, fiction's the highest form of truth?"

"I wouldn't know."

"Where are you going now?"

"Nowhere. I mean, I've got nowhere to go. Athens, really."

"You live there?"

"No."

"I'm stopping there too."

"Doing a story?"

"A few days off, celebrate my birthday."

"What story you working on next?"

She drew her hem over her crossed knees, her breasts filling her blouse. "Nothing planned—go back to Brussels eventually, see what my bureau has for me. What a strange look—what were you thinking?"

He shrugged. "Remembering that old song—'The ghost of electricity . . .'"

"'Howls in the bones of her face?' How weird—am I really like that?"

"In a way I'm like you—seeing the world as transition." He tried to extend his sore leg. "Where d'you send your stories?"

"Depends how timely, what subject." She screwed the cap back on an empty wine bottle and stowed it in the seat pocket before her. "If I learned a three-star restaurant in Paris is substituting mushrooms for truffles I'd send the story to *Gourmet* or *Newsweek* or *Time*. But a story on diplomatic lying in Washington might go to *Le Monde*. Or *The Nation*."

"Not *The New York Times?*"

"The trouble with our newspapers is by their very existence they represent the status quo of which they're a part. Newspapers're owned by the same few who own the rest of industrial productivity, so little that threatens that industry's profitability gets serious and honorable coverage."

"How do you see the States?"

She thought. "I didn't grow up there, and I see the States as Europeans do, with some nervous distrust. Following the State and Defense departments does nothing to make me feel better."

"Do you ever get—what's it called—a story no one else has?"

"An exclusive? Everybody tries. Enough of them, you're set for life. Sure, I've had a few."

"If someone gave you information—how would you check it?"

"The joke of my profession is that truth's immaterial. What counts is your sources. Basically, I track down as many people as I can who'll verify the story."

"What if that's not possible?"

"That's what I was saying a few minutes ago, about levels of truth. What we read in the papers is often completely off the mark. The true gets stonewalled."

"Ever do anything on undercover agencies?"

"A little. Why?"

"I'd think it might be interesting. I mean, from what I read."

"Very little of what they call 'intelligence' ever surfaces. Just for once I'd love—*love*—to uncover something. Put down all the goody-goody politicians with blood on their hands."

"Suppose such a story were hard to corroborate?"

"Then you float it from the individual source, see what happens. But that's easy to stonewall." She smoothed down her skirt. "So it's best to have another source—even *one* other person—to validate it. If you want your story to be believed."

"How'd you become a journalist?"

"Probably my stepfather. And my mother. I was thinking about it, tonight after I got on the plane. Iran's such a farce—it got me wondering, am I wasting my life? It's a nowhere place, Iran, a spiritual vacuum. People with no leadership, no focus. Did you know the CIA put the Shah in power? That back in fifty-four they dumped the democratically elected Iranian government? When the

76

Shah gets the boot—the people hate him and we can't keep him there forever—there'll be hell to pay. . . . So why am I covering such garbage? As if it were real, had meaning? Who cares if the Shah builds himself another palace or gets more U.S. tax dollars to buy more U.S. jet fighters?"

With one fingernail she scratched the corner of her mouth. "My stepfather—he's like the Shah—he's the one who made me what I am. Not in a good sense, not by example. No, maybe that's it—it *was* by example . . . he gave me an example of what not to be."

"What's that?"

"He's an infinitely devious man with strong scruples. But his scruples are based on fear."

"How did that make you a journalist?"

"Tonight I was remembering one example. He and my mother have a farm near Nemours. When I was at the Sorbonne I lived on the rue de Dantzig; there's an abattoir in the quarter. Often in bed at night I could hear hoofbeats on the paving stones—that was before the riots, before the streets were tarred so Parisians couldn't dig up the *pavés* to throw at the CRS—at night I could hear the hoofbeats of horses being led to slaughter. On the farm I had a horse too, Ulysse, who'd been with me ever since I was a little girl; my father bought him before he died."

"When did he die?"

"He was a colonel under de Lattre, and was killed two years after de Lattre died, at Dien Bien Phu. Well, one night—it was a strange night in my life anyway—I dreamt that Ulysse was with the horses going to the abattoir. In the dream I saw his mane—he had a long silver mane—flapping on his neck as he walked under the streetlight. Three weeks later I went to the farm; Ulysse was gone— my stepfather said he'd run away—they hadn't been able to find him. Ulysse was old and going blind and had never run anywhere. My mother sat beside my stepfather and said nothing, backing him up. He'd sold Ulysse to the slaughterhouse because he was jealous of my father. While my mother did nothing to intervene. . . . That was her politics—her political compromise. I was learning to look beneath words for motives. From there it was an easy step to journalism."

Cohen eyed the darkness beyond the wing. What motives lead

to my truth? Tell me, Kim. Tell me, Alex. "Why was it a strange night anyway?"

"It was the first time I was ever with a boy. A psychiatrist would have fun with that, wouldn't he?" She sat upright. "Must be getting drunk."

"Why?"

"So talkative." She shivered. "I'm cold."

"I'll get a blanket."

They slept not far from each other's warmth under a thin blanket as the plane traversed the starred dome of Asia Minor. He woke with her shoulder against his, her hair tickling his neck. "What you going to do in Athens?" she mumbled, half asleep.

He did not answer. The plane decelerated into dawn that snuffed the scattered lights of Anatolia and cast cinnabar across the uprippling Aegean. Twenty-two more days. Would she believe me? He watched through the plastic window as an expanding haze became Athens, crouched under its fumes like a squid in ink.

8

THE TIBETAN'S LEATHER BAG of hashish tucked beneath his shirt, he stood painfully in the Customs line.

"You aren't afraid they'll find what you're carrying?"

"Sssh."

"Aren't you?"

"Quiet!"

"You're the kind of man who wants a subservient wife. I can see it."

"I don't want any kind of wife."

"Careful. You can't always get what you want."

"You have no baggage?" The Customs inspector had liquid, searching eyes.

"No," Cohen said.

"You stay how long in Greece?"

"A few days."

"You have money to stay?" The inspector's eyes dropped to Cohen's clothes. "Every foreigner must show certain money to stay in Greece."

"I have friends here who will give me money."

The inspector took back Cohen's passport. "You must wait in Customs Office for them to come."

She shoved forward. "What's the matter?"

The inspector scanned her. "You are with him?"

"Yes. And I have lots of money. Want to see?"

"Give him fifty dollars. Then he comes in."

Cohen waited as the inspector rooted through her lingerie and notebooks. She took his arm as they entered the terminal. "What's with your leg?"

He returned the money. "Sprained my ankle."

"Don't walk, then." She pushed it back. "I'm hungry as a tiger. Buy me breakfast."

"With your money?"

"Why not? Feed me!" She hailed a cab and held the door as he eased himself into the back seat. "For a Jew you have a very Jesuit mind."

"Oh?"

"'Oh?'" she mimicked. "That's a priest's answer—the confessional: 'Forgive me Father for I've sinned'—'Oh?'—'Yes, Father, I've had relations with the Virgin.'—'Oh?' You see, it gives nothing away."

"What should I give away?"

"Are you Jewish?"

"My father was. He died when I was six. My mother was Irish, Catholic. Soon after he died, we went to the States to visit family, get away from Ireland. Several years later, over there, she remarried, an American. I grew up Catholic."

"So which are you?"

"Both. Maybe neither."

"That's being cat and mouse. Victim and executioner. Ugh! I wouldn't want that."

His knee pulsed unbearably. Angrily he said, "So what are you?"

"Me?" She laughed. "Tell me and I'll love you forever. I'd like to know." She watched the ugly outskirts of Athens roll by. "Maybe I'm learning."

"We're always learning. But we never learn."

At the café before the Hotel Britannia fragrances of coffee, ouzo, and croissants hovered in the still, smoggy air. She thumped her suitcase down beside her chair. "They have eggs and rashers here."

He ordered ouzos one after the other, resting his aching leg on a chair as she inhaled eggs scrambled and fried, croissants and scones with lime marmalade, bacon, feta, olives, a Spanish omelet, more scones and bacon, cupfuls of cappuccino leaving brown intertwining circles on the gray marble table. He chewed his ice cubes, adjusted his leg, winced. "I've seen a whole village live a week on less than that."

She licked the underside of her fork. "I'm to feel sorry?"

He shrugged. "I'm comparing, not judging."

She grinned. "Like the man said, if it feels good it *is* good."

"That kinda thinking gets you into trouble."

"So does its opposite."

He cleaned his glasses on the tablecloth, aware of traffic and clattering heels on the sidewalk. How good it will feel to kill them one by one. When did I cross the boundary between good and evil? What boundary? Is there good, evil? The waiter brought another ouzo and he drained it before the waiter could leave. "Just bring the bottle," he said.

She pushed back her plate. "Your leg really hurts."

He raised one eyelid. "Less and less."

"Now what are you going to do?" She cocked her head.

"Now?" Now, silly, I'm waiting for Paul. Waiting for the semaphore, the wireless, the subconscious signal that won't come. That says you're alive, Paul, alive and on your way.

She grinned, playing with her hair. "Yes, now. Now that you've drunk nearly a liter of ouzo for breakfast, and, for all I can see, don't have the wherewithal to get as far as Delphi, let alone the physical ability, given that leg, I must admit that my journalistic curiosity is raised as to what you plan next."

He yanked his leg from the chair. Hardly any pain. "Never plan, just do. That's the secret."

"Secret to what?"

He shrugged, a stupendous lassitude descending like the smog and noise of traffic over his shoulders. He emptied his glass and slapped the knee: all better. With her spoon he scraped the sugary grounds from the bottom of her coffee cup and ate them.

"Aren't you hungry?"

He shook his head, stood, then sat at once as the knee pounded with pain. Why's she pushing me? "I'm staying in Athens a day or two, Claire. If I get to Brussels some time I'll call you."

"Why not call me here?"

"Here?"

"Sure. I'm not going to Brussels now. I can't get over you." She leaned forward, hands on the table, "Here you are, can't walk, no money."

"I've got friends here."

"Let's call a cab and take you to them." She folded her napkin as if planning to reuse it, slapped it on the table, and gathered up her things, waving to the waiter.

He felt empty, suddenly appreciating a strand of hair that fell past her ear along her cheek, stunned by her change of mood. I'm hurt, Claire, lost in my labyrinth, fearing everything, nowhere to go, no one to tell. "That's a hassle."

"I'll drop you and be gone. No sweat."

"You must have other things to . . ."

"What's the big deal? Five minutes. Come on!"

He nodded, feeling dizzy, aware of the set of her shoulders as she tugged on her jacket. "Sure."

She smiled. "I used to fear loneliness—sought people out, just to talk. About nothing. Seems long ago." She slid back her chair. "Don't think I'm forward, Sam—no matter how you see me, that's not me you're seeing."

"Nobody sees anybody clearly."

She ran a lock of hair under her chin. "If you don't feel good enough to see your friends right now, you're welcome to stay at my place till your ankle's better. It's right near here, in the Plaka. Nothing fancy."

He shook his head. "I'm not into attachments, anything, right now."

"Nor am I. You shouldn't infer that."

"I didn't."

"You did! You acted as if I were propositioning you."

"It's very kind."

"Greek men are a pain in the ass—literally. Some male company might keep them at bay." She touched his wrist. "Haven't you ever done anything unusual in your life? It isn't something people do, meet on a plane and get off together."

Cohen stretched, testing the leg. "I'm not so sure."

"Don't be lewd!" She adjusted her collar and stood, the bill and money in her hand. "Do what you want."

It was a third floor double in a dowdy rooming house in the Plaka. Leaning against the balcony's rusty railing he could see a corner of the Erectheum and the tilted peak of the Parthenon.

"That stuff that you're carrying . . ." She came up beside him. "How about we have some?"

"The hash?"

"What else're you carrying? Are you an international dope smuggler?"

He went into the room. She was taking off her jacket, her body lithe and lean, breasts full against her blouse as she turned to hang up the jacket. He sat on the bed and flaked hashish into the pipe.

She sat beside him, spilling hashish into his hand. She jounced. "Hurry."

"I can't when you're bouncing."

She nudged his elbow. "Hurry."

He lit the pipe and passed it to her. She breathed deeply, jade eyes widening. The diamond heart below her throat winked in a stab of sunlight. "It makes me feel gorgeous, this stuff," she sighed.

"You are," he exhaled.

"No, no. I mean it makes me feel lovely inside."

"I'm sure you . . ."

"Stop it, creep." She pushed him.

The ouzo and hash made his head buzz. Sorrow was gaining, crushing his lungs. The room would not hold still. Killed them all. Head in his hands, he heard her stand and cross the room, go out onto the balcony. Don't drag her in. He got up, edged round the bed. Say goodbye, thanks. She's so beautiful. Not pretty. Just beautiful. God, those eyes. They terrify.

On the balcony the air tasted warm and polluted, viscous as gray oil. Death in Athens, lungful at a time. "I gotta go, Claire."

She spun round, hands together. "Perhaps that's wise."

"It's not . . ."

"It's not anything." Her eyes glittered, her upper lip caught momentarily on her chipped tooth. "Seeing you, I think there's a reason—I really do—why people get what they get."

Dizzy with pain, he sat. "That's what the Chetri said."

"Chetri?"

"With one eye. Three days' journey in one night." He made to stand. Fucking knee. Fucking goddamn knee. Fucking Gurkhas. "'There's no accidents,' he said. It's been bothering me. Bothering me for days."

She sat beside him. "You're not making sense."

"If something bad happens to you, there must be some reason, why it happened . . . things don't occur without reason."

She brushed back his hair. "And you want to go?"

He stood, feeling jaunty. "I'll come by again."

She held out her hand, smiling. "Goodbye."

He took it. "Perhaps first I'll take a bath."

She giggled. "Bath?"

"Haven't for a while. Come to think of it, nearly two years."

She sniffed. "Yuck."

"Oh no, not like that. Took lots of baths in rivers. Never had a bathtub. Hot water. Want to soak my leg."

"I thought it was your ankle."

"Yes, my ankle." He turned, aiming for the bathroom, but the bed was in the way. Sit here a while first.

She touched his ankle gently. "Here?"

"Other one." He pointed.

"That's your *knee,* not your ankle."

"True." He hauled himself up. "Got to soak it."

She steered him round the bed to the bathroom, holding aside her hair as she bent to open the faucet, water clattering into the tub. "You okay by yourself?"

"Couldn't be better."

She shut the door and he undressed, sitting on the toilet to unwrap the bandage round the knee, hissing with pain as it pulled away the corrugated black-and-yellow flesh. No wonder it hurts. Goddamn pig. Carefully and very slowly he lowered himself into the steaming water, keeping the leg raised till the bath cooled a bit, then let the leg down and passed out.

Her voice beyond the door. "You okay, Sam?"

He raised himself up. "Little nap."

"Need anything?"

He pondered. "Bandage and iodine."

"You want antibiotics? They're over the counter here."

"Yes." He took the soap and, gritting his teeth, began methodically to wash out the wound.

A slamming door and jingling keys announced her return. "Still okay?"

He stood and pulled the plug. "Be there in a minute." He put on his shirt, wrapped the towel round his waist, and hobbled into the room.

"Jesus," she said when she saw the knee.

"Pig tripped me." He opened the iodine, pulled apart the wound and poured it in, eyes watering. She brought him two pills as he secured the bandage. "Here." She pulled down the bedcover. "Lie quiet for a minute."

It was dark, the air thick and still. From somewhere light breathing. Is that me? He slid upward, pain wracking his knee. Shit, forgot about that. His head pounded. More cautiously he eased to a sitting position. The breathing came from next to him, a weight that held down the covers.

Paul, I'm so happy you saw the football. You'll be in Paris. In three weeks. I did the right thing. Kim isn't dead—I just saw her. Kim, oh Kim, I'm so glad. He fumbled on the table beside the bed, turned on the switch. Oh Jesus. Another dream.

Claire lay on her side beside him, still dressed, one hand tucked beneath her head, the other between her knees, a raincoat over her shoulders, her nyloned toes curled inward against the cold. Her mouth was open slightly, strands of hair loose over her forehead and cheek. On the table next to the lamp was a glass of water and a pill.

He edged carefully from the bed, limped to the bathroom. Leg's better. Can go soon. On the way back to bed he bent to check the watch on her wrist. Four-ten. In the morning?

She murmured, looked up. "You're awake."

He pulled a wisp of hair from her lips. "How long'd I sleep?"

"Since yesterday noon." She pulled the raincoat closer. "Sorry about here . . ."

"Here?"

"On the bed, my sleeping—nowhere else—didn't want to wake you."

"You didn't," he answered, but she was already asleep. He tugged the blankets from beneath her and covered her, climbed in his side, took the pill, and fell back to sleep.

Dust motes tumbled steadily through a beam of sunlight; traffic noises percolated up from the street. In the distance a sound of bells, a woman singing, faraway rumble of a plane. "Claire?" His voice sounded an old man's, high and creaky.

The knee was stiff and very painful. He changed the bandage for the new one that was laid out on the dresser top, dressed, washed, shaved, limped out on the balcony and sat in the sun.

She came through the door and tossed him a newspaper. "The *Heralds of Tribulation.* Best I could do."

Sunday, April 1. Three weeks to Easter. He squinted at the somber headlines of war and politics, turned to the sports page. A slim time for football news.

"You hungry?" Her face looked wan, thinner.

"You didn't sleep well, did you? Yes, I'm hungry."

"Can you walk?"

"After a fashion."

"It's lunchtime. I'm starving."

"What did you do," he asked in the café, "while I was sleeping all day and night?"

For a second she did not answer and he had a quick feeling of transgression. Maybe she's got a boyfriend.

"Went out a while, in the afternoon. Just to wander. Mostly stayed at home—afraid you'd wake and not know where you were."

He took her hand; it felt surprisingly hard, the skin dry and worn. "Thanks."

She squeezed his hand. "You'd have done the same."

"Maybe not. My life's been awful lately."

"Eat up. Everything goes in spurts. Things'll get better."

It was true; sitting in a park in the afternoon sun, with the warmth of coffee and food in his stomach, the nagging sour pain in his leg decreasing, he felt less agony. Maybe Paul really did see the football. He dozed, waking to recount in his head. Twenty-one days.

He tried to imagine the hitchhike to Paris. Not yet. Knee won't tolerate. Can't sponge off her. Wish I could tell her. Twenty-three dollars left. Dollar a day keeps the killers away. One more day. That's it, one more day—then go.

She took his arm through the noisy streets, halting before an open shop where embroidered shirts lay folded on a formica table, held one against him. "Your wardrobe's light on variety."

He tugged her hand. "You don't need to buy me anything. Just be yourself."

"Maybe buying you something is being myself. You're afraid, aren't you?"

"Of what?"

"There you go again—the order of Jesus—answering a question with another. Afraid of me, them."

"'Them'?"

"The ones you fought with all night. You're a good person, but you're on a wire—afraid—I can . . ."

He snickered. "So now you're a psychiatrist."

"Stop it! I'd like to know—help."

"So you can sell it? An exclusive?"

"Whew." She shook her head. "I see you can be a real asshole when you put your mind to it—does that make me a shrink?"

"I don't care what that makes you."

"I'm not who I seem. Though the seeming's from you, not me."

Their room was silent, cooler than the street. She sat on the bed, not removing her jacket. He got up and sat beside her. "It's no thrill—having me as a guest."

"That's not it."

"What's 'it', then?"

She smoothed a crease across her knee. "Jet lag." She jumped up. "Going to take a shower." She crossed to the bathroom and shut the door. Through it came the whisper of her unrobing, the faucet roaring, toilet flushing. He stepped onto the balcony and slowly climbed the fire ladder one flight to the roof, where the monoxides of Athens shifted fitfully in dull afternoon light.

The Acropolis expended its tarnished splendor on the facing hilltop. Laughter and a radio echoed in the lightwell; from the street came the voices of children running and the uneven cadence of diesels; against the chipped hilltop columns boomed a departing jet. He thought of his own flight, the miles to go. But when? Get to Paris early and I'm dead—first place they'll look. I'm in *their* labyrinth; they know all the exits.

If I told her? Don't drag her in. Could she suggest someone? Whatever happens, no chancing Paris too soon. Kohler Import-Export? By now the CIA'll be happily sitting in ambush, knowing I have the address. Or did the Tibetans tell them? Better to wait for Paul. No money to get to Fulton Street anyway. So I steal it? That's a laugh, with this leg. Funny how it no longer seems wrong to steal, only tactically unwise. My morality's unravelling like an old shirt. An old hair shirt.

The wisest is lie low in the labyrinth, let the knee heal. Meet Paul in Paris when the time comes; together we'll find the way out. Then we'll be the hunters; we'll plan the maze; they'll be the prey.

A cat yowled in the lightwell. He looked down. The bathroom window was open at the top; he could see her legs extended in frothy water. One leg was raised, indolent. A hand moved down, cupping water over a thigh. His pulse pounded in his groin.

He sat on the parapet and watched the specks crawling antlike round the Parthenon. She joined him, fluffing out wet hair in the sticky air. "Shower doesn't work."

"Greek plumbing." He turned toward her. "You smell like orchids."

"How do orchids smell?"

"I don't know. If they do, it's got to be like you."

She hugged him. "It's time for dinner. Greek lamb, food of the gods. Olives and retsina."

"Are you always this hungry?"

"For everything!"

The restaurant was spicy and cool, with French windows opened on a cobbled lane. "Long live *krasi*," she said, swirling red wine in her glass to throw beams of the setting sun on the rush-mat ceiling. "Wine and blood."

"Gifts of God."

"Life's too magical to be the work of only one god. And a sexually frustrated one to boot!" She giggled. "Hard as He tries, He's not even good at evil."

After dark the stones of the Plaka were splashed white by the rising moon. They turned uphill toward the Acropolis. Cubiform low buildings cut rectangular shadows out of the lamplight.

Steel gates blocked the path. Between the bars gleamed the columns of the Erectheum and the moon-scattered tumult of the Parthenon. A cool breeze descended through olive trees, squeaking the gate. She shoved it gently. "It opens!"

Moonlight ran, white lava, down the marble stairs. The olives whispered new leaves, shadowing them up to the Propylaea. The Erectheum fell below and to the left. Beneath the chin of a goddess, far out in the city, an ambulance flashed.

The aisle between the Parthenon's columns and wall was

striated by shadow and moonlight, the stone cool. She rubbed her chin against his hand. "It's too liquid, time."

"Why?"

She kissed his thumb. "Being here, so suddenly. Time is spilling. I can feel it."

"It never stops."

"Sometimes it runs out all at once." She stretched beside him on the stone, traced a fingertip over his lip. "Aren't you glad we didn't hurry?"

"I've nowhere to go, Claire."

"That's what's so nice about it. It'll be over before we know it."

He pulled her above him, slipping up her dress, cupping her sleekness. She laced her fingers under his head, shielding it from the stone, her belly fluttering against him, her hair a silken, perfumed tent around him, as he drove deeper and deeper into the enchanting, fragrant center of her, into all that was lost long before remembrance.

For a long time she lay atop him, licking at his lips, kissing his eyes, as he felt himself go soft within her and his warm slippery seed flow back from her onto him. Her back was slim, strong, and sleek to his touch, her buttocks small and firm, the hair at their juncture curly and wet.

She wriggled alongside him, the moonlight soft on the wetness of her belly. "In the temple of the Virgin no less."

"Which one?"

"*This* one, silly. *Parthenos* means virgin. You Catholics didn't invent everything." She unbuttoned his shirt and kissed his chest, nipping at the hair around his nipples.

He sat against the column, she in front of him within the hollow of his arms. He tucked aside her hair and kissed her ear. *"Tu portes une petite perle à chaque oreille."*

"It sounds pretty that way—prettier than English."

"'You wear a little pearl at each ear'? It does."

Athens glittered below them, a priceless, inscrutable axiom. *Tod und Verklarung.* Dead, now transfigured. Alchemy: clay into flesh through the medium of love. He felt the world's heartbeat and his own; they were the same. The column at his back was as much himself as the bone that bore against it. Through it his awareness tentacled into the mountain, the city below, the pulsing curve of the earth, the void in which they moved.

For a moment I forgot. The awful sorrow, the anger, hate. Loving does that, gets rid of it. So much can be forgotten if you love. I must not love. He ran a fingertip between her fingers, to the softness where they joined. "Once, long ago, I awoke one morning in a state of grace. I had nothing to do that day but live. I had no plans. Plans are deadly, like wanting. Never again have I had that absolute joy of emptiness."

"That's what Montaigne said: *'Je ne trace aucune ligne certaine, ni droite, ni courbe.'*" She tossed a pebble clinking over the marble. "Which is why you smoke that stuff?"

"It saves me from programs and policies . . . enhances the ordinary, makes transparent the mundane opacity of things."

"It does that for me, too. But by making the everyday quintessential doesn't it reduce the quintessential to the everyday?"

"No doubt. It's not as good as you."

She slid down beside him and tickled his ribs. "Do I strip away the mundane opacity of things?"

"When you take off your clothes."

"Surely I knew you long ago. There's just a little strangeness, an ignorance of recent facts. I wonder what you've been doing lately."

"Up to no good."

"But no good deed goes unpunished, as someone said."

Favoring the knee, he eased down to kiss her belly where the little golden curls began, flicking his tongue along the crease between her thigh and belly, into the softness of warm, damp curls, into the intoxicating essence of her. She arched her back as his tongue opened her and he slipped his hands beneath her thighs, his fingertips against their softest inside skin, holding them apart as he kissed and licked gently and slowly, then more deeply and strongly, then harder as her fingernails bit into his back and she shivered, exhaling, closed her thighs and twisted round to nestle against him.

"God, what a feeling," she sighed.

"You mean 'gods'?"

"You *are* a Jesuit. A Jesuit Jew." She kissed his neck, shoulder, the hard flesh of his stomach, along one thigh, avoiding the knee, then down the other, her hands enfolding him, her fingers lightly

90

urging him up, her lips then moist and full around him, down and up, down and up while her tongue wrapped him in warm liquid folds and her hair moved softly over his thighs. He slipped one hand into the wet softness of her groin and let the other wander across her breasts beneath the uprolled cashmere. She withdrew so just her lips were touching him, drinking him in, her tongue fluttering gently.

She kissed his chest. "I never liked the thought of it, swallowing it. But now I wanted to."

He snuggled her into his arms, not sure where his body ended and hers began. I must not love.

The moon was sinking in the west when they closed the gate behind them. The streets were silent but for here and there a couple hand in hand, a patter of rats in alleys, a donkey snuffing at them through a fence. The room was clammy and constricted after the freedom of the Acropolis, making love less exotic within the walls, two green and two peach, that enclosed them.

When she slept, he arose and prowled the roof. A cat yowled in the street, then another. As a boy I would hold two ants close in my fingertips until they tore at each other, and so began a war between two anthills, countless ant bodies littering the sandy soil. He gazed across the rooftops to the columnar magnificence of the Parthenon, blown up by men of war and rebuilt by men of peace. In which category am I?

Exhaustion washed over him. He imagined her as he had left her, on her right side, hands clasped beneath her chin, hair in abandon on the pillow, the covers lifting gently with her breathing.

Three weeks. Perhaps she knows someone at *Le Monde.* If Paul comes to Paris . . . Then we'll go straight to New York, Kohler Import-Export. But what if Paul's dead under the Himalayan snow? Or in some sordid hovel? Then I'm deceased, adrift in a measureless universe. Phu Dorje, his family, Kim, the monkey man—their deaths'll all be blamed on me. Alex's and Goteen's too, Eliott's, the Tibetan in the Kali Gandaki—where does it stop? His gaze returned to the Parthenon's Olympian luminosity. This is the full measure of my fate, my failure. An outlaw, internationally hunted, an excommunicate beyond appeal, I'm everywhere at risk. How much of this would she believe?

*   *   *

At dawn they hunted the chilled, smoky streets for Turkish coffee and rolls, returned to bed and made love quickly, slept and made love again, floating exhausted in each other, and slept again.

Church bells woke them. She watched him dress the knee. "Still bad, isn't it?"

He shook his head, then nodded. "Yes."

"A friend of mine in Brussels has a place near here," she said, slipping into French jeans and a silk blouse. "In Crete, on a primitive beach." She stretched to snap her jeans. "Let's go there for a few days, sit in the sun, till it's better?"

He finished the bandage, stood to test the leg. She watched from the mirror, head tilted as she brushed her hair. "I have to go," he said.

She swung her hair back. "So go."

"Yet I don't want to—already getting pulled back."

"To what?" She tossed the brush into her handbag, bent and pulled a maroon silk scarf from her suitcase, knotted it round her neck.

"Back into life. Being with you I forget what's happened, start to live in the moment."

She raised one foot behind her to hook a high heel strap round her ankle. "You were in Vietnam—some horror you can't forget?" She crossed to him. "It's okay to fear—takes time to forget."

He kissed the tip of her nose. Just flesh, we are—pores and bones and death. Her eyes seemed distant though not harsh, as if she pondered some weight unknown to him; her body moved lean and lithe against his. So beautiful, so fallible, so short-lived, so caring—this is what I've forsaken. "It's more than a personal horror, goes beyond forgetting, makes a parody of life."

"So it's a good story?" she grinned. "Come, tell me!" She sat on the bed, pulled him down beside her. "You've been holding out on me, Sam Cohen!" She licked her tongue into his mouth. "You tell me. Right now!"

Such lassitude—a warning? Claire's face superimposed by Kim's. "God tries," Kim said. "I'll try," he answered.

"Fine!" She sat up. "If it's a good one we'll split the proceeds and spend months making mad mucking love *en Maroc!*"

He tried not to smile. "It's a sick story, Claire. After I tell you, if you believe me, you'll never feel the same."

92

"Was my life so great as it was? Tell me!"

"Nor was mine. But I'm not giving you anything better."

When he was done she sat still, head down, hands clasped between her knees. He felt like a seashell unearthed in the desert, as if the dry dust of Athens could blow him away. Her breathless charm was gone, her eager asperity, her Vassar cynicism. As if we've been married years and just admitted to each other that all our years were charade. He limped onto the balcony, squinted into the glare. When he came in she had taken her handbag from the chair. "I'm going for a walk," she said.

"You don't believe me."

"Yes." Her voice was ancient, as if from a tomb. "Perhaps I do. What reason would you have . . .?"

He took the key from the dresser top. "Can I go with you?"

Gaily dressed strangers jostled them in open markets. She followed him into the cool albumen of a church. Kneeling figures mumbled before altars; a skinny man lit a votive candle, his careworn face lambent.

"All of this," she said as they emerged. "Transitory. Dreamlike."

"It's worse than a dream. We don't wake." It's that strange passive leadership of hers, he thought, that has me going where I never intended, as if it were my choice. "I want to go my own way. It was a mistake to tell you."

"So what do you plan to do?" she yelled in the bustling street. "Be a lone ranger—a solitary hero? In the real world, heroes get eaten alive! Don't you know that? What tapestry are you riding through, my solitary knight? Or shall you forget it, pretend it never happened?"

"I have to meet my friend in Paris. Then we'll see."

"And like you said—what if he's dead?"

He shrugged. "We'll see."

"See what?"

"How to reveal it and when." He avoided her eyes. "My concern's revenge not publicity. I don't care any more about the future—there isn't any."

"So where does that get you? Besides dead?" She shook his

arm, forced his face down into hers. "You're going away from me—
I won't let you!"

"You can't stop me."

"Oh yes I can! Don't you *dare* tell me what I can't do."

"And you're still trapped." He dropped his hand from hers.
"I'm gonna sit in Syntagma, think for a while, plan, be back about
two."

She pulled back. "*Ciao,* then," she turned and shouldered
through the crowd.

Feeling dull and shallow he limped to Syntagma. Shadows lay
corpselike on the square. He ordered a *raki* and sipped it ven-
omously. Finally he rose, threw some coins on the table. Don't take
it out on her. She'll help if I let her. Couldn't be a safer place than
Crete. Lie low in the labyrinth.

He returned to the hotel. The room retained her fragrance but
her things were gone. On the bed lay the embroidered shirt. He
hobbled quickly down to the lobby and called the airlines; she had
just reserved a seat on the Olympic flight leaving in forty minutes
for Paris and New York.

It took ten minutes to find a cab in Syntagma Square. In a side
street off the square a fat truck blocked the way. Cars behind them
cut off their retreat. The cabbie jumped out and pounded on the
truck's horn, invading the street with raucous echoes. An unshaven
man with a dirty undershirt riding up his belly yelled and shook his
fist out a doorway. Horns wailed behind them. Finally the unshaven
man climbed into the truck and drove it gratingly away. Cohen sat
back in exasperation. Traffic gathered ahead behind black-belching
buses; the taxi cut nervously from one lane to another, making little
gain.

Near the airport exit the traffic slowed, then halted. The cabbie
stood on the front bumper, shading his eyes. "*Disti'chima!*" he
called, banging his fists together. He motioned Cohen up.

Through the crepe-paper rippling of exhausts ahead he could
discern the silver oblong of a tanker truck, on its side. Behind them,
a siren howled.

"Airport—how many kilometers?"

The cabbie raised four fingers.

"Forget it," Cohen sighed. He sat back in the cab. And forget her. Now there's all the time in the world for a cautious trip through Yugoslavia. Wait there two weeks, then quick to Paris. No money, but I'll make it. Some day find her in Brussels. He shook his head. Don't lie to yourself.

He picked at the seat's worn vinyl. "Even in accidents," Hem had said, grasping his horses' reins by the cyclone fence in Pokhara, "there is purpose." Suddenly he hungered for Hem's one-eyed face, for his calm acquiescence in a deeper life. Deeper than what? Than ordinary turmoil? How can I be sure what's ordinary, what's deeper, being only myself?

Cars ahead began to budge. The taxi started with a hoarse crepitation. How long was it since the woman's voice on the telephone had said, "In forty minutes, sir"?

They cleared the overturned truck on the right. Half-crushed beneath the truck's chrome torso was a taxi. Its passenger lay in a pool of blood and oil on the pavement. A policeman was covering his face with a piece of cotton, not before Cohen glimpsed the vacant, white-eyed stare of a lean, nearly familiar face, almost recognized the rictus beneath a trim, thin moustache.

I recognize the dead: they're my people. I never knew that one, but I see my death in him, everyone's. Caught in the labyrinth. Without exits.

The taxi halted nosedown in a shrill of tires before the Olympic terminal. "Two hundreds drachma," the cabbie said.

He fumbled in his pockets. His few dollars were tucked away in the room, under the mattress, with the bag of hash. All he had was a hundred drachmas. The driver took them and reached back for more. "Wait!" Cohen pointed downward. "Stay here."

"One more hundreds drachma!" The cabbie wiggled his fingers. A plane rumbled in the distance. A woman dragged a suitcase loudly across the sidewalk. Within the terminal a loudspeaker bellowed.

"I come back," Cohen said. The cabbie shook his head. Cohen yanked out his passport, handed it to the cabbie. "You stay!" He pointed down. The cabbie nodded.

He limped hurriedly through milling crowds, stumbled over a poodle on a chain, its owner snapping at him. The Olympic flight had left seven minutes earlier. He wandered dizzily, seeking her in the throng, without hope. When he returned to the sidewalk, the taxi was gone.

9

HE HITCHED A RIDE toward Athens in a garbage truck, its un-shaven and obese driver gesticulating largely and breathing onions across the seat as his truck jounced and clattered through the streets, melon and squash rinds rumbling disconsolately in the back.

Cohen nodded uncomprehendingly. He was left at a traffic cir-cle and retrieved by a gray Mercedes, whose silver-haired, gray-pinstriped owner spoke English easily. "Odos Apollonos? It is quaint, the Plaka. I will drop you." The car shifted easily. "Have you been in before, Greece?"

"Once."

"Most of us live in our own little corners, never seeing the world. Travel's exciting, opens the eyes."

Sunlight had retreated above the storefronts; Odos Apollonos was rank with cooking smells. The landlady came ranting at him, her pink fists raised, "Out! Out!"

Nodding, he edged by her, limped up the stairs and unlocked the door. Claire sat reading by the window.

"I thought you'd gone."

"I came back." She closed the book. "Though I can't really say why."

"I thought you'd gone," he repeated. He entered the bathroom, slipping. "Why's the floor wet?" He sat on the bed op-posite her.

"When I came back the shower was running. I was happy you were there so I undressed and got in the shower but it was the plumber who had come to fix it; he was so shocked he fell and sprained his ankle. Now he's going to sue the landlady and she's thrown us out." She began to giggle, biting a finger.

"So why'd you come back?"

"I said I don't know. Do you always need a reason?"

96

"I went to the airport to stop you. I've never done that before."

"What," she laughed, "go to the airport?"

"Come off it! I've never gone after someone, if she left, tried to keep her."

"Oh, Sam," she got up and held him. "You must've had a ragged life."

He stood and took his hashish and money from under the mattress. "I lost my passport."

"Sam! Where?"

"Cabbie stole it. Did you see the accident?"

"I saw the mess, coming back. It must've happened behind me. Sam—what are you going to do?"

"I just remembered who he was."

"Who?"

"The dead guy beside the cab. He was on our plane. Got on before you, in Teheran." He sat, his knee throbbing. "So why was he following you?"

She knelt before him. "I don't know. Let's go quickly! Go to Crete, out of the way—it's dangerous here. Now you don't have your passport! How can you escape?"

"Why's it dangerous here?"

"Can't you tell? Maybe I'm getting shaky—picking up on you—but I'm afraid, afraid for you. You said you've got time—why starve in Yugoslavia? No one'll follow us to Crete—we'll have time to find you new papers, figure out something—then fly to Paris, just before Easter. Please?"

From the wet stern rail of the steamer they watched the darkening bones of Greece sink into the sea. Shivering, she leaned against him, shoulder to shoulder. "It's so awful."

He cupped her chin in his palm. "Your face's cold. We should go in."

"You stay out—you're enjoying it." She turned into the oncoming wind. "I'm a little sick."

"Seasick?"

"Crossed the line, maybe. So much has happened today." She vanished through the bulkhead door.

He paced the slippery decks, ducking beneath gently swaying life-boats. In the lee of the fantail he smoked a bit, eyes on the phosphorescent wake, mind on the dead man. He wasn't following me—obviously. An accident? A toothbrush salesman, functionary . . . Arab, Jewish, Greek? Could've been anyone. What brought him across Persia's eroded expanse to death in Athens?

The death of this man with the rimless spectacles and black moustache seems strangely preordained. The labyrinth of fate's otherwise too complex. And I'm no doubt fated to seek a certain exit, and death's fated to be waiting. He drew a finger line along the wet rail. My own death, swifting toward me, equally preordained. Like most men, I don't mind death as long as it stays away.

The ship's engines pulsed through the rail into his elbows. Above him Orion extended over half the sky, gathering stars, worlds, void into his arms. How many winter nights have I watched your hunt across the darkness, while coyotes yapped on the Big Hole benches and owls talked in the lodgepoles? The wide Montana starry sky came back to him; he lowered his head onto his folded arms.

The wind changed and cut into his ribs. Fate is too complex for any understanding. Before all this, in Nepal, I felt that understanding was not important, that since it was doomed to failure no time should be wasted on it. Was that not wisdom? Now I'm forced to some attempt—an attempt doomed to failure. Weary and unsleepy, leg aching, he limped the tilting deck. Twenty days more. She'll be warm, blankets up around her chin. For a while, perhaps my enemies will look elsewhere.

They docked in Heraklion at first light. "I'll rent the car," she said in a harbor café reeking of ouzo and soggy cigarettes. "And I'll go to the bank—let's meet here at ten?"

Sun gleamed on the pebbled beach westward of town. Seagulls and sandpipers kept pace along the water edge. A man with furled trousers led a donkey cart across a tidal stream. Cohen took off his shoes and waded it, the cold shocking his knee. A slight figure approached from the west.

He halted to skip stones. It was a pudgy young woman with windblown rusty hair, in blue jeans. "Hi," she called, approaching. "You American?"

"Australian."

"I'm Budgie. From Canada." She grinned roundly. "Where in Australia?"

He shrugged. "Sydney."

"What's your name?"

"Clyde," he said lamely.

"I seen you before." She peered sideways up at him. "You on television?"

"Me? Never."

"I seen you somewhere. A jock, aren't you? That's what you are." She nodded. "I remember faces."

He smiled lopsidedly. "Never even owned a jockstrap."

"I remember faces. I'm with a bunch in the Hotel Europa. Mostly Yanks but three Canadians. One's a Canuck, really. You talk a lot."

"Too early."

"The beach is good for sleeping. I'll show you where it's warm and dry."

"No thanks."

"It's nice here, the sea, the town, the hills." She blinked. "Lie on the beach, Clyde. Good for your heart." She trudged eastward, Cohen noticing her again when she was the size of the avocets pecking at the waterline, her splayed footprints paralleling the donkey cart tracks that merged into a single line that vanished beyond her in the morning maritime haze.

Budgie's led them to me: Gurkhas closing in over the dunes, Enfields sparkling. Dry-mouthed, he woke, the sun high. Ignoring the knee, he trudged quickly along the hard sand by the sea, scattering birds. Claire was not in the café. Above the square, a chipped clock showed twenty to eleven, the side streets half-shadowed. He saw her through a pharmacy window, left hand at her waist, right holding a telephone. Her eyes widened; she turned away, nodding, and hung up. "You're late."

"Fell asleep on the beach. Who was that?"

"Getting directions."

She accelerated the white Peugeot through the outskirts of Heraklion, white roadside stones flicking past, bearded goats inspecting them with slanted almond eyes, into a countryside jaggedly iridescent with spring.

"You drive pretty well for a woman."

"History *has* passed you by, hasn't it?"

He smiled, bare feet on the dashboard in the windshield sun, tugging last night's hash, malodorous and crumbling, from his shirt pocket.

In the grip of the hash he tumbled into the color cacophony of Crete, its flaming yellows, rubbled greens, cobalts of air and sea, its thorny earth browns, grays of granite and volcano, its limestone houses attenuated like bleak cattle round sparse alluvia, its alien and anciently evocative odors, its hazed panoramas of tilted ridge and plunging valley, its intimations of paths under the hunched, prophetic brush. I've been dead to this, too.

Knee feels better in the sun. She's right—to be here's good. Getting over this. What, though, do I hope to get over? Not the deaths; they'll never be "over," nor will the fear and running, ever. It's a life sentence, that. A death sentence. He glanced at her. "Ever been married?"

She geared down into a turn. "For two weeks." When he said nothing she added, "We met when he was on leave from Vietnam. I knew him for ten days before I married him. We had five days and then he went back—he'd already extended his tour. They sent him right up to Khe Sanh. He was killed three days after he got there, by one of our own shells."

Cohen watched the landscape passing like the cheap backdrop of a film. "And you never let on."

"All I have left is this necklace . . . and a few memories that seem more and more like fiction—though I always think about him—habit, I suppose. Recently I've realized he died for nothing. It's as if they took Tim and fifty thousand other young men, lined them up against a wall, and shot them." She turned. "Did you go?"

"Me? Never. The whole thing filled me with hate. I refused to go; the Vietnamese weren't threatening my country. I lost my job and had to go to Canada. The whole thing made me bitter, about the States."

"What job did you lose?"

"Playing football. I'd just signed on, out of college. I got hurt and had to sit out the season, got drafted. I was furious that we

100

were picking on a tiny country like that, said I wouldn't go. So the team dropped me—everybody in sports was hot for the war except Muhammad Ali. I went to Canada, played a while, got hurt again, had to quit. Couple years ago I was going back, to coach, but never did."

"I know."

"What do you know?"

"You talked a bit, the other night; you were pretty out of it. About the girl in Paris."

"She was from Quebec. What else did I say?"

"Nothing too specific. Enough for me to guess what you've been through."

"She died, in a plane crash with my mom and stepfather. They'd picked her up in Montreal in their plane, to bring her to Quebec for the wedding. It was a freak storm . . ."

The car swerved as she reached for the pipe. "Life's a horror, Sam."

He shrugged. "It makes its own rules. We get to watch."

"This landscape's fitting. Something evil, terrifying, out there." She returned the pipe. "It was here Theseus killed the bull-man, the Minotaur. In the Labyrinth."

"More of your Classics?"

"Theseus would have died without Ariadne, the daughter of the Sun. She turned against her own people to help him slay the Minotaur and escape from the Labyrinth. Then he went off and left her."

"You're the one who said no good deed goes unpunished."

"You almost walked on his grave. On the Acropolis, in the shadow of the Virgin's temple—remember?" She licked her lip, smiled. "So what would you do?"

"At what?"

"Here, in the Labyrinth. Against the Minotaur? Seeking darkness at its core?" Her feline gaze crossed his, against a rushing backdrop of scrub and rock.

"You've got a crooked smile."

"Tell me."

"Who knows? I wouldn't approach him rationally. I learned that from football. When you think things out you expose yourself to the same options as he. I'd stick to instinct."

"It's crude, football."

"Sometimes it's pure feeling, the joy of doing, acting deeply, without consciousness."

"That's romanticizing!"

"So? What's wrong with romance? There's a magical, instinctive place into which you flow, playing good football, so afterward you wake up and wonder where you've been. Somebody once said if there are angels then the loss of the body is their supreme regret. Well, in the moment between a pass and its completion, time stands still. Thanks to football I know what that timeless world is like . . . that heaven is of the body and the body alone. Heaven has nothing to do with angels."

Sitea appeared below, a brief valley shouldered by hills, white masts copsed along the sea. In a café by the dock they ate octopus and drank retsina. A white pelican stood beside a boy fishing from the dock. The boy unhooked a flake of wriggling silver and dropped it in the bird's gaping mouth.

She pointed her glass. "The lion lies down with the lamb."

"No one's lying down with the fish."

"You see only the dark side."

"I'm with the little guy." He drained the bottle into their glasses. "Where now?"

"An hour from Sitea, Etienne said. At the eastern tip of the island, a place called Vye."

"Etienne?"

"An architect in Brussels. He's buying up all the land there, to build a resort."

"Funny word, resort."

"As in 'the last . . .'?"

Vye was one street, a clump of silent whitewashed houses. She swerved north on a cart track, thistles raking the car. The house lay in a gorse valley draining eastward to a beach fringed by palms and flanked by crumbling cliffs, waves crashing loud against the sloping sand.

It was one room, one door, and two narrow windows set in foot-thick walls, a sink, a bed, a table, a hearth of sour ashes. She slipped her arms around him. "Sanctuary!"

A fire of palm fronds and thorns gave the hut illusory warmth: the walls stayed dank. An east wind banged the door on its thongs and hissed through the thatch, thrashing the palm trees and snapping at the waves as they thundered on the beach.

"Make it last, last, last." She settled beneath him, the silver chain of the diamond heart crumpled on her neck.

Once, he thought, if just once I held nothing back. No self, no awareness. He tousled her hair; it was so supple and silken, he wondered is it real? He tugged.

"Ow!"

He could not stop watching her eyes, azure green pools in the half-light, translucent and opaque, tranquil and seeking, their lashes wide, without flutter. He felt her hips one with his, their flesh not a barrier but a juncture, stretched his whole long body as tightly against her as he could, touching every inch of her he could, trying almost to turn inside out in order to cover, wrap, her completely.

The inside of her thigh was lithe and satiny; he raised it and slipped against her cleft, feeling her lips open, wet and grasping. She twisted slightly to bring her downy pubis against him. He pushed and she recoiled, wincing. "You're too big," she gasped. She slid her thigh over his, her breasts solid against his chest.

"You're so tight, so lovely." He moved his tip inside her and began to rotate within her lips, slipping out to caress its underside against the swelling softness atop her cleft. She raised her waist, thrusting her pubic bone against his, her tongue inside his throat, her mouth widespread against his.

He rolled her on her back, her other thigh now enlacing his, penetrated her as she unfolded wider and wider, felt himself endlessly slipping inside her, her lips endlessly sliding up over him. "You're so hot inside."

"You make me." She shivered, her waist twining to him as he drove so deeply within her it seemed she would never end. Out he pulled until she lifted up to grasp his tip and sucked him in again and they roared down her vortex together, through burning joy to a high silent meadow of pollened sun, warm and fertile.

He became conscious of her lying beside him, their shoulders, hips, and legs touching. Sweat glistened beside the pearl in her earlobe. She twisted against him. "I love your body. All muscled but slender. Gentle steel."

Words and ideas and lovely feelings tumbled through him, un-curtailed: like two wild creatures we have stumbled on one another, yet with trust, without fear. He thought of death with peace, almost friendliness.

He rubbed the upslope of her hips, nuzzled her curls, kissed her gently, as if she could break, down the tendon of her neck, across the breasts so full and hard and yet so soft and obedient to his lips. She raised herself on one elbow, shook back her hair, her breasts jiggling tightly. He felt desire begin to throb in him again, leaned down and kissed her belly, licking between her legs. She pulled his head up. "You're going to screw me to death."

"It's *immortality,* screwing."

She kissed him sleepily. "It *is* lovely."

"It's life's deepest good—because it contributes most to life's continuance."

"I don't care what it does. I just like it."

"But even without procreation it's life's greatest good because it gives spiritual continuance, it . . .."

She ran her tongue down his sternum and over his belly, took his upraised penis fully in her lips and swallowed the tip till it lodged deep in her throat, her fingertips lightly teasing. He reached down but she pushed his hand away and knelt between his thighs, her hair tumbling over his waist, sliding her lips up and down, wrapping his tip within the underside of her tongue, nibbling, nipping, licking, and sucking him to a spurting, burning joy that left him aching and empty.

She lay next to him, kissed his shoulder. "I want to tell you everything, but there isn't time. There never will be."

"We'll make time."

"We can't. Only the gods can make time."

Before sunset the wind died and he followed a deep-cut trail to the beach. The earth was punctured by goat prints and peppered with droppings. On the beach, palm stalks crunched underfoot. The palm crowns overhead burst outward like green suns against the cooling sky. The sand was still warm; he sat against a rippled dune, feeling incomprehensibly at a loss. Water rushed up, white, to his feet. Removing shoes and socks, he watched it run between his toes.

How many times each day have I tried to fathom it? The deaths, the bomb, the lethal Australian with his lemur skin and motorcycle—none of it makes sense. She can't make sense of it either. At least she believes. Sand ran between his fingers.

Stones rattled upslope. A goat, bell clinking, trotted down the path. Others followed, kids hopping behind, and began to nose among dry fronds on the beach.

A white-haired man punched a knobby stick down the trail. He wore a loose goatskin cape that fell to the tops of worn wool leggings. His calves were gaunt, his ankles bony. Without words he crossed the beach and squatted beside Cohen, staring seaward. A breeze tufted his yellowed beard. He pointed at the sky. *"Vroxi."*

Cohen shrugged uncomprehendingly.

The goatherd stared whimsically, as if Cohen had misunderstood a simple joke. From the goatskin cape he withdrew a lump of bread wrapped in linen, broke away a chunk and offered it. The bread had a flaky, soda tang. He split a fragment of goat cheese, dry and tasting of olives. *"Tedesco?"* he said.

Cohen shook his head.

The goatherd grinned tobaccoed, stump teeth. *"Bambino, Benghazi."* He pointed to himself, then held a hand out, waist-high. He tipped his head, pointed at Cohen. *"Americano, bene?"*

Cohen shook his head. The goatherd shrugged one shoulder. A sharklike cloud cruised the metallic, white-tipped horizon. The goats were nibbling their way up the northern cliffs. The goatherd stood, jabbing the sand with his stick. His yellow toenails protruded from his rope sandals like claws.

"La pioggia, stasera," he said, and trotted after the goats, stick over one shoulder.

Cohen returned his gaze to the sea. Why didn't the monkey man kill me? Was he hoping I'd lead him to Paul? But why kill Kim, or Phu Dorje, or Seral? To silence them? As punishment? Punishment for what?

Cohen climbed the path. Late afternoon silence saturated the heath. The gleaming scrub rolled upward, breaking on rocky, serrate heights. To the north a vulture wheeled, minute, above a stunted ridgetop pine. Nineteen days.

The Peugeot was gone. Inside was smoky and warm, coals red in the hearth, the floor swept, but she was not there. Her clothes hung on pegs beside the bed; he fingered a flesh-colored camisole faintly fragrant of her, broke a handful of grapes from a clump on the table, glanced out the window.

He took the Tibetan's pipe and followed the cart track northward. Greasy clouds were collecting over bare, barbed ridges. The track split into tributary goat trails sharded with stones and droppings. Two ravens played, diving on each other, in thermals over an outcrop. He walked until the knee raged with pain but found no solace.

When he returned the Peugeot was parked in the scrub; smoke trailed inland from the chimney. "I feared you'd turned into a goat," she said, twirling from the hand pump by the sink to the table with a handful of spinach.

"Where'd you go?"

"Vye, but there's no food. Back to Sitea."

"We have food."

"I forgot greens—for salads."

"I've been watching the ocean . . ."

"Oh? What's it doing?"

". . . and trying to figure out why we're here."

"Haven't we been through this?" She took his hands, her fingers cold and slippery. "It's so short, what we have."

"Why did you come here?"

She sat beside him on the bed. Water gathered beneath the spinach on the table. She retrieved it and began tearing the leaves. "I wish you could see how pointless your questions . . ."

"Why do you think I'm here?"

"To get away, get laid."

"Away from what?"

"From them." She came and put her arms around his neck, palms outward. "I'd rather be with you than do anything else right now. That's why I'm here. Not for a story. Not even because you're afraid and that makes me want to be with you." She wiped her hands. "There are things going on with me you couldn't dream of."

"Such as?"

"My life's changing all around me—I'm losing everything I

106

used to want." She tossed black glistening olives from a white paper sack into the salad. "Purpose without substance, all these years since . . ." She let out a breath. "Since Tim died. Things've happened, in Africa, Thailand. I've been a fool; now I feel bad." She went out, closing the door.

He picked an olive from the salad, bit it away from the pit, stepped outside to sit beside her on a stone wall. Her face was angled away. The reddish aftersun on the hard straight line of her jaw made him think of her dead, of her face rotting in the ground. "What about Africa?"

"It taught me despair."

"Why?"

"I was tricked. Someone died." She rubbed her chin on his shoulder. "Afterward I found out who he was, as opposed to what I'd been told. Now I can't dismiss it. His face bothers me. Last month I spent a night with a man—one of those lonely interludes. In the middle of the night he woke me—I'd been crying out the dead one's name." She snickered. "The guy was jealous." She lifted the back of her wrist to show him a tiny lens of water between amber hairs. "Rain."

"I think the goat man said it would."

"You think?"

"Couldn't understand him, but a word or two of Italian. He learned it in Libya, as a *bambino.*"

"*Bambino.* A nice thought. Beyond having."

"It's all beyond having, Claire."

After midnight the rain came in earnest to shatter the palms and tear the thatch. Candle shadows stumbled wildly on the walls. He awoke and wanted her and she came to him readily, groaning in the depths of her throat, her hair lacing over his shoulders, her tongue full of saliva and licking his mouth and throat and teeth and lips, sucking him down into her gorgeous tight vastness, her other lips licking and kissing at him as he sank more quickly and heatedly, harder and harder into her, yet seeming gentle for she was so ready, so accepting, and it never ended, he driving harder and harder always, wrapped in total consciousness of her sexual magnificence, her lovely hair twined everywhere, her breasts stabbing him with pleasure, their rounded contours silky on his chest, her belly rippling, quivering, her navel pooled with sweat, her blonde curls meshing with his darker coils each exquisite time they came together.

Again as she slept beside him he had no sense of boundary. Her cheek in the candlelight was luminous as bone china, her breathing light and steady as a child's, her lashes shadowy as forest. He snuffed the candle. Why does loving her leave me so free of fear? How is it I forget, even for a moment? Where does the pain go? Where do the dead go? Where did my own death go? Soon I'll leave her, start for Paris. She and this will be memory. Like Kim, like Seral, never to return. Eighteen days to go. Paul, where are you now? Will you be there? Stretching beside her warm nakedness in the narrow, lumpy bed, he listened as the rain hungered for them in the vastness of the night.

In garnet first light they walked the sea-edge strewn with kelp, torn rope, a splintered board with blue Arabic letters, a cormorant drowned tangled in fish net. In the hearth he boiled water for Bravo coffee and goat milk to go with bread and sticky fresh dates from Egypt. On the rickety table he shaved fresh chunks of hash into the pipe.

"I've been planning," she said, "how to release your story. Maximum impact, minimum danger."

"Nobody'll believe it."

"They will when I'm through with them. I can prove it."

"How?"

"Your friend—when's he due in Paris?"

"Couple weeks."

"We'll be waiting. We let it out—one big bang. Set them up to come after us. When they do, that'll prove it!"

"Prove what—that we're dead?"

"No—we'll be safe. I can manage that. This could turn the whole bomb thing around—when people see how much at risk they are—what a bunch of murderous nitwits the CIA is—how much lying there is in the States, the ugly politics . . ."

"They're endemic." He opened the door. "Want to walk?"

"I've got this." She held up a blue paperback. "Did you know '. . . *aucun art ne saurait être vraiment notre s'il ne rendait à l'événement sa brutale fraîcheur, son ambiguité, son imprévisibilité, au temps son cours, au monde son opacité menaçante et somptueuse . . .'"*

"How can you read that shit?"

"It's another person's mind, revealing itself as honestly as it can."

"You sure?" He scowled at the blue paperback. "You always just assumed it, on the plane from Teheran."

She giggled. "Assumed *what*?"

"That I speak French. You never asked me—I've never said one word of it."

"Surely you must—somewhere? Maybe I just presumed. I mean *darling*, I'm *half* French—why should I assume you speak English?"

"Some of my teachers would've told you I don't." Still scowling, he took the goat trail to the beach, its sand already dry and warm in the hollows. He smoked, feeling its excellence distill in his bones, sharpen his muscles, lend credence to his deepest perceptions. In the sun, in the sand vibrating to the tumble of waves, there was peace.

And I'm being shitty and cross. Have to go soon. Tinkling bells disturbed him; the goatherd's steps lisped across the sand. Cohen covered the pipe with his palm. The goatherd squatted, wrinkled his nose. *"Giorno."*

"Fumare?" Cohen uncovered the pipe.

"Sì."

They faced the sea, without words. The old man smelled of goat, sweat, sun, and the minty sage heath. The beat of the sea on the sand was hypnotic. *"Due tedeschi—amici,"* he poked Cohen's elbow. *"Perchè con boomboom?"* He raised an imaginary gun to his shoulder, sighting out to sea.

"Dove?"

"In Vye."

"Chi, amici?"

"Chi? Vostri." He fingered Cohen's arm. *"Vostri."*

"Non sono miei amici, tedeschi."

"Amici con la signora . . ."

Cohen leaned back into the warm sand. Two Germans with guns and wives, that was another thing. *"Turisti,"* he said.

The goatherd shrugged one shoulder, reached for the pipe. Cohen relit it, watched a curlew stitch a wavetop to the sky. The old man exhaled. *"Non sono turisti."* He raised the imaginary rifle.

Cohen sat up. *"Due tedeschi, con due signore, allora."*

The goatherd shook his head. He poked a finger in the sand. "Vye," he said.

"Sì."

The finger moved a few inches westward. *"Qui voi ed io."* He punched a second hole, pointed to himself and Cohen. Beside this second hole he punched a third. *"Vostra signora."* He pointed up to the hut.

"Sì."

"Allora, due tedeschi," the finger ran westward, dove into the sand. *"Con boomboom."* He pointed to the hills. *"Amici con vostra signora."*

Cohen nodded, feeling a breeze run up his back. He fought the urge to turn around. The goatherd motioned with the pipe; Cohen relit it; the man inhaled and passed it back. *"Perchè boomboom?"*

"Cacciare," Cohen answered. He tried to think of the Italian for rabbit, made a rabbit ears gesture. *"Lapide."*

The goatherd's eyes widened momentarily.

"Non si preoccupi," Cohen smiled. *"Domani."*

"Domani," the goatherd echoed. Cohen watched him mount the cliff after his goats, first his legs disappearing beyond the crest, then his trunk, till only his head, whitely reflecting the sun, was left.

He forced calmness on himself, back against a palm trunk, its fronds a parasol, a downy feather twirling down the breeze. So Claire had not gone to Sitea; she had met with two Germans in the hills, two Germans with guns. How many more the goatherd hasn't seen? I am a fool beyond belief. As the untouchable said, I am blind in both eyes. He ambled through the palms and up the slope. Bitch. Bitch. Bitch. Woman of death. Death woman. Kali. You'll die now.

She was sunning herself against the hut's white southern wall, Sartre in hand, in view of the hills. "You must be hungry again," she smiled. Beads of sweat had gathered below her hairline.

Her thighs were amber in the sun; between them, under her skirt, a cooler whiteness. Have to get her inside, out of sight. Make her talk. Oh bitch. "C'mon inside."

110

Quickly she stood. "I'm happy here."

He rummaged for his wallet, counted the money, forgetting the amount. "What are you doing?" she called.

He took a knife from the sinkboard. "Getting lunch. Where's the bread?"

"In that cupboard thing."

"Can't find it. C'mere!"

"Don't be blind."

He edged toward the door; she was striding for the Peugeot. "Get in here!" he yelled.

"Going for a drive."

"I'll go with you." He stuck the knife into his back pocket and moved into the sun, eyeing the hills.

"You're a crosspatch—I'll go alone."

"How about a kiss?"

She opened the car door, bright in the noon light. "Don't forget your lunch."

"Where to?"

"Away from those smelly goats." She stood behind the Peugeot's open door. "*Ciao,* Theseus."

She reversed down the cart track, backed into a thicket, and accelerated toward Vye. Now I'm dead if I don't move fast. Should've killed her. Then they'd have shot me, and I'd have missed Paul. He glanced quickly at the scrubby, dark, ominous hills. Where are you? In the scrub? Coming up the trail? On the cliffs?

Breeze in my face. Nobody on the cliffs. Terror in the back. Expecting a bullet. That crushing pain. No way out. God, in the trees. Safer now. Have to cross the beach. They'll shoot me. Can't stay here. They'll shoot me.

He stepped out of the palms into sunlight. Waves glistened. White, blinding sand. No one. Can't see. Show no fear. He ambled along the beach. No terror. Little excursion. He forced himself to kneel despite the knee and found a flat stone. A booming breaker startled him; he dropped the stone. He forced himself to pick it up again and scaled it. It slapped the first wave sideways and sank.

Hot white sand. They're leading me on. Finger tightening round the trigger—now! Boom! Christ, a wave. Can't breathe with the terror. Sand like soup, can't walk. Run—no, God, don't run!

Shadowy wet kelp-smelling barnacled cool rocks. He sprinted through them up a ravelled goat trail and around the cliff.

10

KILLING ME, THE KNEE. How far can I go? They're coming now. Now they come. Past the house, over the beach. Running. Up the rocks, around the cliff. Matter of minutes.

Far above, a notch of sunlight. Gripping the knee he stumbled up the goat trail. It caved in and he fell grabbing handfuls of grass, snatched a root, arm tearing from the socket, muscles snapping, mouth full of dirt. With the dislocated arm he levered up the cliff, switched hands—they're coming now—wormed onto a ledge, raised the arm and twisted it back into the socket, biting his lip against the pain, and scrambled along the thin ledge up a ravine. Coming now, coming.

Up the ravine over a ridge, running crippled into a meadow studded with oaks, up a dry waterfall and around a table mesa, falling in holes, knees and palms scarred, ankles thistle-torn. Can't go more. The end.

Sun masked, black clouds. Sea and sky dim, wind damp. Southern hills, jumbled blocks, giant's ruined house, shadowed scarps, black brush whose sinister leaves the wind slashes against the ridgeline. Where are you?

A rubbled isthmus striding northward into the sea—Are you there? Westward quilt of gray shadows over restless hills—Or there? A bird sprang from an oak branch and was torn westward by the wind—Was that you? I can't kill you all. Kill you with what?

Biting down the pain he ran westward, thorns ripping his shins and waist. Reach that ridge. Never stop. Outdistance them. Always could. No matter the pain.

He forced himself faster each time he stumbled, fell. They're on foot too. Watch for them ahead—road's up there somewhere. For an hour the ridge drew no closer. Suddenly it hunched its bony back up and blocked off the wind. He collapsed under an outcrop. Count to a hundred then go. One—two . . .

The air redolent with sage, the coast rippling aqueous, the sea slick and restless gnawing its flank. Twenty-one—twenty-two—rain falling in sunlit smoky slanting curtains—forty-seven—forty-eight— forty-nine—jumping at her voice but it was only a falcon hunting, "Scrreee, scrreee,"—Seventy-three—seventy-four . . . You'll die, I promise you. Dance on men's bodies, Kali, dance—you'll die too, their flesh in your teeth—seventy-one—seventy . . . No, counted that already—I'll draw you into your own Hell and keep you there till *it* kills you. Ninety-seven—ninety-eight—he tore himself to his feet and plodded into cold, sharp rain.

Toward sundown the rain slowed. Atop the next ridge a stone wall; he fell against it, weeping with pain. Am I crying about her or the pain? Or the failure? The stupid, childish mistake? Or the dead? Death?

A rooster crowed beyond the wall. He lugged himself up and peered over it. Last daylight was sliding across the sea to pool beneath the western clouds; wind out of the east carried odors of thyme, oleander, and wet lichen. Beyond the wall the ridge fell down a green valley, in its center a yellowed church cloistered on its far side by two-tiered cells. Clumps of grass sprouted like warts from its terracotta rooftiles. Chickens scratched in a bare courtyard before its portals; its nearest wall supported a broken-backed thatched barn with a puddled sheepcote where a few wet ewes huddled. From the courtyard a dirt road coiled southward into the hills.

My shield, my high tower, my refuge. Can they come after me here? Am I safe?

No one moved along the colonnaded cloister, or settled the quiet sheep into the barn for the night. No lights stole through the small, thick windows; no vesper tolled from the pitted belfry. The rooster crowed again, his stony echo bouncing up the valley. A meager puff of white eased from a rock chimney at the far end of the barn and dissipated in the paling light.

He slipped and skidded down the flinty slope and across the barnyard, thin yellow chickens trotting like heralds before him. A door at the barn end was ajar; from it emanated a smoky glimmer. He knocked. A chair dragged on stone; a shuffle approached. A muddy-eyed crone with silver chin hairs opened; she tripped backward, crossing herself. She wore a black smock, her white hair plaited in a sooty bandanna over one shoulder; in one claw she held a half-plucked chicken, its head bobbing, its glassy eye protruding like a marble. He made a motion for food and rest; she leaped forward and swung the chicken to bar the door; he wedged it open.

She crossed herself again and backed away. Cohen glanced down: his trousers were bloody, his arms and chest mud-streaked and torn by thorns, his shoes rain- and blood-filled. A hesitant step returned, a grimy, crooked-shouldered man. Cohen repeated his request.

"Sitea," the hunchback whispered, pointing westward over the valley rim. Cohen shook his head, nodded up at the clouds, fished a handful of coins from his pocket. The hunchback retreated. "*Padre*?" Cohen said, glancing at the church.

The hunchback pointed him through a door into a spacious, frigid baptistry. Before the nave an oaken table was graced by a single candle. In its unsure light glimmered a plate, fork, knife, and white napkin. A breeze toward the door brought the aroma of stale incense and the enclosed fetor of damp stone and rotting wood.

Beyond the baptistry a plank staircase led from the cloister up to a tier of empty cells. In the first, coils of dry thorn atop a board bed, an icon weeping rain. He started up to the second tier. A young, bearded priest wearing a threadbare cassock and pendulous silver cross met him halfway. For a third time Cohen made his request. The priest scowled and shook his head. He spoke quickly, Cohen understanding only "Sitea."

"*Vroxi*," Cohen answered, remembering the goatherd's word, pointed to the black sky. Again the rooster crowed, muffled by the claustral walls. Cohen rolled up his trouser leg to show the priest his wound, offered coins from his pocket. The priest crossed himself. "In the time of trouble," Cohen whispered, "He shall hide me in his pavilion," but the priest shook his head uncomprehendingly and remounted the stairs. Over his shoulder came the words, "Sitea," and "*trianta hiliometra.*"

He dragged his injured leg up the dirt road into the darkening hills. Thirty kilometers by road—twenty miles—how many through the scrub? The Lord is my light and salvation—whom should I fear? The Lord's my life refuge—He will conceal me in the shelter of His tent—though war be waged upon me, even then will I trust. Preserve my life and rescue me—redeem Israel, O God, from its distress.

Light raked the slope, catching out bushes like sentries sleeping at their posts. He dove from the road, the light dipped over his back, crossed the road, mounted the far slope, and traversed back, snatching yellow from spiky leaves. Rocks rattled on steel.

With a flash it was on him again. A rumbling engine and the

crackle of gravel as a car crested the ridge and nosed down the road toward the church. It was long and light-colored, its engine fighting the transmission on the downgrade. It dropped beyond a hillock into the valley of the church. Night returned; he waited for his vision to renew, jumping as a bird twittered cautiously.

He crawled from the road into the scrub. The headlights darted back over the ridge, the car moving slower, black shadows flitting before it. He squinted to see better. The black shadows were two men running before the car, their heads bent to peer at the road. He stumbled to his feet; pain knocked him out. He woke lying in thorns. So intimate, earth. This brush—no pain at all. Will it be like this at the end?

Voices on the road, play of light over the scrub. They see me? English!—they're speaking English! Help—save me! No. Be still!

"Here!" That word—someone's coming. "Sam!"—they're calling—"Sam!" Coming to save. He pulled himself free of the thorns, up on his feet, wavering.

"Sam Cohen—you out there?" A sepulchral voice, made ghastly by night, a man's barrel voice. "Sam, you need help! We've come to save you!"

God of my salvation, my light, my tower . . . He grabbed the thorns, tripping. The light swept past, blinding; he fell covering his eyes as out of the blackness came thunder, the air hot with zipping, pinging, shattered earth and singing stone, wailing of smashed branches, tintinnabular stacatto of rifles dying into the hills. "That's him!" a voice screaming. "He's down! He's down!"

Another voice: "Move in, move in."

Oh God the silence. Now swish of branch on clothing. Light, probing like a dentist's tool. Save me, lamb to be slaughtered. This terrible strength to snake through the thornscrub, each curling leaf and stem bright overhead.

Running feet, crunching boughs, voices everywhere. Now a streambed—dry—crawling like a gutted bear down this stony, scaly, choking earth. Nearest voice fifty yards and closing—"No blood!" it yells. "Can't find no blood."

"Not here," another voice. "Not here neither."

Again the sepulchral basso profundo, further back but louder, everywhere. "Split up and comb it good! He's on his last legs—the priest said so—I want him now!"

Easy, really, to keep going. Place one hand ahead, hoping for a rock, root, anything to hold. Pull with that arm, dragging this heavy body, this ruined leg, scrape the earth, dragging thorn and bones of long-dead scrub. Switch hands, do it again. Oh Christ that's the bad shoulder—reach out the other hand and pull again. Voices closer. Find a rock, anything. Kill them. Into the bushes—goat trail. They won't see it. Jesus—footsteps behind me.

"Whatcha got, Tony?"

"Nothin'—old gully."

"Zig's split to bring the dogs. Be here by two."

"From where?"

"Ankara. Flown in. Kaynines. Be over by morning."

"Still no blood?"

"Shit, man. No blood. Musta missed."

"For sure, man, he went down with the first round."

"It was a long shot—"

"Yeah." A low chuckle. "Shoulda had nightscopes." Down the gully the voices travelled, softening. Dogs. Dogs at two A.M. Be over by morning. My last night.

Keep going you cowardly bastard. You little legpissing chickenshit mommalicker pantysmelling meatbeater. Don't you dare ask God for help. You *lache—froussard—poltron—trouillard*—don't ask anyone! Depend on yourself. Alex's shiteating Polack grin, "Either your body's your friend or it ain't." Body, be my friend. Take me, save me.

The goat trail wound tighter and tighter into the scrub. Up now a gentle slope, rain on his shoulder like the lightest embrace. Easier for dogs now—wet smell. Voices back there, half mile behind. Waiting for the dogs. With a stick clenched between his teeth to bite back the pain, he drove himself to run, down a long brushy slope northward toward the sea.

Clouds clearing, shiver of moonlight over the sea. To the right, a blinking buoy. Wind shifting, warmer, from the west. It's two now? Where's the dogs?

Smell of cold foamy waves. Rumble and thrash on rock, shudder of earth. Can't follow my scent into the sea. Think I've drowned. He cut eastward, leading the dogs back toward the church valley, a great wounded circle.

Can hear sea down there. He peered over the cliff. How far? With each thudding wave, pebbles fell from the edge. He reached out and down: Nothing.

Distant baying—the wind? He scrambled from the cliff, leg jammed in brush. Down this edge. Toward the sea. Dogs—can hear them now. Quick, lower. Steeper. That flash of white's the sea. So far down? Christ, too steep. Dogs homing in. It's a cliff. Can't get down.

A roar, boulders bonking down as a dog cleared the brush and tilted headdown above him, gnashing, panting, slavering. "Come here, boy. Don't growl—they'll hear you. Let me up!" Up this hill, dog roaring, going for his throat, knocking him back; he slid to the edge, dog at his face, legs off the cliff he sprung backward, outward, spinning, down through rushing cold blackness toward the boulders below, crashing into choking sea and with its shock swimming hard and steadily outward and west, the waves against the cliff a white line to his left.

So good, the sea. So fresh, clean, cold. Swim forever. Live.

The shoulder began to dislocate and he swam slower, tucking it in, but the waves then swamped him, dragging him shoreward. Go with them, he told himself, but closer were rocks and waves thundering like falling houses and he paddled westward till the waves were softer and brought him into a stony bay, where he drifted to the shallows and watched the hills, waves rippling coolly over his shoulders.

Lights—on the cliff where I jumped. He clambered to his feet and ran west, from the lights, through the shallows.

An hour lter he flopped into the tidal pool of a mountain stream, gulping its sharp, half-salty water, stood, took a breath, and began climbing its steep cataract, keeping feet and hands in the water. After a quarter mile it near-levelled through a valley lush with grass and flower smells, the moon bright above him. He slumped to the earth. Ten minutes, then run.

He woke suddenly—scrunching earth, something sliding past a branch and waiting. This fist-sized boulder. Heavy in my hand. Kill.

It halted, neared, pinging a twig. So stealthy. Dog? Gently he stood, aimed the boulder. Die with me. Further uphill, pebbles rattled, thunked to a stop. Others.

Against the first carmine edge of day a blunt shadow inching closer. In his ears the stream's dulcet trill. Far laugh of a gull—early morning. Boom of the sea. Die with me.

Diktam odors on the dewy air. Dawn breeze from the east. I do not regret. The shadow slipped closer; he hurled the boulder, hearing it smash as he spun and rolled from the bullets that did not come.

Feet pounding in all directions, branches crackling. Downhill a sheep bleated. Another answered from above, a third. Gravel crunched; sheep outlines cut the red horizon as they quick-stepped past. His lip hurt. He relaxed his bite on it, tasted blood.

He wormed through the damp scrub to where a lamb lay, one rear leg quivering. His fingers found the gelatinous bubbly mess where his boulder had crushed its skull. Ten feet away the sideways outline of a ewe. Everything I do is evil.

The east was red and lavender, then orange, then yellow, then white. He moved westward through the thickets, until above him rose the ridge before Sitea, the road a pale suture across its dawn scrub. He crawled to the ridgetop and looked over.

Sitea crouched against the sea's frontier, its houses bunched like bones on a riverbank. Yellow scrub flowers glittered like daytime fireflies in the sun, warming his chest and face; sage, mint, cardamom, and diktam odors swam round him in the breeze. A truck backfired on the steep road down to the far side of town. At the edge of town a boy with a pitcher of milk stopped to pee on a wall. A shopkeeper was sweeping his sidewalk. A ship's officer in a blue sweater and black peaked cap walked purposefully out the dock toward a lighter nodding on the swell. Further out in the misty bay a tacky freighter slouched at anchor. I'm still alive, Paul. Seventeen more days now.

A dusty white Mercedes slid down the mountain into town. A tall man in a red beret stepped from it and tugged at the telegraph office door. It was locked; he checked his watch and glanced up the mountain. He crossed suddenly from view to the closer side of the street. Cohen wormed tighter into the brush.

The man in the red beret reappeared, bending to speak with an ancient woman in black. He kissed her on both cheeks, went into a shop, and came out with a paper bag. The persian shutters of the telegraph office rolled up and the man entered, tugging a letter from his pocket. He emerged and drove away.

A bell sounded eight; somewhere a goat was complaining. The white Mercedes came back down the mountain. It was cleaner and Cohen saw it was not the same. It halted behind a red Datsun pickup parked under plane trees in the town square. Three men left the pickup and leaned into the Mercedes' passenger window. A huge bald man in a brown suit got out to speak with them, four others remaining in the Mercedes.

The freighter's whistle echoed over the bay. The fat man gripped the shoulder of one of his companions, with his other hand shielding his eyes as he scanned Cohen's ridge. Checking their watches, the men returned to the Datsun. Four dogs, three black-and-tan, one all black, stood up quickly in its rear, tails flicking. The men drove the Datsun east, out of town. The fat man crossed the square and entered a squat building with a blue police sign over the door.

The Datsun stopped on the ridge road a mile above Sitea, glinting red in the early sun. Cohen trotted down the ridge away from the town and sight of the truck, and followed a gully down to the sea.

From the sea edge, the freighter was nearly obscured by a gauzy mist glued to the bay. He limped rapidly eastward along the waterline and around a stony headland.

The freighter lay opposite the headland, severed from the water by the mist. Waves rolled past, refulgent at their tips, green and murky in their troughs. He removed his shoes and tied them round his neck, buttoned his glasses and wallet into his shirt pockets. Salt seared his knee as he waded into the water and struck out northwest, left of the freighter, the steep frigid waves slapping down his throat with each breath. The freighter kept its distance as currents forced him back to shore.

He turned north, directly into the waves. Almost imperceptibly the land slid past, a bent pine on the western horizon inching southward against a distant cloud. He raised up to check position, inhaled cold, salty water. He had moved east again, away from the ship. His feet touched the beach below the headland.

In the shallows he caught his wind, then set off northward, shoulder aching, lungs burning with briny water and oxygen thirst. Each time he tried to rest the waves yanked him down or rolled him shoreward. He floated gasping on his back, gray sky spinning, white crests in his face. When he turned to swim the shoulder slipped out; he dogpaddled one-handed, dragging the arm. Waves drove up his nose and down his throat; in all directions they blocked the horizon.

He dove beneath them, frog kicking, rising for breath every stroke. The mist shifted like a veil, the freighter vanishing and reappearing. The current pushed him northward out to sea, the freighter sliding away, the land with her.

11

IN THE HOLLOW OF a wave he twisted the arm again into its socket and pounded savagely against the current until the ship's starboard, seaward side grew tall above him. On her stern canted slightly toward him he could read part of her name, chalky against rust: "*AZEMSKI*," and "nbul." A wave took him away; he fought toward the bow and its anchor chain frothing the sea.

A man moved along the starboard rail, lingering aft where the rail was broken and linked with rope. The current coiling round the bow began to push Cohen sternward; he grasped the stern anchor chain. It was greasy, pitted with rust, unbelievably cold.

Metal clanged distantly from the port side, voices called. He dove, the water overhead an opaque green as if below ice. He climbed hand over hand up the starboard anchor chain. His hands numbed; he squeezed the chain between his thighs, willing himself upward. When he was ten feet below the rail, a voice called from the bridge, another answering from the stern above him. He hugged the chain, not daring to drop back into the sea.

The freighter's screws were turning to a deep hum in her hull and a roil of dirty bubbles at her keel. He reached eye level with the deck, the rope rail swaying above him in the wind. The deck shuddered as the anchor chain lurched upward. Feet echoed toward him. He grabbed the deck rim, feet slipping from the chain as it ground past him. Hand over hand he retreated behind the upraised lip of the stern. Two voices argued above him in Arabic and Greek. With a swoosh the anchor broke the surface, grated upward, and clanged against the side. The winch screamed and halted. The voices diminished, still yammering.

He waited until he could wait no longer, then waited more. The sea swayed trancelike, licking the stern, urging him to look down. He mustered every trick he could remember to avoid it and the agony in his shoulder, to ignore the frozen finger ache and relentless shiver that threatened to shrug him off the rust-flaked lip of the stern.

The town, under its green and granite mountain walls, boats bobbing like gulls before it, was sliding behind him. Figures stood on the dock. One, bulky and tall, pointed toward the freighter. Cohen swung along the starboard edge, chest scraping white rust from the letters of her name, lunged over the side and darted to the cover of the stern crane. Portside, aft of the bridge, hung a canvas-shrouded lifeboat, the words "*PETR VYAZEMSKI*" and "Istanbul," on its stern. Yanking loose two stays on its outboard rail, he squeezed beneath the canvas into its musty warmth.

Through a gap in the canvas the leopard sprang; he fell tripping through vines into quicksand. The leopard leered down, a grinning lemur's face. Mire choked him, the leopard snaking after him; he woke banging his head on a thwart in the blistering blanched light of the lifeboat.

The sun's yellow orb bore through the tarpaulin like an ingot; the airless space stank of lead paint and stale canvas. He pulled the water jug from under the gunnel and drank half its rusty contents, and slept.

It was dark. He sat up shivering. His knee throbbed. A running sea smacked the hull; the diesels hummed distantly and surely. He raised the outboard lip of the canvas. Heading west. After tonight, it's sixteen more days, Paul. Closer all the time. But where the Hell am I going? An indistinct white edge at eye level denoted, he decided, the remote attack of the sea on the headlands of Crete. Mountains loomed against the shattered starlight. To the west, a faint mass of light waited in the ship's course. Heraklion? After perhaps an hour he chanced another look. Beyond the bow the lights of a city poured down hillsides, white tracers of auto lights nipping in and out.

Will the ones who hunted me in Sitea be waiting here? The fat one in the Mercedes? Maybe he was a nobody. Whose voice did I hear, last night, giving orders—"I want him now!" Maybe Claire and the CIA are still wandering the bush. Thinking I fell off that cliff and drowned. No—the guys in the Datsun were looking for me this morning. The diesels accelerated into higher pitch, then slowed. The ship began to rock, swaying the lifeboat. The lights drew closer, clarifying flotsam and oil streaks on the black roll of the waves.

Heraklion's stone jetty curved out to them, its spine lit by vertebrae of humpbacked, pallid lamps. The ship docked under the

gleaming waists of larger freighters. She rang with voices and movement, quieted. Can I go? Where? Not safe to move, not safe to
stay. The engines stilled. Waves fussed steadily at the hull. A chill
vapor sank through the canvas. He huddled his shirt about him.

Like a cat, he thought, how she arched her body under my
hands, the purr in her throat as orgasm drew her inward then out in
shuddering gasps. She and Stihl and the monkey man killed Alex.
And I'll kill her. He changed position, bitten by cold.

Morning rose with a steely mist and the odors of coffee and smoke.
Trucks banged on the quays. Cranes boomed and whistled; from all
sides came the clatter of feet on steel and voices of command.
Heavy, large things were being unloaded from the rear hold; the
men were nervous and yelled frequently. He rubbed himself steadily
to warm up. Take me away, ship, far away—I'm free; no one
looked for me; they thought I drowned! Now they think I'm dead,
they'll stop looking for me. I'm free!

Soon the sun once more burned whitely through the canvas, the
lifeboat again a sweat bath. Then Heraklion was behind them, the
fresh sea breeze nipping through a crack he had opened beneath the
canvas. Gulls overhead cried out the course. The engines chugged
regularly; waves swished under the bow. It was impossible not to
think of food.

Day's heat became evening's chill, then night's frigidity. Unable to
sleep from pain, cold, and hunger, he recalled each of the best meals
he had ever eaten, evoking the nuances of each dish. He tried to
count all the women he had ever slept with, beginning with the first,
ticklish, nervous high-schoolers, tried to remember each one's name,
the look and texture of her body, her face within the grip of wanting.

His body hardened, the flow of blood warming him. He felt sad
at all the lives he had touched, each woman in the act of love, many
now nameless to him, so many now forgotten, when each had been
so precious, had he known. And it was sad to think that many
would not remember him either, that he no longer existed for them,
or only as a casual, unvalued fragment. Yet in coming, loving each
other's nakedness, in the moments when the barriers to awareness
had fallen, how close they had been, to each other and to something
far beyond, then almost palpable and now beyond reach.

The cold seeped back. The knee had brought on a quaking

122

fever. Where am I going? His hunger and shivering grew stronger. What day? How many till Easter? Is it sixteen? Fifteen?

He slept, shaking, awoke. Darkness. He slept again, woke in darkness. Feet pounded the deck. Voices. The lifeboat shook. Ropes slackened; a flashlight danced over the canvas. Its beam crashed in on him. A shout. He sat up, transfixed by the light. Strong hands grasped his wrists, dragged him over the gunnel and held him fast against the lifeboat's side. An unshaven face snarled at him out of the blinding light. Spit sprinkled his face, a finger jabbed his chest.

They yanked him forward to a companionway. The captain in the blue sweater and black peaked cap came up the passage, sleepily rubbing the back of his neck. He barked at the crew. "I tell them," he yelled, "to throw you over."

"That seems excessive."

"You a pain in the ass."

"I'm sorry. I mean no harm."

"You plenty time no harm now." The captain's scar was white. "In Algiers jail."

"Please let me work. I need to go to Africa . . . see a girl."

"I make you work first, then throw over."

"I can't swim that far."

"Why you pick my boat?" The captain was unshaven, with glaring, pitted eyes under thick, ridged brows, a narrow prow of a face, teeth bending sharply inward. "How you get my boat?"

"Swam." Cohen used the word with reluctance. "Climbed the anchor chain."

The captain rubbed his face, glanced at his watch. "For damn hippie I get up two A.M." He muttered at the two sailors holding Cohen. They led him along the passageway, down two flights of stairs, past the galley, its food odors screaming at him. He stopped them, pointed at his mouth. They jerked him forward.

At the end of this passageway a closet. He saw pails and mops, a sink, and boxes of plastic jugs, before they pushed him in and slammed the door. A bolt slid home.

The air was warm and fetid. He pushed aside a bucket and sat. Steps approached; the bolt slid back. One of the sailors handed him a cup of Turkish coffee and black bread smeared with grease. The door shut.

Coffee spilt stinging his fingers. He devoured the bread, swal-

123

lowed the remains of the coffee and licked out the grounds, felt his way to the metal sink and drank. It was warm, stinking of bilges.

In the morning other sailors took him to the captain, who sat smoking, coffee by his elbow, at a table in the mess.

"How you like you cabin?"

"Better than the lifeboat."

The captain stubbed out his cigarette. "What we do with you?"

"Let me work."

"You got money?"

"Twenty dollars, maybe."

"You be in jail long time, with only twenty dollars." The captain relit his cigarette, puffed hard.

"You go to Algiers?"

"What that matter you?"

"I'd like to go there, too. Where are you from?"

"She is of Istanbul, this ship."

"You are Turkish?"

"They." The captain waved his hand at the two sailors still watching from the passageway.

"*Petr Vyazemski,* that is a Turkish name?"

"Does it matter . . ." the captain grinned, sucking in his lips, ". . . to you, in Algiers jail?"

"Is it your name?"

"You are dumb. You think we not read Shakespeare, Byron, Hemminghvay?" He puffed smoke.

"He is a writer?"

"Ah, the ignorance of world make me weep! A king of poets he was. You like Pushkin? He's nothing. You think Yevtushenko is poet? It's a laugh."

Cohen inhaled the freighter's carious odor. It was as if all the rats of Alexandria had gone to sea in her. Tan paint curled down in broken blisters from the ceiling. "I have read others," he said.

"Who?"

"Anna Akhmatova, Mikhail . . ."

"Communists. Kept poets."

"Nabokov."

"He terrible. He too leave Russia."

"Why did you leave?"

Again the indrawn, acerbic grin. "For my health." The captain drained his cup, slapped it down on the table. "What I do with you?"

"I'll do whatever you need, clean, polish . . ."

"You would polish this old whore?" The captain stood and slammed his chair against the table, hollered into the galley. "This Dmitri," he said to Cohen. "He give you food. Then you go bridge. Look for me, Andrev. I tell you work."

"Can you tell me first what day it is?"

"Day?" A rapid explosion of Cyrillic sounds at Dmitri. "*Subbota!* He say Saturday. So! You work good, go Algiers. No work good, go Algiers jail. Capeesh?"

"Capeesh."

Rotund, hairy, blue-tattooed Dmitri served him a large platter of rice with small lamb chunks, black bread, and Turkish coffee. Saturday. Two weeks and a day. When the food was gone Dmitri motioned for his plate and refilled it.

Cold sea air washed the open bridge. Next to Andrev stood a bearded giant. "This Isom," Andrev stated. "He show you work."

Isom, wordless like Dmitri, hurried Cohen through a rusty labyrinth of passageways back to the mop closet. With hand motions Isom indicated each passageway to be cleaned, the galley, the mess, and, on the deck above, the crew quarters.

He scrubbed furiously, dragging the agonized knee behind him. By the noon bell he had finished everything but the crew quarters. These he completed after lunch, reporting to Isom. Isom went down on one knee and ran a finger over the floor. He indicated the portholes along the crew deck, the stinking lavatories, and the walls of the mess. These Cohen completed by dinner.

"Good work," Andrev mumbled. "Isom give you berth. Tomorrow, new work."

"Good," Cohen said. His knee and shoulder ached unbearably, but his stomach was near bursting with Dmitri's rough stew, his heart felt eased. For a whole day I've been too busy to fear. Fourteen more days. CIA's lost me now. I'll make it, Paul. He sat drowsy in the humid mess while sailors played cards and drank coffee. They invited him in but he could not grasp the game. He left them and limped onto the forward deck.

The air was sharp and clean after the congested mess. Seagulls coasted alongside the boat through the rushing darkness. How hungry they must be, to have followed all the way from from Heraklion. A sweet pine odor emanated from the forward hold. At the bow rail the wind struck him fair in the face. The moon was still down, the Milky Way a clear band of white belting the sky, its powdery stars reflected in tilted sheets of glistening sea.

The following day passed quickly, jammed with work. At dinner Andrev said, "Tomorrow this time, Algiers. You see you girl. Where is?"

Cohen cleared his thoughts. "Morocco."

"*Serdenyi droog, ti nezdorova,*" Andrev sang, "*Ostav menya, ya vleeblenya.*" Isom guffawed, glancing at Cohen, who reddened, not knowing why. Andrev smiled gently, patted Cohen's arm. "Love is good thing. If all the world love, good world."

"But it doesn't. There is no peace."

"In my language, one word, *mir,* means both peace and world. But Russia no more my country. I carry Turkish passport." Andrev puffed. "I have no love for Russia, but it is America will end the world. One dollar from every three, in whole world, one third of all money, spent now on war, things to kill people." He sneered. "That good? Some day now—Hah!—last war of all!"

"Do you think it can be stopped—the last war of all?"

"Stopped? No chance. No chance for *mir*—peace or world."

Cohen shrugged. "Would you go back?"

"To Russia? My father, he go back, after Nazi war. We live in Stamboul then, but he want some things buried when family leave Petrograd."

"Things buried?"

"It is rich, my family, before Civil War, with castle in birch forest named *Tanistveniye Zavesa,* Mysterious Veil. These words are Vyazemski's: 'Where my eyes seek deeply, world is covered by mysterious veil.' But Bolsheviks burn it to ground."

"He got the buried jewels?"

"He never come back. They shoot him or send to Sibír. To jail for life." He patted Cohen's hand. "Is why, when I say Algiers jail, I fool only. I not ever send person in jail. Not even you." He grinned. "But if you not work good, we throw you over."

Cohen smiled. "Tell me one thing?"

"What is?"

"How did you find me?"

"We not. You find us, remember?"

"No. In the lifeboat."

"Ah. You give you away."

126

"How?"

"How you say, *schnarchen*?" Andrev made a loud snorting sound.

"Sneeze?"

"No. *Schnarchen*." He snorted again, closing his eyes.

"Snore!"

"Yes," Andrev laughed. "You *schnarchen* so loud, they hear you on Crete."

While the sailors played cards he went to the stern and watched the wake vee out and immerse itself in the star-struck, wavering sea. Thirteen days more. He retrieved the Tibetan's pipe from his pocket, thumbed in a pinch of hash and lit it, hiding the glow with his back. Its smoke trailed after the wake. The stars danced on the sea. The ship rumbled contentedly, a friendly old man mumbling. Above the eastern wavetops waxed the faint crimson-yellow pall of a soon-rising moon. A great bulk leaned over the rail at his elbow. He contained a startled impulse to drop the pipe into the sea.

Isom held out his hand. Cohen handed him the pipe. He gestured for the matches, lit the pipe, and breathed a long sigh into the darkness. He poked Cohen's arm and pointed to port. Far to the south the regular flicker of a beacon masked itself as a star shuttered by wavetops. "Bizerte."

He finished the pipe and knocked it empty against the rail. Cohen refilled it and they smoked in silence.

Isom chuckled. Cohen peered up at him, got no response. Isom began to laugh. He shook his head, as if to say, don't mind.

He laughed harder. Cohen pocketed the pipe. Isom's laughs were surfacing in great guttural bursts, like tears, racking his body over the rail.

Cohen patted Isom's quivering shoulder and stepped away across the deck. The shuddering laugh receded; from the back of the bridge it was inaudible and Isom's hunched form barely discernible against the sparkling black horizon.

Cohen leaned against the lifeboat, remembering his hours within it. So many wrong turns. But I've survived—I'll reach Paris. Once it was home, all I loved, espresso under leafy plane trees in sidewalk cafés, red wine and fresh bread, dark-eyed girls with slender hungry thighs on the Champs Elysées. Now it's death. For Paul, too. Planning our enemies' deaths.

Algiers thundered in the day's last reddened light with its diesel belches, barge rumblings, truck backfires, ceaseless klaxons, sirens, whistles, catcalls, radios, and the rumpled ardor of sea on stone. Traffic banged along the boulevards beside the docks. Above them the city lay on the hills, lights winking, pale facades tesselated vertically in a random mosaic. With the port pass and handful of dinars Andrev had given him, Cohen passed easily through customs, ate couscous in a café with blue tablecloths, found a room, and dove into dreamless sleep.

A wail erupted outside his window. He leaped from bed and dove behind the door. The corridor was silent. Beyond his cobwebbed window dawn lit the sea with iris greens and purples. The cry returned, above and behind him, quavering, imploring. In the street, a bearded man in a gray djellabah knelt with bowed head. Grinning at his own simplemindedness, Cohen sat listening on the bed as from their minarets the muezzins called the city to its first prayer of the day.

He shuffled down the hall, scratching his head, to the w.c. It was a hole in the floor with a white porcelain foot imprint on each side. With a last squirt of pee he knocked a cockroach off the left side of the hole and into the odiferous Styx below. Going to be a good day.

His café table abutted the sidewalk; beyond the thin, cobbled street of scuttling white-robed and white-veiled women, donkeys, and braying trucks the city fell away sharply to the sea. With some effort he located the diminutive, reddish presence of the *Petr Vyazemski* among her larger, shinier cohorts, the black mantis of a crane tugging pine logs like white entrails from her belly.

Maybe I'm disembowelled too. Gutted. Dead, but don't notice. Numb. Death lacks awareness, being—I still have that. Though I wouldn't mind the nothingness. Not afraid, almost insouciant.

Twelve days. A boat to France? Am I safer here, sticking out in a place my enemies don't expect me? Or in France, where I fit in but where they'll be looking?

Rather than fear, anger, or regret, in the morning's surging warmth, with its lemon and diesel odors, whitewashed luminosity, and clash of foreign voices, he felt pursued only by a cool, exquisite freedom. I'm not dead—I'm happy to be alive. Even if those I love have died. A tattered, pocked woman held out arthritic hands, grinning widely as he dug a few dinars from his pocket. Brown-legged boys were kicking an old ball through an alley; he hobbled after them and stole it, dribbling it over the stones as they pursued laughing and yelling. He let them catch him and then feinted it away, they screaming with glee at his skill, grabbing his elbow finally to get the ball back, then showering him with recriminations when he moved painfully to one side and would play no more. Another boy, legless, pushed himself by on a board with wheels. A calico cat rounded the corner and the boys left the ball to stone it, the cat darting to cover, the boys switching their attention to a starved dog nosing trash, who fled yelping, tail between bony legs. A man pushing a refrigerator on a bicycle inclined his head and blew his nose on the pavement, a lovely, dark-eyed woman in a diaphanous veil stepping round him. An ancient lady carrying planks of wood wrapped in a blanket on her back bent to snatch a soggy heel of bread from the gutter.

Another world. Maybe safer here. To Morocco to Spain to Paris. Not expecting me that way. Christ, why did I ever tell Claire about Paul?

Traversing yammering markets and arm-wide alleys hung with wash and scented with myriad unknown spices, he gained the main avenue westward toward Oran, hitched a ride in a potato-laden, cranky Peugeot van that gasped up the first coastal hills and roller-coasted down their backs.

His knuckles whitened on the door handle as the vehicle caromed discordantly through lizardlike twists in the narrow, undulating road, and as he stared through the paneless window at the whirring Algerian landscape he was forced to wonder, wryly, if perhaps his foes had not finally captured him, and his companion planned to execute them both in a roadside catastrophe.

But the driver did not look the suicidal type: jowly, chuckling, his comfortable body draped over his stool like a sack of tubers. He spoke rudimentary French with a harsh accent, conveying his meaning primarily by gesticulations that involved removal of both hands from the wheel and revolution of his torso and head toward his listener. This behavior Cohen found profoundly agitating during periods of plunging descent, and so their conversation became limited to uphills, where the rumble of readjusting potatoes cut out many of its finer points.

At a place called Tipasa the truck turned south toward distant furrowed fields, leaving him by a broken villa with pockmarked, viny walls, where dusty chickens, dogs, and children watched from a back street. In a store he bought a bottle of Algerian red, a chunk of white cheese, a stick of bread. Books were racked among faded postcards on one counter; he read a title mechanically. "What did Camus have to do with weddings?" he asked the shopkeeper.

"It is not solely of weddings," the man replied in careful French. "It is of this place, . . . *sa qualité ancienne. Les ruines . . .*"

"Where?"

"Going down to the sea."

Cohen tugged the book from the rack and patted dust from its cover. "I am going to Morocco to be married—perhaps I should read it?"

"For some things it does little good to be prepared." The corners of the man's mouth dropped. "To see the ruins, take the path through the villa gardens."

"No one lives in the villa?"

"Not since the revolution. They were all machine gunned, against that wall."

"The whole family?"

The man held out change. "*Pieds noirs.*"

"Children, also?"

"To be sure." He inspected Cohen through old, dark eyes. "It seems sad now. But then? My son, too, he died in that war. He was fourteen. You do not want it, your *Noces*?"

"I must save my money to get married."

"You are the first to look at it in years." The shopkeeper slid the book across the counter. "Take it."

A small burr-eared dog followed Cohen across the road, under the leafy villa gate and through the overgrown garden. Corners of glass peeped from broken windows. He ducked under incandescent purple bougainvillea, their trunks writhing like serpents over caved-in walls, their overflung boughs and mottled, mamba-green snakeskin leaves a canopy of coolness and shade above him, and took a path over a meadow leaning down to the sea. Bone columns towered over yellow trees. The air, charged with the aromas of absinthe and sage, clogged his lungs. Trails bordered by wild roses and studded with goat droppings twisted among piles of broken marble.

He picked up a palm-size piece. It had four inch-wide grooves, smooth as glass. The flat surfaces between were slightly rougher; in places their white sheen had decayed to the darker, unfinished marble beneath. A crack ran half way down one groove like a river through a wide, U-shaped valley, fed by tributary cracks half way up the groove.

Fingering the grooves, he tried to invoke a breath of the past, tried to imagine who had chiselled them. *I can taste the olive oil he ate, the wheaten bread from the slopes of the Djebel Atlas, can feel the cool kiss of the sea on his body as if it were mine. What was his fate? His children, lovers, hopes? Did he love his work or was he a slave—a Sisyphus? What did his struggle matter, what does it matter now?*

Limping to a sunny section of entablature presided over by a large, humped shrub with involute aqua leaves, he sat where the sea breeze carried wildflower and salt smells, the rustle of bees, susurration of leaves on stone. Solitary columns jutted like dinosaur ribs against the black volcanic beach and the blue sea with its white boundaries of surf and cloud. The blue, cool wind off the sea rippled the pages of *Noces* and feathered the hair over his forehead. *"C'est dans la mesure où je me sépare du monde,"* the book said, *"que j'ai peur de la mort . . ."* Only as I separate myself from the world do I fear death: death, then, is part of the world. Without death, life is nothing.

And the bomb? *It's Kali, Death. To ignore it is to separate ourselves from the world, to hide trembling like Nepali villagers while the man-eater stalks them. Better to go out and hunt it down. But the villagers don't believe there is a man-eater, a bomb, and when I tell them that there is they'll laugh at me, call me a fool, have me killed. While the man-eater stalks closer and closer.*

He drank the tanniny wine. *So long without peace. Here, in vitro, in this moment, though, I'm happy. I declare to the sun and to you, blue sea, that I'm happy. Only in this moment. Not in what went before nor in what will come.*

The dog came from foraging in the brush and wagged its knotted tail. Cohen scratched behind its ears, tugging at burrs; it whimpered and pulled back. "I'm not like you, *mon vieux,* content to be. What d'you care about the world invented by people?" He gave it bread and cheese; it ate the cheese and carried the bread away.

A distant thrum of engine. *Car on the road? Fishing boat? Getting leary of everything. Relax.* Far glint in the eastern sky, closer, above the purple cliffs, the windtossed bougainvillea. A plane, paralleling the coast, angled against the wind.

Don't move. Hide, and they'll see me. Act natural. Coming closer. He dove behind a cornice as the plane slid overhead, low,

131

banking, a throttled-down turn past the western rocky headland. Returning. Can see me this side. He bellied under a flat bush. The plane banked, circling now, the pilot's sunglasses flashing, the copilot peering down.

The plane climbed away, going east toward Algiers. He crawled quickly from the bush and stood massaging his knee. An old Arab, face darkened by a white djellabah, sat eyeing him from the back of an ass. The Arab kneed the ass and they trotted away through the scrub, shadows of the columns drifting down his back.

Run. Where? Run, run, anywhere. Who'd hide me? He stumbled breathlessly toward the villa, shoes crunching glass. Not here.

By the store four men were gassing an old Peugeot 403. He limped to them. *"Vous parlez français?"*

They stared at him. Finally one grinned. *"P'tit peu."*

"J'ai tombé, je suis blessé—ne peut pas marcher—Je peux aller avec vous?"

An embarrassed smile. *"Je ne comprends."*

He repeated it, slower—Fell and injured my leg. Can I go with you?

One understood. *"Oran—Nous allons à Oran."*

Going to Oran. *"Je peux y aller—avec vous?"*

A shrug, a moment of Arabic, a smile. *"Pourquoi pas?"*

They drove westward to Ténès, then inland through verdant hills to Chlef. They were young, exuberant, and uncaring, striving to share their few words of French with him, singing bawdy Arabic songs and laughing, each new song or dialogue leading to more laughter. At sunset they halted by the roadside and knelt praying to Mecca, stopping again a few minutes later in a palm-shrouded town before a low building with an unlit gate.

"La femme," one of them said, holding up five fingers. *"Cinquante dinars."*

He answered no and curled up on the back seat. They returned in half an hour, their chatter and song soon louder and more cheerful than before. One turned to him, tears of merriment glistening with dashboard glimmer in the corners of his eyes. "Sad you are *étranger,*" he sighed. "Sad you not understand."

Cohen watched the desert pallor of a single passing window. "Yes," he answered, "I wish I could."

132

12

"WE SEE FEW STRANGERS in Les Champs Elysées." The colonel raised his glass. "We are not like our namesake."

"Food's good," Cohen answered deadpan, glancing past his rickety table with his plate of beef toward the door filling with soldiers.

"American?" The colonel gave a humorous lift to his eyebrows.

"Irish."

"You speak French well. But with the American accent."

"I studied in Grenoble."

"Ah! I would have thought Paris."

More soldiers moved toward the back of the bar, some eyeing him curiously, others watching their commander. "You like him?" the colonel said, jerking his glass at *Noces* lying open on the table.

"Yes."

"A half-friend. We had few half-friends, even in those days."

Cohen surveyed the soldiers for a way out. Too many, too tight. The back door? He did not dare turn to look. "Have you read it?"

"No, but I have *La Peste,* that takes place here." He eased into the chair opposite Cohen, put down his glass. "A vast pestilence consumes Oran. Everyone will die. Perhaps justly. There is a doctor who battles the plague until the end, not acceding to his fear. *Justement,* perhaps, he lives."

Feeling an itch on his ankle, Cohen glanced down. A yellow-spined cockroach fat as his thumb ran under the baseboard. "Life's a punishment, then, visited on survivors?"

The colonel laughed lightly. He spoke in Arabic to the soldiers grouped behind him. Indifferently they moved away; four settled by the door, rifles at ease; the others clustered at the bar. The colonel faced Cohen. "Now, where do you come from?"

"Now? Why?"

"Few *étrangers* come to Algeria. Since the tragedy last year at Munich our borders are difficult to cross." The colonel slipped his olive kepi back from his forehead, exposing inky curls. "Where did *you* cross?"

"I come from Morocco."

"Ah, *vraiment?*" The colonel slid down a little in his chair. "A Fascist country. The King and a few who drive Mercedes. The hungry millions. Soon we'll be at war. *Vraiment,*" he sat up, "you come now from Maroc?"

"*Vraiment.* Why should that matter?" Cohen's stomach tensed round his meal; wine burned his throat.

"That border is closed. *Normalement,* it is impossible to cross." The colonel's fingers flitted like spider legs over his glass. "So where *did* you cross?"

Cohen yawned, covering his mouth. "Don't remember. Some sleepy little town."

"Ahh. We seem a nation of sleepy towns? It must have been either Taourirt, Nador, or Sidi bel Abbès?"

"Can't recall. Maybe Nador."

"Ah, my friend." The colonel's black eyes brightened beneath their hooded lashes. "Nador's a hundred kilometers inside Maroc, not on our border."

"I must've come that way."

"So—you come from the south? You don't look so tanned to have been in the Hamada—the desert."

Cohen shrugged. It was twenty feet from the table to the soldiers leaning against the bar, another ten feet to the four waiting by the door. No back door, either. Can't run anyway. It's over, Paul. You're on your own.

"Did you like it in Nador, the desert?" The colonel's aristocratic features were equatorially bronzed, his nose narrow and pinched at the bridge, his slender mouth animated, almost friendly.

"Yes."

Sadly, the colonel shook his head. "Nador's on the coast, *mon ami,* not far from the Spanish colony of Melilla. There's no crossing in the Hamada." He sighed reluctantly. "Now I *must* see your passport."

"Why?" Cohen shoved forward. "Why harass me—I'm a visitor to your country—don't read Arabic. *Merde de Dieu*—one name's the same as another!"

134

"On the visa in your passport will be the name of your sleepy village."

"I got my visa in France!"

"Surely they stamped it at your sleepy town!"

"It's with my things—at the house of my friends. They brought me here, in a 403, from Maroc."

The colonel raised his eyebrows, nodded as if in understanding. He drained his glass, stood. "Can I get you one? It's tea."

Cohen shook his head, pushed aside his plate, tucked *Noces* into his shirt. The colonel halted to speak with the soldiers at the bar, returned with another glass. "We must talk."

"I have to go."

The colonel raised one finger. "I'll tell you an interesting story . . ." He dragged his chair closer to the table. "Nearly twenty years ago, when our revolution began, I was a student in Algiers, intending to learn many languages and cultures, for I knew all humanity was one. Our differences were only . . . misunderstandings." He fingered his breast pocket for a cigarette. "I returned to Ghardaia for holiday. My family and their home were gone. Also the neighbors." He glanced at the match in his fingers and dropped it to the floor, leaned forward to crush it with his boot. "French bombs. There was nothing to bury. I joined the maquis." He waved away smoke. "I've been a warrior ever since."

"So the killing of your family made you also a killer?"

"But never of women and children, of families. Only of other men, other killers with weapons."

"Why tell me this?"

"Now another country, a 'great' country like France, bombs women and children—in Asia for instance—and they hunt someone like you. They will not say why, so I am curious to know whether he is a warrior, too, in his way."

Cohen laughed. "No one's hunting me, thank God. I'm a simple wanderer, hardly a warrior."

"How good. How much safer." The colonel wrinkled his aquiline nose. "Tell me, what could a young American do that his country would hunt him? With unusual ferocity—intensity."

"Not being American, I'd hardly know. He must've broken some law."

"Yes—you're Irish! Right?" Squinting against the smoke, the colonel finished his cigarette and dropped it with a hiss into the dregs of his tea. "Kennedy was Irish, too. He's still loved in Algeria." He put on his kepi. "When we Algerians began winning our revolution, the French screamed to the Americans for help. Terrible days those were! True, we were winning, but everybody was dying. Everyone who did not die lost a brother, a sister. More than a million young people died; *vraiment,* we could not have fought much longer. Then Kennedy told the French no—that Algeria should be free! How often I've wondered . . . Eh, *mon ami?*"

"Wondered what?"

"Who they are, and why they killed him."

"I still wonder."

"I thought so. In many countries, Europe, Latin America, Africa, it is said by those in the intelligence services that your CIA killed him."

"Ireland has no CIA."

"True. But then, it is that same CIA that now hunts one Samuel Cohen—a half-Jew born in Ireland—stating that he last was seen near Tipasa, having arrived by ship in Algiers."

Cohen suppressed another yawn. "Very interesting, but I must go."

"Wait, there's more. I'll get another." The colonel took his glass to the bar, smiling and jostling with his men, Cohen suddenly aware of their jibing laughter, the nasal yowl of Arabic music from the juke box, the pinging of pinballs. Why play with me? Get it over with. You waiting for me to break, run? So your men can shoot me?

"Why all this talk?" Cohen said when the colonel returned.

"*Que c'est compliquée, la vie!* So few things what they appear. Kennedy's death, and then his brother's, seem to have passed into history. But they are enduring tragedies for the people of the world. Since then, your country has descended into the abyss, become the enemy of peace and fairness, the enemy of liberty and evolution. Evolution, *mon ami,* is life!" He lit another cigarette. "How many children did America kill in Vietnam? Hundreds of thousands? A million? In our own revolution so many little ones killed by the French . . . Do you know, my friend, children die better than men?" Ashes fell from the colonel's cigarette; with the side of one hand he gathered them over the table edge into the other palm and dropped them in the ashtray. "It's why I don't believe in a God—no God could allow what I've seen."

In the lateness of the evening the bar had quieted; beyond its steamy windows, wraiths of mist converged and melted in the street. "How much better," the colonel said, "if just one more child had lived and I'd died. After our victory I found I had lost everything. Since then I've never wanted children, not in this war—not waiting for the bombs to fall."

"Bombs?"

"You Americans. The great big ones. The last bomb, the last laugh. Do you realize, *mon vieux,* there *will* be a last bomb, a very last one? Will it be, I wonder, Russian or yours?"

"I am Irish."

"Yes, I forget; my mind wanders. I say those years are gone, then I sit alone and they all come back. Sometimes I return to Ghardaia—it's always a mistake but I do it—and I see those years haven't passed at all. They're still here. Right now inside me! Ah!" He crushed out his cigarette. "*Mon ami,* time's a fiction." He sat forward, grinning. "So why does America hunt you?"

Cohen looked round the Les Champs Elysées. All in a moment he felt homeless, not solely in this sleazy foreign waterfront bar with its jagged Arabic accents, its wailing music, its strange odors of khaki, mint, kefta, sweat, and seafoggy dirt, its truculent soldiers and the insidiously friendly colonel. Homeless not only in Oran, city of *La Peste,* or in Algeria, where the Christians had persecuted then fled the Moslems, not only on this arid edge of Africa lured by the sea and tortured by the desert, not only far from the country he had once loved and that now hunted him. No, he realized, I am a homeless in the race of man—a stranger there, alone. He smiled at the colonel. "It's kind of you to worry for me. If I were this person, I'd imagine they hunted me because I'd interfered, perhaps by accident, with a secret operation hostile to another nation, and that my friends have all been killed. But I'm a tourist, a wanderer, an ' étranger', and I wish only to pass peacefully through your country."

"Ah, *mon ami,* as an *étranger* you stand out here. Why not travel to another place where you speak the language, where you fit in?"

"I'd imagine they'd be hunting for me there too, with greater intensity."

"For tonight, then, where do you stay?"

"A hotel."

The colonel noted his watch. "It approaches midnight. The hotels are closed." He removed his kepi, fingered the rim. "You are the guest of my country, welcome at the home of my uncle."

"You are kind, but no."

"*Vraiment,* it might be safer. Wandering the streets you might be taken for that American. Your CIA works closely with our criminal element—drug smugglers, prostitution, the like—they call it 'liaison with private enterprise,' I believe." The colonel chunked down his glass. "Since you resemble this . . . this Sam Cohen, you'd be wise to avoid them." He stood. "The Irish are great soldiers. The wild geese, were you not called? It will be my uncle's honor for you to stay in his home."

Cohen stood also, pain shooting through his knee. "Thank you. I'm happy to sleep on your floor."

The colonel scoffed. "In a Moslem country one does not treat a guest so." He paused for a moment with the soldiers, then held open the door. A smile glinted at them from the cluster at the bar.

They climbed through twisted, wet streets into the city's core. There were no cars, few faces. The colonel's boots crunched on the paving stones. "When I walk these streets at night I live it again: the sirens, bullets, plastiques. Corpses, bloody holes in the walls. Here," he swung his hand at a street corner where the cobblestones shone dark with mist and thick in their seams with ordure, black rotted banana peels, goat manure, the wind-borne plastic and sand of the city, "here died my closest friend. At twenty-two he spoke five languages, an economist. He was crippled—couldn't walk without crutches. A week before the end, the French propped him up against this wall and shot him. At the end they were shooting everyone, everyone. So many times I've passed this corner, looking for him, wondering why, why, why? Do you know why?"

It was a place where men and dogs urinated, a whitewashed wall pockmarked as lava. In its center, at chest height, the concrete looked like bread gnawed by a rat. "Thousands of bullets it took, that wall. Where's the blood of all the young people who died against it? What's it nourished, their blood?"

"You don't speak like a revolutionary."

"I was never a revolutionary. I fought because the French killed my family and a million others of my race. But I believe in revolution."

"So do I."

"Ah." The colonel leaned back. "Why?"

"Because the world's divided into a few who eat and many who are hungry, because the few won't turn from their pursuits to share equally with the hungry. Because democratic governments, in that they're susceptible to manipulation by money, become little more than devices to protect the rich from the poor."

"You speak of America?"

"Particularly, yes. But other places as well. No doubt Russia, too."

"Surely." The colonel turned and continued the climb. "How war simplifies! Live or die." He breathed heavily. "Later, it's easy to miss that simplicity. Words lose their meanings."

"I do not believe in words."

They entered a dark, unpaved alley, at its end a dimly lit doorway, and above it a tall, concrete silhouette. The elevator entry was open and smelt of urine. "My uncle," the colonel said, "is away in Constantine."

The apartment was large and well-furnished in French colonial style and Arab carpets. There was an odor of incense and a vague reminder of broken sewer pipes. The city glimmered through fog-stippled windows.

"I do not know your name."

"Joe."

"Come, Joe, have a glass of wine with me." He grasped Cohen's wrist as they sat at the flecked formica table in the compressed kitchen. "I would do anything for peace."

Under the fly-specked kitchen bulb Cohen could not ignore the bfearied eyes, the black stubble, the sour breath, the sallow undershirt with coiled hairs peeping from its neckband. "It's just a word, peace," he said. "It doesn't mean anything."

The colonel lit another cigarette, pinched a fleck of tobacco from his lip. "One night, when I was a boy, I was studying French, lying before the fire in the room where my mother was weaving and my father mending a donkey saddle, my three little brothers playing beside me—and I was caught suddenly by a page of vocabulary. There were words for different things, like spoon or mirror or tree, and in the midst of them was *mort,* as if death were only a thing like a mirror or a spoon, of no greater significance." He blew smoke upward, away from Cohen's face. "Right then I realized only two words count, in any language: life and death." He rinsed the glasses in the sink, put away the wine, showed Cohen to a plushly curtained room with a velvet comforter on a double bed, and clumped away down the hall.

Cohen tucked aside a curtain and looked down on the quiet city. A shabby man descended through a dim arc of streetlight, a burlap sack over one shoulder. A rat scampered along the curb behind him and into a gutter drain. A distant ship hooted.

The door swung open and the colonel entered in yellowed long underwear. He crossed to climb into bed. Opposite him, Cohen edged toward the door. "I'm not to sleep here?" he said.

"I also. You're afraid?"

"It's not my style." Cohen felt his face flush with anger. The small, tanned face beamed up at him from a flounced scarlet pillow. "In truth, it's normal," the colonel said.

"Not for me." Pulling on his shirt, Cohen stepped into the darkened hallway, bumping a plant stand that fell with a crash.

"Stay here." The colonel leaped from the bed. "I shall sleep elsewhere."

A voice yelled angrily from the floor below. Cohen bent to retrieve the plant; his glasses slipped from his pocket and clattered on the floor. He fumbled for them, fingers sticky with loam.

"It's useless. There are no hotels." The colonel flicked on a light and followed him into the living room, shrugging on a purple robe. "You'll be caught, *mon ami*. That'll be the end."

Cohen reached the door. The colonel came up behind him. "I have this."

Hand on the knob, Cohen turned. The pistol in the man's hand was small, nickel-plated. Cohen let out a suppressed, irritated breath, gauging the distance between them.

"Don't be foolish. I have killed so many men I do not even know the number you would be."

"You would kill someone who won't go to bed with you?"

"Perhaps we might sit." The colonel tipped the barrel toward the kitchen. "I'll put this away." He flicked on the kitchen light. "There's something I would learn." He padded barefoot to the sink, retrieved their wine glasses and set them with the bottle on the table.

"What do you want?" Cohen fingered his glasses furiously. One lens was cracked across the middle, the fissure dark with loam.

"To hear your story. My uncle, who owns this place, once was saved by the briefest of warnings. He was an engineer in the public works, under the French; when the French were pulling out they called together all the Algerian personnel, supposedly to discuss the transfer to Algerian management. It was a big room—every Arab who'd ever worked for the public works was there, everyone who'd know where the pipes and cables were laid. A French friend yelled a warning to my uncle and he dove under the table as French soldiers ran in spraying everyone with machine guns. . . . My uncle lay under that table for five hours, shielded by the bodies of his co-workers, then crawled through a window and found his way home past French patrols shooting everyone on the streets. So his wife got two horrible shocks—first she was told he was dead, then she opened the door to find him standing there covered in the blood and brains of his coworkers." The colonel laughed. "They burned all the plans and blueprints, too, the French. For months nothing in Oran worked and no one alive could fix it." He tilted his chair forward. "Perhaps you have a warning, too?"

"Who'd listen?"

"A few. What if you die before it's told?"

"I'll tell a friend first. He'll speak for me." Cohen stood. "May I go?"

"A moment." He left the kitchen and returned with a white silk shirt. "A gift?"

Cohen glanced at the colonel's threaded bathrobe, the undershirt grimy between its lapels. "No."

"Go, then."

He descended the stairs rapidly, listening for the elevator's hum or steps behind him. In the alley the air sang with hyacinth, lemon, and sea fragrance cut with whiffs of fresh sewage. Twelve days, Paul. I'm still with you.

The sidewalks rang out his steps. The lights of the port wavered behind curtains of mist. As he crossed the seaside boulevard the still-bright windows of Les Champs Elysées called out. He turned his back and climbed a cyclone fence guarding a long dock. Between two warehouses stood a pile of bald truck tires, one in the center large enough to stretch out on. "It is in giving that we receive." Saint Francis said that. Perhaps, then, in receiving we give. And I am becoming one who does not exist except for himself, who lives on the leavings, the unreal, who wants nothing more. With *Noces* as a pillow, and breathing shallowly against the worn rubber, rat shit, and oily dirt smells, he fell asleep.

Once he awakened to brush a cockroach from the corner of his mouth, and slept again, dreaming he lay in a pathless forest. A bear circled him in the darkness, loomed over him. He roared in anger and terror. It slashed at him and was gone. He lurched up holding his chest as footsteps sifted into silence along the warehouse walls.

His neck was sticky and hot. His wallet was gone. He ransacked the grime beneath the tires, stood and squinted into the darkness, hearing only the slap of waves on pilings and the solitary clatter of a truck on a distant upgrade. Sweat poured over his stomach and widened across his belt in a clammy black line. He rubbed his neck and pain shot down his throat and through his chest. Dizzy, he sat.

The pain came from a deep slit running from his neck across his right shoulder. Blood dribbled through his fingers and down his arm, pattering on the ground. Taking a splintered board in his good hand, he padded down the corridor between the warehouse walls, listening for a step, a breath, the rustle of cloth or skin on canvas.

142

13

LOADED PALLETS TOWERED LIKE abandoned tenements above him, infiltrating the chill with odors of sea-wet canvas, tarry wood, and grease. He moved forward to listen again, hearing nothing. At the boulevard he stopped. Les Champs Elysées winked through shifting fog. He returned to the tires and rummaged about them, but his wallet and the tall Tibetan's bag of Endless Snow were gone.

The bleeding slowed. I should have taken the shirt. Dropping the board, he crossed the boulevard. A phosphorescent clock in a petrol station window said 3:35. Again he felt dizzy and sat on a doorstep. Mists were shifting like windblown veils across the port lights. A fat rat slipped out of the gloom, sniffed his toe, and scampered away. Standing carefully, he emptied his right pocket with his left hand. Seven dinars. Really nothing.

A door banged as a man in a white cap left Les Champs Elysées. Cohen staggered past the wet tables chained to the sidewalk and peered through the steamy window. A dark-haired boy was mopping the floor. The door was open. Warm air hit him like a blanket. Fighting the need to fall, he moved across the room toward the boy. The room wheeled; the watery floor zoomed up and slapped him in the face. The boy bent over him. *"Vous êtes blessé,"* he said.

"J'ai tombé." Cohen drank the glass of water the boy brought and sat up. His palm felt wet; he raised it and stared at its dirty smear. He wiped it on his jeans and rose to a squat.

"What happened?" the boy asked.

"J'ai tombé," Cohen repeated. "Fell and cut my neck."

The boy had golden, freckled eyes. Cohen stood and went to the bar. "Can you make me an *express*?"

"Aussi un cognac, peut-être?"

The room was stationary now. The taste of the espresso and brandy sank into his tongue. The boy, wordless, was reflected from the waist up in the bar mirror as he bent over his mop and pail. Cohen watched his dinars sitting on the counter. The boy finished the floor, put the mop and bucket in the back. *"Ça va mieux?"* he said.

"Yes, better."

"American, you are?"

"Oui."

"De quel partie?"

Cohen was too tired to lie. "Montana."

"The mountains? Close to New York?"

"Far from it."

"Some day I will go to New York. Do you want a sandwich? It's yesterday's bread—the new comes at seven. Otherwise I throw it away. You like pâté?"

"That too is yesterday's?"

The boy smiled. "There's no charge. You fell on the wet floor."

"Not because it was wet."

The boy made him another espresso and the sandwich and left the cognac bottle on the bar, next to Cohen's glass. "You will see the doctor?"

"No."

"You like music?" The boy thumbed a coin into the jukebox. "When I get to New York, I will listen to this song, 'Strawberry Field'—it's big there, *n'est-ce pas?*"

"Don't know." When the boy seemed hurt Cohen added, "Two years I have not been there."

"Allah! What a long time to leave home. My brother has been nine months in France; he wishes to come back."

"Why does he stay, then?"

"He makes much money, sends it here. He works, like me, cleaning a bar in Lyon. He was very lucky."

"Lucky?"

"To get such work." The boy took away Cohen's plate, refilled the brandy. "When will you go back to America?"

"It costs money."

"That's easy for you," the boy laughed, "you're American. In the world it's easiest to be American."

The door squeaked. An old, turbaned man in a tan, worn djellabah slippered across the floor. "Abdul, *salaam*," the boy said.

144

The old man stared at Cohen with currant eyes. "*Salaam,* Hassim," he nodded to the boy.

Cohen sat half asleep as the old man slurped his coffee with nervous, shuffling motions. A sailor entered, doffed his cap with a smile at the boy. They talked in Arabic by the jukebox. Cohen ignored the urge to drop his head on the bar. He could not remember, already, what the boy had just said. "*Tu peux me faire un autre?*" he called, lifting his cup.

Beyond the café windows night was surrendering to the first mist of day. A white-robed woman crossed the street, a black sack balanced on her head. "How exciting, to travel," the boy said.

"You don't like it here?"

"This country's like my family: good but poor. I want something besides work and sleep. And always, hunger."

Cohen nodded at the bread, cheese, and pâté behind the counter. "You haven't enough to eat?"

"Of that, yes. But we always hunger. We hear about America, Paris."

"In America is the same hunger, even worse."

"You tease me. In America, everyone has a car, *n'est-ce pas*?"

"Some have two or three."

"So they are happy."

"Many perhaps less than you."

"They have each a house?"

"Many. Some have two houses, even more."

The boy laughed. "So they are very happy."

"You will go to France?"

"Like my brother, I will invite myself on a boat."

"You'll be caught. It happened to me, now, coming from Greece." Cohen described the *Petr Vyazemski.* The boy's eyes, with their shifting yellow flickers, stayed on his. "But they let me work," Cohen added.

"And now?" the boy raised his eyebrows.

"Now, as you see, I am hurt."

"Your money?"

"Stolen." Cohen nodded his chin at the dinars on the bar. "That is my all."

"*Alors,* you are poor like me."

A beetle-browed policeman entered and waited, fingers tapping the bar, until the boy served him café au lait. He watched Cohen, wiping his moustache after each sip. Cohen tried to lean naturally over the bar and not reveal the blood down his shirt.

"He asked about you," the boy confided after the policeman had left. "I said you're my friend from the mountains of New York." The boy leaned over the bar. "You're going to take another ship, aren't you?"

"Perhaps."

"I'll go with you."

"Hassim, you're too young."

"I'm nineteen. I'll show you *mon certificat.*"

"I don't believe you."

The boy leaned over the bar, whispering although no one else was in the room. "Every morning the *paquebot* leaves at ten for Marseille. We can stay with my brother in Lyon. He will find me work. He has a Deux Chevaux. I've saved nearly a hundred dinars."

Cohen stilled his shivering. "France is a very expensive place. And cold. Bring a warm coat." Thinking of the lifeboat on the *Petr Vyazemski,* he added, "and food."

A tremulous wail echoed through the street's tenuous light. An old man put down his bundle and knelt toward the east. "Excuse me," the boy said, and went into the rear, behind a bead curtain. "We can leave at seven," he said when he returned. "I will make you some breakfast. *Oeufs plat.* Every American likes *oeufs plat.*"

At seven the owner appeared, pulling at his moustache. Ten minutes later Cohen and the boy stepped into the soggy, sharp morning, their pockets jammed with bread and pâté. "I asked him for my pay, until tonight." The boy grinned. "Told him I wished to buy a bicycle."

"*Alors?*"

"With my pay, he should know I cannot afford a bicycle."

The scent of sea, wet garbage, and docks hung in the air. The boy's apartment was in a streaked stucco building above the waterfront. "My mother will cry," he said. Cohen waited outside. The pain in his chest had expanded to a crushing, nauseating ache that filled his whole body, triggering a spasm of dizzy agony with each breath. "I'm not afraid to pray," he decided. "I pray we get to France. I do." The boy came down and gave him a coat and a small piece of paper with Arabic lettering. "A port pass, old, of my brother. I have one also."

"They'll notice me."

"It's no matter. Anyone may unload the ships. Pull the coat collar, so, around your neck. Face down when you show it."

The civilian at the booth said nothing. They entered the port. Freighters lay, hatches gaping, aside oily quays. Strange flags dropped from their masts. Seagulls complained overhead or sat stoic in the seedy water. Men in worn djellabahs waited by canvas-wrapped pallets.

The *paquebot* was old and rusty. Several people were mounting her forward gangway. A man in a blue shirt gathered tickets. The rear gangway was chained off. At the top, a sailor leaned on the rail, smoking.

"Wait." The boy pointed amidships, to a door open just above waterline. A man in a black stocking cap leaned out of it and spit into the water. A gull dove at the white speck, veered away.

"There's no gangway."

"One can jump!"

A swell rocked the *paquebot*, squeaking her gangways against the quay.

Behind them a warehouse ran the length of the quay, a single line of cars and panel trucks parked along its middle. In the warehouse, stairs descended to an unlit corridor beneath the quay. The boy lit a match. Compartments lay off the corridor to the seaward side. He entered one and unbolted a steel plate door. *"Merde,"* he whispered. "My finger."

In the expiring matchlight Cohen saw gouts of blood piling on the floor. "Now we are both poor and hurt," he said. The boy shoved the door open. The *paquebot*'s black hull faced them, its door to their right. They stumbled into the next compartment. Its door would not unbolt.

"Should've brought more matches," the boy whispered.

The next door was also rusted shut. They found a scrap of iron and wedged it between the door and the wall. The door gave. The *paquebot* again faced them, the open door in her hull to their left. Above them a whistle blew. Feet ran up the forward gangway. With the iron scrap they levered open the door of the middle compartment.

147

The steamer's hull tapered up like a canyon wall into a slit of sky. The gangways soared, concave like high wires, against the glare. The boy leaped and grabbed for the door's rusty sill, one foot sloshing. He faced back at Cohen out of the ship's cave gloom. *"Avancez,"* he hissed. *"Vite!"*

Cohen glanced up. The gangways were empty. He dove for the door, snatched at a hinge, knee-deep in greasy chill, pain wrenching his chest. The boy yanked him into the shadows. *"C'est ça,"* the boy panted.

Stairs ascended into darkness. Oil smells and chugging came from below. Cohen swore at the sensation of blood coiling down his arm. They felt their way down a dangling catwalk into the lightless hull. The boy lit a match, illuminating the metal grid of the catwalk. Cohen noticed with annoyance that his wet shoelace had untied. Roaches stippled the flaky walls like beads of rain, their antennae flexing in the sudden light.

Voices rose and fell behind a bulkhead on the deck below. The boy backed up. Cohen moved to step around him and fell off the catwalk. The bulkhead boomed against his head.

The boy was pulling him up. There was a reason to do something, but he could not remember it, nor the thing there was to do. Claws tore into his shoulder; he fought to brush them away but found nothing. Perhaps I'm shot, he wondered, giggling.

Brightness and voices poured in on him. I've caught Isom's laugh. Pain doubled in his shoulder as someone lifted him. The light was glazed with silence. *"J'ai attrapé son rire,"* he giggled. *"C'est fatal."*

Dark angry faces hammered at him, out of the cottony glare, *"T'es fou, toi? T'es fou, toi?"*

"Je m'en fous, moi," he answered.

"Il est malade." It was a faraway voice, the boy's. Someone shoved them together. Pain cut like a razor, sharpened his sight.

"Christ, *tu m'as blessé,"* Cohen said to a thick-lipped, bearded face. "See, I'm bleeding." Pipes receded whitely into the horizon. His shoulder banged against the bulwark as they hustled him up the catwalk. Stained water flashed through an open door. The boy was talking loudly beneath him.

Sailors held them on the deck until a tan Land Rover, klaxon welling, dodged through the pallets and stopped at the forward gangway. Four soldiers ran up and handcuffed them. One spoke briefly at Cohen in Arabic and called to the others. "He's decided you're not Algerian," the boy said. A soldier slapped him, pointing a finger into his face.

Each jolt of the Land Rover across the potholed quay drove new, impossible pain into his shoulder. The mountain city before him misted over and reappeared gleaming like shattered wineglass. "Neither is true," he said, and began to laugh. They gained the boulevard and swung west. Buses, trucks, and taxis flew past. The Land Rover tilted them crazily to the left as it cut around a guard post and down a narrowing roadway gauntleted by cyclone fence.

The soldiers pushed him up rickety steps into an office. A moustached man glared at him out of a nicotined photo. A grilled window gave on a courtyard where men paraded with their hands atop their heads. "It's over now," he said. Dead flies lay on the window sill and on the floor below. A few bumbled weakly against the glass; one brushed his wrist.

In the center of the room a desk and folding chair. He leaned on the desk. It moved, one leg splaying. He sat in the chair. The world was still. He felt grateful. Isom was leaning beside him on the rail of the *Petr Vyazemski*. Isom faced him and spoke, but he could not understand the Arabic. Or is it Russian? Isom's black-bearded shape swelled into a bear that slashed at him. Isom nodded at the window. "Go," he indicated with his chin, "go there."

Cohen went to the window. The parading men were guarded by a soldier with an automatic rifle. One momentarily raised his head, and in the man's eyes Cohen saw the cause of Isom's laugh: the awesome indifference of the universe to individual pain.

The door grated. With difficulty Cohen turned. The Algerian colonel, a clipboard in his hand, stood grinning beneath his narrow moustache. "It was good, your hotel?"

"I didn't have a ride to Algiers—I came from there, in a 403. I wanted to go to France, but my money was stolen. My visa, my passport, too."

"Your visa, from the sleepy little town? *Que c'est triste.* And your *Noces*?"

"I wasn't going to be married."

"Where'd you get that cloak?"

149

"From my friend."

"You'd take a loused coat like that from him while refusing a shirt from me?"

"He didn't pull a gun."

"He'd fuck you, though, just like me."

Cohen felt his sole smack on something sticky. He leaned giddily on the sill.

The colonel caught him and pulled open the coat and shirt, glanced at the wound, and pointed at the chair. "Sit down." He placed his palms on the table. "Shall I give you to them?"

"Who?"

"You pretend not to know? I shall, then."

"Then I'm dead," Cohen said flatly.

The colonel ran a slender finger along the wound. He wiped it on Cohen's shirt. "Alas for your self esteem, it's not fatal. But," he smiled, "we'll have to send you home."

"As I said . . ."

"Why lie to me? I checked France. They've no interest in you . . . a common sailor. And your accent—Grenoble? Fuck Grenoble. You're from Toulon. Joe? Fuck Joe. You're a nothing named Luc Seghers, a lousy sailor!" The colonel shook his head in disgust. "Perhaps a medic can lend your emblem of courage, there, a little honor." He halted in the doorway. "Then we'll return your *Carte d'Identité* and money—and insist that you leave Algeria at once, or stand trial for trespass on a military port and for attempted *passage clandestin.*"

He called in a stooping, bespectacled youth who inspected the wound with agile fingers, then smiled and said perhaps three words. "It's deep," the colonel translated, "but he affirms my belief you won't die. Perhaps you'll find aid in France?" A soldier entered with slips of paper. "It's the law to deport stowaways to their country of origin. You leave at once on the *paquebot* for Marseille." The colonel glanced at his wrist. "You have twenty minutes!"

The soldier handed Cohen a French identity card. Folded inside it were a hundred-franc and a fifty-franc note. He held out a pen and a yellow form. "A receipt," the colonel said, "to affirm you've received your valuables. Sign your name, Monsieur Seghers." The colonel grinned. "You are suprised we caught the *mecs* who beat you up? And that they still had your *Carte d'Identité* and money?"

150

Cohen gritted his teeth to slow his dizziness. "Please. Tell me who they are! They've killed my friends . . . everyone."

"Nonsense. Give up your past, become a new man, and you never need fear them again." He grinned, bowing slightly. "Stay off docks at night."

"No, I mean . . ."

"I understand." The colonel pushed Cohen toward the door. "Your boat leaves."

"But Hassim?"

"*C'est un arabe.* We will deal with him according to law." The colonel waved his hand at the exercise yard. "You're lucky you're French and deportable." The soldier tugged at Cohen's arm. Pain soared up his neck.

"He's a boy!"

"Forget him. Do not establish contact." The colonel pointed at the soldiers. "I've told them to shoot if you run."

Cohen turned. "I'm sorry. About the shirt."

"Shirt?" The colonel smiled at the soldiers. "I know nothing of any shirt."

The Land Rover bounced over the quay to where the *paquebot* had dropped her mooring cables and lay churning at her stern waters. "*Billet, quatrième,*" a soldier said to the clerk who was closing the gate where the forward gangway had been.

"Too late," Cohen mumbled.

"Your money?" the clerk asked.

Cohen handed him the hundred-franc note. The man gave him change and leaned over the quayside to call down at the water. The *paquebot* was perhaps two hundred yards out, her bow swinging northward, stacks smoking, froth building up behind her screws.

The clerk led them down the stairs under the quay, flicking on a switch that illuminated the corridor and its series of compartments. He unbolted a door. As daylight jumped into the compartment, Cohen saw dark circles on the concrete where the boy's finger had bled.

A dory pulled alongside the compartment; a soldier pointed to it. "*Depêche-toi!*" He planted his rifle butt in Cohen's back and shoved him into the dory. It lurched away, forcing him to sit. One of the soldiers laughingly saluted him.

The dory putted to the side of the *paquebot*. The door in the hull was opening. A rope ladder uncoiled to waterline. Heads were silhouetted above at the rail, small ovals against the sky. He mounted the ladder one-handed. Sailors pulled him through the door. *"Merci!"* he called, but the dory had already pulled away, its engine sputtering in the roil of the *paquebot*.

"Billet?" A sailor regarded him impassibly. *"Quatrième?"* the sailor snorted. *"Là-bas."* He pointed down. Another sailor took him down a foul companionway to a slatted bulkhead door that he opened with a key, shoving Cohen inside. "It's for the animals," he said, and locked it.

Cohen stood at the edge of a wide, low room. The moist, un-swallowable air reeked like an *abattoir*. The hot metal walls vibrated unevenly. Beyond him, figures shuffled mechanically in the jaundiced light.

14

HE TOOK THREE STEPS down into the hold. Cold water sloshed obscenely round his ankles; he backed up the stairs. A woman's laugh. "No illusions here, *mon brave*," she called. "It's not First Class."

The water in the hold rocked gently with the to-and-fro motion of the hull. Mounds of straw floated in it amid bulging, dark globes. Out of sight from the far side came a braying followed by shrill laughter. Cohen sat on the stairs.

"One must not station oneself there," the woman said. "It's an exit, in case of fire. Or need to abandon ship."

"Where can I sit?"

"Demand of the master. Perhaps he'll favor you with a chair such as mine, for only ten francs."

From the obscurity came a tall, bowed Arab in an undershirt, pyjamas rolled to his knees. His bony feet unleashed wavelets under the straw. He grinned, spittle sliding down the corner of his mouth.

"You *are* fortunate," he said, distending his jaw to twist a tooth deeper into the gum, and led Cohen down an aisle between rows of chairs. In each chair was an Arab, some old, some young, some with children clinging to the chair arms. As they moved further from the light the room closed around them with Arabic gutturals, the whine of a child, the lap, lap of water on chair legs. The laugh burst out again.

"He's caught it, too," Cohen said. "From Isom."

"Far enough," the master answered. "How lucky: the last chair. Your ten francs?"

Cohen fished the pieces left-handed from his pocket. One coin splashed at his feet. He knelt fumbling in cold ooze for the coin. A scream spiraled up a staircase of frenzy and burst around them. He jumped and dropped the coin again. The scream cascaded from laughter into silence. Once more he found the coin. "Who's that?"

The master's fingernails scratched his palm. "A passenger, taken from his native land to work out his days in France."

"Why do you laugh?"

"Why not? It's so serious, life? Here you'll have a good seat for the circus. To hear the elephants when they shit." The master guided him by the elbow to a canvas deck chair and sloshed away through the gloom.

He woke shivering. His clothes felt chilled and outgrown. The crash of his skull against the bulkhead door echoed in his temples. The shoulder pain was awesome but alien, beyond personal concern. Faces danced before him like horses on a carousel: the colonel, Hassim, Isom, his mother wiping troubled hands on a flowered apron. "All the good ones die," he said to them. "Who doesn't?" they grinned in response. Weird laughter rolled toward him, a monstrous wave erupted inside him, burst out to meet itself, tears watering his cheeks. Pain cut it short.

"It's just Isom." He rubbed his face, astonished at its asperity. A rumbling spatter filled the darkness with a foul, sweet odor. It subsided in random droplets on the straw. He held his breath until his forehead pounded but the smell remained. Eleven days, Paul. Easy now. Last quarter. Almost.

Lulled by the engines he dreamt of glaciated granite ridges cleft by green rivers, where dogwoods dropped white petals in rushing, lucid water. The petals tossed boatlike on the current over shoals of golden mica and stringing algal tresses. Small cutthroats flexed red gills behind crumpled boulders. Gratefully he leaned down to drink. The reflection rising to meet him was a deer's, luminous brown eyes in which his features were miniaturized. He jumped back. Claire sat on a downed log, her hair tied up.

"You'll drown," she said, loosened her hair and unbuttoned her blouse until he could see the diamond heart winking like a beacon.

"I saw that," he said. "The coast of Africa."

"It was a passing ship."

"Isom said . . ."

"You're a fool, believing what's false, ignoring what's true. Life's truly too complex for you."

She was gone. Ash leaves rustled across him. He waited for the

154

coolness of the wind but it did not come. A leaf tickled his neck. He raised it to the light. Its feelers wavered; its legs pushed against his finger.

He tossed the roach into the water, brushed at the others. They ran up his trouser legs and down his collar. The water was flecked with straw to which roaches clung like sailors to the flotsam of a shipwreck.

A sink was bolted in the corner by the bulkhead. As he approached it a man was drinking from the faucet. When he had finished he hitched up his djellabah and urinated into the sink. He nodded to Cohen as he stepped past. Globules of urine lingered in the sink and spattered up as Cohen turned on the faucet. The water tasted of dead fish and old boilers, reminding him of the closet on the *Petr Vyazemski*. He vomited into the sink, drank more water, and was sick again.

He brushed roaches from his chair and sat. At once he stood, unbuttoned his jeans, and squatted in the shifting straw by the elephant cage. "Transitory, no mind." A child was whimpering beyond the elephants. Cohen wiped himself with soggy straw and hitched up his jeans.

The whimper came from a large cage. He lit a match. Beyond the bars monkeys huddled in thigh-deep water, their eyes rubied by matchlight. In the middle, a smaller monkey clung to a dark blob that he saw was the body of an older one. "Get him," he whispered to the other monkeys baring their teeth and clinging to the bars. "Get the baby!"

In the further cages an elephant defecated again with a rumbling splash. With each shift of the hull, waves of bilge water broke over the young monkey's head and knocked it from the corpse. Each time, it flailed screaming at the water, found the corpse, and clambered back. Cohen pounded the bars, but the lock would not budge. He crossed to his deck chair and pulled a strut from the canvas, returned to the monkey cage and inserted it through the bars. The monkeys jabbered. The young one was unable to keep its head above the water, was washed again from the corpse and fought back. "Here," Cohen hissed. "Take it!"

The monkey found the corpse and pulled itself up. Cohen extended the strut. The match fell into the water. The strut jabbed the monkey in the ribs; it leaped howling from the corpse, thrashing the water with tiny hands, mouth stretched wide against the water. Cohen reached out blindly, dropped the strut to light another match. The monkey was underwater, a foot from the corpse, the swell eddying over it. "Get it!" Cohen screamed at the other monkeys; he battered the bars with his fists, picked up the strut and threw it but it landed short and sank. The match went out. "Master!" Cohen called, shaking the bars. He lit another match. The corpse nodded sedately in the flow; the crimson eyes of the other monkeys glared back at him from the sides of the cage.

He pulled his chair from the water and sat. His fists stung from battering the bars. Laughter from the monkeys rose around him. "They've caught it," he said, and fell asleep.

A monstrous spider descended upside down before him, its brown legs wriggling up over an orange stomach. A harsh voice issued from it. Something touched his shoulder and he jumped at the pain. The spider lisped at him, swinging closer.

A hand shook him gently. A second set of brown legs encircled the spider's orange belly and tore away its skin. Falling skin hit Cohen's knee. Inside, the body was lighter orange, serrated. The legs tore it apart, carried a section to his mouth.

Orange sweetness stung his lips and squirted down his throat. The face of the master regarded him. "You were speaking to no one," he said. He broke off another section and pushed it between Cohen's lips.

Time passed or did not pass; he could not tell. It seemed he dreamed the same dream over and over: Sylvie turning her head to look at him, an orange in her hand, the side of her face cut by a line of dark hair, asking, *"T'en veux plus?"* But each time he went to answer the dream faded, and so he never knew what his answer would be. Perhaps I only dreamt I dreamt it many times, while it was just once. I'm going mad, forget what I'm dreaming.

Twice more he sloshed across the hold to drink at the sink; innumerable times he crouched in the corner by the elephants. Often the laughter of the monkeys awakened him from something that he had resolved to remember.

Voices took spark, feet pattered through the water. The Arabs clustered by the door, women chirping lightly. The shudder of the hull had silenced. He crossed the hold and followed the last Arab up a cliff of stairs toward a bright oblong that became the hull door giving on a gangway to the blue resplendence of Marseille.

He leaned against a lamp pole at the end of the dock and counted the money in his palm. Fifty-three francs were left from what the colonel had given him. There were the now-useless dinars Hassim had pushed back at him across the bar of Les Champs Elysées, a few centimes. It was shocking to think how meaningless centimes had once seemed: flat, light, and tinny, in mute testimony to their own worthlessness. Now, with so little company in his palm, they had more weight. "Liberty, equality, brotherhood," they said.

La Canebière pointed northward from the Old Port like a cannon. In the first side street was an open market. He picked out a banana. "Fifteen centimes," a kerchiefed woman said. He put it back. "And take your roaches with you," she called.

In the next street he found two bananas for ten centimes at an Arab shop and sat wolfing them on the curb. "Where is a cheap hotel?" he asked the shopkeeper.

"French, or Arab?"

"Somewhere to sleep."

"La rue Thubaneau, two blocks. If you reach la Providence," the Arab called, "you've gone too far."

La rue Thubaneau had grim facades and narrow sidewalks; paper rustled in the gutters. An old woman swept flashing glass into the street with a straw broom. "Good morning, grandmother," he said. "Do you know who has a cheap room to rent?"

She peered up at him, fingers gnarled on the broom handle. A thimble-sized wart bristled on her chin. "You're not my grandson. One would not find him on this street of whores and Arabs, stinking like a dead mullet! Beat it!" She shook the broom.

"Does he shit, this grandson of yours? If he does, he's surely like you," Cohen laughed, dodging the noisome swipe of her broom. Further along the street, a slip of cardboard hung in a window: *"Chambre meublée—à tout confort."* A spare woman in black answered the bell.

"It is how much, this room with every comfort?"

"Ten francs the day, fifty the week."

It waited atop four perilous flights, the banister tempting but unreliable, the tin-edged treads shifting under his steps. Its door had recently been punched in and had three planks nailed across it.

It was L-shaped, filled by a bed and a dresser, a chipped sink backed into the corner between them. A four-paned window cast cobwebbed light over fissures in the dresser's veneer. The mattress was slitted and stained. "There are no blankets?"

"Ten francs deposit, each."

He tested the faucet. The water was tan-colored.

"It's not drinking water, that," she said. "I bring one bottle each day." She indicated a dusty wine bottle on the floor by the bed. "Extra water, five centimes the bottle."

"I'll take it for a week, if you throw in the blankets."

"You have a *Carte*? You don't look French. You must register downstairs. No food in the room. W.C. in the hall. No toilet paper in the toilet—it blocks the flush. No fights in the room."

"Believe me, I have no one to fight."

"I believe no one who says that."

He awoke at dusk, head throbbing with hunger and fever, shoulder aching. He drained the water bottle, tugged on the light and stared at the flecked paint. Voices and car noises bounced up from the alley below the window. Vespers bonged out of the vermilion west through the cracked window of the w.c.

What was I dreaming? Oh God, if I could be in Montana now. April and the snow gone from the south-facing meadows of the Tobacco Roots, the streams high and full of rainbows, achingly cold. The grass starting so shiny, and new green pushing out the tips of the lodgepoles, delicate outfolding leaves on the aspens, the willows already in leaf, green-tipped cottonwoods standing haughty as Blackfeet along the arroyos, elk feeding on the bright grass below snowline, the sleek swift patter of coyotes over last year's leaves.

He stared out the window. Silence is Montana. The freedom of silence has nothing to do with man and everything to do with life. That's why I left Montana, too—I couldn't stand to watch it die. Couldn't go back to the forests where we'd hunted sun-gilded elk through cool towering pines, where now there's only chainsawed stumps and sun-charred bulldozed earth. While the Senators, Congressmen, Forest Service, and loggers divide up the public forest like the Mafia divide up some heroin network in the Bronx . . . When once Montana was God's magnificent gift to the entire uni-

158

verse, His most precious, beloved jewel . . . Why's the world like it is? No—why are we men what we are? When we don't need be?

He spread his money on the dresser top. Eight francs, twenty-one centimes. He ran water into the sink, stripped, and washed. Yellow pus and a nauseous odor ran out of the cut in his shoulder. Exhausted by the effort he fell back on the bed. After a while he sat up and slapped his good knee. "I need food. Paris in ten more days."

In the darkening street, a woman watched him from a doorway; a cat hissed and ran behind a garbage can. A truck passed, "A. Trimestre, Carcasses and Tallow," painted on its door. In an Arab café at the corner, he ate *bifteck frites* for three francs fifty. The horsemeat was tough but juicy, gone before he knew it. "Do you have any work to be done?" he asked the austere owner.

The man put his hands flat on his apron. "Alain," he called.

A head, roughcut and weepy-eyed, jumped through the kitchen window. *"Oui,"* it said.

"This one seeks work."

"Voilà," said Alain. "So do we all."

Slowly, like an old man, Cohen walked along la rue Thubaneau. *"Allô, mon mec,"* a voice called from his shadowed doorway. He looked up, expecting the tall concierge. "Have some fun?" the woman said. She was dark and overweight, breasts sloping down her dress.

"I'm queer," he answered, and slipped past her down the half-lit hall.

As he reached the fourth landing a door slapped open to the wall and a man in a sailor suit sprawled into the hall. His sailor's hat rolled across the landing and bounced bounced bounced down the stairs. He lifted his head. "Cheap cunt," he said, yelling as a booted toe caught him amidships, below the ribs.

"Beat it, pansy!" The woman turned fierce eyes on Cohen. "So you think he should have his money back when he can't get it up?"

"I think he's crazy if he can't get it up with you. I'll show him how."

She snorted. "Not without your fifty francs, just like him." She kicked the sailor again, who rolled away.

"I'll owe you fifty francs," Cohen offered. She was slight and pretty, sable hair trailing over one shoulder, breasts nipping up into her blouse, a green slit skirt accentuating the length and promise of her thighs above her calf-length boots. "I'm getting a job tomorrow," he added.

"Come see me tomorrow, then." She stepped over the sailor, who grabbed her ankle.

"Return my money," the sailor moaned.

"Let go, or I call the dog."

"Even a dog couldn't get it up for you!"

"Wait a minute," Cohen said. "She's my sister."

The sailor sat up. He scratched his thin reddish curls, felt round for his cap, stood. He belched. "Thy sister pisses blue," he said evenly, unzipping his fly.

Cohen gave him a quick left-handed tap and he toppled in a slow, inebriated backward handstand down the stairs. His feet came up and went over his head and he crashed against the third floor landing wall.

"You killed him?" she whispered. "Shit, that's trouble."

The sailor sat up and vomited.

"Creep," she spit. "Faggot bastard. *Maricon!*"

Cohen walked down the stairs and knelt over the sailor. "You can find the door, you?"

"What's the matter up there?"

"*Madre!* It's the concierge," she hissed. "Make him stand!"

"What's going on?" The concierge's shriek was a floor closer.

"You can find the door?" Cohen repeated.

"I want my money."

"It's finished, that."

"What's going on?" the concierge screamed.

"I'll tell you," the sailor stood but slipped on his pool of vomit, cascaded down the stairs on his rump and piled into the concierge.

"Get out, get out," she bellowed, twisting herself from under him. "Oh, you stink, Good God, you stink." She wiped at herself hurriedly. "All of you, out!" she yelled.

"I just got here," Cohen said.

"Out anyway."

"I don't even know who he is," the girl added.

"You—*saloppe, putain,* whore, trollop . . ." The concierge halted, panting for words.

"I did nothing!"

160

"I did it," Cohen said. "He's my brother. We always fight."

"Out. All of you, out, no matter what. Out! Out! Out!"

"My money back."

"Money nothing."

"I paid for a week. Fifty francs. I have no more."

The concierge shoved the sailor down the stairs. "Ten minutes." She glanced at an imaginary watch on her wrist. "Then I call the police."

"They'll arrest you for stealing my money," Cohen yelled.

"Mine, too," called the sailor.

"She will, she'll get the gendarmes," the girl said. She ran back into her room, calling, "Here, Lobo!" Cohen shut his door and stared stupified at the blanketed bed, the already familiar sink and dresser. "When you're going down," he muttered, "it's so hard to stop." There was nothing to pack. Ten days to go, no food, no money. No place to stay. Oh Jesus find me a haven. As he left he looked in the girl's open door. She was throwing dresses on the bed. An Alsatian watched him, ears forward, from the doorway. "Where will you go?" he asked.

"Who knows? Another hole like this, with another *grande dame* concierge and another Samaritan to get me thrown out again."

"He insulted you."

She flung a hand at the room. "This is the insult, to have to go like this. I should be working, not moving."

"I have to go too. She took all my money."

"Good." She jammed dresses, underclothes, a mirror and brush into a cardboard suitcase. "Serves you right for sticking your prick where it doesn't belong!"

She caught up to him in the street, walking lopsided from her suitcase, Lobo trotting at her heel. "What'll you do?" she said.

"I'll sleep in the street. And eat rats."

"They need a strong wine, plenty of body. A Spanish wine."

"You have one in mind?"

"*Sangre de Toro.* Come!"

15

LA RUE THUBANEAU RIPPLED with movement: neon glittered, cars prowled the curbs, young sensual eyes challenged them. He limped painfully; twice she waited for him, shaking her suitcase and stamping her heel on the sidewalk. Up greasy stairs, at the end of a dim corridor, she rapped on a door, bracelets jangling.

"Who's there?" A man's voice.

"Police. Open up." She rapped again. "*Salaud,* open up!"

"It had to be you, Maria." The man closed the door to unlatch a chain and reopened it. "The whores say they're cops and the cops are all whores. It's hard to get things straight."

"Keeps you on your toes, Léon."

Léon glanced at the suitcase, at Cohen. "Planning to elope?"

"This white knight saved me from a sailor, and got me thrown out."

Léon snickered. "What should I do, give him a medal?"

"Let us stay the night. Tomorrow I'll find a new place."

"You have work tonight."

"You want me to bring them here?"

"Absolutely not."

"So?"

Léon sucked his upper lip and pointed to a collapsed rattan couch. "Honeymoon suite's there. If the dog bites me, he dies."

"The bite would kill him."

"It's good you remember."

"Give us some wine."

"In the kitchen." Léon looked at Cohen. "You come from where?"

"Toulon."

"You're not French."

"I live in Toulon now."

"Travelling for pleasure?" He grinned at Cohen's clothes. "Got a gun?"

"No."

"Good. Guns are forbidden here. You have work?"

"I'll find something. I told Maria I did because . . ."

"No lies. Absolutely no lies. You have no money?"

"The concierge took it when she threw us out."

"How much?"

"Fifty francs."

"You are arrived from where?"

"Oran."

"There's little work in Marseille."

Maria stood the wine bottle on a crate near the couch. She patted the floor. The dog went to her, turned round, and lay down.

"You, Léon?" She was pouring wine into water glasses.

"No."

"Here," she said to Cohen. "Blood of the Bull!" It was thick, almost black. She refilled his glass. "To Andalucía."

"Piss on Andalucía," Léon said.

"And piss on Corsica," she answered.

Cohen felt dizzy and sat on the couch. "It's not that strong, the wine," Léon said.

"Americans have no head for wine," Maria answered.

Léon was shouldering on a leather jacket. "You're lucky I was here."

"I could have gone to Mamette's."

"Stay clear of Mamette's." He unchained the door. "Hook this behind me."

Maria sat beside Cohen on the couch. "I can't sleep so early." She stood and shifted her skirt. "You should shave," she sniffed. "Go in the bathroom and shave. And take a shower."

"Take one with me."

"For fifty francs."

"I've something better."

"Nothing's better. Go."

The hot rushing water was hallucinogenic, searing his knee and shoulder. He shaved left-handed with Léon's razor. She came in, tucked up her dress and squatted on the toilet. "You smell better," she said. "What's that?"

"I got knifed."

"Ugh. It's infected." She stood and flushed the toilet. "You should go to the hospital. The nuns, they are free." She ran a finger-tip along his reddened wound. "Did some sailor stick you, for defending a fair virgin?"

"I was robbed."

"You and money don't get along. I'll have to stay clear of you. Tomorrow you should go to the nuns."

"It's getting better."

"Nuns don't bite. What're you afraid of?"

He slipped his left hand along her buttock. "I'm afraid you won't make it with me."

"I don't do it for fun."

"You must, sometimes."

She pinched his chin. "It's work, *mi calentorro.* Keeps Lobo and me alive."

"There's surely other work in Marseille."

"For me, coming by *la miseria,* from Spain?"

"Then why did you come?"

"With this work, each month I send money to Andalucía."

"And Léon?"

"What do you think? That I could last on the street without my *chulo*? Without Léon or someone? He's my patron, protects me."

"From what?"

"You don't know? You're truly dense." She tossed her head, walking into the hall. "Get dressed—it's cold."

"Tell me." He followed her.

"*En verdad,* you *are* stupid. *Majadero*!" Her bracelets jingled. "You get robbed. You fight a dumb sailor and get thrown out. You lose your money. You do not understand about Léon. You—*you* need someone like Léon!"

He dressed. His clothes smelt like the hold of the paquebot.

"*Qué desgracia*!" she wailed. "Never will you find work looking like that. What can you do, anyway?"

"Anything that'll pay."

"Hah! You ask about me?"

He took her hand. "I don't ask. I thank you for taking me in."

"Léon takes you in." Arms akimbo, she tilted back her head to inspect him. "He's partial to *bobos*—'A los bobos se les aperece la madre de Dios,' we say in Andalucía—fortune favors fools. With my *mala fortuna,* though, I must be very wise! So Léon might find use for you."

164

"What could I do?"

She glanced under her lashes. "How *canuto* you are! *Mignon*! You could work the boys for him." She pinched his chin. "If you work for Léon, I get a bonus for bringing you in—I'll split it with you."

"Doing what?"

"What do you suspect, *mi calentorro*?" She rattled her bracelets. "Léon'd dress you up and rent you to the old queers of la Ciotat and Cassis."

"No chance."

"Now it's for me to ask why."

"I like women, not men."

"A hole's a hole."

"The one's more natural to me."

She reached between his thighs. "If we went to bed, I could drive you crazy with my mouth. You would not fight that?"

"Hardly."

"You would do that to me, also, *sí*?" She sat back. "So what's the difference?"

"With what?"

"*Pues*! You're not too bright! Between a man and a woman?"

"I wouldn't put my mouth on a man there."

"It's for both the same exit."

"You—you'd do it with another woman?"

"I haven't been asked. But I would. It's a job, like mending the street, driving a bus, being President."

"Men don't excite you?"

"When I was a girl that excited me, a man. After I've made enough money, I'll return to Andalucía, find a good husband. Perhaps then . . ."

"You have what age, Maria?"

"Eighteen."

"When did you come to Marseille?"

"It makes eight months. You are so old?"

"Twenty-seven."

"You're younger than I, *calentorro*."

"For Léon, there's nothing else I could do?"

"He's afraid—*Qué comico*!" She carried the wine bottle into the kitchen. "Listen—it's Léon. With someone."

Léon tweaked her ear as he came in. "Don't open the chain till you know who it is."

"I can tell your smell. From afar."

A thin, chestnut-haired girl, perhaps sixteen, stepped into the room behind Léon. She appraised Cohen and Maria, shook her hair back on her shoulders, and slipped off her black *imperméable*.

"This is my new *cocotte*, Thérèse," Léon smiled.

"We're not that busy," Maria said.

"Some of us aren't busy at all, are we, *chérie*," Leon countered. He turned to Thérèse. "Take off your clothes."

"Already you have had me. You saw nothing?"

"Take them off."

The girl gave Cohen an exasperated look. Her eyes were very large, pale brown, long-lashed. Her graceful mouth curved down. "*Zut!*" She unbuttoned her blouse, slid it from her shoulders. She wore no bra and her breasts were small and round as peaches, a tiny gold crucifix dancing in the satiny cleft between them. She stepped out of her red shoes, unhooked her skirt and let it swing free, slipped her thumbs under the hem of her silver panties, pulled them down, and tossed them to one side with her toe. She shook her hair forward till it fell to her belly like a glowing brown waterfall. "*Voilà*," she smiled. "Enough?"

"*Qué puta!*" Maria sneered. "She's too thin."

"Go over there, Thérèse," said Léon, pointing at Cohen.

She approached. Her sex smelled sweet and dark. Pink lips showed through her feathery vaginal hair.

"Let him try her," Léon said. "You, Little Flower, fifty francs for him." He bent and tucked a note in her pocketbook.

"She's too young," Cohen said.

"Make him happy, Thérèse," Léon said. "If you don't want to go back to Manosque."

"No." Cohen stood.

"My dear white knight," Léon whispered, "you need work? Huh? I'm trying you out. Don't muff it." He stepped into the hall. "I'm going to sleep. Watch them, Maria, see they do the job."

"If I can stay awake," she muttered.

Léon tossed blankets from the bedroom onto the floor. "Some of you'll have to sleep on these. In the morning, Maria, find her a place."

166

"There's a kindergarten in la rue d'Isoard."

"Be gentle, Maria. You were young once, too."

"Not such a skeleton as this."

"When you first came from your blessed Andalucía? I should've taken your picture."

Maria grinned at Cohen. "You were so quick to get it up? To yank out *la pistola*? Give this girl a chance."

"I can't just like that."

"You'd expect it of a whore."

Thérèse was unbuttoning his shirt, her eyes faraway. She stopped when she saw the wound, then pulled down his pants and began to kiss and lick at him.

He tucked her hair aside from her breasts. The little brown nipples were pliant; he played with them until they began to stand. Her hair tickled his stomach; he brought his hands down the curve of her waist to the widening of her hips. "Your skin's so soft, Thérèse."

"It's how *le bon Dieu* made me."

He slid his fingers across the chestnut down of her belly and along the insides of her thighs. Her skin was like scented silk, yet softer and warmer, damask but smoother. He could not keep his fingers from the crease between her thighs; gently he spread the matted hair and ran his fingers up and down it. She kneeled above him and swung her hair gently round and round his penis. She moved forward and nudged her crease against it, soothing the front of her lips along its tip, backing away as he tried to enter.

With one hand behind her thighs he lifted her so that he could move his tip back and forth along her crease, making the lips wetter and wetter, rubbing against the softness of her cleft. She sighed, biting her lip, as he eased her down upon him, and she began to move in gentle rising circles, urging her hips forward and back, letting him slowly further and further inside her until his tip forced open the second mouth deep within her and she winced with pain and drew upward.

"Hurry," he gasped, "I can't stop."

She pulled up and rotated round his tip, pushing him down each time he tried to drive into her, teasing him again with her crease, her schoolgirl's belly indenting with each thrust, her hair swinging like a veil across her breast and tangling in her gold crucifix, her eyes still faraway, until he came surging into her. She expelled a breath and moved aside. *"T'as un cigarette?"* she asked Maria.

"Non."

She turned to Cohen; he shook his head.

"Merde. Where does one piss?"

"Half way down the hall. Don't wake Léon."

"The way he screws he won't wake till Easter." Thérèse crossed the hall, her slim cheeks shadowed by the ceiling bulb.

"When I first met Léon," Maria yawned, "he did me four times in a row. Said I had promise."

"This was strange."

"It was to see she could do it, just like that."

Cohen stretched out on a rough blanket, Thérèse lying curled with her back to him, the second blanket over them, and slipped quickly down a long slope of fatigue into darkness.

He wakened as Thérèse stepped across him. "I've got a weak bladder," she said when she came back, a trickling toilet in the distance. "From sleeping on cold floors."

"I'm sorry about tonight."

She sniffed. "What for?"

"It wasn't much, forced like that."

"Life isn't always what you want." She began to snore.

He could not sleep. What if I fail—if all this horror comes to nothing? All these deaths drowned out, no one ever knowing? If I've been hunted so hard, how could Paul escape?

Morning sun splintered dusty windows; traffic filled the room with clatter and rumble. "Will you fuck me now?" Cohen asked Maria as they ate croissants with café au lait in a corner café.

"All you think about is fucking."

"You must have a boy friend."

"Léon doesn't favor it."

"You always do what he wants?"

"Of course." She raised one eyebrow. "He protects me from the cops, the syndicates."

"How does he protect you from the cops?"

"You don't know?" She wiped sugar from her mouth with the back of her hand. "They import the drugs and he distributes. Every-

168

body knows that." She gave him a girlish grin. "You're too curious."

"A stupid habit."

"A fatal one, with Léon."

"The cat in the proverb had nine lives but curiosity finally killed him. Once I was curious about a place few people ever see. As a result, seven of my friends died. One more lives, perhaps. I'm the ninth. All my troubles derive from curiosity."

"We don't have that proverb in Andalucía." She tossed back her head. "Yet you're fortunate."

"People tell me that."

"But you're such a virgin. Now you're feeling sad for yourself, caught up in yourself like a boy fucking for the first time. A virgin in life . . . as if nothing ever happened to you."

He leaned across the table, shouting over the roar of a bus. "Too much has happened to me."

"Pah! You are playing at poverty. When it becomes tiresome you can return to America, drive your car, have enough food. You know, in Andalucía my brother prays for no children, fearing they will hate him as he hates our father?"

"He hates him?"

"*Claro que sí!* For bringing him into the misery and hunger of Andalucía. When I was a small girl, *calentorro,* I begged in the marketplace on Wednesdays, or before the church on Sundays, sitting on the concrete while the well-dressed and pious stepped around my dirty little gypsy body like a rat squashed on the pavement."

"Perhaps I suffer from too little acquaintance with sorrow, you think?"

"Sorrow? Hah! Sorrow's a luxury. Even the rich have sorrow. I speak of when each day is so arduous that many can't survive it." She snatched his hand. "I'm not angry at you, *calentorro,* but angry when I think of those times." She held out her sweater with her fingertips. "Now look—I've clean clothes, food to eat." She fingered her glistening black hair, smiled, "No lice!" leaned forward, bracelets scrabbling the tabletop. "I don't have to walk everywhere but can take a bus! No one in my family's hungry anymore. Sí! For the first time in memory." She crossed her legs, bumping the table.

"And you make difficulties, when Léon wants to give you a chance."

He perused her fine, youthful features: her nose with the miniature concavity of its bridge, flaring below into the elegant curl of her nostril, her wideset Moorish eyes the color of fresh olives against her tea-colored skin, her glittering teeth, her serenely arched, raven brows, her ears sculpted like little conches under her sparkling hair, the elegant gypsy cast of her jaw which made her infinitely approachable and unconscionably mysterious. Her exquisite small mouth articulated words, he thought, as if they were grapes, as if searching for seeds.

"You don't listen," she said.

"You were detailing my good fortune."

"*Alors,* you will, or not?"

"Of course not."

"Why!"

He took her hand. "Maria, I'm grateful to sleep on your floor. In a day or two I must leave. When I was in Africa, I got hustled by a guy, and had to sleep out on the docks. That's when I got robbed, got knifed. Besides, the whole thing seems gross."

"Gross?" She giggled. "For me, when a client sticks his tongue in my ear, that's gross. I draw the line at that."

"Why?"

"I don't like the noise."

He watched her with appreciation. "You're innocent too, my sister of mercy."

She made a little moue. "Then we're both saved."

Her new apartment, on the Boulevard d'Athènes, was a wide building of cracked parapets and serpent gargoyles with laughing lion faces. Her casement window opened over the street, its sill calcified with pigeon droppings yellowed by rust from a broken gutter. The room was square, a carmine drape across the closet, a hunchbacked bed waiting sorely in the corner, a rusty sink on iron legs, a cold faucet, gray linoleum. Beyond a thin partition was Thérèse's, little different.

He leaned on the sill, smelling the traffic exhaust and sour fresh odor of the bakery on the corner of Boulevard de la Liberté. Below, a man tinkered on a worn Panhard; it sputtered with flat froglike noises. Oh to be away, away from everything. He jumped as Maria edged beside him. She nudged his elbow. "*Chouette*, what? Though tonight I give you some sous, and throw you out till two."

In midafternoon Thérèse brought home two tricks from the railroad station; he could hear them panting and wheezing over her through the wall. When they left he knocked on her door. She sat cross-legged, smoking, on the bed.

"*Ça va?*" he said.

"*Oui.* You think I can't handle two fat pharmacists from Arles?"

"I heard you cry out."

She held up a folded note. "Made me a ten-franc tip." She brushed ashes from her pubic hairs. "Men are so innocent."

"It sounded real."

She leaned back against the wall, knees apart. "I would have moaned more, but one was in my mouth."

"How does it taste?"

"Taste yourself. Like old milk, the kind a cat won't drink." She snickered. "It's not so romantic."

When dark fell he roamed the friendless streets. Nine more days. He hid in the back of a café, nursing his leg and a cheap cognac, gazing at the young and pleasure-seeking, the bodies hunting bodies, the red lips and smirking teeth.

Dance of life. A medieval painting, those men and women at the next table mere skeletons in animated conversation, one with a bony finger to her jaw, another casually caressing the femur of the cadaver beside her—their grinning skulls with gaping eyesockets and hard bright teeth glaring out of tongueless jaws. She in the short blue dress, her slim thighs peeping through, a white crack between them—she's a bony pelvis and a crooked, notched spine, her elegant legs naked cartilage. Embrace me, my darling, rattle thy osseous fingers round my ribs.

He withdrew to a cinema, not remembering the movie the second he left, something about lovers and car racing. Why isn't every movie about the bomb? Why doesn't it scream across every head-line of every paper in the world, every day? Day after day after month after year until not a single bomb is left? Why this solemn complicity, this lover's dalliance, with death? Are we too fearful of Kali even to speak her name? Isn't that the final cycle of despair, when we're too craven to defend life? Aren't we then already dead?

Then I'm no longer one of you—I'm another species, from another world. Perhaps you're right to be living so heedlessly, but you don't seem happy, you don't seem alive. With all my fears, my deadly knowledge, my foreboding—I'm more alive than you. Perhaps because of my fears, my knowledge. Because of my pact with Kali. Once I was dead, like you. Now I live.

He chanced ducking into a quiet bar called *La Caserne*. It was dim and near empty, *"L'amour est comme un jour"* on the juke box, two thin men dancing in an unlit corner, *"Ça s'en va, ça s'en va . . ."* The first stool was tippy; he tried another. "It's a test," the barman said. "The ones who try to sit there—I can tell they're new."

A boy sat on the next stool. *"Un whisky,* Maurice," he called. "It's not easy to come here," he said to Cohen.

"Oh?"

"It's a confession. The moment I decide, each step I take is resolved. It's not as if I were overcome, swept away by the force of it."

"What's wrong with deciding?"

"When it's conscious, it's different."

"Is it wrong, then?"

The boy turned up his hands. "Is anything wrong?"

Cohen pushed the base of his glass in little wet circles on the bar. "Only to kill, to cause sorrow—that's wrong."

The boy laughed. "Some parents would prefer their sons to be murderers than gay."

"At least a few folks," Cohen smiled, nodding goodbye, "get what they deserve."

Traffic had dwindled in the Rue de Rome: here and there a Citroën or Mercedes, sleek unreachable faces within them, faces shielded by glass, fine clothes, and fine opinions. In a jewelry store window a gold necklace hung on a manikin's truncated neck—its brightness so much more self-assured, more permanent, than life. A skinny cat miaowed at him from an unlit alley; he knelt calling to her but she would not approach.

172

Light shone beneath Maria's door. He waited a few minutes, then knocked. "*Mi calentorro,*" she grinned as she opened. Her room smelt warmly of wine and grass, the bed sweaty and rumpled. "What did you find?"

"It's lonely out there."

"*Sí?*"

"All those people trying to have fun. So lonely."

"That's why they stick together. I like loners, *los solitarios—* like you." She took a wine bottle from beside the bed. "Want some? A trick left it."

"It's *Nuits St. Georges.*"

"*Maldito sea!* It's not good like Spanish wine." She lit a joint and passed it to him. "Body and blood!"

The grass and wine brought him peace and an absence of sorrow. Her face seemed soft, naked of care. The smoke from the grass ascended round her face as a veil being removed. She tossed back her hair; darkness had gathered like mascara beneath her eyes.

"This work," he said, "you don't mind it?"

"It's a beginning."

"Of what?"

"I don't want to live like the others—no money, shitting babies, a man who thinks because he's male and works five days a week he has the right to a fuck every night, and three meals every day on the table." She stood yawning and began to unbutton her blouse. "I'm tired."

He watched her dusky belly under the unbuttoned blouse, his throat thickening. "You want to sleep alone?"

She dropped the blouse on the chair and hooked her thumbs into the waist of her skirt. "Seven times I got it tonight, one of them rough. I'm sore; I want nothing else to do with men." She tucked herself into the covers, opened her arms wide. "But lie with me, *mi calentorro.* Keep me warm."

He stretched beside her into the scanty, squeaking bed. Her body seemed long, yet with her toes against his ankles her head came only to his shoulder. "Soon, *mi calentorro,* I'll give you a good time."

"You've already saved my life, sister of mercy." He kissed her smooth forehead. "Nothing more do you ever need to give me."

She snuggled against him. "You have a sister?"

"I did. In a way."

"What's her name?"

"She's dead."

For a while Maria said nothing, then, "What was her name?"

"Kim." Feeling unutterably sorrowed, yet comforted by her nearness, he lay sharing with her the late-night silences of Marseille, in the little human island of her bed, while Lobo snored and farted peacefully on the floor beside them.

He awoke at ten with church bells pealing, flies buzzing on the window, sunlight rippling on the floor. The blue through the upper panes was merciless, untrammeled. She was gone; twenty francs were tucked into his pocket.

Sun gleamed on the café au lait and the sugary crusts of the croissants in the Café Voltaire. Feeling reckless, he blew two francs on *Le Méridional,* sun soaking him as he read it, laughing loud enough for the couple at the next table to peer at him.

"It's the comics," he explained, smiling.

The man patted his graying moustache with a paper napkin. "There are no comics on the front page, what?"

"Ah, monsieur," Cohen held up the newspaper, "there's Pompidou *et sa cocotte, la France*. . . . Nixon, a painted whore lying to his countrymen." He shook the paper. "Nothing here is real! The true world coils underneath, like a snake. This is comics."

The man snuffed a cigarette into his saucer. "Why read it, then?"

"I am like you, dear friend. I wish to laugh."

"Laugh, then." The man rose and put on a small black hat. He led the woman away.

Sunlight glissaded fiercely down the facades across la rue Lafayette. New leaves of the plane trees glittered like emeralds. Seven more days, baby. I'll make it. Sucking in gritty exhaust and swift sea air, the sour bread and sweet coffee fragrance of the streets, inhaling even the staccato of spike heels on the cracked pavements and the swishing hustle of auto rubber on cobblestone, he limped the greening streets. At the post office he sent a mailgram to Hassim, care of Les Champs Elysées, asking for news and promising that soon he could send him bail and passage to Marseille. Exhausted and dizzy, he returned to Maria's apartment and fell instantly asleep.

174

She woke him at dinner. "Time for your evening stroll, *mi calentorro.*"

He sat, stretching. "Each day I feel stronger."

She poked him. "Quick—out of bed! I have to use it soon. Lobo, come! Lick his face till he gets up!"

His wandering passed quickly. At two, he knocked on her door. "*Ça va?*" she asked.

"*Sí. Toi?*"

"An easy night. I made only three hundred." She handed him a wine bottle as he sat beside her on the bed. "One just wanted to look and beat off."

"Don't complain. Love me instead."

She wrinkled her nose. "I don't really want to."

He kissed the soft skin over her temple. "I'll owe it to you. With interest." He took her hand and kissed her fingers one by one. "Such a little hand, such slender fingers. Lend me the money and I'll pay you right away."

Lazily she stripped, tossing her clothes on the chair, and slipped into bed, watching him undress. "Come *mi calentorro,* come," she whispered, wrapping him in her arms, opening her legs, "not waiting, not stopping, not anything, ever, never. Come!"

Heedless, enraged, he drove into her like a bull, bent to lick her crotch; it was tart, metallic. "Don't," she said, "it's my time."

"I don't care." He raised her buttocks and drove into her anus, playing with her crack.

"Easy," she gasped. "I'll charge you double."

He pulled out and went into her again. She began to moan. "Don't fake it," he panted. She came, stiffening her back and sinking her nails into his ribs, the skin above her breast pulsing. They lay side by side, his head spinning.

She raised up, kissed him. "With you, *calentorro,* I do not fake. You aren't a client." She tickled his inert penis. "Look at *le petit,*" she smiled. "Who used to act so tall and proud."

175

16

"WAKE UP! It's Palm Sunday."

"So?"

"*So?* What kind of a question is that! It's time for church."

"I'm not Catholic anymore."

"Come, anyway. Even Jews need God."

He wriggled further down in the bed, ran a finger over her belly. "I'm not Jewish, either. Piss on both their houses."

She crossed her breasts, nipples wiggling. "Come, *mi novillero,* and listen to God!"

Day shone like ambergris through the tall cathedral windows. "Resplendent and unfading is Wisdom," intoned the priest. "She is readily perceived by those who love her, and found by those who seek her." Cool lavender light fell across the altar. Cohen changed position on the hard pew, his knee aching. "He who watches for her at dawn shall not be disappointed, for he shall find her sitting by his gate."

"But is it Wisdom," the priest continued in his homily, "when women work, leaving their young at home? Is it Wisdom that the young stay out late, using drugs, having illicit sex, laughing at their parents, at their Church? That which begins at home finishes in the streets, in sinful living, pornography, prostitution!"

Cohen nudged Maria. "You listening to this *merde?*"

"Silence!"

At communion she gripped his hand, stood. "Come!"

"You go," he snickered, "I haven't confessed."

"God knows your sins."

"And I know His." But he stood with her, wondering why, and walked beside her up the aisle, his head bowed, hands loosely folded before him, fighting the old feeling of an aching moment

176

approaching completeness. The soothing tones of the organ and the high soft voices of the children's choir, the silent lines of worshippers, the nearing drone of the priest, *"Le Corps de Dieu . . . Le Corps de Dieu,"* were all hypnotic. Lulling me into the old dance, the old psychosis. The death I escaped was certitude. Never believe. He stood before the priest.

The priest raised his bit of bread. "The Body of Christ."

"Amen." Wafer softening in his throat, he limped slowly away, light brightening around and above him, tears waiting behind his eyes, Maria's glistening black hair proceeding down the aisle before him. I have long been dead. It's so good to be alive. In this moment—though I'll deny it later—I *know* this *is* the body of Christ, that this *is* God, who is. Despite all. Despite all.

He slid along the pew to Maria. Her head was lowered, her hands clasped. Whatever you pray for, Maria, I pray for it also. To God, Jehovah, I pray that He take you into the strength and caring of His hands and protect you, sister of mercy. Protect you and always care for you.

Outside the cathedral, she squeezed his arm. "Don't blame God."

"What—for all that *merde* about sin and pornography? For that priest beating his meat about sex while the world's readying to blow itself up?"

"Silencio, mi calentorro! God's not responsible for what a stupid priest says. God has nothing to do with the Church."

"Why go, then?"

"To be with God, be fed by Him."

He kissed her forehead, smelling the rich earthiness of her hair. "God leaves me hungry."

"Because you don't live in the spirit—in the spirit of life. That's where the hunger for God comes from!" She took his arm, walking him away from the cathedral. "Today, *mi calentorro,* I would be in Andalucía—where there's much spirit."

"I too, though I've never been there."

"Oh!—It is mountains—mountains sharp as lion's teeth, soaring cliffs, the sea, the sea wind. The mountains are blue. The sky's blue. The sun's so fierce even the *los olivos* are blue. Oh!—I would be in the mountains today. There are some not far from here. Will you go with me? We'll take Léon's *bagnole.*"

It took a half hour to clear the suburbs. At Aix they turned east into the foothills of Mont Sainte Victoire. Bleak rocks and stunted pines chased along the road. "The sun's in my blood," she said. "In the mountains I'm closer to it, and am happy."

"You're not happy otherwise?"

"*Sí*, in a partial way. Like most humans. Look! The mountain has a cross atop it."

He snickered. "Today was the first time in years I've been to church."

"That's bad, *mi calentorro,* You should go every day, or at least once a week."

"If there is a God I don't think He even notices us."

"You care too much for being noticed. We owe God thanks for life itself. He owes us nothing, not even notice." She caressed the inside of his thigh. "God creates us to expand His life, to live a billion little lives in Him, expanding Him. If *we* choose not to live fully, as deeply as we can, it's no wonder God gets bored and forgets us!"

"For a whore, Maria, you are very philosophical."

"*Escucha, mi calentorro*—there's more religion in a good whorehouse than in the grandest churches of the world!"

They parked before a dam in whose chalky blue the white mountain rippled. She shouldered their lunch sack. "Hurry! I won't wait."

Blanched rock gleamed with heat; the mountain air glimmered like a halo. A hawk soared in porcelain heights. She ran ahead through green oak, wild pear, and pine woods, through fields of carmine poppies and red and yellow betony, then sat panting in the shade of a spreading hawthorne whose roots clutched the calciferous soil. *"Qu'est-ce que c'est, les Brigades Mobiles?"*

Cohen read the splintered sign nailed to an oak:

Ste. de beaureceuil
CHASSE GARDÉE
par les
BRIGADES MOBILES
de la FÉDÉRATION

"I don't know. It says no hunting; perhaps the *brigades* are a national guard."

"Piss on them and their guns. Here's mint! Smell it. How like Andalucía!"

"Is every beautiful thing like Andalucía?" Cohen caressed a slender purple thistle.

She jumped up. "Catch me if you can!"

On the peak a rusty cross shivered in the wind over undulating green and whitecapped mountains. The wind worried at them, snatching sleeves and yanking hair. They retreated eastward along the mountain's spine, white stegosaur backbones of limestone ridging up from green oak scrub, to a sunny bowl overlooking white-ribbed cliffs. Dark tufts of bush obtruded from the vertiginous rock face that plunged distantly down into oaks and pines falling away to white-bouldered basins.

She sat cross-legged against the round back of the cliff and opened the sack. "I've been thinking about your future."

"I have one, then?"

She passed the wine. "How's your wound?"

"Less sore."

"How quickly you heal."

"I've been happy, these few days."

"You're a curious one, *calentorro*. Arriving from outer space, refusing to speak of your past. Now, tomorrow you'll leave."

"And my future?"

"You could be safe here."

"Mountains are never safe." He flinched as rifle shots burst like ragged firecrackers in the canyons below. "The *Brigades Mobiles,* no doubt." He sank back into the cliff. "Shooting practice."

"In Marseille, you could be safe. You could carry drugs for Léon, work a ring of girls or boys on the Côte d'Azur, anything . . . Léon protects his own." She drank from the bottle and gave it to him. He nudged against her, his back to the rock. *"Un sandwich pâté,"* she said.

How funny, the simplest words sometimes have most meaning: food, woman, sun. The thin air magnified the red taste of the wine on his tongue, the sting of mustard.

"But you won't stay." She took a joint from her shirt pocket, lit it and passed it to him.

"I could return, some day."

"Why would you?"

"I like it here. I like you." He stretched out on the warm, blanched soil next to her, inhaling the denim odor of her blue cotton shirt. He kissed her neck where the collar opened.

"Are all Americans single-minded like you?" She tickled his cheek with her chin. "I could make a fortune over there." She kissed him tentatively, drew back. "I'm not comfortable." She rolled aside, slipped her fingers under his shirt and slid it up his chest, kissing him there. "It *is* better, your wound."

Lying under his kiss, she licked her tongue softly over his teeth, under his lip, ran fingernails down his neck. As he unbuttoned her shirt she lay back on her sable hair, eyes crinkled against the sun. "You'll come back?"

"To Sainte Victoire?"

"Don't tease me." Her body surging up was white softness in the sunlight, bright from the delft sky. Crushed scrub and limestone dust fused in his nostrils with her jasmine odors and the musk of her hair. There was no end to the deepness of her, or to the pressure of her slim channel that gripped him in its delicate, hot grasp, her thighs clenching his back. *"Dios,"* she moaned, *"Dios mío,"* her head twisting in the chalky dust.

They leaned together, overlooking the tumbled ruin of cliffs and green ridges. She drank from the bottle and red spilled on the pale inside of her thigh, against the black curls. *"Sangre de Toro,"* he said, wiping it away with his finger.

"Buena suerte," she answered. "In the *corrida,* it is always good luck when the bull's blood spills."

Lobo rose whining beside them; Cohen rubbed absentmindedly at his ruff. The world felt in place again. The jumbled landscape of lilting blues, emeralds, aquamarines, and limestone was tranquil, unthreatening. It's true, I'm sorry to be leaving. "Caring," he said, "what a difference it makes."

Her ribs touched his elbow as she inhaled. I will always love this one, he thought, for who she is. It's not romantic, love. What matters is not being loved but loving, a gift that in giving we get. A cool breeze played with her hair against his cheek and baptized their nakedness in thyme, juniper, and aphyllanthe. A red-roofed castle in a far green valley wavered in the heat. Swallows burst from the ridge below and blew past them, chittering. Lobo whimpered. "He wants to play," she said.

Cohen pulled loose a sharp bright pebble that had poked into his knee. It was the color of the Mediterranean, a pool of hardened color reflecting a miniature sun. "It makes the sun far away." He showed her the tiny reflection.

"But the sun *is* far away," she remonstrated.

"It is not of Sainte Victoire, this rock."

"It is *el jade*. I do not know the word in French."

"The same." She leaped forward to grab it as it slipped between his fingers. Her head exploded, her body smashing into him, her blood and brains spattering him. A second bullet smacked above his head and screamed stinging away like a hornet at the mountain. He hugged her, screaming, "Jesus, Jesus, Jesus!" Blood was pouring down his face and over his arms. A bullet knocked white splinters into his eyes. On his stomach he squirmed over her body to the far side of the bowl. Maria's crushed head spun before his eyes. They were making love but she had no head. Pebbles rattled downslope. Lobo crouched snarling beside her.

He leapt into space, air rushing between his naked thighs, skidded down the cliff, jammed his feet in a crease. Emptiness below. He grabbed a shrub rooted in the cliff. Its bark was peeling: umber on the outside, lizard yellow beneath. "Jesus! Stop! Oh Jesus Jesus Jesus . . ."

Pulse thundered in his temples. Releasing the shrub he scrambled along the crease, his hand feeling blindly overhead for another hold. The crease ended at a vertical fracture. Ten feet farther it resumed, following the cliff's curve out of sight. He could see nothing; with one hand he wiped the blood and tears from his eyes.

Lobo snarled. He glanced up, losing his grip, the cliff yawing. He clawed a fingernail's hold in the rock and looked down, the rockface undercurving, vanishing between his naked legs.

Stones crackled on a talus slope below and to the right. He backed up to the shrub, sprinted for the gap in the crease but stopped at its edge, scattering pebbles that faded, tiny and white, dipping back and forth till lost in the rippling void. Stones rained around him. He sprinted, ignoring the emptiness and the sharp wham that spattered the crease between his feet. Again the rifle fired. His foot bounced off the far side, his fingers caught. The crease broke away like cake, chunks of it hitting his knee. Bullet splinters whined past his face. Nothing underfoot, one hand clutching pebbles. He grabbed a hold, dragged himself two handholds further, groin scraping the rock. A voice yelled in the bowl, Lobo snarling. A different gun fired. Lobo squealed. Dangling in emptiness he swung hand over hand along the crease. The crease widened, his fingertips no longer bumping the cliff behind it.

A bullet sucked at his head. He hauled himself onto the crease and ducked round the bulge of the cliff. An overhung chute blocked his path; below it was space. The chute was streaked with water; grass grew in cracks along its edges. Beyond it the cliff was straight down and smooth. Voices came from above and below. Under the overhang the rock was dark. They were making love but she had no head.

He stepped into the emptiness of the chute. The sole of his left foot against the wet rock at the far side of the chute, he leaned out and planted the fingers of his left hand. Sliding his right foot to the near edge he slowly increased his left hand pressure on the far slimy wall of the chute, pushed his right hand against the slick near wall, swung his right foot into the chute, and hung facing outward over the void, supported by the pressure of his palms and naked toes against the slippery vertical rock.

Voices rattled off the rocks. Ignoring them he inched backward up the chute, one pressure point at a time. The wet rock smelled stagnant and glistened with algae. His thighs trembled. Footsteps closed in along the ledge. Climbing faster, he slipped, pushed out frantically. He was down where he had begun, toes and hands skinned and rubbery. His knees would not stop shivering.

A thousand feet under his groin the foothills began to dip and swim. Steps halted at the gap in the ledge, around the cliff from the chute. *"Ist er abgestuerzt?"* yelled a voice.

"Vielleicht," answered another from below.

The overhang was near. He jammed himself against the chute, slipping, the lip of the hole above and behind his head, glanced at the tiny ridges a thousand feet below. Plenty of time to think before I hit.

He spun in empty air and scrabbled for a hold on the slippery stone, fingertips skidding down. Tearing with his nails he pulled one arm above the lip then the other and swung himself up into the hole, twisted round to stare down the chute past the glissading rock, below the vast, aching space to the rolling tiny panorama of forest and hills.

The voice came frequently now from the ledge, answering questions poised from below. He slid further up the hole, cradled himself shivering and fetallike into a crevice of icy stone, head on his arms, his cheek wet from the sour, calcifying seep. "Oh my God," he begged. "What have I done?"

The voices dimmed, returned, moved away again. The wind rose, quickening the faraway tree canopy, agitating the grasses that clung to the chute. The sun fell to the bony hills, bleeding red-brown down their slopes and carmine on their peaks.

17

S⊤OP NOW. JESUS I will. Every move causes more horror. Stay here, let them come to me. Finish it.

Down the chute dark sickening emptiness. In Athens once I almost jumped, from a roof, but it wasn't far enough to kill. Not for sure. A warm feeling it gave, though, the thought of death. That's what the bomb does—makes horror seem normal. Numbing. Don't let it.

Maria, to bring you back I'd die a thousand tortured deaths. Each step I murder the innocent. Phu Dorje, Seral, Kim. Captain Andrev—what's happened to you now? Everyone I touch turns to clay. I'd be so happy now to jump into this darkness, but I can't leave you, Paul. Not till I know for sure you're dead. Seven days more. Trapped here now. In this mountain.

He edged downward to the lip of the hole. The trickle of water had frozen in the shadowed chute. No sound from them lately. But now with ice in the chute I can't chimney down. Trapped here till the sun melts this ice. Tomorrow midmorning. By then they'll have finished searching below the cliff for my body, will be looking here again. I'm trapped.

Cold as the tomb. He rubbed his feet; they were too numb to tingle. His shoulder was immovable with pain; an icy, feverish sweat dribbled from his forehead.

He squirmed up the hole, bumping his head in the blackness. The hole seemed to end in a vertical slit between two parallel planes of rock poised directly above the chute. Reaching in darkness for the cold slippery edges of these planes, he swung under the slit, feet hanging over nothingness. Come down, called the darkness.

Exploding sound and dark forms beating his face, whirring wings and whistling, scratching claws, his fingers skidding, darkness sucking him down. Spinning by two frozen fingers as the bats clattered past shrieking and battering their wings on the icy rock, he

184

held gasping, expecting the weightless moment of fall as his other hand scrabbled uselessly at the fissureless stone, his legs pinwheeling wildly. The two fingers weakened; he reached out with his toes for the side of the hole but could not reach it. Feeling the rock like a blind man he found a hair-thin seam and steadily raised his foot till his toes were planted against it, then forced himself up till his shoulders jammed against the slit. It was too small; his toes slipped from the seam and there was no other handhold, his feet kicking frantically, touching nothing, fingers skating down, snagged on one side of the slit and he pitched dangling.

No terror to die. Any moment. Let go this hold. All it takes. I won't. Don't look down. Move one finger. Feel for a grip. Oh God my shoulder. Here a crack. Fingernail in. Second fingernail. No room.

Other hand now. Forget the shoulder. Lift. An inch. Another. Keep going. Oh God the pain. Here a little bump. Slippery. Hold. Slipping. Other hand quick up an inch. Why am I doing this? Dead—nothing lost.

New crack. Get in one fingertip. Hang. Other hand. Oh Maria. No grip here. Higher. Still nothing. Finger dying with pain. Shoulder jamming. Force it. Here a seam, handhold. Up and in. Sideways— don't jam. Gasping and shivering he waited ten seconds, rock constricting him on all sides, darkness total, the mountain icy on his stomach and heavy on his back. Made it—but to where? Oh Maria. The slit had the odor of old roof drain, of trash left to rot in the snow.

Higher. Twist. Feet touching now. Push, toes. New hold. Pull. For you, Maria. For you, Paul.

The slit tilted from vertical, narrowing to a glacial funnel with a rippling, rifled bore. For several hours he forced himself up this tube, stopping constantly to gasp for breath, never able to fill his lungs against the pressure of the rock encasing his chest. A coffin, a tomb. "This is what it'll feel like," he reminded himself. "Forever."

The funnel narrowed, jamming his shoulders; he beat it with his fist, jammed one shoulder through, then could not back up. He rested, licking water from the stone. A week of hunger and I can get through. Don't have a week. Again and again he drove against the scaly stone, twisting and wrenching his body through the distortions imposed by the funnel, wriggling finally into a chamber smaller than a car trunk. Icy air entered from a crack in the ceiling.

It seemed this crack opened on another narrow space between parallel walls of rock. He thrust his head through it, then one arm and shoulder, waited to catch his breath, and wedged up it for another hundred feet until it tightened.

The rock had a mica, mossy taste. His thighs and stomach were scraped raw, wooden with cold. Forcing the air from his lungs, he rammed himself through the crack into a slightly larger chamber. Here the draft was stronger, falling on his neck from a gap at the top. The draft was chill and tasted wet. His fingernails slipped, he crashed down to the floor of the chamber. He felt round the chamber but could find no other draft, no other exit.

The gap was barely larger than his head, the ceiling four inches thick. His fingers found a seam in the floor. Clawing away the dirt, he dug out a chunk of limestone and hammered it left-handed against the gap.

The limestone crumbled. He found another and smashed it to bits on the gap. But the edges of the gap also were crumbling. After an hour he had used up all the chunks in the floor and began to pummel the gap with the side of his fist. It gave way and he elbowed up and into another round room, this one taller, again ventilated by a hole in the ceiling through which he corkscrewed into a perpendicular chimney. After an endless time of working his way up this chimney he was shocked to see the faint outline of his hand on the rock. With a snarl and flailing claws a dark cold hard body thudded into him and he smashed it away in terror, slipping down the chimney away from its weasel's rancid odor, its nails slashing his frozen skin, and it turned and scrambled upward into the silence, leaving him swearing and shivering. Badger. Goddamn badger. Means there should be an exit. Where are you, badger? He inched forward; there was no sound but a distant hissing.

The chimney was lightening but closing in. His head caught sideways. He reached up for a handhold and found nothing, wind and wetness flitting through his fingers. His head was free. He saw a shallow valley blanketed by snow; stars glittered overhead. The wind smelled of new grass and snow.

Orion lay on his side like a dying warrior; from his position over the horizon there seemed perhaps three hours to dawn. Cohen twisted his body from the chimney and ran through shin-deep snow to the edge of the valley. The white summits of Mont Sainte Victoire undulated westward. Above the horizon, under Orion's dagger, rose the crucifix.

Frozen-footed and shivering, he loped along the ridge to the crucifix. From it the mountain tumbled down, shimmering cliffs under star-bright snow. The red-yellow glint of a fire flickered among boulders on a saddle five hundred feet below.

He stumbled numbly down over slippery rock toward the wind-fitful fire, halting when he saw two men hunched in its light. One crossed the fire's gleam and began to climb toward him. Cohen wriggled into a snowbank; the man yanked a dead juniper from the snow and returned to the fire. His tracks left shadows in the snow; other such shadows fanned out from the fire across the saddle.

The man broke up the juniper and cast part in the fire, crouched on his heels before it. Cohen dug a hatchet-shaped rock from the snow. Masking his naked darkness behind boulders and brush he inched closer. The juniper's snapping boughs threw flaring shadows on the snow and reddened the crouching man's face. The other man, his back to Cohen, did not move.

There was no sign of others. The crouching man stood several times, turning his back to the fire, slapping his hands on his thighs. Cohen beat his frostbitten feet and legs, crawled back up the slope, turned north and down the ridge, switching eastward again to pass below the saddle. Downhill from the fire he ascended the ridge. Firelight licked the boulder tops. Windblown snow needled his groin.

In a sudden scrunch of snow a man was on him. Cohen leaped aside and smashed the rock into his face. The man spun grunting; he slammed the rock against his head, fell on him holding his mouth, the man trying to scream as Cohen pounded his temple with the rock, then hammered the rock against his spine at the neck until the man shivered and lay still. He stood silently, looked round, then bent down to beat the stone against the man's temple until a wide badge of blood blackened the snow.

Shivering uncontrollably, he tugged the man's jacket and trousers free and yanked them on. Again he peered toward the fire, ducked down, and tore off the man's shoes and socks. He looked at the corpse. "The least of my brothers." He moved to smash the corpse's gaping teeth but restrained himself, fearing the noise.

In the man's pockets were several cartridge cases, a wallet, passport, and a pocketknife. He opened the knife and crawled toward the fire. The crouching man was gone; the hunched figure had not moved. Was the crouching man the one now lying dead in the snow? Or was the dead man a sentry, and the crouching one circling now in the darkness, coming up behind?

He circled quickly to the ridge above the fire. The stars were slipping from sight, the wind failing. New tracks led away from the fire to the lower end of the saddle. The hunched figure stood, extended his hands and stretched, staring downhill toward the new footprints. Cohen ducked behind a boulder. The man brushed at his shoulders, rubbed the back of his neck, picked up a rifle. Cohen's ankle wedged between two boulders; he squatted to free it and the knife vanished through the snow. Snow stinging his wrist, he felt under the snow between the rocks, the man six feet away and starting to turn.

He found the knife and stood; it was not the knife but a sliver of rock in his wooden fingers and he ducked down, the man still turning, profiled against the firelit snow. The man raised the rifle, opened and closed the bolt. The knife was stuck under the rocks; when Cohen grabbed it, his clenched hand was too large to pull free. It fell again, his fingers too numb to find it. The man cleared his throat. Cohen found the knife and dove on his back, spun him backward and jabbed the knife against his throat as he dropped the rifle and grabbed Cohen's arm, squirming forward. Cohen kneed him in the back and lifted him off the ground, drove the blade deeper. "Want to die?"

The man's feet skidded under the snow. Cohen twisted the knife. The man screamed into Cohen's hand, biting his fingers. Cohen tightened his hold and lessened pressure on the knife. He felt warmth, realized his hand was wet with blood. "Where are the others?"

"Was?"

"Les autres—où sont-ils?"

"Nicht spreche."

Cohen lifted the knife to an eye and pushed. The man moaned. "Tell me," Cohen said, "or I'll kill you."

"You kill, no matter what."

"You're not the one I want."

"Who you want?"

"Your boss."

"I not know."

"Who else's here?"

"No one."

Cohen twitched the knife; the man gasped. "Don't lie," Cohen said. "Who else's here?"

"Just Dieter. He by cliff."

Cohen touched the blade to the other eye. "Don't learn, do you?"

"I not know where."

"Where was he?"

"Here, at fire."

"How many?"

"Just us. No time for others."

"Where are they?"

"Who?"

"The others."

"Aix-en-Provence."

"Where?"

"I not . . . No!"

"Where?"

"Hotel Metropole."

"How many there?"

"One."

"Who?"

"Mort."

"Who?"

"The fat man. You kill me now?"

"I won't kill you if you talk."

"Yes. You kill."

"You talk, I'll let you go. I swear to Virgin Mary." Cohen lowered the knife to the throat.

The man relaxed slightly. "You swear by Virgin? You Catholic?"

"Yes. Why'd you shoot at us?"

"Oh, dat was Dieter."

"Where's Dieter?"

"He gone, I not know. He supposed to be here, at fire."

"How many, yesterday?"

"Just Dieter, who shoot, and me."

"Why'd he shoot?"

"Mort say follow you. You leave in car from Marseille. We follow. Call Mort from dam. He say he coming Aix. He say shoot if you go away."

"Who told him about me?"

"He hear from Oran. Then he talk to man in Marseille."

"Who?"

"The Corsican."

"Why?"

"Why what?"

"Why kill us?"

"Mort say, ten thousand marks. Just to kill, that is a lot." The man tried to shrug but Cohen held him tight.

"Did you ask why?" Cohen repeated.

"Mort never say why."

"Who do you work for?"

"Like I say, Mort."

"Always?"

"I work the drug, here to Köln. No harm. No harm to anyone."

"What drug?"

"From Stamboul."

"What kind?"

"Hash, only."

"Heroin?"

"Oh, that, never."

"Who's Mort?"

"Like I say, fat man. American. I not know other name."

"Where's he now?"

"Like I say, Hotel Metropole." The man was shivering now in his own blood.

"Who killed Maria?"

"*Was?* Maria?"

"The girl, yesterday."

"Oh, dat was Dieter. He aim for you but she jump in front."

"You killed the dog, then."

"Dat was Dieter, too."

"It was different guns."

The man thought. "I must kill dog. He was bitting me. I sorry."

Cohen thought back to Nepal, the beginning. "Who's Stihl?"

"I not know that name."

"Claire? Claire Savitch?"

"Sorry. I not know." The man waited. "You kill me now?"

"I kill you now," Cohen mimicked as he drove the knife home, twisting into the jugular while the man writhed and squealed. He stood and spat into the snow. I become like you. Executioner and victim. Catholic and Jew.

From the body he took a passport, wallet, box of cartridges, and car keys. In the snow nearby he found Dieter's rifle and threw

190

the bolt over the cliff. He checked the magazine of the scoped custom Mannlicher carbine the second man had dropped, loaded an extra clip, and climbed quickly back up the mountain to the bowl.

Snow had covered everything; it took time in the still-dim light to find Maria's frozen, abbreviated corpse beneath its white blanket. Her legs were bent and immovable; her shattered head was locked in a neck-broken, sideways lilt. He dropped the Mannlicher and brushed away the snow but there was no face left to see. He clutched her to him, her hard limbs askew, his tears making small dark spots in the frost on her breast. Tripping over Lobo's stony body, he moved her against the edge of the bowl, dug his own clothes, shoes, and glasses from under the snow and put them on, keeping Dieter's jacket but throwing Dieter's other clothes over the cliff. With a final glance at the ridges and peaks now dusted with day's pink light, he ran down the trail.

Léon's Fiat would not start. He yanked open the hood. The plug wires were cut, the distributor cap smashed. He mounted a boulder and scanned the road from the dam. Two hundred yards below, under oak boughs, gleamed a red door tinged with snow.

It was an Alfa with Rome plates. The dead German's keys opened the door and fit the ignition, but there was no key socket for the trunk. He hesitated, not wanting the Mannlicher to be visible. Finally he dropped it on the jump seat with Dieter's jacket over it, backed the low-slung Alfa into the road and drove to the Fiat. Shivering as much with fear as cold, he switched licence plates and accelerated toward Aix. A black Citroën bobbed over the next rise. Its nose dipped as it braked; its headlights blinked. He fumbled for the headlight switch. The Citroën neared, pulling over.

A man was getting out of the Citroën. He was huge and raised a thick arm in salute. Cohen downshifted and accelerated at him.

The fat man bounded onto the Citroën's roof yanking a gun from his coat. It banged in Cohen's ear and the passenger window shattered outward. It banged twice more, and then he was beyond the rise and out of range, the Alfa slewing, its steering wheel chattering to the whup whup of the punctured left front tire.

He slid the Alfa across a curve, grabbed the Mannlicher and leaped a rock wall into the oak trees. The Citroën roared over the rise and skidded to a stop. Cohen had it blurred in the cross hairs and flipped off the safety.

The man was big as a bear as he danced for the far roadside.

Cohen fired. The barrel leaped and as it came down the fat man was gone into the trees. Cohen fired again, the bullet sang through the oaks. He sprinted across the road and ducked under wide boughs. There was little snow; leaves crunched underfoot.

He was panting. Birdsong filtered flutelike through the clear air. A scratch of bark as a pygmy thrush skipped down a trunk. Far whistle like a train. Touch of a falling leaf, dipping down like a flat stone under water. He dropped the scope to three power. Wind chafed the leaves. He had to sneeze, held it. It came again and he turned his head, choking it in. The fat man was running up the road, dove behind a tree. A crow laughed; another answered. Cohen tightened the sling over his elbow and held the cross hairs on the near side of the tree. He's the one I saw in Sitea, sending out the dogs, the one from the Mercedes. The German called him Mort. A leaf snapped; sun glared on the road. Cohen squinted. He's got me facing the sun.

He fired, twisted and ran head down into the oaks, back aching with expectancy. He stopped, holding his breath to listen, tried to picture himself in Mort's eyes. I missed the first easy shot. Mort'll think I'm scared, expect me to run. Have to wound him, capture him, make him talk. How soon will others come?

Pines sloped southward into a green oak valley. In its cleft a brook and black stones glimmered among tall flaming clematis and creamy poplars. Above the clematis towered a single pine, its bark crusted with age, its far-flung branches weighted down with cones.

He leaped the brook and bolted for the clematis, pushing through them to the pine. Its bark was tangy with pitch and the dry smell of warming needles. He climbed out of easy pistol range, straddled a bough, and ran the scope over the opalescent leaves of the clematis, the poplar trunks, the wider, duskier spaces between the uphill oaks and hawthornes. To the north, the road flashed beyond a gap in the trees.

Mort was running up the stream, steps muffled by flowing water. His bald head gleamed; his brown suit was rumpled. Cohen lowered the cross hairs on him; he was gone behind an outstretched oak. He reappeared uphill, above the clematis. Cohen waited for a leg shot at the crest. Sweat stung his eye, fogging the scope. How soon will others come?

Mort darted into the clematis. Cohen yanked down the barrel. A screen of leaves filled the scope. Mort was edging into pistol range, beneath the cover of clematis and poplar leaves. Cohen checked the breech. Two shots left. He reached into his pocket for the second clip; it was gone. Swearing, he checked his other pockets, glanced at the ground below the tree.

A twig leaped up, a sparrow flashed away. He scoped the spot, first three power, then four, then six, stretched out the bough, leaning the Mannlicher through its prickly needles. With intentness but without direction, he let his gaze find its own way through the kaleidoscope of leaves and stems. In the corner of his eye a blink of color, green to brown, under the crisscrossed branches. At six power, flies danced like points of light above the leaf carpet but the flicker of brown was gone.

Closer he found it again. He followed the direction of its movement even nearer to a clearer spot in the interlocking clematis. A cuckoo called, downhill. Pink flashed across the scope. He came back to it, lost it, cranked down to three power, found it. It was pale with black atop it, moving away under the green and scarlet. It stopped.

It was the finger of a hand, wrapped around a clematis stem. The black was a stone set in gold. The other fingers were invisible. The hand came round the stem and he saw there were no other fingers, only stumps. The hand vanished. He leaned over the pine bough and located a hole in the foliage ahead of the ringed finger. The cuckoo called. His pulse tolled. Car sound on the road, slowing. But now Mort's too close; I can't descend. The car picked up speed and continued along the road.

Darkness edged beneath the clematis stems. He found its center and slowly, very slowly, squeezed the trigger. The Mannlicher's great boom shattered the silence, tearing him back on his bough, smashing to pieces in the hills. The clematis crashed and were silent. Two crows were cawing hurriedly as rumbling echoes died beyond Sainte Victoire. He bolted the last round home. At their upper edge the clematis rustled. He aimed at a flux in one stalk and fired. A brown rabbit zigzagged uphill into the oaks. He shinnied down the pine and broke for the oaks, gained the crest and bolted over crackling leaves to the road.

18

HE DASHED PAST THE Citroën and grabbed the box of cartridges from the Alfa, darted back into the oaks, and reloaded the Mannlicher. Skirting the brook he scoped the clematis, crawled downslope. Muddy tracks spattered with blood led downhill into a bramble thicket; cautiously he edged toward them. From the road came the quick whirr of the Citroën's starter; he jumped up and sprinted toward it, its engine roaring now, but the Citroën was gone when he reached the road, a spot of blood shiny in morning sunlight on the gravel shoulder.

He tossed the Mannlicher into the rear of the Alfa. The tire was torn to shreds. Another car made him duck into the trees, but it was only a Renault 4 *camionette,* an old man driving. Again Cohen yanked at the Alfa's trunk but it would not budge. He jumped in and, clenching the steering wheel, drove as fast as he dared, the front wheel chattering. After a kilometer he turned up a farm road and killed the engine.

The trunk latch was nonexistent. He strained at the lid, but it would not raise. He tried the back seat; it would not move. A toggle switch with a key slot was set into the back of the driver's door jamb; he inserted one of Dieter's keys and the trunk lid sprang up. Beneath two leatherette suitcases were the spare tire and jack.

At a café on the outskirts of Aix he washed the mud and Maria's dried blood from his face, ate, and asked the way to the Hotel Metropole. The waiter tipped aside his tray to peer at him. "There's not one, Monsieur."

"There must be . . . If not, a Metropolitain, perhaps?"

"Nothing like that. It's not the Roy René?"

"I'm mistaken," Cohen said brusquely, standing to toss several of Dieter's francs on the table. I should have got him alive, should have waited. He parked the Alfa in a sedate street of budding plane trees backed by high residential walls, rolled down the shattered

window, put the suitcases on the back seat, and locked the Mannlicher in the trunk. With the keys he gouged "*A bas les riches*," in
the deep cherry paint of the hood. On the trunk he scratched "*Vive
la P. C.,*" and drove downtown.

Near the railroad station he found a nondescript, under-
patronized body shop. "Can you fix this?" he fumed angrily at the
freckled, square-jawed foreman, pointing at the trunk and hood.

"It's my job, is it not?" the man replied, wiping stained hands
on a rag.

"That was my hope."

"What is hope but nourishment for fools, poison to the wise? I
don't like them either, *les Communistes.*"

"The window's broken, too."

"That I'd have to sub out." The foreman scratched on a pad.
"Twelve fifty, including the window."

"The paint'll match?"

The man licked a finger and rubbed it on the hood. "This here,
has oxidized, and'll clash with the new." He fondled his jaw. "Of
course, we'll try to fade it in."

"To do the whole car, how much?"

"The same color, Monsieur?"

"My girl doesn't like this color. She wants silver."

"Women are like that—it's the most expensive. Why not white
or gray? That'd be eighteen hundred, the silver twenty-one."

"And black?"

"Same as white."

"Black, then. How soon?"

"Three days, rush."

"I need it tomorrow."

"For nineteen hundred, five o'clock tomorrow."

He gave the foreman the ignition key only, and found a room near
the railroad station where he searched the two suitcases, finding
nothing but French and Italian clothes and toiletries. At the station
he obtained a map showing all the hotels in Aix. By midafternoon
he had learned that none had a present or recent client matching
Mort's description.

He entered the shadowy coolness of the cathedral and crossed
to the cloister. On the cloister's far side, a door opened to a stair-

way that he mounted to a window giving on the crypt roof. He climbed through the window and up slippery orange tiles to the nave wall, then up a narrow ladder to the roof, up its steep slope and forward on the ridge to a square bell tower guarded by gargoyles. From a narrow stone walkway at the base of the tower he had a good view of the town, yet felt unseen. In the warmth of the sun on the yellow stone he soon fell asleep.

Bells boomed around him at four and again at five. He sat up and rubbed his face. People flocked far below in la rue Gaston de Sapporta like toy soldiers going in and out the doors of the cathedral. What are you looking for? None of the toy soldiers raised its tiny head to answer. He remembered the Algerian colonel's words: "After what I've seen, how could I believe in God?" and Claire's: "A jealous and sexually frustrated one at that." Yes, God of the Bible says do what I say, not what I do, says to forgive, yet He tallies everything and waits. But even more fearful than the vengeance of God is the vengeance of man.

In his pockets, over five thousand marks and seven hundred francs from the suitcases, and nearly another two hundred francs from the wallets of Dieter and his accomplice. He dined mechanically in an obscure café and returned to his room, searching the suitcases again, without result. He woke at dawn, feverish and unrested. After another unproductive round of Aix's hotels, he sat disconsolate in the garden of the Hotel des Thermes. Birds warbled in the trees; beyond the garden's thick and ancient walls the city thrummed like a hive.

With a snicker he remembered Claire's joke—"No good deed goes unpunished." In the moonwashed Parthenon it had been a funny taste of truth twisted from a mouthful of rhetoric. Like the bomb, a brilliant discovery, Nobel Prizes for absent-minded professors, the prize-winning discovery soon to kill us all. Like my mailgram offering help to Hassim, that killed Maria. What a murderous fool I've been. I think I'm learning, but I'm always way behind.

They traced me to Oran and Les Champs Elysées; therefore they found Captain Andrev. Or did they simply check all major ports? Is Andrev dead, too, and the Algerian colonel? For how much did Léon sell me?

Put myself in my enemies' shoes. They've lost me; what'll they do? He motioned to the waiter for another espresso. Knowing what they know, they'll simply wait for me to come to them. But soon I might meet Paul; soon we might reveal them. Five days till Easter. Will you be there, Paul? But if you're not dead, why did Mort tell the Germans to shoot?

Three weeks of running and I still don't know who's chasing me. Who's killed my friends. Yes, it's the CIA: Mort, Claire, Stihl, Eliott. But *who* are they?

Can I reveal them? They'll say I did it all. Was this the only bomb the CIA's run into Tibet? Or are there other nuclear bombs in Tibet right now? Have they been smuggled into China? Ready to go off? If so, what's the CIA waiting for?

Weird to be hunted by my own government. When I did nothing. Would I give up now, if they called it off? Would I? Would I forget the CIA and Stihl and the others who've killed people I love—innocent people? I don't think so.

Today's Tuesday. Five days. If Paul gets to Paris we can reveal it together. Who'll believe us? How long will we live, once we open our mouths? And if Paul doesn't come?

All I have is questions. If Paul doesn't come—if he's dead—I'll go to New York, try Fulton Street. In the meantime, I'll try to track Mort down, here in Aix. Until it's time for Paris.

Why? Because I'm a dead man kept alive by artificial means. Vengeance is my life support system. A breeze stirred the hairs on his wrist. Of all of them, I hate Claire the most, but it's really myself I hate, my babyish trustfulness, the incomprehensible naiveté by which I allowed her to trap me. If it hadn't been for the goat man . . . By such anguish do we become wise? If so, it's not worth the price, this cant of wisdom through the generations. How much better to sit in warm grass by a trout stream, without dread or guilt.

What Hem said, squinting one-eyed through the cyclone fence at Pokhara airport: "Cease to be the person they seek." Cohen smiled and stood, laying coins on the table. "Thank you, Dieter," he said, "for lunch." A woman at the next table stared at him, fingertipping short curls. He winked at her. She faced her plate. Further along the Cours Sextius he entered a beauty shop. The beautician, a short, anxious man, peered at him. "I have a problem," Cohen said.

"Monsieur isn't unique in that respect."

"My girl doesn't like me as I am."

"People rarely want what they have. What's new about that? Without it, where would I be?"

"She says she can only love men who are blond."

"There's no shortage; she should soon be happy."

"Perhaps. But I want her to love me."

"That's something else." The beautician bleached Cohen's hair and coiled it in hot rollers. "You'll be irresistible."

"I think it makes him highly resistible," muttered a graying lady waiting her turn with a magazine over her knee.

"As you know, dear Madame," Cohen answered, "passion has no bounds. Or why come here, covering your gray?"

"When I look younger, I feel younger. When I feel younger, I live longer. You've no need for such concerns."

"Ah, but each of us has the same concern," the beautician said, "to uncover what's inside."

"And men?"

"They're more vain, want what they cannot have. *Par exemple,* only two days ago one man came in, wanted a haircut, was most emphatic, in fact. But he had no hair."

Cohen shrugged. "Can't cut what doesn't exist."

"There were but a few strands, falling away, here." The beautician touched Cohen's temples. "Yet this man—a great fat American he was—inspected every hair I cut."

"The less there is, the greater its value?"

"If that is so, why are kindness and generosity so unrevered?"

"He was of what size, this American?"

"Truly huge. Though not soft for being large, but hard . . ."

"Where does he stay?"

"At the Hotel des Thermes."

"And his name?"

"That I don't know. But my wife, who works there, cleans his room." The beautician broke off to speak to a short, glaring woman who now entered. "Ah, Madame Petrach, as you can see, I'll soon be free."

The woman glowered at Cohen. "My appointment's for one."

The beautician nodded at the clock. "It lacks that by twenty minutes."

198

"You shall not be done."

"Most assuredly I shall. This gentleman's finished. The lady, I believe, requires but a rinse?"

"*Exactement.*" The graying lady began to fold her magazine.

Cohen paid the beautician. "This American, what's his room?"

"I'm not the desk clerk." The beautician banged the cash register closed. "I'm quite busy. It won't be long, Madame Petrach."

"I think I know him," Cohen persevered. "He's still here?"

"The Mirabeau Suite. Madame?"

In a men's store he bought and changed into blue jeans, blue shirt, tan corduroy jacket, and new running shoes. He stuffed Dieter's jacket and his old clothes, including the embroidered shirt from Athens, into a trash can and entered the Hotel des Thermes by the back door.

His hands were sweaty inside his pockets as he eyed the door of the Mirabeau Suite from the end of the second floor corridor. In a mirror across the corridor a blond, curly-haired man in tightcut French clothes mimicked his every move.

The broad, red-carpeted corridor was empty but for urned palms and a chambermaid's cart. He climbed to the third floor, to a window overlooking the veranda of the suite. Boxed cypresses lined the veranda. An empty brandy glass sat on a white metal table beside a single lawn chaise. Haze flooded the city, blurring rooftops, spires, the murky hills.

He descended to the staff lockers, slipped into a white waiter's jacket, and returned to knock loudly on the suite door. There was no answer and the door would not open. He hid the jacket and descended to the desk. The same walrus-mouthed clerk he had interrogated twice the day before glanced up without recognition.

"My friend in the Mirabeau Suite doesn't answer."

"He's checked out, Monsieur."

"Oh? He left a camera at my place. Surely he left a message where he may be reached?"

As the clerk peered in the key box, Cohen searched the upside-down desk register. Next to Mirabeau was one word, Goslin.

"None," said the clerk. Cohen left by the front and reentered the back. The second floor was empty, the maid's cart now three doors away from the Mirabeau Suite.

At a turn in the corridor he waited until the maid knocked at the suite. There was no answer; she took out a key ring and opened the door.

He counted to fifty and went to the door. "Madame," he called, entering. She was stripping sheets from the bed. "Madame," he repeated, breathlessly, "it is your husband who cuts hair, on the Cours Sextius?"

She stared at him with incomprehending, cowlike eyes. "*C'est moi.*"

"*Alors,* you must go at once. An accident."

She dropped the sheet. "*Quel accident? Charles!*"

"It's not grave. Go quickly."

She ran whimpering from the room. Counting the seconds, "One, two, three, four . . ." he ransacked the desk. Nothing but spa advertisements. "Seven, eight . . ." nothing in the closet. An empty liqueur bottle on the bedside table. "Fifteen, sixteen . . ." In the bathroom trash, a paperback. "Twenty-four, twenty-five . . ." With the bottle and the book he dashed down the stairs to the back yard.

The bottle was German, a half liter, dark brown. The liquor-sticky label read, "Belchen Geist, Schwarzwalder Hausbrennerei, Munstertal." The paperback, *Seven Virgins in One Night,* had no underlined passages, nothing lodged between the pages. On a dog-eared page he read:

> With frenzied tears she begged, beseeched, importuned on scrambling knees, nails tearing his sleeve, "Not my little sister!" but he thrust her nakedness rudely away and faced the younger girl cowering with her torn slip clenched over her nascent breasts, blank terror paling her eyes. "C'mere," he grinned, yanking down the slip.

At the hotel's back door, a butcher's van was unloading chunks of red flesh. One chunk fell; a boy in a white jacket glanced round, brushed gravel from it and lugged it into the kitchen. A trash truck backed up, clanging, to gorge itself on barrels of garbage.

Near the university Cohen bought a German/French dictionary and a map of Germany. In a café by a spattering fountain he tried to translate the bottle label. "*Geist*" was spirit, mind, or intellect, but he could find no entry for *"Belchen."* Despite the dictionary, the label on the back, *"Jeder, der recht froh gestimmt, gern den Belchengeist mal nimmt . . .,"* evaded him also. *"Schwarzwald,"* however, was the Black Forest, lying, according to the map, in southwestern Germany about five hundred kilometers from Köln. In the middle of the Schwarzwald was the word *Belchen,* followed by the number 1414.

"You should've left me the key to the trunk," said the foreman at the body shop. "As such, I couldn't reach the red paint on the lid edge; you can see it, thus."

"Ça va. My girl won't care."

"You change everything for this woman?" The man nodded at Cohen's hair.

"I have a twin brother. I'm afraid she'll sleep with him by mistake."

"She could double her fun," the foreman said. Cohen paid him, parked the now shiny black Alfa in an alley near the station, and telephoned the Hotel des Thermes. "This is Mr. Goslin," he said in English.

"Yase, Meester Goslin?"

"Do I have any messages?"

"None, Monsieur."

"Good. Sunday, I think, I made a call, from my room. I need to call again, but have lost the number."

"Un moment. I look in the book." The vacant line buzzed. "Allo, Monsieur Goslin? You call Sunday, to Neuenweg, Germany. It is the one?"

"Yes."

"Alors, c'est 5-1243."

At a café on the Place de la Liberation he ordered an Armagnac and opened the map of Germany. Bells sounded seven; the dewy, echoing streets smelt of early flowers and diesel. Light rain began to patter on the canopy.

Neuenweg lay four kilometers south of Belchen, which was a mountain peak; 1414 was its elevation in meters. A cold contentment overcame him. He asked for another Armagnac. Brake lights flashed on the wet stones; pigeons and rooks complained on the parapets; wrens and starlings were fussing in the evening branches of the plane trees. A line filtered through his mind: "Into the heart of light, the silence," but he could not remember its source. Washed by the warm, bright odor of the rain, he began to plot his route to Neuenweg.

Alone at the next table a tangle-haired woman sat nodding to the music of a man who played guitar on the sidewalk in the rain. People lounged at other tables, most reading evening papers, as if this woman humming and scratching at herself were not there.

The backs of her hands, her face, her arms, were smudged, her worn cotton dress threaded and dirty. She broke into trailing Italian, was silent, then shaking her greasy hair began to sing again, turned wide-eyed to him. "I know your fortune!"

"Non, merci."

She gave him an almost winsome smile, brown stumpy teeth out of coffee-colored gums. "Knowing the future, you've less to lose." He returned to his thoughts. Trickles coated the sidewalk as the rain stiffened. She beckoned with her hand, "Some perils known can be avoided. Some questions have answers."

He drained his Armagnac, counting coins from his pocket onto the table. "The cost?"

"Five new francs." She sat opposite him gathering his coins from the table. "To begin, I see you will not listen." She took his hand. "You're led by your heart, which is strong." She spread the palm open. "You've had much pain in love. But so has everyone. Love can be more destructive than hate, although its purpose is to make you strong. The heart's gone underground, here, see? You're laboring under a delusion, but have power and may overcome it."

"And the future?"

"A waste. I have no faith in it."

"In my future?"

"In the life line. I've held the hands, like this, of other young men as they lay dead after a battle. And traced the long life lines in their palms. There are no promises." She licked her upper lip. "Expectation robs life. Have no expectations."

"My life line's short?"

"You listen to nothing." She twisted up his hand. "You'll die when you've ceased to live."

"For that I must pay five francs?"

202

She stood abruptly and tucked her chair against the table. "Here," she tossed down his coins, "I give you back your fortune." She went asking *sotto voce* from table to table, "Wish to know your fortune?" while people stared into their papers, not answering. After a few moments she was gone through the rain hanging like a bead curtain beyond the canopy.

He drove the damp, reflective streets until he found another black Alfa. With it he switched license plates, bent open the vent window on the passenger side, and removed the insurance certificate and registration from the glove compartment. He closed the vent, satisfied his entry had left no mark, and took the Autoroute north to Lyon.

At six the next morning he left Lyon, the Mannlicher stowed beneath the back seat. He passed through Besançon before eight, and stopped for gas near the border at Mulhouse before noon. The German control-post flanked the road on the east bank of the Rhine. "So, Monsieur Seghers," said the customs officer, "you have this car from a Monsieur Jacques Bonneville, at Aix?"

"He's my friend, who comes by plane next week to meet me in Munich."

"*D'accord.* But I must see your driver's license."

"I was told I wouldn't need it. You see, I lost it and the office in Toulon has yet to send the new."

"Who said you wouldn't need it?"

"The German consulate, at Marseille."

"They've dreadfully misled you." The officer rested his hands on his belt, near his pistol. "You must have a license to drive in Germany."

"I have one."

"In your possession, it must be. You must return to France and get a temporary one."

Cohen re-crossed the river to France. The officer at the French control asked also for his license. Cohen repeated his story.

"But you're not French?"

"Yes, my family is of Toulon, but I have lived most of my life in Canada."

"You have a Canadian passport?"

"No, I'm a French citizen."

"It's a shame, Monsieur Seghers, but one may not drive in France without proof of license. You must leave the car here and take the bus to Mulhouse, to receive a temporary certificate."

The clock inside the control-post said ten to one. Cohen waited until the next bus arrived at one-thirty, and reached Mulhouse at three. It took another half hour to find the license office, where he waited in line until four-thirty to find that there was no record, in Toulon or elsewhere, of a Luc Seghers, born February 12, 1949, in Toulon.

In a bar in the working quarter he found a red-haired, freckled teenager named Alphonse, who possessed a valid driver's license. They took the next bus to the border. There had been a change of guard. "Here is my friend, who will keep the car at his place, until my new license arrives," said Cohen.

On the way back to Mulhouse he paid Alphonse. "Want two hundred francs more?"

"Depends for what."

"To go to Germany."

"I'd be liable to arrest. Four hundred."

"Three's all I have."

"Three fifty, then, and bus fare home."

They traversed the Basel bridge in early darkness. A line of taillights led to the German post. Dark tree forms surmounted the far riverbank; black water coiled under the bridge. The north wind was sharp in their faces. Twenty minutes later he deposited Alphonse at the Riehen bus station, then found a drafty room in a back street hotel in Lörrach.

"Do you know this stuff?" he asked the bartender in the hotel bar.

The bartender raised Mort's liqueur bottle to the light. "It comes from Belchen? That's a famous mountain—you can drive to the top from Schönau. A hotel's open there in summer."

"You sell it here?"

"I never see it before."

Cohen ate dinner and nursed a beer while a man and two women squirmed naked on a movie screen that the bartender unrolled above the cash register. A man across the room snored loudly, his head flopped back on the naugahyde. The waitress leaned her bosom over Cohen's table.

"Sie englisch?"

"Nein. Français."

She smiled. *"T'es seul? Solitaire?"* She nudged down the top of her tights to reveal a few sweaty blonde curls. Cohen shook his head.

After another beer the movie stopped and the waitress stripped to carnival music on the bar, flesh puckering round her navel. A man was speaking French in the next booth, gesturing with florid, spatulate hands: "Last week, my brother parks his car, in Zürich. Late at night he has a bad feeling about this parking spot. So he dresses, goes out, and moves his car a few streets. In the night a building burns down at the new spot; his car's destroyed."

The man's companion chortled quietly. "Second sight."

"A Four-Fifty. Fifty thousand marks."

"He has insurance, so?"

"He'd lost his license; the insurance was kaput."

A light rain tinkled on the tiny, square windowpanes of Cohen's room. He lit a candle on the dresser, extinguished the electric light. Candle glow wavered on the ceiling. The room softened. Above the radiator the steam-yellowed wallpaper had peeled, disclosing an earlier layer with vague vistas of flowered fields, their edges overlapping. Four days to Easter. Raindrops fell into the ashes of the fireplace.

By dawn the rain was gone, the cobblestones shiny and unlittered. He drove northeast into hills dark with spruce and fir. Willows bloomed in the ditches, grass a brilliant emerald round their stems. Water sparkled in valleys edged by stone walls, in culverts, in spurts tumbling down needled banks between thick conifers.

The road nicked a saddle and dove between two black ridges split by a stream. It chased the stream down to a valley where the forest cleared and white-and-black cows grazed on a steep slope above tall, narrow houses. Over the cows, the trees closed in again, spiring toward a high, naked summit.

Two inns faced each other across a fountain in Neuenweg's trapezoidal square. There was a storefront, closed, and about fifteen other houses, most with barns and fenced livestock. Chickens poked at the street. A pig called, raucous and aggravated.

He drove for several hours round the mountain, checking slate-roofed villages rimmed by firs. The grassy, rocky peak was rarely visible, and then only distantly. In midafternoon he drove from Schönau to the top, the road slick where trees blocked the sun. At the peak was the hotel, shut, and an empty parking lot. The wind rattled a chairlift, scurrying snow around the corners of the hotel. In all directions swept away a bitter panorama of ice, rock, and evergreens. Water sparkled in the valleys; contrails fractured the frigid sky. On the southern horizon the chrome backbone of the Alps split the earth's crust. It was too much like Nepal; he returned sadly to the car and drove part way down the mountain, below the snow, cut east on a rutted logging road along a forested ridge, hid the Alfa behind a mound of bulldozed stumps, and descended on foot through the firs to Neuenweg.

A white rooster stood on the lip of the fountain; three brown hens scratched the gravel below it. The store was now open, a smocked woman inspecting him from its window. In one inn he asked for a sandwich, beer, and, haltingly, a telephone book. As he had expected, the number given him by the Hotel des Thermes was not in the village listing. He considered asking about Mort, but concluded it too risky.

A tank truck stopped at the store. The smocked woman carried out milk cans which the driver siphoned into the truck. A wrinkled man in a wrinkled cap and a pink-faced boy drove lowing cows through the square. A school bus came, flattening the piles of fresh manure. Children flew from the bus chattering and scattering like larks.

He walked eastward out of town, climbed the spruce-thick slope to a point exposing the valley, and watched until dark, ascended to the Alfa and drove to Freiburg, where he bought binoculars, dinner, and lodging. Tomorrow's Friday. My last try. Then Paris. Our backup at Le Serpent d'Etoiles. Something tells me, Paul, you'll be there. Before dawn he returned to the hill above Neuenweg, parked the Alfa behind the stumps, hid the key under the tire, and descended to the point.

The village sat quietly in its cleft in the hills. A window opened, a flash of hand and shimmering draperies in his binoculars. A dog paused to lift a leg against the concrete border of the fountain. A farmer in yellow coveralls poured grain from a white plastic bucket into a trough behind his barn; brown ducks and white geese came quacking and honking to gobble at the trough. The farmer stood watching, arms akimbo, the bucket by his heel.

In late afternoon a black Citroën halted before the store. Mort sprang from it and dashed up the stairs, his right arm in a sling. Moments later he emerged with a plastic sack, waved to the smocked lady and swung into the Citroën.

The Citroën swerved uphill at the edge of town, ascended a pasture road past dappled cattle and over a brook, continued to the topmost switchback under the forest, and stopped at a house commanding the apex of the pasture. Mort entered the house, the car door echo ringing after him into the valley.

Trembling with excitement and anger, Cohen ran up through the forest until he was above the house. He angled westward and dropped through the spruce until the rear of the house and the black Citroën were a hundred yards below. Next to the Citroën were a silver Mercedes and a yellow Golf. Westering sun glared in his eyes and threw prisms into the binoculars. The pasture gleamed in the reddish light, shadowed along its western forest edge and in the grazing paths of the cattle.

Through binoculars it seemed a normal home: square couches with muted plaid fabrics, off-white walls, a fishbowl lacking fish, a sword-leafed plant. A shape glanced across the lens—a man's chest and arms, gray suit, hair on the backs of his hands. Cohen retreated into deeper forest and down its eastern edge until he could see into the larger windows facing the valley. The front door squeaked open and the man in the gray suit stepped onto the deck. He was well-tanned and half-bald, of medium height. He placed his palms on the banister and watched the valley. Mort joined him, glass of beer in his left hand. The man in the gray suit took it, raising an eyebrow in salute. Mort spoke and the other laughed, pointing his glass toward Neuenweg.

Two others came out of the house, carrying beers. They were younger, dressed in slacks and pullovers. One gave Mort a beer. Cohen fine-tuned the focus until the suited man's gray herringbone leaped out at him. From Neuenweg rose the tolling of five bells. The gray-suited man glanced momentarily toward Cohen, turned away, pointing again into the valley, his hand on Mort's shoulder.

207

Mort laughed, his cheeks pouching redly round his small, round mouth. A few minutes later he slouched into the house.

The others finished their beers. Mort emerged, swinging car keys on the single finger of his left hand, and gave them to one of the younger men, who glanced at his watch and nodded. All four descended the stairs, entered the silver Mercedes, and drove down the mountain into the shadowed valley. The car's taillights blinked as it slowed for the square, then zigzagged over the hills toward Müllheim.

The house lay in shadow. The forest approached it closest on the west; he circled around until he could see in the windows on that side. He thought of returning to the Alfa for the Mannlicher, decided it would take too long. He ran doubled over to crouch by the foundation. When his breath calmed he stood and glanced in a window. Couches extended across the dim room. At the back, a door stood ajar. From a table came the silver sheen of a lampshade. The window was locked. He ducked round the rear past the warm rubber and polish odor of the Citroën. The back door was locked; the window over the sink slid open. He retreated for a last glimpse of the valley now spattered with lights.

Empty glasses smelling of beer crowded the sink. He slipped through the window; linoleum creaked as he dropped to the floor. A newspaper on the couch. Two bedrooms, a mildewing bathroom. Women's clothes in the dresser, a faint, nagging scent. Beyond the living room window the town twinkled soundlessly. A truck's red taillights chased the twin beams of its headlamps over the Müllheim hill.

Nothing in the kitchen but cutlery and the faded odors of rust, soapflakes and rat poison under the sink. A gleam steadied on the ceiling, vanished. He ran to the living room. Two points of light flicked up the mountain, glanced into his eyes.

The back door would not open. He dropped the binoculars on the drainboard, twisted the handle, felt up and down for bolts. Light climbed the walls. He clambered over the sink out the window and sprinted into the forest.

The headlights neared. He swore and ran back to the house, stumbling in sudden brightness as the lights washed over him, leaped the stairs and reached into the window for the binoculars, knocking them from the drainboard to the floor. Headlights filled the windows; beer glasses smashed in the sink as he fell to the floor, grabbed the binoculars, wormed back through the window and dashed for the trees.

Over the pounding in his ears came a gear rattle and the valve knock of an aging engine, moving from left to right along the slope below the house. The lights picked their way over a track that traversed the slope. They flashed unevenly on the forest, giving the trees an affronted, startled look. Gears ground disconsolately as the lights hesitated, dipped, and centered on a brown cabin sheltered by the trees. A dog barked. The truck door slammed. The dog quieted. The cabin windows glowed.

He reentered the window and opened the refrigerator so its brightness filled the kitchen. In a drawer he found matches, closed the refrigerator, struck a match in the living room. The lights clicked on.

"You should've stayed away, Sam."

Blinded by the light, he turned.

"I'll kill you!" Claire smiled, twitching a stubby shotgun.

19

CLAIRE FINGERED THE TRIGGER. "You're so undeniably dumb! Where's Paul?"

"You expect an answer? Whose dick are you sucking now? The fat guy's?"

"Don't move! It doesn't matter—about Paul. Christ, here they come."

"Paul's dead?"

"They can't find him."

Footsteps thundered on the deck. Mort banged through the front door, panting, his forehead glistening. "Saint Augustine of Marseille!" he grinned. "Good!" he nodded to Claire.

"That truck almost blew it," she said. "I saw something in his hand—those silly binoculars—but I thought it was a gun and kept waiting for him to put it away so I wouldn't have to kill him, and then the lights came and he was gone out the window in a flash. I thought you'd pick him up outside. So I . . ."

"He fell for the window?"

"Then he came back through it. I waited for him to light the matches—you should have seen his face!"

One of the younger men entered, panting hard. "This him, Mort?"

"Yup."

The younger man kneed Cohen in the groin. "That's for Dieter." As Cohen doubled with the searing pain the man kneed him in the chin. "For Willi."

"We've got time, Tim," Mort said.

"He's a pansy," she said. "Don't break him yet."

Tim pushed Cohen against the wall, holding his palm under Cohen's chin, staring up into his face. "I'll break him in pansy little pieces." Cohen spit in his face and Tim kneed him again, Cohen twisting to take it on his thigh.

She giggled. "I'm going to cut his prick off and feed it to him."

"What'd he do," Tim laughed, wiping his face. "Make you eat it?" The other younger man ran in. "All clear—he's alone."

"All the way from Aix," Mort boomed, "following his bread crumbs. What a bore it is to deal with assholes. The cuffs, Tim."

Tim wreathed Cohen in sweaty arms, clicked the cuffs behind his back. "Put him in the bedroom, Ruby," Mort said. "Use your set to hitch him to the bed."

She put the shotgun on the couch and took Cohen's arm. "No," Mort shook his head. "Upstairs. We'll talk more openly." Tim pulled down a drop stairway in the hall. She pushed Cohen up it and across the attic to a bulb which she lit. They readjusted his handcuffs around a post, cuffing his ankles to it also. With his good arm Mort tucked aside Cohen's shirt to inspect the knife wound. His odor was beery and sweaty. "One of the whores claw you?"

The Mercedes rumbled to a stop outside. The man in the gray suit, shorter than he had seemed through binoculars, mounted the stairs. "You call yet?" he said.

"Not yet, Lou," Mort answered.

"I'll do it." Lou went down.

Mort pulled up a crate before Cohen. "Now," he said. "Get the machine, Ruby."

She returned with a portable tape deck. It had a long cord that Tim draped over a nail in the ridgepole. Mort spoke into the microphone, "Red Dog first interrogation of suspect Samuel C. Cohen, 8:42 P.M., Friday, April 20, Neuenweg, Federal German Republic. Run it back, Tim."

Tim played it back. "Up the volume a bit," Mort said. He smiled at Cohen. "Well, son, where shall we start?"

Cohen shuddered. Now that it was over he had a fierce urge to cry, to fall into their arms, beg understanding, protection. "If I only understood . . ."

Mort nodded sympathetically. "I've been burdened by this, too." He glanced up. "Sam, let's make a clean breast of things, you and I? You're here with us now, and I'd be less than honest if I didn't tell you there's some very hard feelings against you. But maybe together we can sort things out, huh?"

Cohen licked his dry lips. "You're American?"

"I am," Mort said. "And Tim and Jack here, and Lou downstairs. Ruby, here, you already know."

"Then why've you murdered my friends? Other Americans! Innocent people for no reason?"

"Nothing's ever done without reason. Sometimes mistakes are made, and you've made some beauts, but that doesn't mean it's the end."

Cohen laughed. "Sure it's the end, you fat pervert. How dumb do you think I am?"

Claire laughed too. "Very dumb, Sam."

Cohen smirked. Now that it was over he felt weirdly whimsical, capricious, insane. "Make your clean breast," he said to Mort.

Mort dragged his crate a little closer. "A long time ago, you and your friends decided to make a little money on the side. Now, now, wait!" He raised his hand. "Hear me through." He sighed. "I understand who you are—you refused to serve the country that adopted you, you're an expatriate with little love for the land that gave an immigrant like you a home—but why, *why*, would you get yourself into a scrape like this?"

"Does it occur to you that if I loved my country less I would have cared less what it does? And I didn't get myself into this scrape, as you put it, you people did."

"I see." Mort rocked back on his crate. "You'd have me believe that you and Paul and Alex accidentally slipped into this, this escapade, of yours? Like the guy caught with ten pounds of heroin at Kennedy who doesn't know how it got into his suitcase?"

Cohen dropped his head in disgust. "Why am I talking to you, wasting the last hours of my life on shit like you?"

Mort brayed. "The last hours of your life! Give me a break! We're officers of the U.S. Government—we don't go around murdering people in German attics. Even if *you're* a killer, we don't have to be like you."

Cohen said nothing, staring toward some point invisible beyond the poorly illuminated rafters.

"So what're you saying, Sam?" Mort prompted. He tugged at his trousers crease where it flattened over his huge bent knee. "Do you want to tell us your story? Isn't that what Lekbir El Khebib wanted, in Oran? To hear it?" Mort grinned. "Remember him—the Algerian colonel?"

Cohen turned back from the darkness. "What did you do to him?" I *am* the Plague. Everyone I come near dies.

"*Do* to him? Nothing. We had a little conversation, like the one we had with Captain Andrev, who at first was quite hostile. But he came round."

"Did you kill him?" To Cohen, his own voice was like the narrator's in some movie out of childhood—a voice with no person attached.

A mincing grin. "You've been reading too many novels. We've killed no one. Though I understand Andrev was so distressed when he found out who you really were that he killed himself. You've done quite a bit of damage to innocent people, haven't you?"

"You murdering bastard!" Cohen screamed, writhing against his cuffs. He fell silent in a twisted clump at the foot of the post. "God what have I done?"

In the attic all was quiet; Mort watched him with a quizzical air, reached left-handed for his handkerchief and wiped his neck. Lou came up the stairs. "Der Kapellmcister says Bravo!"

"And Dr. Schwarz?" Mort asked.

"They got him."

"Where?"

"I didn't ask, Mort. He's at the Chapel."

Mort put away his handkerchief. "Okay, fella," he said to Cohen, "you can get up now. It's a good act, but I've got work to do. What I want from you, right now, are the reasons why you were running guns into Tibet. I want your contacts in Nepal, your source for the guns, and the names of everyone in your team. Right now!"

Cohen stared. "You're insane."

An empathetic smile. "It was insane to do it, that's for sure. Did you need the money?"

"I did nothing! Stihl hired us to guide him to Mustang—I waited till I saw his permits—he had them! So we took him up the Kali Gandaki. The three of us, for twelve grand, and . . ."

"That's a lot of money, Sam. Nobody'd pay anybody twelve grand for a trip up the Kali Gandaki."

"We thought he was crazy! But we were delighted to have the money. Up in the Kali Gandaki we joined a Tibetan caravan—because Stihl insisted on it—and the same day, four of their horses . . ."

"You never saw these Tibetans before?"

"No. And the same day . . ."

"That's funny. Several of them, including their chief, say you came to them offering to sell arms. Or trade arms, rather, for hashish."

"That was later."

"That was *later?* So you *were* trying to sell arms! To run drugs back to the States."

"No—I was making that up! To find out about Stihl's operation."

"And what did you find out?"

"Nothing. The Tibetans said they didn't know about the bomb."

"What bomb?"

Cohen sighed. "The one Stihl and Eliott were sending to Tibet."

Mort shook his head. "You're leading me down the garden path, Sam. Here's the scenario: You and your friends were caught running guns into Tibet; you killed an American government employee, Roger Eliott, as he and Clem Stihl were trying to apprehend you on the Kali Gandaki. In the process, one of your partners, Alex Vlasic, was killed, also a Nepali whose name's in the file somewhere. But . . ."

"Goteen. His name was Goteen. Stihl or one of your Tibetans shot him."

"Goteen—whatever! But you and Paul Stinson got away. You then killed Clem Stihl in Katmandu, *in front of the American Embassy, no less,* but not before he told us what happened on the Kali Gandaki.

"Then," Mort continued, pursing his lips, "you murdered everyone in Katmandu who might help us find you—an American girl, Kim Davidoff, and four Nepalis related to that dead Nepali, Gowloon or what's his name. In escaping from Nepal, it appears you also murdered a British zoologist solely to acquire his motorcycle, which was later found at New Delhi Airport. We traced you, with Ruby here's help, to Athens, closed in on you in Crete, but you got away—you're a smart one—and by the time we'd found you in Algeria you'd gone to Marseille. Through French sources we tracked you to the whorehouse on Boulevard d'Athènes, but you made a break for it, taking one of the whores with you. Two of our people closed in on you in the mountains; you shot the girl, a Spanish girl—so now Franco's agents are after you, too—and then you doubled back in the middle of the night and beat a German agent's head to a pulp and cut another's throat. That sound pretty accurate?"

Mort pinched his lips in the thumb and forefinger of his left hand. "Then you tried to kill me, a U.S. government official, wounded me, in fact, in the woods near Aix-en-Provence. In the dead German agents' car, with stolen plates, you travelled to Germany, where we finally apprehended you." Mort sat back. "Quite a scenario."

Cohen relaxed his arms, the pain of the cuffs subsiding. That's how it *will* sound, when they tell it. If they ever do. All I've done has been a waste, will come to nothing. He raised his head. "What do you want, fat man? You must want something, or you'd have killed me by now."

"For a start we'd like to understand your motives."

"Tell me, why were you sending a nuclear bomb to Tibet?"

Mort dusted off his knees, stood. "That's a fantasy. To cover up what you've done. *Not one person* in the world'd believe you. Even Paul doesn't hand us that!"

"Paul?"

"Yeah, didn't you hear Lou? We have Paul, or Dr. Schwarz, as the code goes, back at the office. He's singing quite a different song."

Cohen retreated to the darkness, his mouth and eyes dry, a curious buzzing in his ears. How should I feel when the world's ended, when the last hope, the last child, dies? I feel nothing. I don't even care I don't care.

From the death soon to come I resurrect the memory of the good I've known: mother, with her blue Kilkenny eyes; my father, with me on one knee, the Talmud on the other, teaching me what I've long since forgotten but still live by. My stepfather, robust and hard—like the battered toes of his boots the horses stepped on, the white barbed wire scars on his brown hairy arms—the man who taught me to win in a new country. Sylvie, who gave me her life until it wasn't there to give any more. Alex, eaten by the pain of Vietnam. Kim, gentle sister, who believed in the goodness of God. Andrev, who "not ever send person in jail," who did not know his father's grave. The sad colonel in Oran, who tried to give me his best shirt, and when I wouldn't take it, gave me my freedom. Maria, sister of mercy, whom I dragged to her death at eighteen. My brother Paul, bound now in some hellhole of a torture chamber, in the hands of the white men who killed the woman he loves and make our country what it is today.

He felt a nudge, glanced up. Mort stood there. "Speak. If you have anything with which to reprieve yourself, we're prepared to be indulgent."

"What do you want?"

"Tell us your story—Paul's too."

"Perhaps you don't have him."

"Oh we do, we do. That's why we don't need you any more. Do we, Lou?"

"They don't need him at the Chapel. But they want to know who he's talked to."

"So who've you told about all this?" Mort smiled patiently. "Let's tie up loose ends, shall we?"

"This bomb, Mort, it'll end everything, including you. Don't you have kids? Don't any of you have kids?" Cohen looked at them. "What's so important it's worth killing everything?"

Lou chuckled. "He seems stuck in a groove, Mort."

"Yeah," Mort sighed. "Let's get him out of it." He went to the head of the stairs. "Tim! You're on!"

Tim carried a suitcase up the stairs and opened it, a combination doctor's bag and electrician's kit. "Shall it be the trappings of honesty," Tim grinned, "or the essence of pure truth?"

"There's not much time," Claire said. "If he's spoken to someone . . . he's got a big mouth. We'll have to cover quickly."

Tim unlocked a side pocket in the suitcase and filled a long syringe from a sealed vial.

"What's that?" Cohen said.

"Call it a little icebreaker," Tim answered as he rolled up Cohen's sleeve, "to ease communication among relative strangers." He shoved in the needle.

"He's afraid of drugs," Claire grinned.

"Speak the truth and there's nothing to fear."

Mort glanced at his watch. "We've got a half hour to grab a bite in town. Jack, you stay with Ruby. We'll bring you something."

"Fuck kraut food," Jack said.

She crossed to Cohen, stared into his eyes. How evil now she seemed, although it was easy to remember what had trapped him in her pale luminosity, her high straight cheekbones, her amber-lashed eyes, the angle of whiteness narrowing from her neck past the diamond heart to the pearshaped breasts pushing out the fabric of her blouse. The whites of her eyes were veined with red. "I'm going down, Jack," she said. "Just let him be."

Her tawny hair disappeared down the stairway. Jack sat on the

216

crate picking his nose. Cohen tried to break the mood of help-lessness seeping into him. Is it because I've failed? Does it come from seeing her? Or is it already the drug? He tried to remember what it had felt like when he was first captured. It was beyond re-call.

He fought the urge to smile at Jack. They didn't seem so bad, these people. Hadn't Mort said, "We're all Americans?" Maybe the fault was his own, for not trying to help. Something was biting at his wrists; he tugged but they would not be free. "Jack," he said. The word sounded thick, as if he had been drinking. He'd have to do better. "Jack?"

"Yeah?"

"Can you help me? Something's hurting my hands."

"Sure." Jack stood, his face in shadow. "I'll take your mind off it." He kicked hard into Cohen's crotch. Cohen tried to double up but could not with the cuffs holding his arms. Pain roared through him, awful. He threw up. Jack took a black stick from the suitcase. "I used to play Triple-A ball. Could hit it four hundred and twenty feet over the left field fence. Know how?"

Cohen tried to focus.

"The trick is just a touch of uppercut. Like this!" Jack whirred the stick into his ribs, snapping the handle. He could not scream; he could not breathe the red waves of air that crushed him. Jack had picked up the broken stick and was hitting his head, his shoulder, his ribs, his shins. Someone was screaming. He tried to close his mouth, stop it, but the screaming went on. The hitting stopped. It was not his voice. He vomited, blood.

She had the broken stick. She was screaming at Jack. He could not understand the words. Jack was shaking his head, looking away. She slapped Jack; it made a flat smack.

She kept yelling and Jack went downstairs. He brought up a coffee pot of warm water and a towel and washed Cohen's face, rubbing blood and vomit from his shirt.

"Asshole," she was saying. "Asshole, asshole, asshole!"

"He has it coming," Jack mumbled.

"First we need answers. Then do what you want. Asshole!" The word seemed to calm her in its repetition, and she sat on the crate, yanking at her hair. Cohen spit on the floor. "Clean up the floor, Jack," she said.

The room had changed colors. The wall behind her was a waterfall over which a rainbow cascaded. He closed his eyes but it was pouring down inside his eyelids too. Voices. Mort stood before him, a great balloon. "Do you know what Jack did?" Cohen tried to say, but the words were scrambled.

She was talking to Mort. Jack was nowhere. The one with the hairy hands was peering at him. The face was wizened, an old monkey's. Cohen glanced down to keep from vomiting. The floor planks diverged like tracks in a switching yard. Their cloak of dust was marred by scuff marks and wetness. There were hammer marks around the nail heads.

Mort would help him. He could see that. It was just a question of being honest enough to satisfy Mort. In his heart he sought something Mort might need.

"Bring him water, Ruby," Mort said.

The water kept falling from his mouth down his chin. Mort sat on the crate, said, "Interrogation of suspect Samuel C. Cohen, continued 10:57 P.M., same team, place, and date." Mort stretched. "How did you get here?"

"I took Dieter's car to Basel." Cohen smiled. Mort did not smile. "Did I say something wrong?" Cohen's voice seemed disconnected from his throat, as if it issued from the top of his head.

"No, no. Continue."

Cohen remembered about Alphonse. He had promised the boy he would not tell, but Mort needed help. "Alphonse came with me."

"Who's that?"

"Don't know. He was just here."

"Shit, where?"

"In . . . that town by the border, where they kept the car. I can't remember it."

"Basel? Rheinfelden? Säckingen?"

He strained in his effort to help Mort. Glee erupted in him. "Mulhouse!" Once more Mort was not elated. Maybe he's just pretending to need help. He tried to remember who Mort was, where he came from. "I can't place you," he mumbled.

Mort was taking off his suit coat. He removed his shirt. His enormous, glossy shoulder was swathed in white. "You did this," he said. "I know it was an accident, but you hurt me."

218

Cohen was stunned. How could I hurt Mort? "I'll make it up somehow."

Mort looked happy. "Who'd you speak with, in Aix?"

"Lots of people!" He would recall them all, for Mort.

Again Mort seemed upset. "Did you tell them about what happened on the mountain?"

"What happened?"

"Sainte Victoire. You killed the girl."

Cohen saw a headless doll. Its neck poured blood like a faucet. "I did?"

"A Spanish Gypsy whore—it doesn't matter." Mort's voice was consoling. "But did you tell anyone?"

Rafters wavered in the pullulating heat. The heat itself was visible, waves of motion pouring thickly from roof to floor, rising then in steady spasms to swirl against the rafters. Now the rafters pulsed like rocker arms; the floor blistered, its boards wracked upward. Red slipped up between the boards, engulfing his ankles. He tried to scream.

"Yes?" Mort asked solicitously.

"The fire!"

"Fire?"

"The floor."

Mort nodded, glanced down. "Who'd you speak to, about Nepal?"

"Nepal?"

"What you and Paul did there, and how you were punished. If you talk about it, it'll be better, and you can see Paul."

"I can see Paul? Where is he?"

"He's staying with our friends. He's very angry. You were supposed to meet him."

"It hasn't come yet!"

"He says it's passed and you weren't there. I hope he forgives you."

"But it hasn't come. It hasn't." Tears ran down Cohen's face.

"Tell me about it. I'll try to explain it to him." Mort seemed unafraid, standing in pools of fire. If I could be like him, Cohen thought. "It was on the Kali Gandaki ridge," he began, "after we'd run."

The fire was rising, but Mort did not flinch. "Were you to meet in Nepal?"

"In Katmandu, but I couldn't stay." The heat was tearing at his throat; he twisted his head away. "I left him a message, for a fall-back. The Serpent . . ."

"The serpent?" Mort swam before him, in pools of fire, their eyes locked.

"Stop it!" Cohen screamed. "Stop the fire!" It closed over Mort's head.

She stood before him. The flames were enveloping her, yet she seemed calm. Her touch was sandpapery. "When you see clear light," she said, "you can tell me." She fell away into the fire. He writhed, holding his breath against the heat, tearing at the thing that pinned him until his chest and arms could no longer bear the pain.

Through a veil in the flames he saw her sitting atop the crate. His vision cleared. She was unmarred. Heat roared in his ears. Past moments darted through his head. She was holding water. The flames subsided.

Everything was sharp: a mole on her neck, her cracked tooth, a nail half sunk in a rafter, the bulb's filament. It was yellow, that filament, now white, now stationary, now dancing, in its sea, its universe, of light. Its echo rumbled in the floorboards, slower, duller. The nail hummed, motionless with speed.

"He's shot till morning," she said. "Jack blew it."

"I'll strangle the little cocksucker," Mort rumbled.

"No, no, we still need to know. . . ."

"I mean Jack." With his good hand Mort patted her head. "Getting protective, aren't you, Ruby?"

She started down the stairs. "I want him to live." She laughed, sardonic. "For a while."

Mort switched off the tape recorder. "Uncuff his hands, Tim, so he can lie down. Cuff one leg to the post. Then cuff the hands again. You and Jack split the watch. Any way you like. If he gets away, or if one of you hurts him, I'll kill you both."

Blackness descended, an all-forgiving blanket. It would be centuries, perhaps never, till tomorrow.

A quiet presence at his side. "It's you," he said. Hem did not answer. A brown-white bird drifted down beside them.

"You and this killdeer," Hem said, "have an eternal relationship. When you were eleven you shot her with your twenty-two, in Montana. She wants to know what matter of overwhelming importance made you take her life. Were you hungry?"

"No."

"She's come to remind you that your task's unfinished, Koan. That every being is precious. Your task's to nurture life, nurture good, to battle evil. That's what you're doing now—although you feel you've failed. If you die, then die combating evil and nurturing good, nurturing life! Fulfill the will of God, Koan, who desires only good and not evil."

He awoke in the deepest depression he had ever known. His head ached; his mind whirled. His tongue pounded like a drum inside his teeth. The weight of the floorboards beneath him was monstrous. Each breath caused pain. He tried to stop breathing but that made the pain worse. His eyelids came unstuck.

Jack sat half asleep on the crate under the patient glare of the bulb. Clattering dishes and aimless conversation percolated from below. Jack stood and rubbed his face. Footsteps mounted the stairs. Cohen blinked and tried to move his head. Glossy brogues approached. Mort's voice, "Get him up."

Jack shoved him against the post. They cuffed his arms behind it. Mort adjusted himself on the crate. "Turn it on, Jack. Continuation of conversation with same suspect, same place and team, Saturday, April 21, 7:15 A.M." With a rheumy gurgle he cleared his throat. "Ruby, bring up my coffee, will you?"

She stepped into the attic, humming.

"Do you remember," Mort asked Cohen, "a children's game called Twenty Questions? We'll play it this morning. If you do well, you'll end the day as an animal. If you don't, you'll be a vegetable, and soon after, just mineral. Let's begin with the simple. Where were you to meet Paul?"

"Ask him."

"We have, and he's told us. Now we're asking you. Wouldn't it be a shame if someone were lying?"

"You going to kill him?"

"He won't die at our hands. Nor will you, unless you remain silent. Think of it: a life's in the balance, and you have the choice."

"We have no meeting. The last time I saw Paul he was headed north on the Mustang trail."

Mort scratched his nose. "Get Tim."

Claire shook her head. "If we want to shoot him again, that will wreck it."

"On the double."

Tim came up, frowsy and unshaven.

"Wire him," Mort said.

As Tim attached wires by stainless steel clamps to Cohen's fingers and ears, Mort twiddled dials on a console that he took from the suitcase. "We have nineteen questions to go, after you answer this one," he said. "Now, where were you two to meet?"

"You don't have him, do you, fat prick?"

Fire screamed in his face and arms. Arching his back, twisting from it, trying, begging to talk—nothing changed it. His tongue choked him; he could not see.

It went away. "Where was it?" Mort whispered.

"It wasn't."

It returned, insupportable, eternal. After a long time, he could speak. "I can't stand this," he said. "I want to tell you, tell you anything."

"The fallback, son. Paul says you missed the fallback, this serpent thing."

"That's a lie. It hasn't come yet."

"When is it?"

"Ask him." A yell tore from his throat as the searing whiteness ate his bones, burned out his eyes and brain. "Sorry," he gasped.

"When and where?"

He caught his breath. "It hasn't come yet," he repeated. "Yes, it's due, in about a week, I think."

"You think?"

"What day is it?"

"The twenty-first. April."

"We kept it loose, for the last week of April, in case one of us had trouble."

"Where?"

"If I tell you, you'll kill him."

"No, no, no. If Paul's lying, we'll be angry with him, but we won't hurt him."

"Then why'd you kill my friends?"

"We didn't, son." Mort drew the crate closer, his hand on Cohen's knee. "We're fighting a ruthless enemy, terrorists who'll do anything, anything. *We're* the ones trying to save *you.* You've gone astray but we'll still help you; we're all Americans. Had we known in time, perhaps we could've saved your friends." He leaned back on the crate, sighed. "But it's natural for you to fear, given what you've been through. Now let's sort out this fallback problem once and for all. Where's this meeting?"

"In Colorado."

"Where?"

"South of Carbondale. It's hard to explain."

"Try me."

"In the mountains—a place we both know, from several years ago. I could show you on a map."

"This is Germany, son. We don't have a map of Colorado here at the moment."

"If you get one I'll show you the place."

Mort retreated to confer with the others. Tim descended the stairs. Mort sat on the crate. "Give me a description."

"There's hundreds of square miles there; I don't even know the name of the road—it's just a dirt road—that goes near it. Then you have to walk, or ride a horse."

"Why call it serpent?"

"That's our name for the little plateau there. It's loaded with serpentine—Colorado jade."

"Why'd you pick such a lousy place?"

"Because it'd be difficult to find. Paul should remember."

"I'll talk to him," Mort said.

"I don't think you have him. Otherwise you'd kill me, wouldn't you, fat prick?"

"Please get it through your head, Sam," Claire said, calmly, "we haven't killed anyone. I was supposed to keep you safe, and I blew it."

"Fuck you."

Mort tut-tutted, shaking his head. "Let's get some background, while Tim's finding a map. Now, how long have you known Paul?"

"Since college."

"You played football together, as I remember."

"We were on the same team."

"And so are we. We're on your team now, Sam."

"Yes."

"What did you do, on the team?"

"I was a quarterback; he was a defensive back. We were friends outside of that. We didn't work together; he wasn't a receiver or anything."

"Like Alex?"

"Yes, he wasn't like Alex. Alex and I worked together, almost every day, for years."

"You miss him, don't you?" Mort patted Cohen's thigh. "I'm sorry for what's happened, Sam. Believe me, I know. I know . . ." He cleared his throat. "Tell me, as you remember Paul, was he willing to see both sides, when things got rough?"

"Only the impossible attracts him. Some day he'll piss on your grave."

He was ready for it this time but it made no difference. It could not be worse but it was, mashing each separate anguished cell, burying him in a choked, heat-glassy ocean. "It's just pain," he told himself and tried to think like the Blackfeet who laughed in their torturers' faces, but that only made it worse, and he knew it would kill him and hungered for death.

"Is this how you get it up?" he lisped at Mort. "Wire one to my dick—maybe it will make you come!" Mort nudged the rheostat. Pain was everything, pain and only pain, but still he did not die. Higher and higher the pain lifted him, until he stood alone on a plateau where he had never been.

It was fading. He stared at Claire. "And may you ever live, every moment, the first moment of the death of your husband." She blanched, briefly shook her head. "May it be all you know, especially if it isn't true."

"Enough, Mort!" she said. "You're gonna lose him." The world began to circle, gained speed, sucking him down a ravenous whirlwind.

Her mouth was moving. Words hissed in his ears. Behind her a line, dark below and white above. Humps of trees on the horizon. Grass tossing in the wind, October stinging his nostrils. Femur of a moose aslant the sandy soil, its grain weathered like barnwood. "Transitory," it said. "All transitory."

By degrees the heat grew bolder. Time followed no pattern; this day had lasted weeks, had not occurred. They came rattling a sheet of paper and asked him questions that he did not answer; they went away.

224

*   *   *

Thirst awoke him. His voice issued in faint crackles, the sound of a
mouse in sawdust. Jack hovered at the far end of the room.

Claire dipped a handkerchief in a glass, squeezed it on the floor.
Drops beaded the dust. She touched it to his lips. He sucked ec-
statically. She tipped up the glass. The water evaporated in his throat.

Time waited. She shifted on the crate, or paced the floor. He
counted the pulses in his head to a thousand, then again, and again,
again, and again, all the while images, memories tumbled through
his mind.

I'm here and now I understand. I understand that everything
I've ever done has lead to this moment: this is the product of my
life. I'm paying for some monstrous thing I never understood: a
killdeer's death, death of all life. We all have to make payment.
Now I'll die, in their hands. But I'll die by my rules, not by theirs.

Paul walked toward him through late afternoon shadows of the
stadium wall, the first lights coming on, roaring voices in the background like a radio unheard, hands slapping Paul's shoulder pads as
Paul grinned at him. "It was *there*," Paul said. "It was easy."

"You won it, Paul."

"It's a game. We all win or lose it, together." Paul took the
football he had just intercepted and with a fluid motion hurled it far
up into the stands.

Thirst spread inside him like a cancer; his chest burned with each
breath. Blood vessels were splitting in his eyes. The world danced
before him as one level of illusion over another. People sat on the
crate and were replaced by others.

Coolness pervaded the attic. Jack sat on the crate. After a time
Mort came up and they wired thin electrodes between Cohen's
teeth, then to his testicles, questioned him again with the electricity,
and left unsatisfied. He heard the Mercedes purl away. Jack rubbed
his chin, a raspy sound. She climbed the stairs. She wore a suede
jacket. Blue-black glitter of the little shotgun in her hands. He
tensed for death. This moment. Barrel blue with two black holes.
Steel to come out of it, shatter my head, shredding my eyes. One
breath. Now. Please not in the eyes. Another breath. Sylvie, this is
Maria: I love you both. Give me a moment—my father—I hardly
remember . . .

Jack turning slowly on his crate. "We're not 'sposed to fuck with him, Ruby." Jack starting to stand. Now! My chest heaving. I see them all—this moment. The shotgun roared, crushing his ears. Jack flew sideways off the crate and rolled along the floor leaving watermelon blotches. Cohen backed against the post. "You can't kill us all."

She caressed his face. "God, Sam, I'm sorry." He recoiled; she knelt and uncuffed his ankles, bent over Jack's body, her shoes squishing in the new blood. She took keys from Jack's trouser pocket and uncuffed Cohen's wrists.

He fell down. She tugged him up. "In half an hour they come back—they'll kill us both. I can't carry you. You have to run!" She shoved him down the stairs.

"Where?"

"Forest—hide!" She shoved his arms into his jacket, yanked it on him. "Come, darling, run!"

"My glasses . . ."

"Hell with them."

"Car."

"Can't—Mort's got the keys."

"No, Alfa. In the woods!"

"Show me!"

He was running along the slope beside her in the early darkness. Is this it, after death? He pulled her to a halt. "My father—needed to speak . . ."

"Sam! Sam!" she kissed him, hugging him, crying, "It's over, we're getting away—you're safe."

"Wanted to tell my father . . ."

"Faster!" she shouted.

Forgetting already what I had to tell him . . . Lights far below, a tiara nestled in blackness. "Neuenweg!" he said, stunned.

"They're eating dinner down there right now—with a team come from Frankfurt for you." She hurled him up the prickly slick slope onto a narrow track. "This it?"

He felt for tire marks in the duff. "Maybe." He grabbed her. "What about Paul?"

"They don't have him! Never did. Hurry, twenty minutes already!" She encircled his waist, half-carrying him.

The track stopped at a wall of trees. "Higher!" He dove up-slope, running now. Nothing mattered, not pain, not exhaustion, not even fear. Tomorrow, Paul. I'll be there.

226

20

RAIN SLUICED OVER THE windshield like waves across a deck. Bough-shaped arrows of darkness stabbed out from the roadside. The Alfa rumbled like a ship, its motion grasping him, releasing him, grasping him again.

Today's the day. He sat in knee-deep grass at the base of a ruined rockpile. Stones crouched in the green heat. Oaks clung to them with scaly exposed roots. Above, where vestiges of a castle wall slinked along the crust, he peered through a window slit at the rubble beneath. Pink and yellow daisies burst from a fissure in the wall. A brown moth buzzed round them, wingbeats blurred. It darted up, down, became a hummingbird the size of his thumbnail.

The black Alfa glinted from a fold in the hills below, beyond sight of the country road where a single bicyclist pedalled up a gentle grade. Cohen descended granite steps where fat black ants scurried over strawberry runners. She sat against a south wall, under a *meurtrière,* drinking wine from a bottle.

"Long live *krasi,*" she said. "And happy Easter."

"Are you Ruby or Claire?"

"Take your pick."

"I'll take the real one."

"There isn't one. Claire was for you. Ruby's my standard."

He sat beside her, woozy from the sun, and fell asleep.

The sun had slid behind a broken wall. She pushed white-covered bread at him. "Goat cheese from the village," she said, pointing down at an intermission in the hills tiled in faded orange. "Go easy on the wine. I refuse to carry you again."

"Did you?"

"You passed out three times between the house and the car."

"When?"

"Last night, at Belchen. We're two hours from Paris."

He scrunched his body around to lie in the sun, the back of his skull on the warm, worn stone. Above the abbreviated wall the sky was blue, cloudless. "I'll stay here."

"You need rest; the city's anonymous. Here we'd be noticed. The police are looking for us."

"The police are always looking for me. I don't give a shit."

"If I'd known that, I'd have let them have you."

"Who is 'them'?"

She fished a crumb from a fold in her jeans, tossed it in her mouth. "There's time in Paris for all that." She pulled him up and took his arm. They descended to the Alfa; she backed it speedily out the narrow trail, weeds lashing its sides. She slowed for the village, then accelerated down a long roadway where leafing trees met overhead, their white-painted trunks flicking along the shoulders.

He awoke to the rumble of trucks and the downgearing of the Alfa. "Where are we?"

"Autoroute du Sud—Orly. Too risky from the west."

Paris was stunning, its crowds, traffic, clothes, and vistas of trees, its columns, and glowing facades. The Parc de Montsouris throbbed with hallucinatory colors. The Boulevard St. Michel rippled with moving bodies: girls in flashy dresses and quick stiletto heels, dark-suited young men shaking hurried hands outside leaf-shaded corner cafés, families coming home from church with daughters all in white. The ripe, almost cheesy aroma of bread floated in the fumes of taxis and the blue glare of truck and bus exhausts.

Not since Sylvie have I dared to be here . . . not since I turned around and went to the Himals to climb until I died up there somewhere. That's what I wanted: to die up there in the cold. But Alex and Paul came over and after a while it was fun, the climbing. Trying to find a place no one'd ever been.

"If you were trying to hide in Paris," her voice broke in on him, "where would it be?"

"Where I wouldn't stand out. St. Germain, with polyester tourists, down-at-the-collar poets, fifty-cent guitarists and fifty-dollar whores, South American exiles . . ." Not the Ile de la Cité, down the alley and up the narrow stone stairs to the room curving out

228

over a view to the river? Where she dressed before the chipped old armoire, turning this way and that in its flaky stained mirror, asking, "Does it go with the part, *Chéri*?" How bad would it hurt to see it again?

"Too many cops, mostly plainclothes. It's the most logical place for us, and the most logical place to look for us. There's nowhere cheap to stay and the food's lousy. If these are the last days of my life I'm going to eat well."

"Don't be heroic—it's ludicrous."

"Don't be foolish enough to disbelieve me." She turned left on Des Grands Augustins. "We'll go to the eighth. The American Embassy and the Elysée Palace, bastions of freedom in an unfree world . . . we'll fit like peas in a pod. Perhaps we should be from Des Moines."

"Look, why are you doing this?"

"Doing what?"

"This—Paris, 'escaping' with me, and all that?"

"Cool down, Sam. I want to tell you, step at a time."

"It will have to wait. I'm splitting."

She looked over, her voice suddenly contralto. "Leave any time you like. But what I have to say could make it better."

"Make what 'better'?"

"Either the going or the staying."

"You're full of shit," he said.

"You could work for the local bank, and I'll give my time to our PTA."

"What the fuck're you talking about now?"

"Des Moines. What we *do* there. Our cover."

"I never intended to see you again except to kill you."

"Would you?" She nipped her lip.

"The last morning in Vye."

"That's why I left. The old man told you?"

"Were they the ones I killed on Sainte Victoire?"

"No." The Seine furled jadelike under Le Pont Royal. West of the Louvre, the arbors of the Tuileries and the Champs Elysées. The clothes were richer now, the cars lower and faster. She swung left on rue de Rivoli.

La rue Jean Mermoz was inconspicuous even for the quarter. Dress shops, front-room restaurants, and inexpensive hotels jostled for space along the narrow tarmac. Opposite their hotel window children played on an ornate, peeling balcony. "You dye your hair black and grow a moustache," she told him, "and we'll get you a blue sweater and leather jacket. You'll pass for Lebanese." She rattled the room key. "I won't be long."

"Where to?"

"Arranging a new persona."

"Perhaps I should go, to see who you call." He watched the inexpressive ovals of her eyes. "But I'm past caring about all that."

"You're already dead," she grinned. "I reincarnated you."

"I'm not sure why."

"Neither am I." She kissed him, fished in her purse. "Here's two hundred francs in case I disappear. In the meantime, get some sleep."

When she returned, he did not know her, but started in fear from the bed. Her hair was short and black, her face Eurasian in color, seeming rounder. Under black brows her eyes were betel nut. Her lips were broadly carmine; she wore a dumpy black sweater above tan slacks and worn buckle shoes, held up a wrinkled paper sack. "Been to the used clothing stores." In the sack were sandals, a blue sweater, a gaudy chest amulet in fake gold, a Japanese chrome watch and watchband. At the bottom was a small furry object. "Your moustache, until the real one grows. Let's do your hair." She sheared his Aix-en-Provence curls, daubing black dye in the remains.

"I look like the Corsican who turned me in."

"He had no choice."

"Tell me about it."

"Shave your beard every other day." She rubbed dye into his stubble and stuck a pack of Gauloises into his front jacket pocket. "Keep one in your mouth. You look positively awful." Her voice took on a rough, Arabic twist, "Speak French with harshness, like this." She handed him cheap sunglasses. "Put these on when you go out."

"Christ, I'm already half blind. What did you do to your eyes?"

"Colored contact lenses I've had for years and never used. We'll get you some."

"I'm fine like I am."

230

"I want us alive." She pulled the dumpy sweater over her head and slipped down the slacks. Her body was long and slender. "And I want to lie next to you, breathe you, kiss you. This thing has almost killed me."

"Me too, actually."

"Don't be snide, darling. I'm going to die for you."

"Bullshit."

"Love me."

"Not a chance." He turned away. "I'm not the least bit interested."

"From being kicked?"

"And beat, and punched, and drugged. But mostly because your friends killed Maria, and I remember her right now and don't care for anyone else."

"You don't remember me?"

"You're evil, as far as I'm concerned."

"But I love you! Touch me a little with your hand, I'm going crazy. There's so little time, darling."

"Maybe they won't get us."

"They will, I know them. But it won't change things if they don't."

Late afternoon traffic in la rue Mermoz woke him. She sat reading *Le Monde* in a tattered lilac chair. "I've been here before," he said. His mouth tasted awful.

"Where's that?"

"Sleeping in an unknown bed, hurt and exhausted, while you sit over me. Where was that—Athens? And Marseille, too—no, that was Maria." The thought of Maria brought pain and he lay silent waiting for it to go away. "It seems I'm always getting better, about to get up and fight back; then suddenly I'm lying here again, trying to heal and gather strength for the next round."

"What's amazing is that you've lasted. That you've overcome."

"Overcome what?"

"The diligent efforts of several countries' intelligence agencies to crush you into nonexistence."

"What other countries, besides the U.S.?"

"West Germany, Turkey, France, Spain, Morocco—those are the five I'm sure of."

"What the fuck do they care?"

"You're a terrorist, dear—a dedicated killer. The intelligence community clings together against people like you; they feel they're entitled to a monopoly on terrorism, don't like competition."

"So why didn't they kill me in Neuenweg?"

"They needed you, darling, to track down Paul."

"It irritates me, that word. 'Darling.'"

"You'd prefer I called you 'Prick'? Because that's what you're being."

"Fine." He sat up licking his fuzzy teeth. "Old blood and vomit—caked on my teeth."

"How charming. You could consider brushing them. Or should you keep them like that to remind me what you've been through?"

He grinned. "Right now I'm considering how to get rid of you."

"It's easy to get rid of me. Just walk out that door. I'm a lot safer without you."

"Then why don't *you* go?"

"Unless you stop laying your trials and tribulations on me I will." She sat on the bed beside him. "You've been through Hell and that's a shame, but it ain't my fault. I was trying to get you out of it in Crete. I failed, but I was trying. Now I've written my own death warrant—no, don't you dare laugh at me!—by hustling you out of Neuenweg, so I'm unlikely to take any puerile remonstrances from you about the holes in your hands and how heavy your cross is. It's your cross, Prick, so bear it!"

He swung his feet out of bed, sat scratching his balls. "Glad to."

She crouched before him, fingers biting into his thighs. "Don't be cute! This is awful, where we are. Can't you see that?"

He stood massaging his ribs. Body feels like it fell down an elevator shaft. God, she's ugly. Hate her. Hate them all. "Fuck you, Cunt."

She tousled his hair. "It's the romantic in you I can't resist. Prick and Cunt—we should do well together."

He limped, exasperated, to the window. "No matter what I say you turn it somehow."

She folded *Le Monde,* slapped it emphatically on the dresser. "Let's eat. And talk."

Lifting his jeans from the foot of the bed he slipped one leg carefully into them. Then, sitting on the bed, the other.

"Can I ask a question?" she grinned.

"Might not get an answer."

"Why do you never wear underpants?"

"Haven't owned a pair since '69. They overheat the balls—kill all those little squirmy things."

"What need do you have of those little squirmy things right now?"

"Question of morale on the lower forty. Keeping their pecker up. Sense of optimism, infuses the whole *corpus delecti.*" Wincing, he pulled up the pants. "I have the collective miseries of every halfback who ever played the game."

She kissed him. "I love you when you let even a little of yourself show."

"Ever since you've known me, ever since that day on the Kali Gandaki, I've been a wild man, a stranger, out of myself." He shrugged into his shirt, buttoned it and stuffed it into his pants, buckled them. "Now I've got to do these goddamn shoes." He tried to bend over. "Please come tie them, will you? My hands won't work—fumbling the laces."

She knelt and tied them. "Maybe it's the shock treatment—it was agony watching, pretending to be with them, knowing you were dead unless I played along till I could get you free." She pulled him up. "But you're going to be fine, Prick, and we'll vanish somehow, once we've found Paul."

He turned from the door. "Who said anything about Paul?"

"You did. You have to meet him in Colorado, in a week. I've already figured how we can fly from Madrid to Buenos Aires to Mexico City and drive from there. But we have to leave tomorrow."

"I'm going alone."

"They'll be waiting for you! I can help you slip through."

"Like in Crete?" He walked out the door and started his awkward, painful descent of the stairs. Why the fuck she take a room on the third floor? Shit, it's *troisième étage*—the fourth goddamn floor. Fuckin' French with their *rez de chaussée.* Why can't they be like everyone else? I'll never make it back four floors. Not without a gun up my ass.

She's glomming on real friendly now, but it's bullshit. This's how they hope to get Paul. Crazy that she shot that Jack guy. Blew his lungs all over the attic. They must want Paul bad, to do that. Gotta pretend I trust her. What if she's straight? Can't take that chance. Should walk her into some alley and strangle her. Can't do that. Not to her.

But I have to get rid of her soon. Don't make Paul wait—that's terror.

At the corner a front-room restaurant, its curtains shutting out the street. "How'd Mort track me down?" he asked her.

"There was a real hunt for you in the hills of Crete. After several days they were sure you'd drowned—I learned all this later. But Mort kept checking every other avenue—nothing escapes him—and he finally ran down the freighter he remembered had left Sitea the morning after you escaped into the hills. Then they tracked you by plane to some place on the Algerian coast, lost you, and found you again in Oran." She bent to clear her throat. "Then, idiot, you wrote that letter, from Marseille!"

"And what were you doing while I was having such a good time in Africa?"

"After my snafu in Vye, they stationed me back in Brussels till they caught wind of you. I was on my way to Marseille when you shot Mort and disappeared. Then they found you'd called that hotel in Aix, and figured you were on your way to Neuenweg, so I was switched up there. You got there faster than they expected." She slipped a stockinged toe up under the cuff of his jeans. "But you'll never make it as an *agent clandestin.*"

"Oh?"

"In Neuenweg you were staring right into the sun with your binoculars. Lou saw the reflection. They figured you'd want to search the house, and left me there to capture you, since I was the only one you hadn't seen out on the deck. They drove back uphill with the car lights off. I knew they didn't trust me, after Vye, that they wouldn't go far enough away for me to warn you off. I was so happy when the truck came and scared you out. When you came back I couldn't believe it."

"I shouldn't have been surprised to see you there."

"I almost killed Jack, when he beat you, but my mind was so scattered. I hadn't worked out a scheme yet. But by the end you were mentioning things I'd told you that were true, and were not in the persona I was supposed to be with you—about my husband and stuff—and I knew that soon they'd kill me. And I was afraid you'd tell them about Paul."

234

"What's Paul to you?"

"Nothing, except your friend. But I knew once they had him you'd both be dead."

"Why?"

"You're the only ones, Prick, who know what went on. Once you're dead they're safe, forever."

"What about you?"

"I don't even know why they want you . . . that's the chance I'm taking. I've got nothing to expose but hearsay."

"I'll tell you."

"Let's just drop it, find Paul, and get away—please?"

"And let them stay safe, forever?"

"So what? Let's live, not dig up their sordid lives."

"Who'd send a nuclear bomb to Tibet?"

"Ah, that's the story you're supposed to be spreading, that's what they said you might tell me. It was your role."

"Jesus. They did it, Claire, I saw it."

"That's idiotic! Who'd dare to start that?"

"Maybe they thought it wouldn't cause anything—or that it'd be localized. A way of putting pressure on the Chinese, chasing them out of Tibet, subtle victory against the worldwide specter of communism."

"Who would they blame?"

"The Chinese? I don't know. The Russians, the Indians, us . . ."

"Never in my work did I come across such a scheme. When you told me in Athens, I only half-believed you." She tugged at her short hair. "But then, I never knew what was going on anyway. They certainly wouldn't have told me."

"So what's Neuenweg?"

"A safe place, for meetings. I never knew of it before. One of the higher ups was there—Mort must have called him after they found you in Marseille."

"Who?"

"Lou. He's from D.C."

"Mort's American?"

"Who knows what anyone is in this business?"

"I have to know."

"I can't help very much. I've been in Brussels for them for three years, supposedly as a freelance reporter, but actually prying loose whatever secrets I could on the EEC, on all the NATO members except the Americans."

"Secrets?"

"Troop strength and deployments, technology transfers, missile locations, who's sleeping with whom, that sort of thing. I assumed the U.S. was just checking up on its allies."

"You never cared to ask who you were working for, or what they were doing with your information?"

"After my husband's death I didn't care. I really loved him, Sam."

"No one said you didn't."

"A year after Tim died I was still heartbroken, hating the people who'd killed him. I saw an ad in the *Times* for a researcher on international affairs, 'excellence in languages a must.' I spoke French and German like a native, being French and having grown up here."

"You had an American passport in Athens."

"It wasn't real."

"Are you American?"

"The real me?" She dimpled. "She was a French citizen."

"What was her name?"

"She's dead and buried. Take me as I am."

"You've just grown a new head."

"I'm the snake eating its tail, darling."

"So you answered this *Times* ad?"

"And they called me back a month later; I was to work in Brussels. It was soon boring, but it helped me forget. It became my world, a world of no absolutes, of forces and counterforces with no rights and no wrongs except the underlying hatred that forgave all, allowed all. It was perfect for me. But over the months I began to heal, began to see things that shocked me, that I couldn't forget. I was changing, but I didn't realize how much until I met you."

"'Till I met *you*,'" he sang in falsetto. "Crap!"

"You're not the world's sexiest man, Sam. I hate it when you squint without your glasses, or when you're brusque, like you are now, and think it's masculine. In some ways you're so dumb . . . and you're going to lose your hair." She reached across the table and pinched his side. "You're going to seed."

"Keep to the subject."

"And now I've hurt your feelings. You've got no sense of humor. Try to take yourself less seriously. Though I love you, anyway. On the flight from Teheran I was supposed to stick with you as a way of finding Paul. But in Athens, in that hotel in the Plaka, I kept seeing a person who didn't fit the description I'd been given. I had to know, you see."

"Had to know what?"

"Who you really were. After you fell asleep that first day in Athens, I got to thinking it over, and decided I couldn't take their word. I'd begun to like you." She grinned. "Don't ask me why—I can't imagine."

"Back to your story."

"After a year in Brussels, translating silly dispatches and wiretapped phone conversations, I was sent to Kenya and told to call myself a stringer for *Le Figaro,* which no one ever questioned, amazingly. Out of Kenya I gathered info on leftist figures—politicians, editors, military people, and sent it back to Brussels in the diplomatic pouch. In Nairobi, though, I began to have doubts."

"Regarding?"

"Just exactly what I was doing. And whom I was working for. I wanted to tell you about it in Crete but you didn't listen."

"Try again."

"One of my tasks was to interview an American who was trying to stop the elephant slaughter. You know about the ivory trade, don't you, how all the elephants are being killed for their tusks? The elephant poachers have strong ties to the Kenyan government—at one point the president's sister was head of the largest smuggling group. Well, I spoke with this American. It was one of those persona assignments, I thought, that you file and forget. But he was on to something."

She filled his glass and he pushed the bottle away. "He was trying to force the World Bank to hold up development loans to Kenya until the government began to enforce its elephant poaching laws. In the course of the interview, I established his daily routine as well as his intentions for the coming months—he was very honest about how he planned to put pressure on the World Bank."

"Well?"

"A month after the interview he died in what was described as a car accident. I think the people who sent me . . . that my information was used by the killers. So, in a sense I killed him. And I really liked him."

"You keep saying 'really.'"

"An affectation, in a world where nothing is more real than anything else. Pretences, facades, covers, roles, ropes, feints, doubles, faking, disguises, masks—how many words are there for lies? I'm sick of them!"

"Since when?"

"For months I've been learning what my job really is, and wondering who, underneath it all, wants the results of it. One night last year I got stoned, alone, and while doing the dishes and listening to music I began to think what I was doing in the world—was I making it better or worse?"

"Why care?"

"For such a long time I'd wanted only to kill those I imagined responsible for the deaths of my father and Tim—when my contact called I'd beg for something more crucial, impacting, and he'd chuckle and say, 'in time, in time.' But every chance I got I'd ask, or read, or figure out, how American intelligence was structured, what we were doing against the communists. In my three trips to Thailand I met with newspaper editors in the guise of a free-lancer doing stories on the Cambodian refugees beginning to pour into Thailand. My assignment, of course, was to find which editors and publishers were hostile to the States, but as part of my persona I had to spend some time with the refugees."

She pushed her plate away. "I've had it." She put both hands over her face, silent. He watched her short black hair, tarry in the mirror behind her, the mirror put there to make the room seem larger. Why do we manipulate the world? In the mirror's reflection an obese man leaned into his meal at another table, a white napkin over his belly—like spring snow on a north-facing slope. Oh, to be in Montana again, or in the Himals, far from the cities. To be in the cold October wind off the Beartooths, the scent of elk and lodgepole in the high sharp air. Christ, she's crying—tears sliding down her hands. "C'mon Claire, don't reduce us to this. A lovers' quarrel. *La chamaille imaginaire.* Don't make me leave."

She laughed, wiping her cheeks with the backs of her fingers. "You're crippled, silly. You can't leave."

"It seems you're always dependent on my being crippled."

She reached out a tear-wet hand to his. "Why are you so mean to me?"

"I don't trust you."

"Don't you see how *I've* been had? By them? Myself? Unlike you, I'm not accepting it—interviewing those Cambodian refugees, all the things I'd been avoiding began to take form in my mind. Here were survivors by the thousands: shattered, bereaved families who'd been bombed by the U.S. Air Force every day for months, *in a neutral country!* At first I dismissed it as lies, but the more I *saw* the wounds, the agony, the heartache, the burned children and starving parents, I . . ." She shook her head. "It wasn't just they who suffered; I did, too. And I judged myself by the rules the U.S. taught at Nuremberg."

She squeezed his hand. "Since then I've learned more: the CIA battle to take over opium smuggling out of South Vietnam and Laos in the '60's—how we—the CIA—sold heroin to pay for operations Congress wouldn't fund, assassinations Congress didn't know about—the same heroin that ended up on the street in New York and Chicago and a thousand other places, addicting young Americans. And the Vietnam War, which killed my husband, was unleashed by the CIA yelling 'Wolf! Wolf!—Communist! Communist!' and the gullible Americans came running to protect the enormous CIA heroin networks and profits in Laos, Cambodia, and South Vietnam . . ."

"Why are you telling me this?"

"Sam, try to realize the implications: I've been working for the very people responsible for Tim's death, and the deaths of fifty-five thousand other Americans! All these years, I've been living a falsehood, not just in the roles, the covers, but in my deepest motivations! I was living with a stranger, lying to myself while my self was lying to me. Sex, an occasional orgasm, hunger, thirst— they were the only parts of my life I couldn't prove false."

"Nobody's who they seem."

"Maybe. But good people don't *try* to be false—not to anyone! CIA people, and their likes in the KGB, in British Intelligence, any undercover operative of any sort, are *consciously* false. It's a way of life become a habit they can't break. With so many identities they lose the real one; there becomes no person underneath, just roles on top."

"That may be easier."

"But it's not *alive*! It isn't good."

He sat back. Her face, rouged by emotion, seemed swollen, her look accusatory, hounding. What right does she have to criticize me? Again she's twisting things—I'm on the defensive. Is she straight or playing me? Until I know I have to assume the latter. "Tell me about *Der Kapellmeister*."

She paused. "Where'd you hear that?"

"Answer me!"

"I don't know *who* he is—but that's the name for the MAD liaison. It means bandleader."

"What's MAD?"

"Acronym for West German military intelligence."

"Bandleader?"

"*Kapell* in German means chapel, so it's chapel master, literally. Where'd you hear it?"

"Mort mentioned it once, to Lou." He smiled. "I've gotta tell you, I don't buy your change of heart."

She sat more upright. "When?"

"In Athens, for one. When suddenly you decided not to spy on me but be my buddy. 'I'd begun to like you—don't ask me why,' and all that."

She smiled. "I did a horrible thing, but I'm glad I did it."

"What's new about that?"

"You don't have to be such a bastard, Sam. I do believe you feel sorry for yourself."

"I certainly feel sorry, but for other people. So what did you do?"

"With your antibiotic I gave you something to make you speak openly—that you wouldn't remember the next day." She snatched his hand, "I had to! I *had* to know if their story was real! When I learned who you were—that's when I decided to help you. My mistake was I should've told you right then. But my trade makes me hungry for reliability, for sureness, makes me conservative. Most everything I face is false; when I find the true, I don't trust it."

"After Africa what happened?"

"Two weeks after that American died in the World Bank incident I was pulled back to Brussels. I spent another year and a half there, travelling occasionally to Thailand, and recently serving as girl friend to a British major."

240

"Fucking for secrets?"

"You would put it that way. He knew all along, I'm sure, and fed me tidbits just to keep me. Then one Sunday morning at 6:30 I was called and told to be on the eleven A.M. plane to Delhi. At each stop I had to call Brussels, and when I got to Teheran I was met by a man who spoke German with a South American accent— Raoul was the only name I got—who gave me a ticket back on your flight and a file on you."

"What was in it?"

"A passport photo, your college transcript, handwritten notes on your whereabouts since graduation. It told about the football in Canada, your injury, and about the deaths of your parents and fiancée. I never could say how sorry I feel."

"Keep going."

"You doubt I love you. That's one of the reasons I do, that you never mentioned the pain you've suffered, but only paid attention to mine."

"What was your job?"

"You were an American-born Russian agent gathering information on the Chinese and acting as an American climber. You'd been trained in North Africa and Paris, and were suspected of having traveled in and out of Russia via Odessa and Vladivostok. You'd just finished an assignment in Nepal that resulted in a worsening of U.S.–Chinese relations, and had killed three Americans there in cold blood."

"Three? I killed only Stihl."

"According to the scenario you also killed Alex and the other American—what's his name?"

"Eliott?"

"Yes. If Interpol or the CIA ever get you, that's what the story will be. That you killed those three, and a bunch of Nepalis. And you'll be killed trying to escape."

"Go on."

"I was to get involved with you, on the plane if I could, try to keep you on the back burner in Greece; if not there, then in Paris or New York."

"Why?"

"Till we could track down your partner. I was to try to get his whereabouts from you, stay close to you, find out if you planned to

241

meet him. Raoul also gave me a file on Paul, a known anti-American and presumed saboteur of American bases in Europe."

"That would please him. Like Alex, he was in Vietnam. It made them both dislike a lot about the States." Cohen brought his hand quickly down on hers. "I need to know who these people are."

"I'll help you where I can. But it's not my choice."

"Why?"

"I know where it'll take us. Dead. With no good to come of it."

"I'm going to get them back for Alex. And for Maria and Kim and Phu Dorje and his wife and daughter and son, for . . ."

"Who's Phu whatever you said?"

"A Sherpa whose brother was killed by your friends on the Kali Gandaki trail. And whose crime was to be told about it. You should've seen the children, lying beneath their mother with their throats gaping, flies swimming in their blood . . ."

"Don't prey on me."

"These orders—to go to Calcutta, Nairobi, and such. Where did they come from?"

"I was attached, rather loosely, to a press bureau in Brussels. I'm sure they didn't have the faintest idea what was going on, though they may have wondered about my schedule. I worked hard at my persona. I never met the man who called."

"Called?"

"Every Monday evening I had to be at my apartment. It was one of those new yecchy buildings in the suburbs. Sometimes he'd call, give me some information, ask me questions, have me pick something up in a locker for which he'd mail me the key. Occasionally he'd call at other times, too. For all the wiretapping they did they never seemed to worry about my phone. The first ones I met face to face were Raoul, then Max and Emil on Crete."

"Where are they?"

"Heaven knows. They were backup. When I drove off that last day in Vye I went to their hut, to pull them off you long enough for you to disappear. Later, Emil was very angry and kept muttering in his lousy English that I'd ruined him, that he was finished."

"He was German?"

"Argentine. I could tell it when he spoke German, as with Max, who also said he was German. So I stayed at their hut until they came back swearing and sweating and started calling on their car radio. Emil took the Peugeot and put me on the next bus from Sitea to Heraklion, where I was told to take the first flight to Athens, and then to Brussels. I thought a lot about breaking free and trying to find you in Crete, but doubted I could and knew I might lead them to you. Also, you'd probably have killed me before I could open my mouth, and I knew I was in danger with them as it was. So I decided to tough it out for the present and disappear when a good chance presented itself. I never expected to see you again, dead or alive." She squeezed his hand. "Let's walk—we're honeymooners; it's April in Paris. In a few days we head back to a lifetime in Des Moines, you to your bank, me to my PTA."

"Honeymooners aren't in the PTA. What happened back in Brussels?"

"The voice called and said they were considering firing me. I knew that 'firing' meant an execution somewhere—car crashes seem to be their favorite. So I told him how angry I was that Max and Emil had blundered and revealed themselves, almost getting me killed, that I had had you wrapped up until they blew it, and that I hated you and would do anything for another chance. The same line I used with Mort."

"And the guy under the truck?"

"In Athens? Maybe he was one of them, what they call an insurance rider, whom I would not know about, on purpose. Or maybe he was from some other group, checking up on you."

"He was following *you* to the airport, not me."

"Maybe to get my destination, call it in, go back to you. Or maybe he was just a poor schmuck who got crushed by the world."

"Were you really leaving?"

"I was going to run, run, run. From them and you. I was so confused. I thought you'd be safe without me, that I was endangering you—yet I couldn't go back to them if I left you. I tried to think of a way we could disappear together, but knew you wouldn't go for it. Then when I called in I found they wanted to drop me and move in on you and so I pushed you toward going to Crete, telling them you insisted on our going there. God, it was a strain—it's all been such a strain, let's enjoy these moments." She took his arm as they stepped from the restaurant into the lamplit penumbra. As they crossed la rue Mermoz a black-uniformed policeman halted them with an upraised submachinegun. "Your identification?"

Cohen stared into the mean dark hole in the barrel. She grasped his arm. "*Pourquoi, Monsieur?*" she said.

The policeman leaned forward to look into her face. "Arab, aren't you?"

"Certainly not. Why do you ask? Why point a gun at us? It's the custom now in France to harass tourists in the street?"

"You know where you are?" The policeman swung a black-gloved hand toward the side street opposite them. "Isn't that the Israeli embassy? Am I not here to guard it?"

A blue and white flag drooped before a long yellow building half way down rue Rabelais. "We didn't know," she said. "We're even Jewish."

"From where?"

"England."

"Your friend?"

"He doesn't speak French. He's also English."

"Your passports, please."

"We're Common Market . . ."

"Your identification?"

"It's in our room. Shall we get it?"

"Where?"

"In this street, at our hotel."

"I'll go with you." He crossed the street, bent to talk with another policeman who also carried a submachinegun.

"Whose fucking idea was it to be Lebanese?" Cohen whispered. "The Eighth, so quiet and unsensational—right around the corner from the Israeli fucking embassy." He bit his lip. "It's the goddamn CRS, too."

She smiled up at him. "Calm down. We'll think of something."

The policeman crossed back to them. "*On y va?*"

They reached the hotel under the curious glances of passersby. The policeman clumped up the stairs behind them, gun at the ready. Outside their room Cohen bent to insert the key. The policeman stood on the stairs, front boot on the landing.

They entered the room. "*Entrez,*" she called.

"I'll stay here," the policeman said.

She stood behind the door pulling off her sweater and bra. She snatched a brochure from the dresser. "Give him this. When I follow, hit him."

244

Cohen advanced toward the black muzzle. *"Voici, Monsieur,"* he said in flat French, proffering the brochure. The policeman leaned forward, his eyes widening as Claire came through the door. Cohen grabbed the gun, the policeman tumbling off balance, swearing, the sling catching his neck. Cohen slammed the gun butt down on him. "Careful," she hissed. Hand over his mouth they shoved him into the room, lashing his wrists with the bra and stuffing an undershirt in his mouth. Claire pulled on her sweater and coat. "We've got two minutes."

"No we don't." Cohen ducked from the window. "Here comes *L'Ecole Militaire.*" He shoved her into the hall and up the stairs to the fifth floor and then the roof, hobbling fast across sticky tar through warm cindery smells of the chimneys and jumped a half-floor down to the next roof. Its door was locked; they leaped to the next building. Its door hook snapped. Whistles screamed in the street.

21

DOWN THE STAIRS THEY dashed past an astonished woman holding a pail of water on the third floor landing. On the main floor a courtyard opened to the rear, beyond it a wall then the back of another building. He boosted her on the wall and she pulled him up; the top of the wall was inset with broken glass. *"Salauds,"* she swore, sucking her bleeding hands.

They ran through a lobby past a man reading a paper by an elevator door, halted breathless on the sidewalk. Whistles and sirens at the corner. "Miromesnil's closest!" she yelled, bolting down the street.

"The Alfa!"

"Later."

The métro was jammed with people who stared at them openly. He faced the floor gritting his teeth against the pain in his knee and trying to breathe easily. She sat with bloody hands tucked in her sweater, under the "Reserved for Mutilated War Veterans" sign. "If I sit here," she grinned, "everyone will think I'm French."

"I feel sorry for that *flic*. His head's gonna hurt."

"It's his job."

"No, this wasn't his fight."

At Trocadéro they switched to the Nation line. "Gotta get off this thing. They'll be watching every exit."

She stood as the train slowed. "I'll get off here; you go one further to La Motte Picquet. Meet you at 143 Emile Zola, on the roof." She ducked out the door.

The train picked up speed. Cohen stared away from a young man in army fatigues and a painter's cap who smiled inquisitively. I must look weird, hobbling about. Christ, already's after nine. Late for the Serpent. What if I made it all this way only to get nabbed the day I'm to meet Paul?

Wincing, he stood and crossed the aisle to inspect the Métro

246

map on the wall, the train knocking him off balance and into the man in the painter's cap as it slowed for the elevated station at La Motte Picquet. *"Pardon,"* he said, grabbing the center pole. La Motte Picquet flashed into view—a tanned naked woman's back on a suntan billboard, another ad of a boy smiling as he brushed his teeth. The métro map showed a different line from La Motte Picquet to Odéon. Can I risk it? Nothing else's any safer. Here I come, Paul.

He stepped through the train's hissing doors. Three policemen in black uniforms with Sterling submachine guns watched the turnstile. He turned and walked quickly back toward the train. *"Attends!"* yelled a policeman. *"Toi!"* The doors shut in his face; he drove his fingers into the rubber seam between them and tore them open. A policeman hurdled the turnstile running for the train. The doors reclosed. The train jerked; the doors shuddered as the policeman battered against them; he ran alongside the train smashing his gun stock through the glass. *"Arrêtez-le! Arrêtez-le!"* he screamed at the other passengers, "Stop the train!"

A tall man with spectacles stood and yanked the emergency stop; Cohen shouldered past him into the next car and through people scrambling and stumbling as the train squealed to a halt. He dashed to the front car, the engineer opening his door, surprise on his face as Cohen slammed through a window and dropped to the tracks. Watching the electrified rail he sprinted along the ties, glimpses of city streets shuttering between his feet, the policeman behind, gun in hand. Jumping over the rail he dropped down a girder into the shadowy substructure, the policeman's gun clanking against metal as he aimed over the side.

Away now and running. Running hard and free, no pain, faster than they, round a corner and no touching me now, free in wind-floating face-tightening hair-tugging fleetness. Down the sidewalk and over the street, cars screeching, blue lights flashing, no stopping now. This alley, through a garage where cars sit feeding from gas pumps, my feet spinning on oil stains, here another street, pounding through a church yard into a bar, panting, quickly to *Hommes* in the back, stand before mirror, face red, chest heaving, sirens wailing in the street.

Cop car outside. Two-way voices. Hop out of Men's Room—corridor leads nowhere but to the bar, policeman coming through the door as I back into *Dames*: two stalls, one shut. Step into empty stall and lock door. Sound of heavy feet in the corridor, a voice: *"Vous avez vu quelqu'un?"*

The floor of cracked concrete rivuleted with leaks from the john, a brush and a basket of used toilet paper to one side. At least they can't see under the door. Odor of fresh excrement from the next stall, tearing of paper. Clatter of doors from *Hommes,* zip of a zipper in the next stall, sucking roaring of its toilet, click of high heels, banging of the stall door, spatter of faucet into the sink. If she tells them someone else came in . . .

Ripping sound of long hair being combed, a young woman's voice—*"Vache!"*—snap of pocketbook, squeal of door opening, voices drifting out onto sidewalk, sear of tires as a car pulls away.

He dropped his head, took a breath. For this moment safe. Hunted the second I leave. Get to Odéon, but how? They're watching the subways, buses, taxis, sidewalks . . .

Above the stall a window. He prised it open, diving through it as a woman entering *Dames* shrieked into the bar. Landing in an alley of dogshit and trash cans, he sprinted to the corner where he walked steadily but relaxedly along Avenue de Suffren, past UNESCO.

Restaurants were closing; *flaneurs* ambled hand in hand before darkened shop windows. At a kiosk on rue Perignon a blue Lancia idled while its owner rummaged through magazines. Cohen jumped into it, the owner running for him as he peeled round Place de Breteuil down rue de Sèvres. He ditched the Lancia in a deadend off St. Sulpice and strolled casually toward Place Odéon.

Le Serpent d'Etoiles was a scruffy, unpresentable bar with a long, battered zinc counter, shabby chairs, and a sticky floor. The tables outside were empty; several people sat inside with espressos or drinks. Paul was not one of them.

"Has a tall black guy been here?" Cohen asked the woman behind the counter.

"Not that I've seen, Monsieur."

"Perhaps earlier?"

"I've been here since two, Monsieur."

He lingered with an armagnac till the bar closed at midnight, but Paul did not come. Now I'm alone. He's dead. All this horror, Paul. All this misery and death had a reason: to see you alive again. So

248

they wouldn't win everything. But they have. They've killed you, and everyone else who knows. Except me. And they'll run over me like a truck. They've got the power to see that no one listens, no one believes. It wasn't worth it, Paul. All this death, your death. But we never chose it, did we? That's how totally I've been defeated—I sometimes forget even how innocent we were. . . .

It's not over till it's over. I almost didn't make it here on time—maybe you've had troubles too. Tomorrow you could be here. He glanced up from the table. Unsafe here. Unsafe on the streets. Claire's waiting, worried, at 143 Emile Zola. Do I trust her? He paid for his armagnac and wandered into the night.

Give Paul another day. No rush. The CIA'll be looking for me in Colorado soon, thinking Paul's there to meet me. Cohen stopped dead on the sidewalk. If Mort swallowed that story I gave him in Neuenweg about my meeting Paul in Colorado, that means Claire didn't tell him the real meeting was set for Paris. So she's not lying. Should go to see her, see she's okay.

On rue Vaugirard he snagged a taxi to Place du Commerce, and descended empty and silent rue Violet to 143 Emile Zola. It was a tall narrow building set back from the street. No one waited outside or in the unlit foyer, or in the dark corners of the damp and windswept roof. Where are *you* now, Claire? Do they have *you*, too? I've failed again?

Dawn smeared the eastern sky. The horizon was a maze of cranes, tiled roofs, steeples, and hotels backlit by a smoggy mustard preglow of the sun. He shook himself from a dream in which someone was always near death. His back ached; he wriggled tighter into the cold concrete corner of the roof but could not sleep. From the apartments below rose the smell of coffee and the drowsy voices of men and women.

He combed his hair with his fingers, rubbed his face, and descended the stairs of 143 Emile Zola, stopping once more to watch the entrance in which she had never appeared. A girl came in carrying a *baguette,* jumped with surprise as she saw him. "Ça va?" he said.

She ran past him into the building. He crossed the street, wandered toward the Seine, ate without hunger in a nameless café, bought a razor, scissors, and a woman's blonde wig in a Monoprix.

In another café restroom he shaved, trimmed the blonde wig with the scissors and put it on. I look like Doris Day. Like Doris Day in drag. He threw the wig in the trash and walked out into the sun.

In the Bois de Boulogne he sat on a bench watching a mother Rouen duck shepherd her children through muddy rushes into the discolored water. The ducklings cheeped and paddled round her, splashing their backs, diving under, and coming up sparkling with droplets.

A breeze wrinkled the water. The duck and ducklings had left; on an island in the center of the lake waiters were setting out tables and chairs before a fake Tudor inn. He stretched, rubbing his chest, patted suddenly at his coat, removed it, feeling the lining.

Inside the lining was a black plastic and metal device the size of a watch face. He stared at it, slowly nodding his head. So that's it. Schmuck, schmuck, and schmuck again. Schmuck and schmuck again. How conveniently she disappeared when things got hot! He froze and dropped the device back in his pocket. Somewhere right now they're watching me. From behind some tree, from some car, watching, waiting, following the signal from this beeper. And I almost led them to Paul. He stood, settled the coat on his shoulders, and strolled casually from the park.

Bitch beyond bitch beyond any human possibility. Horror, nightmare; love is death; death loves with a woman's kiss. Chest aching with fury, he walked blindly through the sunny Paris springtime streets, his hands trembling with the strangled images whirring through his mind. In rue de l'Assomption he glanced back for the first time, seeing no one. A hundred yards back a gray Simca halted at the curb. Three blocks later it was the same distance behind him. He darted across the street, dodged a white *camionette,* sprinted up rue Boulanvilliers, knocked down a schoolboy carrying a blue briefcase, and crossed Ranelagh, glancing over his shoulder. Cutting through Place Chopin, he ran down rue de l'Annonciation, up rue Bologne, and down rue de Passy. There was no sign of the Simca. He waited panting in the Trocadéro métro station for the sound of an incoming train. It was headed toward Pont de Sèvres. At the last moment he ran down the stairs. A girl in a black raincoat trotted alongside him; when he reached the train he pulled up, letting her enter. As the train pulled away she peered through the window at him with surprised foreign eyes.

He took the next train, direction Etoile. At Kléber he waited until the doors began to slide closed, then jumped from his seat and jammed them open. The platform was empty but for an old woman in a blue apron who swept listlessly at cigarette butts. The doors shut behind him and the train slipped away. The old woman stared, chewing on a butt that hung from the corner of her mouth.

A taxi took him over Pont de l'Alma to Place de la Résistance. He ran through parked motorcycles on rue Cognac-Jay and caught another taxi to métro station Duroc. At the Gare de l'Est he bought a second class ticket to Strasbourg.

"It's not worth it," he said to the ticket seller behind the plastic screen.

"*Quoi—ça?*"

"This lousy ticket—it's too dear!"

"Talk to the Pope."

"You hear that?" Cohen called to the man behind the next screen. "I make a complaint, and what does your buddy do, he tells me to get fucked."

"Perhaps you should, then."

"I'll report you guys when I get to Strasbourg."

"Do that, *couillon!*"

Turning away to hide the grin on his face, Cohen crossed toward the Strasbourg platform. He bought a paperback *Bonjour Tristesse* and wrapping paper in the station bookstore, and a pocket knife and stamps at the *tabac*. Dropping a franc in the saucer at the men's room he shut himself in a stall. Cutting the center from *Tristesse,* he took the small black plastic device from his coat and placed it in *Tristesse,* wrapped the book and addressed it to an imaginary name and street in Strasbourg.

The platform was busy. With ten minutes till departure he approached a dark-haired young man reading *Le Canard Enchaîné*. "I'm looking for someone going to Strasbourg."

"I am," the young man said.

"My sister lives there, and I want to send her this book, but it'll take a week from here. Would you be willing to drop it in a mailbox there?"

"Sure," the young man smiled. "If it's not a bomb."

From the station he took several more taxis and métros to arrive finally at Place Odéon. The windows of Le Serpent d'Etoiles

251

opaquely reflected the early afternoon sun. Inside, a few teenagers clustered round a pinball machine; an old man in a blue beret sat contemplatively with a *pernod* by the door. A man with shirtsleeves uprolled past red elbows, cigar in mouth, tended bar. "I'm looking for a tall black dude," Cohen said. "He been in?"

"Not today, unless he's invisible."

"Nobody black?"

"I said nobody. This ain't Tanzania."

Cohen sat at the bar. "I'll have an *express*."

The man knocked old grounds from the espresso basket, cranked in new, clamped it up and pulled down the lever. "From the number of blacks I seen in here," he said, bringing Cohen his coffee, "you could wait a long time."

After the *express* he had a sandwich, then a *pernod,* as customers came and went. He felt a listless alienation, a numb heartache. You're a day late, Paul. I'm really beginning to think you're dead.

He clutched the table in horror. What if Claire tracked me here with that signal, last night, after we split and I escaped the *flics*? Then I led them to him. I'll kill myself. His hands tore into the aluminum table rim. I'll kill myself. But then why aren't they here now? To get me?

His head whirled. They trap me not only in the physical world but also in my own spirit, confront me with my own failure, my own unawareness. If they don't kill me they'll make me kill myself.

Paul, if you don't come I'll find Claire, no matter where she hides, no matter what country or city in what corner of the world she goes to. This time, kill her right away, before doubt can creep in. She's a master of enticement, of making me believe her masks. Did I love her? Have to be honest and say yes. Fool beyond fool. Maria was wrong: fortune doesn't favor fools, it tortures them in their stupidity as a boy tearing wings from a fly.

Though it's better to love without guile. Love is not love unless, like me and Sylvie, trust is absolute.

Where are you, Paul?

Time creeping by. Like watching someone die. The chance is dying, chance he might still be alive. Working my way onto my fourth *pernod*. Low on money, no more in sight. Rob a bank? Don't have a gun. Can't take the chance I'd hurt someone. Nowhere to go. Who do I know'd put me up, someone the CIA couldn't find?

If Paul came now what would I do? All the cool way we used to be, I wouldn't be that now—I'd grab him and hug him and weep for joy. Even praise God and thank God. Yes I would.

Though maybe God's like Maria said—maybe He leaves us alone and we should just be grateful for the gift of life. Am I? After all that's come down?

Paul strode through the door and Cohen leaped up to grab and hug and squeeze him, to never let go, feeling the fine roughness of his face and the hard barrel of his chest and the long wiry muscles running up his back, feeling the awful harmony of life that kills some people and lets others live, choosing blindly, without justice, and yet this was surely justice to have Paul here—thinner, yes, with purple hollows under bloodshot eyes and a nervous shudder in the shoulders and a way of looking all around without stopping.

"Hey," the barkeeper barked, "I don't want none of that stuff here—there's other places for guys like you—*Vite, vite, sortez, sortez!*"

"It's not like that," Cohen laughed. "We each thought the other was dead—I couldn't wait in K'du," he added, moving Paul to the table, "What happened to you—Christ, tell me!"

The barman came for Paul's order. "This guy thought you weren't gonna show," he said to Paul. "Sure you guys ain't queer? Not that I mind, *vous savez,* but I got other customers, *n'est-ce pas?*"

"No," Paul grinned, "*ça va.* We're your average American motherfuckers. Nothing abnormal with us. And I'll have an *anis.*"

Cohen grinned at the pun, suddenly there seeming nothing to say and no way to say it; he felt close to tears but would never express them, knew that nearly all had been lost but would not now admit it, knew that he felt joy, but a joy compounded of awful memories and a question of guilt that could never be answered. To have Paul here leaning back in his chair asking for a drink seemed no different than years ago, after a game, in some backstreet U.S.A. bar, Paul hamming to the girls and downing Coors while the world spun in dizzy drunken joy, the joy of youth, of innocence. "You okay?" Cohen said.

"Fine."

"Anybody following you?"

"Not a soul, man. I don't leave tracks."

"Why so long, then?"

"I went beserk, didn't know where I was—weeks passed, maybe, don't remember. Finally I pulled myself out of it, got some clothes, bought a British passport for five hundred bucks, took a flight here from Calcutta. Got in this noon."

"Did they tell you I did it?"

"They didn't tell me nothing, man. I missed you by an hour—got to the house as they were taking Kim's body away. I went crazy, tore half Katmandu apart looking for Stihl. On my way to the Embassy I found he was dead and everyone was hunting you. I quick grabbed a flight to Calcutta and there I fell apart; lived in some awful ghetto sleeping on the street, crawled into myself until no one was left. Old guy took pity on me—skinny as a starving rat, he shares his rice with me when he gets any, old mangy rice thrown out from a TB hospital. Fell apart. I really fell apart." Paul bit at a fingertip, staring at the wall with its jaundiced photographs of race horses neck and neck at the tape.

Cohen felt like reaching out and hugging him. "I've got it figured out."

"What's that?"

"If this address in New York, Kohler Import-Export on Fulton Street, is good, we'll follow it from there. When we find out who they're hooked to, in the CIA or whatever, when we have the names and faces, we'll blow them away in the press."

"Why not do it now?"

"We don't have anything but a story. What proof but a few missing people?"

Paul laughed, folding his fingers together like the steeple in a child's game. "Who's *ever* gonna believe you? Who's *ever* gonna believe that the CIA, or some group within it, gave a nuclear bomb to the Tibetans to use against the Chinese?" He leaned forward, hand on Cohen's arm. "Do you really think the Associated Press and the papers it feeds are gonna *print* that?"

"What about what Claire said, and that Algerian colonel, and . . ."

Paul shook his head. "Don't be naive, baby. Look at the world

254

through a black man's eyes for a change. What do you think the States is, man, some international do-*good* agency? Who you are in the States depends on how much you steal—you're a nigger kid and you steal a junk car maybe you get ten years, but you be Vice President and you steal from the whole country maybe you lose your job and get a richer one as 'consultant.' You ever notice that, how all those Senators when they leave government they become '*consultants*'—the sultans of *con*?"

Cohen chuckled. "So what's that have to do with us?"

"'Cause we're up against all that! When sixty percent of the U.S. budget's for war, do you think that ain't the country's biggest industry? Do you think that industry don't run the government? Elections? They're just Roman circuses, baby. The CIA's just the active foreign arm of America's military government—it's the CIA's *job* to start wars."

"So what now?"

"Now? We go home, get out of this shit, start a new life. I got everything to forget and nothing to remember."

"I'm the opposite. I can't forget a single thing out of the last six weeks."

"Then we're different, man; let's each go his own way."

"What about vengeance—about getting them back? About killing them for Alex, for Kim . . ."

"Don't bring up her name, Sam. Not as motivation for any killing. She don't like that. She don't want to be revenged."

Cohen glanced around the bar. "It was another world, when we were here. Only three years ago."

"Remembering Sylvie, aren't you?"

"Let's take a walk."

As Paul tossed crumbs from a dry *baguette* to pigeons in Luxembourg Gardens, Cohen recounted his experiences. When the bread was gone they sat on a bench watching girls double-skipping rope on the gravel walk.

"So what'll they do now?" Paul said.

"Probably they think I don't know about that transmitter, and that I've gone back to Neuenweg. Or that I'm living in a mailbox in Strasbourg."

"I'm amazed they'd sacrifice one of their own people."

"The one Claire shot? That's how much it's worth to have us both; they must be very afraid. Must understand how we could blow their scene."

"And you still think it was a bomb?"

"I believe Alex. It's the last thing he said. You and I are the only ones left who know it, and that's why they want us."

"It's how I always thought it would start—some terrorist thing, some stolen bomb . . . but I never dreamed it would happen now. It was always some time in the future, when I'd have time to get ready . . ."

Cohen laughed. "Ready for what?"

"Remember that poster, the one with ten steps to take in case of a nuclear attack, telling you how to find a safe place, how to lie on the floor, your head under a desk or something, and the tenth thing you do is stick your head between your legs and kiss your ass goodbye?"

"No. I don't remember that."

"That's what it'll be. We'll all be kissing our ass goodbye."

"So we have to reveal this—we have to get them before it goes further."

"No." Paul shook his head again. "Whatever's written's written. I'm gonna live, and learn to love life despite life, like my buddy, that old man in the Calcutta ghetto. I'm not gonna ruin my time running around trying to convince the world how it oughtta operate. If it wants to blow itself up, then fuck it, let it blow itself up."

"You can't mean that."

"I sure's Hell do." Paul watched the park emptying now of children on their way to dinner. A housewife hurried by, broccoli heads peeping from her string sack. An old man in a blue cap tossed bread to ducks along the concrete edge of a pond where the sun threw green, dark shadows.

"If I want to walk due west, baby, and there's a cliff there I can't climb, I got two choices. One, war: to convince my fellow men we must blow up that cliff, dominate it. Two: I can go around it, alone, on my own path."

"I don't give a shit about all that, Paul. I want revenge."

"Yeah, but you're hooking yourself up to the same process. Just like Br'er Rabbit and the Tar Baby, the more you fuck *with* it

256

the more you get fucked *by* it." Paul leaned forward. "Why not step outside it, change dimensions? Why not write a book?"

"Sure," Cohen shrugged. "And give them my address."

"They wouldn't dare touch you. If they kill you, they prove you right. Look at that guy who wrote all the books on the Kennedy murder—they ain't killed him yet."

"Because he hasn't figured out their secret."

"Nor have we. But writing a book might help. I could get behind that—that's not killing anyone."

"I'm not interested. I *am* a killer. They've made me that."

"Then they've already won, Sam. They've taken over your soul."

"Please stay with me on this. Let's go to New York together, find out what's with 293 Fulton. Then we'll decide." Cohen paused at a fountain darkened by tree shadows. "The Medici'd do anything to gain and preserve power: murder, poison, intrigue, war, degradation of the church. Why should our leaders be different? The Medici Fountain—Do you think some day our descendants'll stand before stuff like this in honor of Johnson, Rusk, or Kissinger, and never realize how many thousands of agonized deaths their reputations are built on?"

Paul looked out over the treetops dark in the failing light. "I'll stick with you to Fulton Street, Sam. But it ain't my choice."

Cohen squeezed his arm. "You won't regret it. Christ, I'm hungry. I dread going back to American food. Going back, want to split up?"

"Not again. Somebody has to keep you out of trouble."

"I already got trouble. The CRS wants my bod; I got no passport."

"All in due time. But first the condemned shall eat a hearty meal."

Impetuously Cohen grabbed Paul and hugged him. "I'm so broken-hearted by all this. But I'm so happy to have you back." He felt tears sting his eyes, bit them back. "I'd give anything to have things the way they were—just a few weeks ago."

The streets were dark when they left the restaurant. "Strapping tape and glue, then the two maggots," Paul said.

"You should learn French. It's an ape, not a maggot." They

descended Boul Mich and crossed at the Ecole de Médecine onto St. Germain. A man leaned against a black Porsche, a slim girl kissing him wildly. Opposite the church they entered a large corner café whose tables crowded the sidewalk. After an hour's serenade by a sidewalk guitarist they followed a tall, lanky man downstairs to the john. He entered the stall.

"*Vous parlez français?*" Cohen said when he emerged.

"Huh? *Oui, un peu.*"

"*Américain?*"

"*Oui.*"

"Where from?" Paul said in accented English as Cohen moved toward the stall. Paul grabbed the American's mouth as Cohen twisted back his arms. They spun him to the floor. Paul locked the door. The American was mumbling through Cohen's hand. Cohen whispered, "Shut up, or I kill you," and the mumbling was replaced by wide-eyed terror.

They yanked off the man's necktie, stuffed his mouth with paper towels and tied the necktie tight across it while Cohen rifled his coat pockets, tossing a packet of travel checks and an emptied wallet on the floor.

Paul held him while Cohen took the passport from his rear trouser pocket. They taped his wrists behind him, then taped his wrists and ankles to the stall door jamb, relocked the door, and walked separately up the stairs. Cohen strolled down rue Bonaparte, turned at rue de Lille and crossed the Seine over the Pont Royal, cut through the Tuileries to the Concorde métro, and took the first train to the Montparnasse station.

Outside the station he paid an Algerian vendor sixty francs for a used blue nylon jacket too tight across the shoulders, and bought a second class ticket to Calais. In the self-portrait photo booth he took ten frames. Near the station entrance a *clocharde* was scrunched under a shabby coat over the métro heat ventilator. She reeked of old vomit.

"Hey, grandmother, wake up!"

One eye opened. "Leave me sleep, cuntface."

"Here." He tucked the American's money into her horny hand. "Get a meal and a warm bed."

"Who are you to tell me? Stick it up your ass!"

Paul was in the waiting room but Cohen did not approach him;

258

they entered separate cars on the train. "Third couchette," Paul said when he passed Cohen in the corridor as the train rolled out of Paris. Cohen watched city lights accelerating past the dirty corridor window. A train rushed the other way, shaking the window. He had a sudden fear of being wrong, about Claire, about Paul, himself. "Transition," the train replied, "repetition, transition, repetition, transition," its wheels clicking faster, faster, until half-dazed he followed the corridor to Paul's couchette.

Paul's eyes were hard and black. "Never," he said, "never will I do anything like that again, robbing that poor helpless shit and terrifying him, taping his arms like that! Never!"

Cohen sat, head in hands. "I'm sorry. I'm losing track. But if we don't get out of France we'll both be killed. We had to do something."

"I paid for both bunks," Paul said. "You might as well stay." He reached across and squeezed Cohen's knee.

"The *flics* come an hour out of Calais." Cohen put the passport and the ten photographs on the fold-out table.

Paul was removing the photo of the American from the passport with the blade of his pocketknife. "You've been to England, France, Germany, and, strangely, Zaire."

"Wonder why."

"Charles Russell Goodson, Andover, Mass. Born Tennessee, U.S.A., April 1, 1945. You're an April Fool, Charles. Don't forget to memorize this stuff." Paul began to sort through the photos.

"That one's best."

"Customer's always right." Paul took the indicated photo and placed it under the one he had cut from the passport, trimming it with his blade. "Now comes the tricky part." Gently, with the chain ring attachment of his knife, then with the plunger of a ball point pen, he began to duplicate the circle of depressions punched into the surface of the American's photo. "The jerking of this train doesn't make it any easier," he said after a while.

"Do your best. It's only my life in your hands."

Paul leaned back to survey his work. "Then no doubt this's good enough." He glued the photo into the passport, blew it dry, and scuffed it a bit over one knee.

Cohen stared at his picture, the strange dark hair, in the passport with the strange name and signature. "You do this all the time?"

"Sho nuff. We nigras's born to crime. You should practice signing your name, Charles."

"Chuck."

"The interesting question is will we hit the States before they learn this is stolen?"

"The Sûreté won't report it till tomorrow at the earliest."

"Say eight A.M. Paris time—or two A.M. New York."

"I'll just have to gut it out. You stay away from me at Kennedy Customs, and hope they're not that organized. And hope you don't get picked up, either."

Near midnight the French passport control officers descended on the train. Cohen, back in his own compartment, nodded nonchalantly as the small, moustached officer handed back his passport without comment. "It flew," he said to Paul, once the Dover boat was beyond the last gossamer lights of France, caught in the wrenching cadence of heavy seas on the English Channel.

"A good trap, Sam, is one that's easy to slip into."

The passport passed muster with the English port police. They took the train into London and the A1 bus from Victoria to Heathrow. At Heathrow they bought two tickets to New York with Charles Russell Goodson's American Express Card. By nine they were over Belfast on a TWA flight to Kennedy. Cohen watched through the perspex, but Ireland's emerald lay veiled in clouds.

The Kennedy customs man stared at him thoughtfully. "You comin' back with no luggage?"

"My father just died. I'm returning to France after the funeral."

"Oh. Sorry to hear that. Go ahead."

New York's air was damp and warm, smelling of park grass and bus fumes. They took a room near Grand Central. It began to rain; Cohen stared through the streaking window at the flow of umbrellas far below in the street. "We've been gone two years," he said finally, "but I don't feel home at all."

22

TWO NINETY-THREE FULTON was an unimposing four-story brick building suffering from a century of boredom and neglect, its window sashes rotting quietly, its ripply glass holed here and there by BBs and cornered with spider webs where smog collected like silt on a riverbank. Ravelled wires drooped between a creosoted pole and a pipe knocked horizontally through the brick. In a Chinese clothing store on its first floor ladies in multicolored coats argued intently with the balding owner while children ran between the racks on the sidewalk.

Paul mounted the stairs to the second floor. Cohen fondled the flashy oriental nylons, his eye on the stairs. The quick-talking ladies left, and the owner asked what he wanted.

"A blouse for my girl."

"What size?"

"She's tall." Cohen raised his hand over the man's head.

"That rack in back."

"I'll look here for a moment first."

"That Chinese coats."

"Yes. I'm looking also for my mother. A coat for my mother."

"She want Chinese coat?"

"Yes, she's Chinese."

The man tucked his head back on his neck to look up at Cohen. "You mother no Chinese."

"Yes . . . my girl's mother."

"You make fun? What you want?"

"A Chinese coat . . ." Paul was descending the stairs. "Here she comes now," Cohen smiled. He followed Paul around the corner, the man watching them, arms akimbo, on the sidewalk.

"No Kohler," Paul said, out of breath. "A Scandinavian woolen place on the third floor, everything else accountants, a Chinese lawyer's, or empty. I asked the girl in the Scandinavian place if

261

they knew Kohler, and she said wait and went into the back office. The ugliest guy in America came out—baggy eyes, nicotined lips, round-shouldered, about fifty, a great sprouting red-haired wart on the tip of his nose. He takes off his bifocals and says who wants to know. I tell him some other place gave me the name. He asks who; I don't remember. He listens to my spiel for a couple minutes, then says Kohler ain't there no more, they went under." Paul licked his lip. "He knows, Sam. I watched him sweat." Very deliberately, a truck tractor was backing its trailer into a short space in front of them, its air brakes hissing. "A stack on a file cabinet. One of the files said Kohler."

Cohen sucked air between his teeth. "Time for a trip to the East Village."

"Count me out."

"No violence, promise. Persuasion, Paul, I'm talking persuasion."

A crosstown cab took them to an eroded park at the corner of Avenue A and Seventh. A few mothers pushed strollers, guarding their flanks with a hunted air; several teenagers were throwing knives at a bench. "Want to make some money?" Cohen said.

"Maybe." One squinted at him, wiping hands on his jeans.

Cohen sat on the bench. It was splintery and warm. "I don't have much time, so here's my problem. I need a handgun and some acid and speed. I'll pay good. If you guys can help me, fine. Otherwise I'll find somebody else. Anybody who talks to the cops is dead."

"You think we're criminals?" said the shortest one, missing front teeth. "We don't talk to cops."

"I don't care who you are." Cohen stood. "Am I wasting my time?"

"Nobody say that," the squinting one replied. He glanced across the dead grass at Paul. "Who's that?"

"My bodyguard."

The boys moved away, conversing in Spanish. The short one returned. "Come back this afternoon."

"I need them in one hour."

"Fuck you, man. No can do."

"Thanks anyway." Cohen stepped away.

262

"Wait." More conversation. One boy left, walking quickly. "Where's he headed?" Cohen said.

"Talk to his uncle."

They waited. Bongo drums thrummed in another corner of the park. Two girls with long black hair approached; they sat on the bench and smoked a joint with the boys. One offered it to Cohen. "Your friend want some?" Cohen called Paul over but he shook his head. The boy who had left came back. "We go to my uncle." They crossed Avenue A and turned west on Fifth Street. Ahead an American flag hung from a facade.

"That's the precinct house," Cohen said.

"Easy," the short one grinned.

Two old men sat on the front steps of the police station drinking from a paper bag. The boys walked up the steps of the adjoining building. The short one took Cohen's arm. "Here we meet his uncle."

"You think I'm crazy?"

The boy smiled, toothless. "It's the safest place."

"Leave them outside." Cohen pointed to the other boys.

"With your friend, except Jaime. It's his uncle."

They climbed the stinking, narrow stairs. Wads of bloody cotton lay on the third floor landing. Jaime knocked on a fourth floor rear door.

The room smelt of garbage and roach spray. Behind a door a baby was crying. The uncle was a man in his mid-twenties with a cross-hatched scar on his forehead. In a shoe box he held out a stainless steel .357 Ruger. "Four hundred fifty."

"That's too much; it's just a single action."

"It's what I've got, friend."

"What about the dope?"

"Fifteen dollars a tab, acid or speed."

"The gun's too high. You know that."

"You wanted it quick. Quick costs money."

"Not when you had it here already. I'll go three hundred on the gun, with twenty rounds ammo."

"Shit, man, go to the store and get registered."

"You know I can't do that. But I can go back out on the avenues and get a gun right away. You know that, too."

"Four hundred. I give you a box of ammo, too."

"And throw in five tabs of acid, five of speed."

"Four-fifty for the whole thing," the uncle said. He went into the crying baby's room and returned with a box of factory loads and two plastic bags with five capsules each. The Ruger was nearly new. "Police Special," the uncle said, tossing it gently in his palm. They went down to the first floor landing; Cohen called Paul in to pay. Then Cohen loaded the gun and tucked it in his coat pocket, keeping the ammo and plastic bags in a paper sack.

On St. Mark's Place they halted at a brown Plymouth Valiant with three parking tickets under the wiper, its windshield opaque with grime. Paul flicked his knife blade through the cracked weatherstripping and popped up the door button.

No one passing on the sidewalk seemed to notice through the dirty glass as Paul cut the wires behind the ignition switch, linked two, and touched the third to them. The starter yowled, clacked, and caught. On East Houston Street Paul stopped to remove the parking tickets and clean the windshield. At 11:35 they parked next to a fire hydrant around the corner from 293 Fulton.

At 12:10 a short, heavy man with red hair left the building and walked toward Broadway. Paul intercepted him at the corner. "Sir, I'm the one who spoke to you before, about a job?"

"So?"

"I got one. I'm working for the fellow behind you. He's got a .357 Magnum pointed at your back, and unless you join us for lunch he's going to blow your intestines all over the street."

The man stiffened. "I'm not carrying any money."

"Lunch is on us, beautiful." Paul held open the car door, flipping the seat forward. "Keep your hands on the back of the front seat and slide across. My boss wants to slip in beside you."

Cohen kept the Magnum on him through the Midtown Tunnel's Correct Change lane, and on the Long Island Parkway till the Jericho exit. Near Oyster Bay Paul parked at a For Sale sign by a field overgrown with sumacs and elms. They entered the sumacs, checked the man for weapons, and sat him on the sandy earth. His face was blanched, with red splotches.

"Well, Kohler," Cohen smiled, "this's the end of the line."

"Name's not Kohler."

"Who's Kohler, then?"

264

"It's defunct. We merged, but kept our name. I don't think there ever was a person, Kohler." The man looked up. "What the hell do you guys care about Kohler?"

"Enough to let you go if you're straight with us."

"You don't want money?"

"We want to talk about Kohler."

"Go ahead."

"What did they sell?"

"They bought. Rugs from Iran, brassware and wool from Turkey—all Middle Eastern stuff."

"And from Nepal?"

"Nothing from there." The man rubbed his eyes. "Jeez, guys, mind if I smoke?"

Cohen lifted the cigarettes from the man's breast pocket and placed them out of reach. "He's wasting our time, Paul. Let's give him lunch." He opened the plastic bags and took a capsule from each. "Truth drugs. They'll make it easy, not being able to say no."

The man gagged down the capsules. Cohen tied his wrists to his ankles and waited. After forty minutes he began to sweat and shake, eyes flitting from one to the other.

"You're a real hippie, now." Paul untied him. "What time is it, boss?"

"Two-twenty." Cohen forced two speed capsules down the man's throat. "If we don't have everything we need to know by three o'clock, Kohler, you're a dead man."

By ten to three Cohen had taken the man's belt and was drawing his knife blade back and forth steadily over its machine-stamped western motif. The man sat cross-legged, fingering his empty belt loops. "Can't I please have a cigarette?" he whispered.

Cohen raised himself to a crouch. "I'll kill you unless you speak!"

The man went wide-eyed. "It's before my time, but Kohler dealt with Nepal. I don't like to tell you this, but with a wife and family to support, you know, what can I do?" He cocked his head. "Stihl? He's a tall fellow with a beard? I'll bet he stayed in contact with Nepal; he's worked in the Philippines. But I had nothing to do with the Nepal thing."

"What was the Nepal thing?" Cohen asked softly.

"One word, and as God is in Heaven I'll be dead."

"Leave out one word and as God's in Heaven you'll be dead."

"I'm a gopher, nothing but a clerk. Really . . ."

Cohen shook two acid capsules into his palm and showed them to the man. "This is the end of your mind. Do you want to be a vegetable the rest of your life?"

Paul fished a photo of a slender, chinless youth from the man's wallet. "You'll never even recognize your sweetheart again, let alone get off with him. And he won't want you." He held up a New York driver's license. "Yes, Chester, it'll be the end." He put down the license and opened the wallet further, pulling out a New Jersey license. "Ah, it's Arthur I'm speaking to now, or are you both? How patriotic."

"It's two-fifty-seven," Cohen said. "Time to go."

"What was the Nepal thing, Chester?" Paul tugged the man's sleeve.

The man was shivering like jelly in a vibrator, flushing up into his red hair, pouching his liverish lips, Cohen thought, like a catfish out of water. Cohen placed a hand on the matted red hairs of his wrist. "Look, Chester," he said, "please try to be helpful. We have no quarrel with you. We want the ones you work for." He smiled. "Simple as that!"

The man looked at him hopefully. Cohen cocked the Ruger's hammer, the man jumping at the sound. "Okay, Chester Arthur, you have thirty seconds to explain Nepal."

"Stihl took the orders, from over there. I passed them, up the ladder, you know."

"What orders?"

"Types and quantities. Say, fifty AK 47's, so many side arms, so many crates of grenades, Johnny Jump Ups, you name . . ."

"Johnny Jump Ups?"

"A little fragger, you know, jumps to chest height and goes off, when someone comes near it. Good for gooks."

Paul chuckled. "I don't know that term, Chester. What's a gook?"

"Oh, you know—somebody with slanty eyes—an Asian—not one of us."

Paul smiled, stretching his fingers together. "Like in Vietnam?"

"Yeah—right."

"And you sent out those things—those Jump Ups—to kill gooks."

266

"I don't touch the stuff. A little office, that's all I do, have a little office. Stihl's the one you want, not me; I'm just the contact. I just run a little . . ."

"Stihl's dead, Chester." Cohen shook a cigarette from the man's pack, handed it to him. "So where's this stuff go?"

"Like to fight commies, leftists, that bunch. Some to Tibet. At least it used to, when the Agency was outfitting them."

"Agency?"

"CIA."

"Was?"

"Now, I think, someone else's paying. Please, fella, can I have a light?"

Cohen blew out the match. "Who?"

"Don't know." The man shivered. "The process is the same."

"That's you, isn't it, Chester—the Agency. Isn't it?"

"Well I'm—I mean I was—I mean there never was any proof who it was . . ."

"Who what was?"

"Who set us up, you know . . . I mean, I always thought . . . You see, it was never clear. The State Department, too . . ."

"The State Department?"

"Yeah. You know, how it's really the same, at the top, State and the Agency. State has its own intelligence group, and part of that's Agency people, and then the Agency helps them, and they help the Agency. Like everybody knows, some of the top people in State are really Agency people . . . have always been Agency people, in State."

"What about the bomb?"

"What bomb?"

"Take out the pills, Paul."

"The thing for Tibet that went wrong, that's what you mean? It was a surveillance station. For surveillance on the Chinese. It came through the other way."

"The other way?" Cohen lit another match.

The man leaned forward. "It came down the ladder, you know, instead of up."

Cohen shook out the match. "*Where* did it come from?"

"Alexandria. Where all the rest go to."

"Feed him the pills, Paul."

"It's true, it's true!"

"All the way from Egypt!" Cohen grinned. "You're a real ass-hole, Chester."

"No. Virginia. You know, near D.C. From the owner, you know, of Kohler." The man leaned back, as if he had just finished being sick.

"His name?"

"I tell you and I'm a dead man."

"That's up to you, later. You *don't* tell us and you're a dead man right now."

The man regarded them stonily.

"Chester," Paul said, "I don't want to feed you more acid. You know we can get names and addresses from the files, or from your secretary. I don't want to hurt you; I've never killed anyone and I have no grudge against you. You can save us a little time. Isn't that worth your life?"

The man watched uncertainly, his eyes flat. His forehead crinkled like a dirty undershirt, sending down trickles of exertion along the crevices and blackheads of his nose. He smiled yellow teeth. "You guys'll help me, afterward?"

"What do you want?"

"The regular. Cover and pension. With a new start, you know, I could be real useful to your company."

Cohen glanced quizzically at Paul, who nodded slightly. "I'd like to say yes, Chester, but I can't. We aren't authorized. All I can promise is a ticket and some startup money."

"How much?"

"Ten grand. Plus the ticket."

The man rocked back, hands on his knees. "I'm blowing my whole scene, and you offer me ten grand?"

"We're also offering to blow you completely away. That's the alternative."

"The cops will be on you in a minute." He turned to Paul. "This isn't darkest Africa out here, it's Long Island."

Paul leaned forward. "That was the wrong thing to say, Chester."

"We're asking you to make a sacrifice, Chester," Cohen said. "Ten grand is nowhere near enough, we know that. But we can't commit to more. I'm being straight. We can keep tabs on where you are, try for more. I'll try every angle for you. Please don't be stupid!" He shook the Ruger.

"He codes himself, you know, Blaze." The man was shivering. "But his real name's Marcus Aurelius Clay."

"How do we find him?"

The man silenced, teeth chattering.

"Once we find him, Chester, you don't have to fear him anymore. He'll never trace it back to you. We already knew a lot about him from Mort, though not his name."

"I don't know any Mort. Clay's office is in Alexandria, but he's hardly ever there. You have to go, you know, to his home. It's five Dogwood—I always call it five Dogshit—Annapolis."

"What's he like?" Cohen lit another match and held it out.

"It's been two years, you know, I haven't seen him. He calls on the phone. Tall, silver hair, about fifty-five, a very big man in Washington—I seen his picture, with Senators and stuff, in the paper. That's how I know his name." He inhaled, sighed. "He's been on some Presidential Commission. He goes to the White House. He's got friends in Vegas, too. Big friends. I wouldn't fuck with him unless you've got an army."

"He doesn't have an army, either."

"Oh yes he does. The U.S. Army."

"Where do you want to go, Chester?" Paul's voice was sweet.

"Shit, I don't know. Paraguay, Brazil?"

Cohen glanced at his watch, stood. Keeping the Ruger on Chester, he backed away, motioned Paul over. "Now what?"

"I s'pose you want to go to Alexandria?"

"Yeah. What do we do with him?"

"We don't kill him. Not me. I got through a whole Vietnam tour—fire-fights, search and destroy—without killing anybody. When we attacked a village I'd shoot over the huts, aim for the paddies. Not one person, as far as I know. I'm not gonna now."

"You killed Eliott."

"I don't mind that. But I won't be party to offing this little wimp." He sneered at Chester crouching wide-eyed on the ground. "We are what we kill, man."

Cohen crossed to Chester, extended his hand and raised him up. "How much money you got?"

Chester's face paled. "About forty bucks."

"That's enough to get you home. We're gonna leave you here; we'll drop by your office Friday morning with cash, passport, the whole setup. In the meantime, act if nothing's happened. Want a passport for boy friend?"

"Huh? No, he won't go for that."

"So be it. We'd like you to sit here till dark. Then our backup car will split, at eight-thirty, and you can go. Please for your own sake don't leave till then."

"I ain't goin' nowhere, boys. You can bet on me."

They packed the gun in newspaper in a new plastic suitcase and, leaving the car clean of prints in long term parking, caught the shuttle to Washington. Near the Capitol they had scant trouble locating extra license plates and a recent Chevy Impala with spinners, a vinyl top, and a hole in the dash where a tape deck had been.

Setting sun gleamed on the leafing maples and white houses across the Severn River from Annapolis. Boats crawled up and down, leaving wakes like long feelers behind them. Paul turned to the southeast, to the glimmering deeper chop of Chesapeake Bay. "This here's my last stand, Sam. After this you're on your own."

"What you gonna do?"

"Go down country, work on a farm, save some money and head for the Coast, start over."

"Me too, soon. But I want to find the head of this thing first."

"The head of this thing is America, its way of life, its political system, the money . . ."

"Okay, okay. For now let's just say I want to find out what this guy Clay is about."

The Impala's tailpipe clattered in the narrow, stone-walled lane. At 5 Dogwood, a concrete pickaninny with thick red lips and bulging white eyes balanced a black mailbox on its head. The next gate was two hundred yards further down the lane.

The stone wall was above eye level; behind it, the land seemed to slope down through thick trees to the house whose broad, slated gambrel dormers glinted darkly through new leaves, then to the riverbank beyond.

Dogwood Lane ended in a stone-walled turnaround where two granite lions, each with one upraised paw, watched from the sides of a steel-barred gate. They drove back to the beginning, where only a verge of willows separated the lane from the river. "It's dark enough," Paul said, "we could risk a look from the water."

Cohen snickered. "Shall I charter a boat?"

"Swim, lazy, swim."

Cohen pulled off his shirt. "You did the last one, remember?"

"No."

"The Kali Gandaki? Changtshang." He slid off his jeans, shirt, and socks, slid his glasses into his shoes, and ducked through the willows into the murky water.

Cold was gathering the darkness into mist and casting it over the surface. A gull flapped up with a strange cry. He swam out a hundred yards, shoulder twinging comfortably, and turned upriver. Steadily the well-lit mansions of Dogwood Lane drifted by to his left, till he slowed before an elongated gray-shingled cape with a slate roof and gambrel dormers. A dock obtruded from the rip-rapped shoreline. Behind the dock, a bulb glowed in a boathouse where two kayaks stood racked one over the other, a tall shadow moving back and forth before them. While Cohen treaded water the shadow became a tall man in a light blue sweatsuit who carried a kayak over his head from the boathouse and dropped it gently into the water beside the dock, climbed surefootedly into it, and paddled toward Cohen.

He dove. Below was inky and numbing; his lungs hungered for air. Interminably he waited for the shadow of the kayak to cross above him but it did not; he pushed up frantically against the suffocating cold. The kayak slid by thirty feet away, the man's hair silvered by the boathouse light.

After the kayak had vanished into the mists, he swam quickly to the dock and climbed to the boathouse, lifted the second kayak from the rack and flipped it into the water, tied its bow painter, and returned to rummage in the boathouse for a paddle.

"Who're you?"

He spun round. A girl, perhaps ten, watched him impassively from the door. Her hair was long and tawny. "You startled me," he said. "Help me find a paddle."

She edged closer. "I don't know you."

"I'm Dave Johnston. Friend of your dad's. Can't find a paddle." He shivered.

"You're looking in the wrong place." She crossed to a chest and lifted out a paddle. "When's my dad coming back?"

"Soon. He's helping us with a busted motor on our boat."

"That's why you're undressed?"

"Thanks for the paddle." Cohen untied the painter and stepped into the kayak.

"Tell him to hurry home. I've hardly seen him all day, and he has to help me with my Spanish."

"I'll tell him." He pushed away from the dock and paddled into the mist, turned downriver to the willows and whistled to Paul. "Get your ass out here. I've found Clay. He's out there in a kayak!"

Paul waded out and slipped gingerly into Cohen's kayak. "Let's go have a talk with the man."

They paddled back upriver, the paddle slicing silent dimples in the current. A sycamore's low branches reached out for them. They halted beyond the boathouse light. A car honked in Dogwood Lane, its sound muffled by mist.

"Where'd he go?" Paul whispered.

"Not sure." Cohen explored with his fingers a heartshaped hole in the canvas below the right gunnel.

A boat was idling near the far shore, its motor steady as an electric fan. It sped up, gurgled, and died. Cohen paddled lightly shoreward, thinking the current had dropped them downriver, seeking the outreaching sycamore. A dark lump swam at them; it was a new-leafed bough riding the current.

Drops fell tip tip tip from the paddle. Cohen lowered it but the sound grew. With it rose a hissing, like a knife drawn steadily toward them through water. He touched Paul's shoulder with the paddle and pointed it toward the sound.

The current was easing them past the sound. Cohen backpaddled gently, roiling the water. He twisted his wrist to deflect the kayak inward.

White, in the water. A plastic milk container. Paul leaned out and pushed it; it bobbed back up, the river sluicing round it. Its handle was fastened to a weedy rope descending at an angle toward the riverbed.

"Where was this?"

"Never saw it," Paul answered.

"We've drifted too far down." Cohen paddled toward shore. Laughter ran over the water from upstream. The shore was not there. Cohen dipped the paddle over the side but could not touch bottom. Angrily he paddled thirty strokes ahead and stopped. No bottom. He turned ninety degrees left and took thirty strokes. Nothing. A semicircle to the right and ninety strokes brought nothing more. "We're fucking lost," he hissed.

Brrrap started the boat, to their left and nearer. It revved high and held, then steadied into gear. Cohen drove hard away from it. The boat moved downriver. Dark trees rose before them. The kayak sliced through weeds, paddle sucking on the bottom.

"Upstream," Paul whispered.

Cohen pushed out and paddled upstream, drifted down in sight of shore until they were in the weeds again. "Can't find the dock."

"We must be too low."

Again Cohen paddled upriver. There was the sycamore, its lowest bough diving out over the water, new twigs upraised. He went further upriver. Another thick darkness, another sycamore. He tucked into shore and drifted down its edge to the dock. The boathouse was empty.

He paddled from shore and drove the paddle straight down into the mud, holding the kayak against it. Water riffled under the bow. The paddle thunked on the gunnel. Nervously he pushed off the paddle, then realized it had not touched the boat. He pulled it free and moved them toward the sound.

A black prow across the water, head down like a snake. The man raised his paddle. "Evening," called Paul. "Can you tell us where we are?"

"Where do you want to be?" Clay's voice had a disembodied tone.

"Up the Severn, about two miles from Annapolis."

Clay was gone in a churn of his paddle, his kayak bottom up.

Cohen shoved his paddle at Paul and dove. The water was cold and thick. He felt for Clay's kayak; its seat was empty. He twisted down to guard his flank, but all was black, above and below.

He surfaced panting and dove again, checking all the way below the kayak to mud and creepers at the bottom. A hand grabbed his ankle—a waterlogged branch heavy with weeds. He broke it free and clawed upward, lungs roaring.

Clay's kayak drifted empty, keel up, to his right. Paul had left; he would be checking further out. Cohen breaststroked quietly toward shore. A log shape rode ahead.

Cohen took a breath and slid under the log. It was another kayak, upside down. He peered over its side. "Paul!"

Paul did not answer. Cohen fingered the canvas to the heart-shaped rent amidships, and gently slid away. "Paul!" A motorcycle was working along Dogwood, backing off loudly.

He treaded water. The kayaks had drifted out of sight. He swam toward the sound of the motorcycle and waited. The current carried him downriver; he moved inshore till his feet touched, and pushed upcurrent on the grasping mud, past the first sycamore, until he saw Clay's dock.

The mist was clearing and house lights shimmered in the shallows. Part of the dock's substructure moved and merged with the next piling. It broke free from that piling and moved inshore to the next. He stifled the impulse to call, moved closer, squinting. The water was too noisy; he eased to shore and ran crouching through the trees toward the dock.

A head appeared against above the dock. Shoulders came with it, then arms and a waist, a tall, weaving figure. Cohen pulled a rock from the shoreside riprap. The figure cleared the dock. Cohen barefooted across the lawn and hid behind young birches. Clay stumbled toward him, face down, on the path to the house. In his left hand was a knife; his jaw hung strangely open, his mouth and nose deep-shadowed. Cohen hit him on the forehead with the rock; he fell in a clump.

23

HE TIED CLAY'S ARMS and ankles with strips torn from his sweat-shirt, stuffed other strips into his mouth and wrapped it shut, found Clay's knife, then dragged him to the water's edge. From the boathouse he took a life vest, rope, and spare paddle. Shoving Clay into the vest, he towed him to the kayak lying in a waist-deep eddy between the weeds and lower sycamore. He jammed Clay into the front and climbed in behind him.

Clay began to move and twist against him. "Where's my buddy?" Cohen whispered. Clay moaned. Cohen paddled into deeper water and began searching in runs paralleling the shore, cal-culating his increasing distance from it by the lights now freely dap-pling the black, tossing surface.

Paul floated face down below the lower sycamore. He was still warm. Cohen lifted him to the bow; darkness ran like paint down the canvas. The front of Paul's undershirt was black. It was a small puncture below and into the heart. No pulse, the fingers cold.

Paul felt light, almost alive, as he gathered him into his arms, Paul's blood running tepidly down his stomach. He buried his face in Paul's shoulder; it still smelled like Paul—a musky warmth—and it could not be true that he was dead, that it was too late to love, protect, to say the things that had always been left unsaid. He laid Paul over the bow, the few shore lights clearer now, but there were no people there, in those houses, no people anywhere; the earth was empty.

Dropping Paul's hand he spun the kayak and grabbed Clay by the neck, squeezing the jaw till he felt it break, clamping his hands round his neck and thrusting him underwater as Clay's feet thrashed and thudded against the kayak, twisting out chunks of his hair and throwing them like refuse onto the water. When Clay stilled he dragged him out, pinning him by his ears against a thwart. "Why'd you kill him, you bastard? Why'd you kill him?"

275

Clay moaned. A car's lights flashed over the water. Can't get caught here. He banged Clay's head, splintering the thwart. "Why'd you kill him? He never hurt anyone! Why'd you kill him?"

Clay did not answer. He shoved him into the back and paddled into the river's center, where the current slipped him past the lights of Annapolis and into the Bay's chop. Here Paul's dead weight offset the kayak, forcing Cohen back on the rear thwart. The wind slicing off the wave tips was cold from the south; the water drowning the bows had raised a groaning shiver from Clay.

An hour brought them to the rumbling shore of an island. Cohen turned south, into the wind, where the lowered bow worked to advantage. He crossed a straight between the land and the island, and nudged the kayak along mud flats to a rocky, wooded outcrop far from lights or the sound of traffic. With the paddle he trenched a shallow grave in the mud and dragged Paul into it. He stamped down the mud over Paul's body and covered it with boulders, forced Clay into the shadows of the trees and loosed his gag.

"Oh, God, my arm," Clay moaned. "Untie my arm!"

"It's just a shoulder separation. You like football?"

"God, I can't stand the pain."

"They get them all the time, those guys you watch on TV." Cohen spun the arm like a windmill; Clay shrieked and went limp. Cohen splashed seawater on his face and slapped it until he came round. "Want a doctor?"

"God, yes. Hurry."

"Tell me about Nepal."

"Don't know what—God, stop!"

"The truth."

"I will, God, I will. It was just an operation. I bucked it along."

"How?"

"From the, uh, source, to the folks in Nepal, via New York."

"Names."

"Please, please, stop. Stihl in Nepal, Chester in New York. I just passed the requisitions."

"That's not what I hear."

"Cohen—that's who you are. The guy that killed Eliott and Stihl. Half the world's looking for you."

"Unsuccessfully." Cohen rotated the arm. "And everyone will

be looking unsuccessfully for you." Clay slumped; Cohen shook him awake. "Where'd you get the weapons?"

"Military sources. Captured AK's, that's all they were. There's a place in Istanbul, two places in Switzerland, others. Everybody knows."

"Where'd you get the bomb?"

"What? Wait, wait—it was just a surveillance station."

"Who on whom?"

"Us against them. What's wrong with that?"

"Where'd you get it?"

"It got passed down."

Cohen wrenched the arm. "Clay, you've got a choice: cooperate or die. I've talked with all your friends. They keep naming you."

"They're trying to wriggle out." Clay sat back weakly against a tussock, drew up one knee. "But I've got something on you."

"Do you now?"

"Your girl friend's about to die. Want to stop it?"

"My girl friend died on Sainte Victoire. Your people killed her."

"The Hell. We got her Sunday night in Paris. She's in D.C. now. I saw her this morning."

"You can have her."

"I might, under other circumstances. Right now my circumstances are rather constrained, aren't they? I've killed your buddy, Stinson, albeit in self defense. You've gotten the idea I'm responsible for your recent inconveniences, although I'm not. I've got only one piece of information valuable to you."

"Only thing worth anything to me is the names who run you."

"There I can't help you. Jesus, oh, stop it." Clay sagged into the mud. "Please—I'm a terrible coward . . . can't stand pain."

"Imagine what your friends have endured." Cohen stretched the arm. No one will save you here. You can talk and hope I keep my word. Or you can clam up and die very painfully for a bunch of people who wouldn't hesitate to murder you the moment you're not needed."

"There's another side you wouldn't understand. If I give in and die anyway, I've gained nothing. If I don't give in, even though I die I keep my pride. You wouldn't understand pride, Cohen. It's not in your make-up."

"I have one reason for leaving you alive. That's your daughter."

Clay tried to stand. "What'd you do to her?"

"Nothing. Although you're shit, she needs a father. While I was at the boat house she came down from the house. How old is she?"

"Nine in September."

"How did you ever spawn such a pretty child?"

A bullfrog croaked officiously in the marsh behind them. A powerboat was crossing eastward, its motor laboring in the swell. "If I twist your arm any more, I'll break the nerve. Then the arm will be useless the rest of your life. In a minute I'm gonna start on the other arm. Then you'll have neither." He wrenched Clay's other arm. "Goddamn it—who pulls your strings?"

Clay was gone and Cohen slapped him back. "Unfortunately, no one," Clay groaned. "I'm what you call a self-motivated man."

"Then why do this? Why the bomb in Tibet?"

"Surveillance station."

"A surveillance station's worth this killing? And pursuing me to Hell and back?"

"Security." Clay shivered. "Can't we move to drier . . .? To make money."

"Who pays?"

"I get a commission, and favors in the Senate and House; it's just politics."

"Is this all you do, this stuff?"

"I'm a consultant; I've got contacts. It's how I make the money I need."

"Need for what?"

"Upkeep. My position. Campaign donations, parties, State Department receptions, boats, cars. You think it's easy, being in society—being part of the government?"

"Do you think most Americans would approve of what you do?"

"Why not? They don't give a shit anyway."

Cohen twisted harder. "Names."

"Can't. Help. Don't. have them." Clay tried to pull back. "Trade me for the girl."

"Fuck the girl!" Cohen bit his lip.

278

"It's happening this minute. She's getting it from every guy in the team . . . an electric probe stuck right up her . . ."

"Give me the names."

"It's a voice in the night. I never know who calls."

"Who pays?"

"It's dollars in a pickup packet, or a draft to my bank."

"From where?"

"Banks in Argentina or Uruguay."

"Which ones?"

"Not allowed to keep records. Don't remember. You won't believe it, but the print won't xerox and the paper disintegrates."

"Sure."

"Everything they've sent me, which isn't much. It powders. Disappears."

"Who started you out?"

"I was divorced. Had money troubles. Was with a Senate committee. Got a call from a man who said I was recommended to him by a Senator."

"Who?"

"He didn't say and I didn't ask. You don't know how business is done on the Hill." Clay coughed. "He said he represented associates who wanted to help me out, and would I do them a favor. I said sure, what is it. He sent me five thousand. At first I didn't want to spend it but finally had to. After a couple weeks he called again and asked me to interview a man in New York for an import-export job, and to serve as their representative to that firm. So I flew up to the city and met Chester."

"What about Stihl and Mort?"

"Later they asked me to find a man with a military background to represent the company in the Far East. That was Stihl. Mort was hired for Europe. Same criteria."

"Do you want to live? I need *names*."

"Can't help you."

"Then I'll go through your address book and kill every person in it."

"Waste of time, and a waste of innocent people."

Cohen took Clay's knife and slipped it into his good arm, above the elbow. Clay gasped, tried to scream. Cohen punched him. "I'll twist this arm right off unless you shut up and give me names. I'll cut this nerve too."

"You're dirt. Not even human. I can't stand it. Please, if I knew, I'd tell you, please! Please?"

"I'll count from ten. At one I do it." Cohen shifted to better his position. "Nine, eight, seven, six, five . . ."

"I'll tell you where she is!"

"Four, three, two . . ."

"Don't you care about Ruby? Why won't you make a deal?"

"She works for you. Now and always."

"She went over to you in Neuenweg. She helped you with that cop in Paris. She bought you clothes and kept you from the law. She killed our man in Neuenweg. The Hell she works for us."

"If she doesn't, how do you know all this?"

"Mort found you two in Paris. He watched your room from across the street. He'd planted a bug in your coat in Neuenweg, as a precaution."

"But he was still in Neuenweg when we got away."

"You're an amateur. They found your car in the woods, Cohen. They were going to take it, then decided to wire it, hoping Stinson might show."

"Why didn't Mort kill us in Paris?"

"There were some heavy transatlantic calls about it. Mort wanted to kill you both and I said no, in hopes you'd meet Stinson. We lost you briefly after you evaded the CRS. What was that about, anyway?"

"Keep going."

Clay paused to swallow. "They picked up your transmission again by driving around Paris till they got an echo and vectored it. Then you shook them on the train, and they couldn't find you in Strasbourg. I swear to God it's true—I swear on my daughter's life."

"Where's Ruby now?"

"It's a meat-packing plant, D'Angelo Services, off New Jersey and Third."

"Stay quiet and you might live." Cohen threw him into the kayak. "I should make you paddle."

"Oh God, I need a doctor. I'm gonna die of pain . . ."

280

*　　*　　*

The wind had shifted to the east, pushing them fast across the river. Cohen retied and gagged Clay and left him bound to the kayak in sedges by the west shore, walked to the Impala, dressed, and drove back to him. With Clay in the trunk he retrieved the .357 from under the seat and drove downtown.

Too many people I've deserted, drawn them to their deaths, can't chance Mort has you, Claire, killing you. Paul was right: Fuck vengeance, go and live peacefully, save the people you love. Do I love you? I always have but you've tricked me—have you? Maybe what tricked me was my lack of trust—and now you're paying for it. Why do others always pay for my sins? God's most brutal penance—just like He did to us with Christ.

If you didn't put the signal in my coat and Mort did, then I've failed you, Claire; I haven't loved, for love is trust. They've hunted me so hard I don't trust anyone—even losing faith in Paul because he didn't hate. And he was right, he was right.

In an alley off Third Street, cars leaned curbward on wheelless hubs; soggy newspapers and broken bottles waited in the gutter; the pink eyes of rats ducked from his headlights into the sanctuary of sewer drains. The D'Angelo packing plant had six stories, a false concrete loggia mortared to its face, and a stepped-up facade at the roof. No lights were on and the doors were locked. Two truck trailers were parked along one side; they smelled of sawdust, oil, and rotten meat. The loading doors were locked; like those in front they had thin wires taped inside their small glass panes.

Tossing the extra rope from the Impala's trunk over the lowest rung of the fire escape, he climbed to the roof, lashed the rope to a flue, and dropped over the side. The parapet was overhung; he had to swing back and forth until the rope carried him to a window. It was not wired. As he leaned forward to break it, the rope's arc carried him out again, the Impala spinning way below in miniature circles. He pulled himself to the roof, tied the rope in a sling round his chest, and swung over the parapet again. On the third try he smashed the window inward and grabbed the casement. The Magnum slipped from his belt and fell endlessly, cracked loud against the sidewalk.

He wriggled through the window into an airless office stinking of pipe tobacco and coffee residue. In the corridor he bumped a water cooler that hummed back malevolently. There was no movement on any of the floors. The front door could not be unlocked without tripping an alarm. He considered returning to the roof and back down the fire escape for the gun, but checked first for the cellar stairs. They were hidden behind a fire door with an OSHA poster. Lights were on below.

The stairs creaked as he descended. They gave on a narrow corridor, at its far end a lighted room and the voices of two men discussing batting averages while they bent over a battered, dark-haired form lashed to a chair. One shifted position and Cohen saw a bloody, swollen face as a toilet flushed behind him, lavatory door clanging. He spun round; Mort filled the corridor, grabbed his waist, yelling. He slugged Mort as a crack of pain shot across his skull. He started to run, awareness receding down a wave into frothy vagueness.

24

HE SANK THROUGH ULTRACOOL light, a silent sea peopled by the dead. Horrible pain centered on his neck, inside the spine. A red mass floated before him, a raw-flesh aroma. Rib blades gleamed in its fractured chest. A ghost approached, shook him. His eyes would not focus.

"He's awake." It was a harsh, squeaky voice.

Mort entered, eyes black, nose bandaged. Cohen remembered; he spun himself toward the corpse next to him. It was a side of meat.

"Now you really have something to beef about," Mort chuckled. "With no one to take your side." He punched Cohen's ribs. "Side—get it?" He settled his great bulk on a stool and leaned toward Cohen confidentially. "You know, Sam, my work's often very frustrating. I can spend months, *months,* on a task that comes to nothing. How satisfying it is to have you hanging here with the corpses in the aging room. How'd you find us? Or shall I wait for Paul to tell us?"

Cohen's tried to govern his swollen tongue. "You'll never get us both. I've promised you, he'll piss on your grave."

"Time will tell. In the meantime, we have some entertainment for you." Mort held up the heart-shaped diamond necklace. "Remember this?"

The one with the squeaky voice and two others with beards cut Cohen down and tied him to a chair bolted to the floor. The squeaky one stuck a needle in his arm.

What returned was beyond formulation. It was not color, sound, or heat. It was experienced individually by each cell, he realized, because the structure of his psyche was shattering. It occurred to him distantly that he had become like a nation whose laws were abandoned, and whose citizens, his cells, had reverted to fending for themselves. Beneath this chaos grew a foreknowledge of death, and despair over something irretrievably lost. Intensely he fought back, nurtured a private understanding against the random thoughts unravelling his mind. It was the hardest thing, he realized, he had ever done, and it threatened to slip away the second he gave it less than full awareness.

He heard Mort's voice, and fought the urge to smile, act familiar. "You have been through a mental anguish in the last half hour," Mort said, "that few ever have to endure. However, because you believe you are strong, you have been able to overcome it. Very commendable, but it's only a stage of the drug. In a few minutes the horror will be back, this time for real."

Cohen kept his mind on the purpose growing inside him like a pregnant orange spider swollen and inverted in its web. He called the fortune teller; it was an old French telephone, very crackly, the voice at the other end veiled by a mysterious, inhuman hoarseness. "She is not here," the voice said, "but she left you a message."

"What is it?"

"She said you would not listen."

"I will—I promise!"

"No, no. That was the message."

"What?"

"She said you would not listen." The connection died; the receiver idled like a motorboat in his ear. Then he saw it was not a telephone but an electric drill in Mort's hand. "Where's Paul?" Mort grinned. "We need answers. Or Paul won't be safe."

"He's safe now."

"Not enough." Mort stuck the whirring drill up Cohen's nose. It tore his nostrils and roared against his brain. Mort drew it out, turned it off. The silence and blood were nauseating. Mort smiled. "A taste of the future."

Pain swept him into unconsciousness. Mort shook him awake. "Where's Paul?" Cohen did not answer. "Bring her in!" Mort called.

The two bearded men dragged her into the room and tied her to a chair opposite Cohen. It took him a moment to recognize her, for her face was puffy, bruised and blue, her lips split and blackened with dried blood, her eyes half-shut. Her short hair, still dark as she had dyed it in Paris, was frowsy and matted with blood.

"Wake her," Mort whispered.

The squeaky-voiced one threw a pan of water in her face. It ran down her half-unbuttoned blouse and onto her jeans. Her head wobbled listlessly; she coughed and moaned. "Hey!" Mort yelled and slapped her face.

Cohen lunged but the chair held him tight. Claire raised her head and saw him. "Hello," she rasped. "You okay?"

"What have they done?"

She tried to smile. "Not too much."

"I'm sorry."

"You've got nothing to be sorry about."

"But I do." Beyond the bruised face, the black short hair that had replaced the amber tresses she had once coiled so sensuously about him, beneath the turquoise eyes so clearly regarding him through darkened lids, he saw the person who had tried, as she had promised, to sacrifice her life for his. "I could've trusted you, in Paris. I thought . . ."

"Come, come," said Mort. "It's been a learning experience for us all. But let's get this meeting on the road. Here," he pointed to Cohen, "we have someone with information we need, who will not share it. And here," he poked Claire, "we have someone who has nothing we need, but whose condition may interest the other. In essence," he chuckled, "it's a variable of our original plan." He bent down to Claire. "We will still use you, my dear, to extract information from him."

Claire looked at Cohen. "I've told them nothing."

"Let's be quick," Cohen said. "You let her go, and as soon as I'm sure she's free, I'll tell you whatever you want."

"No, no, no, Sam. I've too much respect for you to ever do that. Once she were free you'd clam up. We've found it difficult to break you; now we'll see if you're cruel enough to sit there and watch her suffer."

"Don't talk, Sam. They can't hurt me more than they have. Keep Paul safe."

"I don't even know where he is."

"The fallback, Sam?" Mort said. "The one you talked about in Neuenweg."

"That was bullshit."

Mort stood, clasped his hands. "Let's not be meretricious." He motioned to the one with the squeaky voice, bowing to Cohen. "Let the show begin."

The squeaky-voiced one brought in the electrodes. He pinned two to Claire's fingers, popped her blouse apart and attached two to her nipples. She watched Cohen with unflinching eyes, shook her head. Mort took the console. "How high shall we go, Sam?" He spun the dial.

She arched her back, gasping, writhing, her fingernails tearing at the chair arms.

"Stop it," Cohen yelled, trying to kick but his legs were tied fast. Mort clicked the dial higher. Claire howled; Mort smiled at Cohen. "Where's Paul?"

"Stop. I'll tell you."

Mort nudged up the rheostat. "Tell me and I'll stop."

"No!" she screamed, writhing. "No! No!" Her head lolled forward. Mort turned off the rheostat.

It was a chill, sunny November Saturday. Paul came into the huddle, mud-stained, winded, bloody. "Let's satisfy their expectations," he panted, tightening his helmet strap. "They expect pass, so we will. But not how they think."

The moment of elation faded. The lovely odors of bruised grass and sweat, the dry-throated taste of blood and exhaustion, were replaced by a sterile fluorescence, a pervasive stench of carcass and sawdust. "I'll tell you where the fallback is if you let her go."

"No dice, Sam. She's our insurance. Otherwise you won't talk."

"I promise."

"Try to understand my position, Sam. If I fail, my ass is in the sling. So far I've failed with you. She's the only way I have to make you talk. How can I let her go?"

Cohen tried to lick his lips but his tongue was dry. "What day's it?"

Mort looked at his wrist. "In a half hour, April twenty-seventh."

"We've got to hurry."

"Where?"

"Colorado, like I said."

"I remember something about a map, and horses. Fill me in."

286

"Shut up, Sam!" Claire had come to.

Cohen ignored her, turned to Mort. "Paul and I once hunted there, years ago. West of the Crystal River there's a place in the aspen near a small beaver clearing where he killed his first elk. It has no geographic significance—there's hundreds like it in those mountains—but we both know where it is. Starting in two days, he'll be there sometime the following week."

"Where is this Crystal River?"

"South of Carbondale. You follow a dirt road to Dead Horse Creek, and go in ten, maybe fifteen miles to a particular saddle between two low hills, climb that saddle, walk for a couple hours, till you reach the Clear Fork of Dead Horse Creek. You follow the Clear Fork for an hour or two and then there's a certain blue spruce to look for, a schoolmarm . . ."

"Schoolmarm?"

"Has a split trunk about halfway up. Like a woman with her legs spread, upside down. Facing it from across the Clear Fork is a parson, and that's where you climb toward a long mesa rising into the flanks of Huntsman Ridge. It's thick aspen with spruce above, and bogs and beaver ponds everywhere. Once you're in the forest you lose all landmarks except those inside your head. That's why we chose it."

"A parson?"

"That's a tree with a strongly outjutting limb about half way up, you know, like a hardon? What you get when you beat off with your dirty books."

Mort rubbed his head. "Can you show us on a map?"

"I could show you Dead Horse. I wouldn't know for sure where the mesa is, on a map. But I could show you Huntsman Ridge. It goes to ten thousand feet, maybe fifty or a hundred miles long."

"And all forest?"

"Nearly all."

"You'll have to show us."

"Sam, don't!" Claire tried to break free. "I can stand the pain. They're going to kill us anyway."

Cohen eyed Mort. "Will you let us go, afterwards?"

"Of course, Sam. Once we get a promise from Paul, and from you two, not to reveal anything that could jeopardize national security."

Claire shook her head. "Don't be stupid, Sam."

Mort called the others. "Take her out of here. Get her some clothes. She's going with us."

"Where?"

"Colorado, Sam." Mort left. The bearded ones untied Claire and walked her carefully into the next room. Cohen watched the wall shudder. The beef sides hanging in the corner seemed to nod on the gentlest of currents. A roach ran into the center of the linoleum, hesitated, and crossed under a sink.

They injected him again; he dropped into choking silence. He had forgotten who they were when they woke him. They untied him and moved him to a room with a table. On it was a green and white U.S. Geological Survey map with ashtrays holding down the corners.

Mort splayed the single, ringed finger on the map. "Here's Dead Horse Creek. Where's the spot?"

Cohen was entranced by the broad, blanched moon of Mort's fingernail. "Like I said." His voice felt crusted and unworldly. "I know where Huntsman Ridge is." He drew a six-inch circle with his own finger. "Must be in here someplace."

"Step at a time." It was Lou from Neuenweg. "Here's the Creek. And the road." As Lou bent over the map his chest hairs, long and black, slipped like coal grass out the breach of his collar. Cohen vomited on the map. They brought out another. "When you went into Dead Horse with Paul, how did you travel?" the squeaky-voiced man said.

"I don't know you."

"This is Stan," Mort said.

"I don't know him. I'm not speaking to him."

"C'mon, Sam, he's a regular one of the guys."

"Fuck him. If he stays, I'm not helping you."

"Want him to leave the room, Sam?"

Cohen nodded.

"Okay, Stan, you heard the man. So," Mort smiled, "how did you get into Dead Horse?"

"We rented two riding horses and two pack horses from a rancher."

"Where could we land a copter?"

Cohen thought. "Maybe on a beaver pond. You can get one

with pontoons? Even on the beaver ponds there's hundreds of standing dead trees where the water's risen."

"On horseback, how long did it take, from the Dead Horse road?"

"A day."

He showered with Lou guarding him and ate the hamburger and fries they brought, dried blood in his nasal cavity crackling as he chewed. They climbed together out of the cool, rancid cellar into glaring midday. Heat danced like flame over the soft macadam, the seedy windows across the street, the smog-coated cars. The Impala sat in the sun's full blast, hot air rippling up from its trunk. I should have killed you, Clay. If somebody finds you alive, Claire and I are finally and truly doomed. As if we weren't already.

He sat wedged beside Claire in the back of a blue Ford Fairlane with tinted windows, bulletproof plastic between them and the front, the two bearded men flanking them, squeezing them together. She faced ahead, saying nothing. A new shot made them both sleep. They were in the back of a small jet. An Air Force C-130, flaps down, rumbled past. New faces looked down at him.

Evening's red sunlight ran up the west-facing slopes above the Crystal River, dyeing the higher trees gold-green, like jade weeds seen underwater. Bleached cliff bones broke through this sheen like fossils through the ocean floor, giving Cohen a sense of unreal hope. They spent the night in cabins on the river, Cohen bound in darkness, listening for Claire's breathing in the next room, hearing only stones clacking underwater on the riverbed.

The next morning they parked on the shoulder of the Dead Horse road, by a livestock truck and jeep. A tall, saturnine man in a western hat sat on the jeep's dusty fender. Another, bent-nosed and chunky, moved from the shade of the livestock truck to shake hands with Mort.

"All set, Walt?"

"You got it," Walt replied, shifted a wad of tobacco from under his front teeth to the cheek, bent aside to spit. They led them to the horses tethered at the far side of the livestock truck, and tied Cohen into the saddle of a brown-white paint. Walt adjusted the stirrups.

"Do'n wan'er ta take a notion," he smiled, a thread of tobacco juice down the side of his jaw.

They tied Claire into the saddle of a slender palomino and rode up a sagey draw into a filigree of aspen shadows. The new leaves were still porphyry along their edges, the peeling white trunks black where elk had winter-gnawed them. Beyond the saddle they zigzagged down into a columnar white forest, leaf shadows flirting with the breeze over a tumult of decaying leaves, bright moss, and purple-brown oakbrush seedlings. The pack horses bunched up and Walt had to ride behind, swearing and pulling them apart.

The forest cleared into a glistening valley with a silvery stock pond in its center, beyond which they forded the dank trickle of Little Horse, and rode north over scrubby, overgrazed hills to the steep, crumbling banks of the Clear Fork. "While a man awaits a time of challenge he places his mind at ease, he laughs, he sings," said Hem, reining his spotted gray closer to the paint. Cohen blinked, but there was nothing save soft dust from the hooves, like pollen filling the air.

"We keepin' you up?" It was the tall, taciturn cowboy. Cohen said nothing. "We keepin' you up, I asked!" Cohen twisted in the saddle to stare back at him, at his small, self-assertive nose, the surprisingly intelligent eyes, the thin lips, the colorless brown hair meager under his hat brim. Cohen shrugged and leaned forward.

After an hour riding its west bank they forded the Clear Fork, horseshoes clanking on its bed. Cohen pointed out the schoolmarm and parson. He nudged the paint with his knee and she turned amiably uphill toward the mesa, her head dipping from time to time to snatch at bunchgrass tufts. She halted, ears perked forward. From the alders came a fading bonk bonk bonk of elk hooves stepping through the down timber.

At the north end of the mesa a series of beaver ponds let light into the forest. The beavers had cut away the willows by a stream, felled the aspen, and worn deep grooves in the earth where they had dragged aspen branches down to the stream. Beyond this perimeter the forest stepped upward in verdant waves to the gray cirques and black spruce of Huntsman Ridge.

Mort rode forward, his horse winded. "This it?"

"Near enough. It's too thick for horses up there. I'll show you tomorrow."

"You'll show us today."

"Up to you."

They tied Cohen's wrists to a young aspen, and Claire to another tree out of sight behind him. They unpacked the horses, set up camp, and ate. Only Walt and the slender cowboy, whom they called Link, seemed familiar with the process. Mort could not pitch his tent and angrily told Link to do it; Lou swore at Walt when a tethered horse shied. Walt grinned. "Sorry, par'ner," he said.

Cohen hunched himself round into the sunshine. The sky through the leaves was ultramarine; a vulture hung on levels in it. What must he see? he wondered. Mort brought him a sandwich and water, and then the hypodermic.

"Forget it," Cohen said. "I'm not going anywhere."

"Keeps us in touch." Mort gripped Cohen's shoulder and stuck in the needle. Cohen waited in the sunlight. The shot seemed more manageable each time he received it. He realized that he almost enjoyed its sudden illuminations, the way it reinforced the physical fabric of the world; he saw that he no longer needed to fear it, and his fear was gone.

The remaining fear's Clay. If he's found alive, he'll send a message over Mort's radio, and Claire and I will be dead and buried in the aspens an hour later. Cohen remembered the heat rippling off the Impala's trunk. Wish I'd killed you, Clay. A camp robber swifted down and stood on the dead leaves, watching him sideways from one red eye. "You here already?" he said. The bird nodded and flitted across the clearing to call from the peak of a blue spruce that stood drowned at the edge of the beaver pond.

Walt was talking about "big city cowboys." He poured Jack Daniels into his coffee. "Gotta have a fur-wheel drive, 'n ruuf lights. Gotta be muddy. Gotta have a rifle rack. They all growed up in Nuh Jersey. Whut the hill're we cumin' ta?" The camp robber swooped down on the far side of the stream and ran along the bank with something white in its beak. A hawk screeched; Cohen looked into the sun but could not find it.

"Time ta go, son," Walt said, pulling Cohen up. "Let's find this meetin' place."

"It's called Paul's pond."

"I don't see it." Lou held the map.

"It wouldn't be there; that's Paul's and my name for it. It's where he shot his first elk. That's how we remember it." While Lou stayed to watch Claire, Cohen led them up a steep, aspeny slope to a higher table of the mesa. It was difficult to walk uphill with his hands cuffed behind his back, but he moved fast. Mort and Link began to breathe hard. Cohen and Walt crested a ridge and waited for them. As soon as they arrived, red-faced and sweating, Cohen set off again.

He maneuvered them up game trails through a mile of thick oakbrush that caught at their clothes and cut their faces. Everywhere was the aroma of fresh elk droppings. Beyond the oakbrush was a vast aspen blowdown, started by beavers. He led them over and under the dusty white logs, Mort swearing with effort. "This better not," he puffed, "be a goose chase."

"It's because it's so hard that we picked it."

The sky was drifting furtively toward gray. Shadows had gone from under the supine trunks. A chill wind began to work on their wet shirts and sweaty necks. "Haw much mor?" Walt, finally beginning to tire, sat beside a serviceberry bush, hat in his lap.

"The first pond's up ahead," Cohen called, forcing them to follow. He came to the lowest pond in the string. It was perhaps twenty feet wide, its dam of mud and sticks barely wide enough to walk on. Brown and yellow aspen leaves carpeted its bottom; stems of new grass leaned over its banks, tracing black reflections.

"Heya?" said Walt.

"It's one up ahead. Let me check."

Walt glanced up. Cirrus tails were yielding the last sunlight. "It's an owuh off this gaddam hill."

Link joined them. "Fuckin' game."

Mort arrived. "We've got time, Walt," he panted.

"In the mawnin', then."

Back at camp they handcuffed him to the young aspen. Claire, still cuffed to her tree, had ignored him when he passed. Scowling in the firelight, Walt cooked chicken-fried steak and potatoes. They ate, ignoring Cohen and Claire. The horses were nickering from the trees where Link had short-roped them. Walt stepped into the darkness with hobbles and a bag of oats.

"When do we eat?" Cohen called.

Lou nodded at the horses. "Maybe when he comes back."

A low whine like a dying alarm clock sent Mort scrambling for his tent. Moments later his voice rumbling soft through the nylon fabric, "Right, right. He did? When?" Cohen felt the night's chill sink into him. The radio. So this is death. In a minute he'll come out of there and walk over here and put a pistol barrel against my temple and the world will explode. And then he'll kill Claire.

Mort stepped out of the tent and crossed to the fire, patted Lou's shoulder. "Daisy says hi."

"No news?"

Mort shrugged. "Nothing. They'll check in again in a couple days. Maybe something then."

Cohen eased back against his aspen. Oh Jesus to live. I thank you God, for this moment, for this life. And Claire's. Maybe Clay's dead?

Walt fed him greasy eggs too hot from the pan, and tossed a horse blanket over him and two more over Claire. "Sorry, you kids gotta stay pinned to them trees." Mort took the first watch. He sat on a log staring into the fire, rousing himself occasionally to gaze at Cohen or Claire, or to rummage in the woodpile Link had cut. He drank whiskey with his coffee, after a while not bothering to mix in the coffee. The others snored in the two tents pitched back from each side of the fire.

Stars flickered through the reflections of the flames on the overhead aspen boughs. The wind, soft and chill from the west, tossed the leaves, altering the star pattern. Coyotes were talking, higher on the flanks of Huntsman Ridge, and closer, in the draws leading up to camp. A beaver splashed in the pond.

Orion strode up the southeast sky, the line of his dagger sharp in the thin air. Mort was replaced by Link, who soon fell asleep. Cohen watched the rhythmic rise and fall of Link's chest, and tugged at his handcuffs.

When Orion had fallen from the center of his arc, Link roused himself and went into his tent. After some mumbling, Walt appeared and sat on the log, rubbing his hands close to the fire. Cohen scratched the back of his head against the elk-gnawed bark.

Orion was dipping toward the west. Walt sat with head sloped forward, hands on knees. His hat began to fall and he roused himself.

"Hey, Walt," Cohen whispered. "I gotta piss. Terrible!"

Walt stood, stretching. He bent over and rubbed his knees, slipped a gun from his coat and stepped round the fire to the tree.

"You gotta what?" His voice was sleepy.

"Piss. Hurry up!"

Walt glanced over at Claire and then stepped behind Cohen to inspect the cuffs. Cohen felt the hard presence of the gun on his spine as Walt unlocked them.

"Quick," Walt said.

Cohen crossed to a willow clump and urinated. Buttoning his fly, he looked up. Orion was hidden.

"Back up." Walt shifted the gun to his left hand. Orion reappeared between the branches. Cohen felt the cuff slide over his right wrist. He spun round the trunk and punched Walt as his right hand grabbed for the gun. It fell. Walt dropped sideways, mouth open to yell. Cohen shoved a fist into his mouth, driving his head back into the leafy earth. He straddled him and squeezed the knobby neck until Walt's hands ceased to beat against his face.

He turned Walt over, heavy as wet garbage, found the gun, and dug a buck knife from Walt's pocket. Downslope a lion screamed like a child dying in fire. The horses whinnied nervously and stamped their hobbles. He could not find the gun's safety. He glanced across the fire at the orange tents, then beyond, where Claire slept against her tree. A coyote barked. The fire hissed. Another coyote answered, to the north. He glanced up at the sky. One hour more of darkness.

He fished in Walt's pockets but could not find a key for Claire's handcuffs. Maybe it's the same one. He found the key to his own cuffs and slipped through the trees to her side, put his hand over her mouth.

She awoke at once. He took away his hand. "Who's got the key to your cuffs?"

"Lou."

He felt her cuffs; they were hardened steel, too thick to break. His key would not work. I could shoot through them but the tents are too far away to cover after the shot. I might kill Link in the closer tent but Mort and Lou'll come out firing and the advantage of surprise'll be gone. He kissed her. "You stay here. I'll get the key."

She kissed him back. "I'm not likely to go anywhere."

He checked the gun. It had a two-inch barrel and a wide bore. Even standing between the tents I can't be sure of hitting either, nor the people in them. So the trick's to kill Link first in the one tent, then concentrate on Lou and Mort in the other. Is it possible? Is it possible soon we might be free?

Moving upslope until the fire was only a glow on the trunks, he crossed the first beaver pond. A great bang exploded on the water; he ducked fumbling for the safety. The beaver that had slapped its tail swam away across the starlit surface of the pond. He lowered the gun and edged downslope until the tents were visible again.

An owl hooted. A trail of sparks ran up from the fire. Wind slipped under his collar. From the trees came a clump, clump of tethered hooves and a tearing of grass. He knelt before Link's tent. Light snoring within, like a child's. He stepped over a white guy line, snapping a twig. The snoring slowed. The word Talon was visible on the black plastic tent zipper. He shifted his stance and bumped another guy line. The tent quivered. The snoring halted. A whisper of nylon, then the scratchy snuffle of a man rubbing his face. Cohen watched his own motionless fireshadow on the tent flap.

Nylon whisked as Link changed position. A coyote yipped. Cohen exhaled slowly. The snoring resumed, first intermittent, then steady. With each snore, Cohen dropped the zipper one click. An oval of darkness grew with each click. Through it came the vapors of clogged sinuses and unventilated farts, of man at his most vulnerable.

He could make out the lumps of two sleeping bags, one flat, one rounded. Cold air rushed past his hand into the tent. The full sleeping bag squirmed, relaxed. Link's mousy hair shone dully against his skull. The zipper was half down. It caught near the bottom. Cohen stuffed the gun in his belt, held a flap in one hand, and tugged at the zipper; the tent creaked. He pulled harder but the zipper was stuck. Its track scraped his shirt as he inched into the tent. His palm crossed the silkiness of the empty sleeping bag. His knee rustled against it, and he was in.

He scanned the sleeper's peacelike face and opened the buck knife. His thoughts fell inward. God's face was averted. Seeking the softness to one side under the chin, he jammed the knife to its hilt, angled into the skull. Link's hand flapped against the tent wall.

The buck knife made a sucking noise as it came out. Blood purled hot and reeking over his hand, up his wrist under the sleeve. He closed the sticky blade, took the gun and ducked from the tent.

It was a hundred feet to the other tent. Mort stepped through its flaps, glanced at the fire and leaped into the willows. "Lou!" he called, "Lou, Lou!"

Cohen ran along a downed aspen trunk, avoiding the crunchy leaves beneath, skirted the fire and entered the aspen as Lou ran out of the tent. Lou stopped by the fire, gun in hand. His face was reddish from the light of the coals. Cohen aimed for his chest and fired. The gun roared, crushing Cohen's ears; the bullet hit Lou's mouth, snapping his neck. He dropped, pieces of his skull ticking down on the dead leaves. Cohen squirmed through the brush, rolled him over, and dug into his pocket for the key.

The reverberations of his shot rattled along Huntsman Ridge. In a crackle of aspen leaves he moved upslope toward Claire. "What's happening?" she whispered. He unsnapped her cuffs and yanked her downhill into the aspens, away from the direction he had last heard Mort. Once out of gunshot they sprinted along the dark trail, oblivious of noise. The ground vanished and they slammed into a pool masked by aspen leaves. He struggled up and pulled her, panting, behind a granite outcrop.

"My knee, Sam!"

"What's wrong?"

"Twisted it. When we fell. I can't stand!"

He forced down a breath and listened. Branches rustled in the treetops. The gun's muzzle reeked of cordite. He checked it; it was plugged with mud. He switched on the safety. Or was that off? Had he knocked it when he fell? He felt underfoot for a twig. Pointing the muzzle away he poked it with the twig. A chunk of mud pattered on the leaves. More inside. The twig snapped, half still stuck in the mud inside the barrel.

He pinched at the broken twig with his fingernails, whacked the barrel against his foot. Something scraped on the trail. Squinting over the outcrop he fidgeted for another twig. Irregular whisper of steps. Darkness crossed the aspen boles. Closer, a white trunk vanished, reappeared. He bit off a willow stalk and shoved it down the bore.

The steps grew louder. Mud smacked as Mort side-stepped the pool. The willow stalk snapped loudly inside the barrel. Cohen pushed Claire down and raised the gun. Mort huffed. His outline turned. Cohen squeezed. Nothing. He leaned forward and with his left hand snicked off the safety. Mort ducked.

25

COHEN'S GUN THUNDERED, SPLINTERING into white fragments and throwing him back on waves of concussion. She screamed as Mort's answered, its bullet tearing his thigh. He squeezed again but the gun was shattered, its grip burning his hand. A bullet cracked off the outcrop; he grabbed her and scrambled into the aspens, bullets pinging through the branches.

They stumbled tripping over blowdowns and slipping on wet leaves into the meadow. With a snort of terror a great form leaped up, hooves flailing. Clenching his thigh with his left hand and circling Claire's waist with the other, he ducked around the horse and staggered along the meadow edge then uphill into the forest.

They fell, panting. He tore his jeans away from the thigh. The wound was oozing blood, but the bullet had missed the bone.

"Where is he, Sam?"

"Other side of the meadow, maybe."

"Did you kill him?"

"Gun exploded. Plugged. Don't think so." He opened the buck knife and cut a tail and sleeve from his shirt, sliced the tail into two pads and tied them against the wound with the sleeve.

"You're hurt!" She reached for his leg.

"Stay away!" He cut off his other sleeve, sliced it lengthwise, tried to wrap it round his right hand where the exploding pistol had torn the palm to the bone.

"Wait," she whispered, and tied it for him, leaning against him in the darkness. "We're a mess, Sam."

"Can you walk?"

"Feels like my knee's broken. Hit it against a boulder when we fell. But I'll walk." She hugged him. "I don't intend to die now that we're so close."

"Close to what?"

"To having each other, getting away."

"Mort's still out there. He's on the radio right now, calling in the troops."

"It'll take them time from Denver. How'll they find this place?" She stood, hissed with pain, reached down and pulled him up.

"Not going to run. Have a date with Mort."

"Forget him. He's the tip of the iceberg. Please let's run while we can!"

He raised his injured hand. Darkness had filtered through the bandage and began to patter on the leaves. Cursing, he peered across the meadow. The ridge above it became a monstrous bear that flexed its shoulders, cocked its ears of wind-rippled aspen tops. "Dawn's coming." He stood; the pain made him sick. He covered his mouth. His hands smelled of blood, cordite, and beaver shit. The lion roared again, a banshee yowl from the far side of the Clear Fork. He hunched his shoulders at the memory of the leopard on Tensan Ridge, told himself, "It's just a silly cougar. It isn't the man-eater." He forced a grin and pulled Claire tighter, limped carefully beside her into the deeper darkness, toward the Great Bear and the higher ground sloping up from Paul's pond into Huntsman Ridge.

The wind-scattered leaves on Paul's pond were locked in ice that he broke with his heel. He unbandaged his right hand and stuck it through the ice; pain roared up his arm. He washed the thigh wound and retied it. They each took a long drink and moved upstream. The night was thick with smells. Something lay wet on his cheek. Another touched his hand. He sniffed, raising his face to the sky. Snow struck his lips and tickled an eyelash. White specks were slipping across the dark branches.

"Oh Christ," Cohen sighed, "if only we'd run off the horses."

Claire halted, gasping. "What do you mean, darling?"

"It's snowing. We'll soon be giving Mort a nice trail to follow. Have to hole up before we leave tracks."

"What about Paul?"

"He's dead."

"Oh good Christ. Oh Jesus. Oh Sam—we have to get away!" She clung to him as they hobbled upstream past the last beaver ponds until the slope flattened and then fell away into a west-facing scarp. Skirting this, they descended to a niche in the sheer northern wall, overlooking a crisscross of elk trails. "If Mort comes this way,"

Cohen said, "he'll ride below us. It'll be the best chance I'll have."
He brushed the snow from her shoulders and swung himself into the
niche beside her. She twisted herself against him, wrapped the torn
shirt tightly around him, and fell into a shivering doze.

The prospect of death, the waning of the drug, and Claire's
presence rendered him fully alive. Life tasted in the snow on his
lips, in the smell of musty aspen leaves, earth and stone, his own
sweat and blood odors and those of the woman beside him. He
watched her. The swelling of her face was receding with the cold,
but she was still far from pretty, and he realized how meaningless
appearances had become.

This is my woman. I am her man. I owe her my life. And I love
her more than life itself. Why don't I tell her? How can I love part
of life more than life itself?

Soon it would be light. Even now, a far blur had resolved into a
cedar, short and vaselike behind a picket of aspen trunks. Snow-
flakes were individually visible, skating down through the still air
like flat stones toward a lake bottom. He looked over the edge of
the niche. Our tracks are covered. We're safe until we move, or
until Mort comes back with others.

It was day. Downslope to the left a branch had snapped. Snow-
muffled hoofbeats. He rubbed his face and watched through willow
stems at the bottom of the niche. A snow clump fell, brushing his
shoulder. The semiautomatic rat-tat-ta-tat of a flicker reverberated
among the cold trunks. In the maze of white columns below a
darkness flashed. A twig popped. The swish of hooves loudened on
snow-smothered leaves. He shook Claire awake, clasped the knife.

The hooves came closer. They thumped over a log. He held his
breath. A stone crunched. The hooves moved past. He tipped his
head up sideways. Aspens blocked the view. In an alley between the
white trunks a bull elk paused, trotted forward, and paused again.
His pelt, varying from gold on the back to burnt umber on his chest,
rose and fell gently with his silver breath. The elk licked his nose. A
drop of moisture hung prism-like on his nostril. He half-raised a
back foot as if to scratch his belly, then dropped it. He rubbed his
head and ear on a sapling, sniffed it, and moved on.

The snow had stopped. The sky above the slender aspen
boughs was milky slate. Wind ran coldly upslope, carrying the roar

of Rock Creek from the gorge below. He wondered if Mort had ridden for reinforcements.

"How's your knee?" he whispered.

Carefully she raised her leg. "Can't bend it."

A bluejay screeched downhill in the cedars. He was surprised, again, at the noises of the forest. Sticks snapping with cold, the soft thump of clotted snow falling from a branch, the yammer of a flicker, the chick-a-dee-dee-dee of that little black-and-white bird, all conspired to rid the forest of silence. Added were the chill, erratic soughing of the wind, the chafe of bough on bough, twig on twig, of dead and leaning trunk in the embrace of another yet alive, the almost silent quality of snow crystals hardening and bark tensing round aspen boles.

When far-off branches snapped he held his breath but Mort did not come. Near midday, when the northwest-tipping aspen shadows lay shortest on the snow, a bough swished suddenly above them and he grabbed the knife. A small owl looked down. It fluffed its wings. One eye closed, opened. It wore a gray business suit and a white collar. Its beak was a flat black nose. Its tiny wirelike talons were black against the pale, mottled bough. Its eye shut.

They did not move. The owl closed its other eye. The sun inched steadily westward. Cohen stretched in the niche and rubbed his feet, flexed his shoulders and clenched his jaw to still the clattering of his teeth. Gently he rubbed Claire's back. She took his frozen hands in hers, opened her jacket, and held them against the warmth of her breasts. He pulled her close and the weird feeling returned, of there being no boundary between them.

He was surprised by a sharp pain in his hand. Over his makeshift-bandaged palm his fingers curled, white and hard. Across one finger was the scar cut by a stone when he had stumbled in an unnamed Himalayan stream, at last light, the leopard at his back. Across the next finger was the redder mark of Clay's knife, cut more recently, also at last light, when he had grappled for it on the bank of the Severn.

Stunned by the full circle of this pain, he tried to count the days since the Kali Gandaki trail. It's another lifetime, not mine. It's a dream to show me the way, and now I know and will awaken. Strangely reassured, he glanced up, but the darkening trunks were the same, the waiting snow, the dull, cold light. Claire shivered beside him. The sun had set, and warmth ran from the deserted earth as from the carcass of a winter kill.

Shivering uncontrollably, he hugged her tight. What if we leave now? Under cover of darkness? How far can I walk, or she, and how soon will our tracks across the crusted snow reveal us? If tomorrow's sunny, the snow'll melt and our chances of escape will be better. As terrifying as it is to sit, it's the wiser choice. And it gives us time to heal, if only slightly.

A fat white moon rose over the cirque, illuminating the snow so that each aspen trunk, willow clump, and cedar stood out in chiaroscuro. He huddled closer to Claire and tried to share his minimal warmth with her. His hands were too numb to move. If we don't go tomorrow we'll freeze.

He awoke to an uphill crackling of brush, barely discernible over the wind. The moon stood straight above them. He cocked his head. He could hear, or perhaps only feel, a rhythmic thudding. It grew; he pulled her down. A branch snapped. A doe, black nose flared, eyes wide, crashed past the niche, bolted over a fallen aspen and was gone in the downslope aspens. Snow skipped after her in little bundles, coming to rest in willow scrub and against aspen boles. The aroma of the doe's fear lingered. He listened for following coyotes but there were none.

Something changed in the air, something bark-like or moldy, a burning. He wrinkled his nose. An unpleasant odor. He licked a finger and wet the insides of his nostrils, sniffed.

Cigarettes. He remembered Mort's yellowed fingernails, the ashy stench of the Mirabeau Suite at the Hotel des Thermes. An uphill stick popped, clear and decisive. A horse snorted. Wind came up and rattled the trees, carrying the odor of manure and the glacial chill of Huntsman Ridge.

Mort appeared in a distant alley of aspens, riding the contour on level with the niche. An owl called.

"It's him?" she whispered.

He rolled into the niche and grabbed her. "In less than five minutes he'll pass right by here." Cohen scooted to the edge of the niche. Too steep a drop. He crawled out one side. "Climb on my back!" he hissed.

"You can't carry . . ."

"Climb on my back! He's got to think I'm alone."

She locked her arms around his neck. He bit his lip, took a deep breath, and stood. Pain roared up his leg, knocking him down. Warm new blood spilled on the snow. He stood again, clenched her legs against his hips, and staggered along the edge of the headwall, away from Mort, pulse pounding in his head, his breath sounding alien, unreal.

Between the headwall and the cirque a steep ravine dropped toward the rushing sound of Rock Creek. He slid over the edge and down into the ravine, each downward jolting step tearing through his thigh. He halted, panting, and looked behind. He had left a clear trail, one foot dragging, blood black on the snow.

"Please let me walk."

"Not a chance." He turned downslope again and soon reached a clump of cedars. Again he looked back. Mort had not yet started down the ravine. He glanced up at the moon. Well past midnight. Rock Creek was louder, like wind in a tunnel.

He began to run, ignoring the leg and Claire's offbalanced weight on his back. A half mile downslope he reached the granite cleft of Rock Creek. In its moonlit cavern, maple and aspen leaves floated over shuddering boughs jammed crosswise in the current, and a water spider cast his solitary wake in a pool rimmed with ice.

He set her down in the middle of the creek, held her shoulders and peered into her eyes. "You do exactly as I say."

"I always said you wanted a submissive wife."

"Don't fool. Mort's ten minutes away. I want you to walk upstream, *in* the stream, until there's no stream any more. Then you'll be on the side of Huntsman Ridge and there's a thick stand of blue spruce you can hide in. I'm going to lead him down the creek and into the canyon, where I can drop on him from above. He won't be expecting it. Afterwards I'll ride his horse up to you and we'll be free."

"You're going to die. I'm going to die with you."

"Bullshit." He put the buck knife in her hand. "I don't think you'll need this, but I feel better with you having it. If I don't arrive by noon tomorrow, I want you to walk east along the side of Huntsman Ridge. In ten miles of hard going you'll reach the Glenwood Springs road, where you can hitch a ride away from all this."

She leaned against him. "Come with me."

"Can't. Unless I leave tracks downstream, Mort'll find us in no time." He pushed her away. "Go." He grabbed her shoulder. "And don't you dare step one foot out of the water, no matter how cold your feet get. Not one footprint!"

She was gone into the darkness, her steps lost in the plashing water. He regained the bank and walked downstream, leaving large, bloody tracks. The canyon narrowed to a tall granite box where juniper roots clung perilously to fissures along vertical walls and brown needles littered thumb-wide ledges and snow-topped stream-side boulders. He descended beyond this place and then stepped into the creek, its cold burning his feet and jarring his thigh. He caught his balance and waded back upstream, leaned carefully across his earlier tracks, grasped a ledge, and pulled himself up. Brown needles fluttered down from the ledge onto the tracks. Swearing, he jumped out from the ledge and landed one-legged in the water, trying not to splash the snow. Supported by one hand on the wall, he leaned over and picked each brown needle from the snow and tossed it in the water. Again he pulled himself up the wall, avoiding the needled ledge, and stretched gingerly up a crack above it. His fingers found a slanting seam that he climbed to a scraggly ledge clustered with junipers. Where this ledge expanded to a hand's width he was able to stand, hidden by the junipers.

He calmed his shivering and took a careful bite of snow. In the moon-bright snowy canyon the aspen trunks stood out darkly; the canyon walls cindery, the creek and its junipers black. His tracks below were a shadowed jagged stitch along the creek bank.

A horseshoe clicked stone. A horse and rider appeared around a curve in the rock wall. Mort was leaning out slightly in the saddle, pistol in hand, eyes on Cohen's tracks. He dismounted, dropped the reins forward, and knelt beside the tracks. He fingered a bit of snow and flicked it away, raised his eyes to the canyon. He moved nearer, watching the walls. The horse sighed. Mort moved under the juniper. Cohen poised to jump. A boot grated on a boulder.

Mort was walking upstream toward the horse. It nickered, pointing its ears toward Cohen. Mort shifted gun hands, patted the horse's neck, tossed the reins over the pommel, and mounted. Cohen tensed for his passage underneath, but Mort tugged the reins aside and rode back upstream.

Cohen was flooded with new fear. Why did he stop? Did he see me? Then why not shoot? Is he riding upstream for Claire? A fist-sized rock bounced over the canyon wall and splashed into the creek. Snow trickled after it, hissing in the water.

He's circling above the canyon. It'll take him an hour to reach the lower end. Then he'll see there are no tracks, put two and two together and hunt back upstream. This ledge won't shield me from his view coming upstream.

Again avoiding needles and snow, he climbed lower and jumped into the shocking water. Oh to hobble upstream after Claire, shelter with her until dawn, hope for another place to trap Mort in the daylight. That's chickenshit. He leaped a boulder and shuffled downstream, watching the dark, high walls. He fell, the current banging him from boulder to boulder.

Near the canyon's lower end a fault forked up its western wall. A chunk of rock had broken loose and half-blocked the creek. Its indentation would hide him from a downstream approach. But here the creek bank was too wide to step across. Downstream beyond the canyon the lower slope fanned wide and gentle, studded with dark pencil lines of aspen.

He scanned the broken wall. A fingernail crevice zigzagged up it. He stepped onto a single baretopped boulder, pinned his frozen fingertips into the crevice and swung up it. Ten feet above the ground he twisted into the indentation left by the chunk of rock and waited. His shivering grew as the creek water froze in his hair and clothes. He clenched his teeth. Claire'll be half way to the ridgetop by now. Soon out of danger.

Moonlight was fading up the opposite canyon wall. Come, you fat bastard, come. Don't go after her. He held his arms around his shivering torso, over the torn and frozen shirt. Not dressed for this kind of shit. Really am not.

Hooves clunked on stone. The horse's head was six feet away. It sniffed him, pulled back. Reins snapped on its flank. It shifted position, hooves tinkling ice on the creek edge.

The horse saw Cohen as he leaped from the wall. Bellowing, it dove sideways, smashing its rider against the far canyon wall. Cohen stumbled after it as it kicked and dragged its rider by one stirrup downstream through pools, thudding over boulders and falls.

He could not see Mort. He clambered from the creek and staggered after the horse, watching the wet lump dragging from one stirrup. They reached the flat, Cohen staying out of pistol range. The lump cleared a dark line through the snow. The horse quieted in an oakbrush clearing. The rider hung unmoving by one leg, on the far side of the horse. The horse nuzzled the snow, its saddle tilted crazily.

He whistled to the horse. It raised its head, bridle jingling. He whistled again, slapped his good thigh. The horse watched, took a step. Squinting at it, he called softly. The horse moved toward him. He slipped into the aspens. The horse passed in front of him. Its rider dragged along behind, face down, arms extended.

The horse snorted and moved a few feet away, still dragging its motionless bundle. Cohen's leg gave out and he sat weakly on a down aspen. The horse nuzzled its shoulder with a snuffling sound, raised its head and nickered into the darkness. "Why?" Cohen asked, but the body gave no answer. He leaned back against a trunk, weeping, for Alex, for Clay's fatherless daughter. One by one the slain stepped past and peered into his eyes: Kim, Goteen, Phu Dorje and his wife and son and daughter, Maria lying cold and faceless on Sainte Victoire.

And you, Paul—if we'd bagged it in Paris you'd be alive now. Mort's dead, and a few other bastards—is the world any better? But you're dead, Paul, you're dead, and the world's infinitely worse.

He wiped his cheeks and stared up through the branches. A star winked in the leaves. He saw himself from the outside: a man slumped in darkness among spring growth. His perception rose and he saw clearly the slumped man and the corpse near him, then also the patient horse, its ears forward, its saddle skewed.

"Look!" a voice said. "Listen!"

Now the slumped man and patient horse were hidden by a canopy of moonlit aspen tops, the slit of the Clear Fork dark within them, a ripple in the flanks of looming Huntsman Ridge. Higher went his vision until he searched for the Clear Fork, found it briefly in the ocean of mountains below him. Dots of light glimmered to the north and east: Glenwood Springs and Aspen. He looked back but the Clear Fork was lost and the pallor of Denver arose on the east.

The continent was edged in silver, the line of the globe itself soon visible, flanked by black. Mars glowered on its nearby traverse. The sun was perfectly round, perfectly white. He lost the earth, still finding Mars by its red gleam. The sun was larger than the other stars, but fell into the Great Bear; the Bear rose and lumbered away. Lastly Orion diminished below him, rolled on one side, and swam into night.

In a silenced world of galaxies and blackness he floated. Terror took him; he began to fall. Gradually he saw there was nowhere to fall, spread his arms, and swam among the points of light as a porpoise in a midnight sea.

The ghostlike columns of the aspen closed in. He took a deep breath and limped through the snow to the patient horse and fallen rider. The body offered no resistance as he turned it over. Walt's raw and empty face stared up at him. Cohen crouched, touched the face. Terror ran up his back.

"Been a long haul, hasn't it, Sam?"

Cohen stood slowly and turned toward the hated booming voice. Mort stood ten feet away, the blued glint of a saddle carbine in his hands. "Should have been sure Walt was dead," he chuckled. "It's a hard thing to choke a man to death. As it was, he came round. When he did he was pretty mad . . ."

"You win," Cohen said. "I give up."

"Where's Paul?"

"I wish I knew."

"I'm not going to wait any longer. It's over. I just want you to know I respect you. You're the toughest man I've ever faced."

"I still don't understand . . ."

"I don't either. Probably the ways of nations are inscrutable." Mort moved a step closer. "Is she dead?"

"You hit her with your first shot." Cohen pointed toward camp. "She's up there, somewhere, under the snow."

"It doesn't matter. She doesn't know enough to cause much trouble. If she's alive we'll kill her when she surfaces."

He tried not to shiver. He kept his eyes on Mort, praying, Dear God help her get away. My last thought—a prayer for her.

Behind Mort, on the aspeny slope, a figure edged between the trees. "Your reinforcements . . ."

"They're hours away. It's just you and me. And I can't let you live any longer. You're too dangerous."

"Let me join your . . . company." Cohen tried to smile. The figure was slipping toward them.

306

"I'd never trust you." Mort raised the carbine.

"You'd have my word."

"Like about the fallback? Perhaps for a while I could. Then one day, when I'd stopped doubting, you'd put a bullet in me, wouldn't you?"

Cohen nodded. "You'll never get Paul."

"I believe he's dead. In any case, you'd never lead us to him. You're too brave for that. I'm sorry to have to kill you."

The figure was still a hundred feet away. "Before I die, please tell me about the bomb."

"I don't originate policy, just expedite it. I know little more than you. In any case, the exercise failed. All evidence of it has vanished. It's not part of history any more."

The figure was directly uphill behind Mort. It hesitated by a long blowdown, moved to one side around it.

"What's the matter, Sam?"

"Please, when you find Claire, bury her here, in the forest. With me?" Cohen tried to keep his eyes off the figure limping softly up behind Mort.

"Agreed," Mort answered.

"She's up the canyon," Cohen pointed, drawing Mort's eye from the hill. She dove onto his back, the buck knife glinting in her hand as she drove it over Mort's bulky coat into the side of his neck. He fell, choking, his red bloated cheeks twisted with pain and rage as he tried to raise the carbine to fire behind him but Cohen was on him, pinning him down while she sawed his massive bulbous neck with the knife.

She knelt to one side and wiped her hands on the snow. Mort's blood spread in a great dark disk. Cohen crunched to where Walt's body lay already growing cold and stiff by his quiet horse. He twisted Walt's boot free of the stirrup. The horse sidestepped skittishly. "Easy," he whispered. "It's all over now." Holding the reins, he led the horse to Claire. "Where'd you come from?"

She stood carefully. "I went upstream a little ways, but then I got mad at you for telling me what to do. So I hid in some bushes until Mort came down to the creek. He started down it but then came back up. He rode above it and I followed him, hoping to be able to stab him. Then Walt appeared, from above. I'd thought you'd killed him! He almost saw me." She shuddered. "I was so scared. Walt rode up the canyon from the bottom while Mort stayed in the trees. I was trying to get close enough to stab him. But then you and Walt came out of the canyon and Mort dismounted and moved downhill to get you."

The leaves were nodding, now visible against the dying stars. Cohen closed the buck knife and gave Claire a hand up into the saddle of Walt's horse. She rode silently beside him as he limped up through the trees to Mort's horse and mounted it. They climbed the canyon of Rock Creek toward the beaver ponds. "Wait," he said, and rode alone into camp.

The campfire and Lou's body were covered with snow. The other horses nickered with hunger from the trees. He dismounted and checked the tents. In one Link lay frozen in his bloody sleeping bag; the other tent was empty. He called Claire into camp. They dressed in warm clothes, ate quickly, and packed paniers for two horses—a tent, sleeping bags, ammunition, and all the food. They dug another rifle and two scabbards out of the snow, loaded up a pack horse, set the others free, and rode through the lightening forest to the Clear Fork.

He turned them upstream, keeping the horses in the water. After an hour they swung westward up a tributary, and a half mile above that left the water to follow a well-worn elk trail. Crimson edged the east as they broke out on a long ridge soaring toward northern crests he had never seen before. They rested the horses in the fresh wind.

I leave all this, Paul. I leave you and Alex and all who have died. Not with joy, not with acceptance. With sorrow and never to forget. To live each day as Isaac and never as Abraham. To ride with her, if she wants to come, deep into Mexico. To heal and think. To write the book you asked for.

As far as he could see, mountains rippled like a forest sea flecked with snow. Orion lay on the southwest horizon, his dagger dimmed. Red grew stronger in the east, outlining individual spruce tops along the nearest crests. A family of coyotes called gregariously from the ravines below. He edged his horse close to hers. "We're like those coyotes," he said. "We're not human, we're free."

"They're hunted too. Poison, traps, guns, planes . . ."

"Yet hear them sing! Grateful for the blessing of life."